RESOLVED

Also by this author:

The Diary of Mrs. Noah

The Transformation

Yesterday and Tomorrow

Alpha & Omega: Book I of the Godmaker Trilogy

Blood Ready

Everywhere & Nowhere: Book II of the Godmaker Trilogy

I Am: Book III of the Godmaker Trilogy

The Ocean Wore Red

It is What it Isn't

Leafy Tom

The Wandering Atheist and Other Stories

Resolved

Robin Buckallew

Saffron Books
2019

First Printing: 2019

ISBN 978-0-359-38071-8

Saffron Books

Cover design by: Matt Jorde

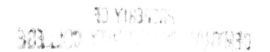

I dedicate this work to all the women who have ever inspired me. It is a list too long to enumerate.

1

The plane was late, very late. Lorelei fidgeted on the hard seat, wishing she could go home and wait for Ogden. Why did she have to come to the airport every time he came home? It was ridiculous, and she planned several ways to tell him so. Should she be sweet? Or sassy? Maybe sorrowful and long suffering would work best. She amused herself for several minutes planning her revolt, and by the time the plane touched down, managed to tease herself out of her bad mood. Ogden expected to be greeted with a smile.

Plastering on a smile required a lot of work when they first got married, but after eight years it was automatic. She pulled out her compact, fixed her lipstick, and turned her smiling face in the direction of the moving stair in time to see her husband step off and move in her direction. She held out her arms and was tucked into his indifferent embrace. The embrace was for the benefit of onlookers more than any undying affection for her. He never hugged her at home, but they needed to keep up appearances. Everyone pretended, and they were no exception.

"Is the mini-transit ready?" Ogden saw no reason to waste words in affectionate whispers.

"It's waiting. I imagine the cost is going to be enormous, with the plane being so late." Lorelei managed to get the words out without sounding accusatory, but it was Ogden's fault. Oh, not that the plane was late, but if he would let her send the mini-transit away and they ordered a new one when he got in…but that would take at least five minutes, and Ogden hated wasting time even more than he hated wasting money.

The driver held the door for them but did not reach for Ogden's bag. Lorelei winced as she saw the look on her husband's face. This would cost the driver big time…possibly even his job when Ogden made an irate call to the mini-transit company in the morning. She tried to deflect his rage by diverting his attention to his trip.

"Did you find anything interesting?" Lorelei wasn't sure what to ask, because he never filled her in on exactly what an archeologist is looking for when they go to a new site. The smile that lit up his face suggested she asked the right thing.

"Oh, this was a very productive trip, very productive. We found the most amazing cache of materials, and preserved beautifully. They

1

were locked in an underground vault that had never been breached. Even the paper materials were preserved intact. We'll get a lot of new information from this, as soon as we are able to analyze it."

"Where is it? Didn't you bring it with you?" Lorelei tried to examine his bag to see if it was in there but he swatted her hand away.

"Of course I didn't. It was huge. It will be delivered to the office. I had it shipped by special transit."

Ogden lost interest in his wife and turned his attention to instructing the driver on how to drive. Lorelei turned her attention out the window, fascinated to watch the world go by, to see the wonderful new structures being built by the busy men who ran the town. It looked like the new shopping center was almost ready. She would have to watch for the grand opening.

"Look, Ogden, a new meal center is going in. We should try it."

Ogden scowled. "It looks expensive."

"I heard it was going to be really cheap. The owners are trying an experiment, providing food that looks and tastes expensive but doesn't cost much. They want the working class to be able to experience life like the rich."

"Why should they? If they want to experience life like the rich, they need to get out of their rut and earn some money."

Lorelei puzzled over that. It was Ogden's answer to any attempt to make life better for the working class, and she supposed he must be right. But if they were working, didn't that mean they *were* making money? So why were they all so poor? She shook her head and gave up on the problem. It was too much for her. She'd just have to trust Ogden.

The couple finished the ride in silence, Lorelei looking out the window while Ogden read his important papers. It seemed as if all Ogden's papers were important, but she had no idea why. He never shared any elements of his work with her, other than answering the direct questions she asked, and even then he didn't tell her much. She knew an archeologist studied ancient cultures but she wasn't sure why. It didn't seem important to know what someone was doing thousands of years ago. If it didn't make life better today, why were men so interested in the past?

It wasn't that Lorelei was stupid, of course. She could read the papers as well as he could, and did read them whenever he left them out on his desk. It wasn't difficult to understand the things described in his papers, she was just uncertain why it mattered. And it wasn't that she lacked curiosity. Why, she was curious about a lot of things! It was just, well, in the past her curiosity was answered with indifference or even anger, and she decided it was best to stop asking questions and just go on with life. It made more sense.

It wasn't as if she had any choice. As a woman, she had her special role to play, and it made her feel good to know she was highly skilled and efficient at keeping the house and raising the children, even if Ogden never noticed. Woman's work was beneath the notice of most men, and he was no exception.

Lorelei dreamed about when she was in school and the teacher gave her a gold star for doing well on her assignments. That was a long time ago, of course, when she was in low school. By the time she got to high school, she got in trouble if she did too well. "Men don't like smart women" was all the teacher said when he instructed her to quit doing better than the boys in the class. "Women should never be good at math; it dries up their ovaries and makes them unhappy."

Lorelei had not yet learned what ovaries were, so she didn't know if it was bad or good to have them dried up, but the look on Mr. Britton's face, and the tone of his voice, convinced her it was a bad thing. She tried all year to fail her math tests, but kept on getting his disapproval because she was just too darned good at numbers. He finally called her parents and demanded they come to the school and take her out of math. The administration was eager to please after Mr. Britton explained the problem; they only allowed her to take algebra because they assumed she would be bad at it and her failure would reinforce lessons about her proper role. They didn't know how to deal with a girl who was good at math.

Since then, Lorelei allowed first her father and then her husband to take over all math functions on the pretext that she simply couldn't understand math well enough to maintain accounts. At the grocery store, she kept her purchases within the budget she was provided, but Ogden preferred not to notice and recognize that she was using math to do what most other wives struggled to accomplish. In spite of all her efforts to be a good wife, she still occasionally functioned as a smart woman.

In college, Lorelei obediently took all the homemaker classes that were the required curriculum for women, but she often would sneak into some of the other classes, those intended for men. Even wearing a hat to hide her long hair, and hiding her figure in loose men's clothes, many of the men in the class spotted her subterfuge. The male students tolerated her because she was pretty, but teased her unmercifully about how strange and weird this must be for her lady brain. She nodded in agreement, and went on entering problems into her notebook to work later in the privacy of her dorm room. She never knew if she worked them right, because it would have been unacceptable for her to turn them in for grading.

The other girls told her she shouldn't be going into the classes with the men, but she wanted more intellectual stimulation than the simple classes offered on the woman's side of the college. Most of her friends agreed, but were unwilling to risk punishment if they were caught.

"If we all go together", Lorelei reasoned, "it will be much more difficult for them to punish all of us."

"If we all go together", her best friend Amity reasoned back, "we will stick out like a sore thumb. You can scrunch down in the back of the room and not be noticed, but seven or eight of us would be harder to hide."

Lorelei realized Amity was right, and didn't press her friends to go to the men's side any more. She smuggled books out of the men's library and she and her friends read them avidly, eager to learn the things the men were learning. In the end, of course, it did them no good, since they all married as soon as they graduated, and turned their college skills into homemaking. She and her friends settled near each other, all of them married to archaeologists because they were the pick of the women, raised and trained to be wives for the high status men.

The mini-transit skidded to an abrupt stop, interrupting Lorelei's memories and Ogden's reading. Ogden glared at the driver and mumbled something rude. The driver missed their home by a block, and was now executing a tricky backing up maneuver to get them back to their door. He moved in reverse for the entire block, and luck provided him with a clear street so there were no mishaps. Lorelei congratulated him on his skillful driving but Ogden scowled and swore at him as the hapless driver rescued the luggage from the trunk.

"Damn foreigners", Ogden growled as the mini transit shot away, leaving them alone on the curb. He did manage to be polite enough not to say such things while the drivers were actually present, and Lorelei was glad of that. She knew many husbands were not so tactful.

"But, dear, if it weren't for the foreigners, who would drive the mini-transits?" As usual, Lorelei's quiet tone had a calming effect on her husband, and he relaxed as he fumbled with the key. Lorelei dragged his luggage up the walk to the porch, reaching the door just as he opened it with a triumphant flourish.

"Home at last." Ogden threw his coat in the direction of the coat rack and headed toward the sofa. "I don't want anyone to bother me for at least an hour. Bring me a hot beverage."

Lorelei nodded and headed toward the kitchen. She stopped the children as they tumbled down the stairs to greet their father. Later, she told them, after he has time to rest. They nodded and silently tiptoed back upstairs. They knew what later meant. Disturbing Daddy could be a painful proposition right at this moment.

Lorelei picked up the errant coat from the floor and put it on the rack. She whipped up a quick dinner and took it to him on a tray along with his hot beverage. He grunted and accepted the tray but didn't look up from his reading. He had important things on his mind, and his wife was already forgotten.

Lorelei hesitated at the door to the study. She hated to disturb Ogden at work, but the men said it was important. She knocked and was greeted with an angry growl. She ignored the rude comment and entered the sacred inner sanctum where her husband hunched over ancient records.

"Ogden?"

"Go away. I'm working."

"There are men at the door."

"Tell them to…"

Lorelei interrupted before Ogden could finish his instructions for the visitors. "They say it is important." She held her breath, steeled against his wrath at her boldness.

"How important could it be to interrupt me on the one day a week I have set aside for no interruptions? You know the drill…get rid of them. Or have an affair with them. I don't care, just don't bring them in here to me."

Lorelei was accustomed to Ogden's rudeness and she didn't let it bother her anymore. She handed him the card one of the men gave her, although she knew she was overstepping the bounds of her wifely duty. Still, if it was as important as they said…

Ogden started to crumple the card and throw it in the trash, but he caught sight of the name and straightened. He grabbed the tie he had thrown against the wall last night when he came home and buttoned his collar. He motioned to Lorelei and she brought him the suit jacket she hung on the coat rack last night after he flung it in the general direction and missed. When he arranged himself to his satisfaction, and smoothed his unruly hair, he growled at Lorelei to usher the men into the study. Lorelei rushed to comply, glad she would not be punished for intruding today.

The men were waiting with something less than patience in the living room. Some of their temper probably came from the fact that Molton was playing in the room and kept dive bombing their feet with his toy airplane. Lorelei grabbed her energetic son with one hand and gestured toward the hallway with the other.

"He's waiting for you in his study", she purred, hoping to placate them so they wouldn't be in an angry mood when they met with

Ogden. He would blame her if they were unpleasant. "I'll show you the way."

Lorelei held onto Molton as she led the men through the hall toward the study. When she reached the staircase, she gave him a gentle swat on the bottom and told him to play upstairs. His mouth opened to protest, so she shot him one of those looks that told him she was serious. He scampered upstairs without another word.

Ogden opened the door of the study as soon as she knocked. He greeted the men effusively, and pumped their hands as he ushered them into the study. "Farnsworth! Masters! Come in, come in."

The men scowled; their mood had not improved in spite of Lorelei's attempts to deploy her most pleasant manner. They marched into the study as though to battle and the door closed behind them. Lorelei debated putting her ear to the door to hear what they were saying, but she had her own duties and had no time for eavesdropping on her husband's private conversations.

Lunch was ready, but Lorelei hesitated to call Ogden to the table. His habits were so regular, and he required the same regularity of his household, that he always knew when lunch would be ready but he still expected her to call him. It was her duty, he explained, on the one day of their marriage she did not call him to lunch, assuming he would realize it was ready.

She was torn between her desire to maintain peace through regularity, and her desire to avoid his wrath at being interrupted. She knew she risked punishment if she selected the wrong choice, but she wasn't sure which choice Ogden would want her to make. She was still sorting out her dilemma when the door to the study opened and Ogden ushered his guests into the hallway.

"Oh, there you are, dear. Would you see the men to the door?" Ogden had a habit of posing orders as requests when other people were around, though the men he associated with no doubt ordered their own wives around. Everyone pretended. And everyone knew that everyone pretended.

Ogden turned to retreat to the study. Lorelei seized her chance and told him lunch was ready. She was rewarded with a faint nod of acknowledgment that suggested he was waiting for her to fulfill her proper function. He headed toward the dining room as she herded the men through the hallway and out the door.

She called the children and the family gathered at the dining room table, waiting expectantly as she bustled between kitchen and dining room bringing in plates of food. Ogden refused to allow her to set the meal on the table until after he was seated because he hated eating cold food.

"Mama!" Molton exploded in excitement.

"Yes, dear?" Lorelei shot an anxious glance toward Ogden. He had high expectations of his children, and remaining quiet at the table was the top rule on his list. He appeared lost in thought, his face marred by a fearful scowl. He didn't seem to notice Molton's breach of etiquette.

"Mama, there were men here."

"I know, dear. They were here for your father and are none of our business. Just eat your lunch, and then you can go outside to play."

Molton and Micra settled in to eat as Lorelei took her place at the foot of the table. She watched Ogden with trepidation; his mood appeared stormy. She had hoped for a peaceful Saturday. He didn't say anything to her, or to the children, but that wasn't unusual. He was not a talker and did not discuss business within the domestic sphere, as he preferred to refer to Lorelei and the children.

Ogden stood and laid his napkin on his plate, a signal that lunch was over. Lorelei put down her fork, knowing that eating one more bite after Ogden declared them through would be met with swift and sure punishment. She had not finished a single meal since they were married, except when he was off on his trips. When he was gone, meals were a much less formal affair.

The children erupted into the backyard where their screaming and laughing would not disturb their father. Lorelei cleared the table, puzzled over the events of the morning. Ogden was in an ordinary, not particularly good or bad, mood at breakfast, and nothing changed by the time she interrupted him in his study. Now he appeared to be in a temper, and she knew the best course was to avoid him until dinner. That shouldn't be difficult, she thought, since he has those new papers to work on and they seem to be taking up all his time.

The sound of a loud thump, followed by another, led her to the study door. She opened it a crack and peeked in, relieved to see Ogden was all right. She ducked just as he pitched a box of pens at the door. It fell to the floor to join the shoes that were lying where he threw them moments before.

"Ogden! What are you doing? I thought you'd fallen."

Ogden turned his back. He hated anyone, even his wife, to see him lose control. She realized he was struggling to get his poise readjusted. When he felt he could comfortably interact without showing inappropriate emotion, he turned back to his wife.

"Nothing is wrong. Go away. This doesn't concern you."

Lorelei wanted to say it concerned her very much, since she would have to pick up the items he was throwing and put them back where they belonged, but one look at his face told her he would not tolerate even the most moderate back-sass today. He was in a fearful mood, the worst mood she had ever witnessed. She shivered.

"I'm just thinking about your health", she murmured, even though she was more worried about her own health than his right at the moment.

"How kind of you. What a dear wife you are." Ogden growled, but she sensed his mood relax as she moved behind him and rubbed his shoulders. "What would we men do if we didn't have our women at home to take care of us?"

Lorelei tensed. It was a common sentiment, one he expressed often, but there was a different tone in his words today. The phrase sounded less automatic, less robotic. Something new entered the room, and she had no idea what it was. Whatever it was, it unsettled him, and anything that unsettled him unsettled her.

"Yes, dear, of course, dear. It is our joy and our mission to make sure you never have a single uncomfortable moment." Lorelei purred out the words she was taught, but she felt even less sincere today than any of the other times she'd mouthed the soothing words.

Whatever was in the air, it was more than just Ogden's mood. She felt it for several days, ever since he came home from his last trip. He spent most of his time since then sequestered in his study when he wasn't at the office, poring over ancient documents and examining the minutiae of ancient artifacts. That wasn't unusual; he spent most of his time at home in his study. But something was different, even though she couldn't put her finger on what.

Something had changed. Something new had entered the world and she felt a tingle of excitement. For the first time, she understood why her husband did the things he did. She wanted more than anything in the world to know what they found, what they were learning about those ancient civilizations, what was so unsettling not only to her husband, but to those men who intruded on his Saturday routine and were admitted into the most sacred of all sacred places, his study.

"Something is about to change", she whispered so quietly that even Ogden couldn't hear. "Something is going to be different."

3

Things remained in their normal pattern for the next several days. Ogden came and went in his usual routines, and remained locked in his study most of the time when he was at home. He didn't say a word to her at dinner, but that was normal. The children attended church and school, and played in the backyard or upstairs so they wouldn't disturb Daddy. Lorelei cooked and cleaned, shopped for groceries, and did laundry on her usual regimented routine, established for her on the first day of their marriage by her order-loving husband.

Thursday came, and time for her woman's group. They were at her house this week so she spent the morning giving an extra polish to her already immaculate house. She fussed for over an hour to make sure the canapés were arranged just right on the plate. To do otherwise would be seen as sloppy, and being sloppy at your homemaking was the absolute worst thing that could happen to your reputation. Women and men alike could forgive a minor intimate transgression, after appropriate shunning, of course, but sloppy housekeeping was the ultimate unforgivable sin. Lorelei never committed that sin, and never intended to transgress. She was the most fastidious woman in her circle.

The group was in a twitter about something. Lorelei could tell from the moment the first woman arrived. They were not themselves, any of them. All of the women were on edge, a bundle of nerves. They settled around the table and nibbled the edges of the food on the tray as though they were three birds. Lorelei bustled in and out, bringing in cold beverage and hot beverage, according to the preference of each woman. It was not until she settled at the table in her accustomed place that the women began to chatter.

"Have you heard the news?" Amity was the first to speak.

"No! What?" Lorelei leaned forward, ready for the latest in gossip, even though she hated gossip. There were certain expectations of a woman and she would live up to them or die trying.

Corinne answered, jumping in before Amity could open her mouth. "Something…weird. The stuff the men discovered? They're all terrified. They're all angry."

Lorelei nodded. That had been her assessment. Even though this past week seemed normal on the surface, there was a noticeable shift in Ogden's mood. Never a cheerful man at the best of times, he was downright difficult now. Her only salvation from his temper was his habit of retreating to his study and interacting with his family only at the dinner table, a habit that gave her much cause for relief this week.

"Ogden has been…tense…about something", she affirmed.

"Tense? Oh, my dear, this is so much more than tense." Grenata was always the most eager to share dirt and she leaned forward, her eyes glistening with pleasure, her voice a near whisper, suitable to the mysterious behavior of the menfolk.

"Yes, I guess. Ogden was in a really bad temper on Saturday, and he hasn't said a word to me all week, except for I need hot beverage or get me something."

"I heard", Amity started than stopped. She leaned forward, gesturing the other women to do the same, until their heads nearly touched over the table. She dropped her voice, a conspiratorial whisper that sent chills down Lorelei's spine. "I heard there is something in those records so subversive, so dangerous, that they fear it could destroy civilization."

Lorelei thought that seemed extreme. "But what's the problem? They just don't tell anyone what they found, and it's fine."

Amity shook her head. "They are bound by law to publish whatever findings they unearth. It's part of their charter, and it's the rule of their discipline. They have to tell."

This was news to Lorelei. How had Amity learned so much? Her husband, Merris, was even more close-mouthed than Ogden. He was also more brutal, and Lorelei noted the deepening bruise on Amity's face just under her left eye.

"How do you know?" Grenata asked the obvious question.

"I listened. You know, through the keyhole." Amity grinned, a grin that managed to be smug and know-it-all without being obnoxious or annoying. Amity had the type of personality to carry that off.

"Watch out. You'll get in trouble if you're caught." Corinne voiced the obvious, something they all knew so well the warning wasn't necessary – well, maybe it was, if Amity was breaking one of the cardinal rules of womanhood.

"Never spy on your husband. Never intrude into his business. Never act like you know more than he does, even if you do." The three women spoke simultaneously, mouthing the familiar mantra they repeated every morning throughout their education, starting with low school. In college, it was printed on every handout, and posters hung in every classroom as a mute reminder of the proper role of a woman.

"I know, I know." Amity brushed off their concerns, even as all eyes were on the bruise. "But I had to know…I *had* to."

Amity paused for effect. It was clear she wanted the women to press her, to ask what was so important about knowing this one thing, this one time. Lorelei decided she wasn't going to take the bait. She loved Amity as her best friend, but they were adults now and needed to quit playing childish games. Corinne jumped in, asking what they all wanted to ask.

"Because I think it concerns…" Amity paused and looked around as if to check that the women weren't being watched even though they were alone in the house. "…us."

"Us? Like, this group?" Grenata always thought in the concrete. For some reason, abstractions escaped her and she never mastered the skill of looking outside the moment.

"Us. I mean, women. All women." Amity sat back and crossed her arms across her chest. She dropped a bomb on the group, and she knew it. This time her smug grin did manage to be obnoxious and annoying.

"What about women?" The group erupted in unison. This was big if it concerned all women, everywhere.

"I don't know. I just caught…you know, the tail end…or maybe the edge…of the conversation. It wasn't clear. I just heard the word women, the word wives, the word disaster…oh, and catastrophe."

The group was silent for the first time since Lorelei had known them. None of them knew what to say. They tried to work their minds around this new bit of information, but it was more than any of them could handle. It was just a hint, a tease, without anything concrete. Lorelei thought about her feeling of something new entering the world, a feeling she experienced frequently over the past several days, and shivered. Something new might be something sinister, she realized. It could be something dangerous.

She decided it was time to change the subject. "C'mon, ladies, let's end the gossip. It's time to get to work. We're here to plan the charity bazaar." She never figured out why, when Ogden hated charity so much, he always insisted on her being on the committee for the charity bazaar, but she was glad. It gave her something to do that was different from her ordinary rut, and allowed her to use her organizing skills for something other than arranging her kitchen.

The group buzzed again as the women turned their attention to the task at hand. There was a lot to do before next month's bazaar, and they couldn't waste time chit-chatting when they were only allotted two hours a week to do their planning. Lorelei found it difficult to concentrate.

"Women", she thought. "Disaster. Catastrophe." The words seared into her brain as the group sorted out tasks and arranged the order of speakers for the event. She could not concentrate on her work, and realized she was drifting into a state of chaos she had never experienced before.

4

Lorelei struggled to regain her equilibrium after the other women left. She had several chores to complete before Ogden got home, and dinner was not yet in hot box. She shoved the meat into the pan and covered it with Ogden's favorite spices. She added a few vegetables and shoved the whole thing into hot box with very little awareness of what she was doing. She set herself on auto pilot and soon had her chores done, though she was unable to remember doing them. She shivered as the day got colder, anxious for the heat that was on only when Ogden was home.

The children raced downstairs, through the kitchen, and out the door. Automatically she admonished them to be careful, not to get dirty, and to be ready for dinner in thirty minutes. She put the last of the clean glasses in the cupboard and set the table. She moved through her chores in a stupor, to a constant refrain of "Disaster. Catastrophe. Women."

When she stood back to check her handiwork, she realized she put Micra's plate at Ogden's place. She grabbed the pink, ribbon-painted plate and switched them just in time. Ogden stomped in the door as she set the correct plate at his place with a thud and disappeared into the kitchen.

"Lorelei?" Ogden stuck his head in the kitchen, much to Lorelei's surprise.

"Yes, Ogden? Did you need something?" Lorelei bustled between hot box and cold box, getting out everything Ogden would want at dinner, planning for his every need before he needed it.

"Nothing. Just…making sure." Ogden withdrew, his head pulling back as the kitchen door slammed behind him.

Lorelei stared at the door where Ogden disappeared. What in the world was he doing? He never ventured into the kitchen once in their entire marriage, and never looked for her when he came home. He assumed she would be where she was supposed to be, and of course, she always was. She learned her lessons well and gave him no reason to watch over her, not like some wives…not like Grenata, who seemed to struggle with the easiest schedule. "Grenata is a dreamer", she mumbled as she moved around the kitchen in a delicate ballet. "She shouldn't be a wife. She should be an artist."

Lorelei stopped short and clapped her hand over her mouth as though the treacherous thought might escape. What in the world was she thinking? A woman? How could a woman be an artist? And what woman ever was anything other than a wife? Well, there was that woman over on Center Street, the woman who never married, never found a man. Everyone said she was crazy. She left the house every morning and went somewhere…no one knew where…and came home again when the day was done. Lorelei wouldn't wish that woman's life on anyone, especially not on one of her friends.

The children burst into the kitchen, four minutes before they were expected for dinner. Lorelei shook her head. Everything was strange today, even the children. They never came in without being called at least twice, usually three times. It was like they sensed the disruption in the universe that was frightening her, and responded to it in their own way. She inspected their hands and sent them upstairs to wash.

Ogden didn't speak at dinner, but he watched Lorelei the whole time. When she got up to fill his glass or to get a clean fork for Micra after she dropped hers on the floor, he watched her all the way to the door and all the way back. When she picked up her fork, he watched the fork move from her plate to her mouth. It was difficult to eat with him watching her, but she knew she needed to behave in a regular, orderly manner, or it would disturb his digestion…and his temper.

Dinner over, Ogden retreated to his study while she washed the dishes and put the children to bed. When she came downstairs, he was standing at the door to the study, watching her. She started to enter the living room for her evening reading, conscious of his eyes on her, but he motioned her to come to the study. She hesitated, her hand still on the doorknob, and he motioned again. She nodded and crept along the hallway toward her husband.

Ogden held the door to the study without a word. She entered, feeling like a little girl going to the principal's office. She tried to read his face but couldn't see any sign of anger. He had an unfamiliar look on his face. It looked almost like…fear? What in the world could Ogden be afraid of?

"Disaster. Catastrophe." The words echoed in her brain as she moved to the far wall of the study and scrunched against it, ready for an angry tirade and the punishment that would follow. She noticed the drapes were closed. That was unusual. Ogden did not allow the drapes to be closed when he was in the study.

Ogden didn't speak. He closed the door and leaned against it, watching her as she cowered in the corner. She cast her mind over the events of the evening, trying to remember what she could possibly have done wrong. His study was clean...no sign of the stuff he'd thrown the other day; she picked the things up and put them in their proper places as soon as he left the next morning. She didn't imagine there could be a trace of dust. She tested everything this morning, using the white cloth she kept handy for the job. The room was neat as a pin, except for his jacket lying on the floor beside the coat rack, as usual. Lorelei started to move toward the jacket, habit driving her to pick it up and place it neatly on the rack.

"Leave it." Ogden's voice was hoarse and low.

Lorelei backed away from the jacket and tucked her hands behind her back. She scooted toward the wall, not taking her eyes off her husband. When her clenched hands touched the wall, she rested against it, trying to relax. Things went better when she relaxed. Pain wasn't as bad when she didn't tense against it.

"Come here." Ogden gestured to his wife but made no move toward her.

Lorelei crept from the corner and dropped to her knees. Ogden preferred her to crawl when he was angry and meting out punishment. Best not to make him ask. She would try to defuse his anger as much as possible.

"Get up. Walk."

Lorelei stood and moved toward her husband. Ogden had not moved since he shut the door. He had a new look on his face, a look she was unable to interpret. She tried to figure out what he was thinking but his mood was closed to her. She thought she would die when she heard him turn the lock. There would be no hope of escape from whatever he planned to do to her.

The journey across the small room seemed like miles. Lorelei watched Ogden watching her and felt like a small child in the presence of a large, angry adult. She hoped he would tell her what she did wrong before he lambasted her. The worst times were when she didn't know what was wrong, because she knew there was no way she could fix things. She stood in front of him and closed her eyes.

Ogden reached for her and she felt herself tense. She struggled to relax, but it was no use. Her traitorous muscles simply would not respond. She didn't struggle against his grip, which wasn't harsh or punitive, but was firm enough she knew she couldn't escape. He pulled her nearer and she found herself locked into his embrace, his lips pressed against hers as he fumbled with the buttons on her dress.

"Ogden! Not here!" Lorelei protested. "Someone might...see. It isn't...proper."

Ogden didn't respond. He continued to unbutton her dress and thrust his hand roughly inside her bra. She didn't return his kiss or his embrace but she didn't move away. If Ogden wanted marital duties, well, it was her job as a wife to comply. She would be a proper wife. It was one of the other mantras that was drilled into them in college: "Never refuse your husband when he has the desire." That one wasn't taught in either low school or high school. Girls weren't supposed to know about those things until they were ready to marry. It was the last lesson they received in college, the day before graduation. They were required to repeat it over and over before they could receive their diploma.

Lorelei stood like a rag doll in Ogden's arms until he grabbed her hand and thrust it into his pants, which he unzipped without her noticing. She wrapped her hand around his manhood and stroked it in the way he liked. He had her out of her dress now and was moving his hands up and down her naked body. She rested against him, numb and obedient, no excitement moving her as it obviously was him. It wasn't expected, because it was widely known that women didn't enjoy marital duties, they just supplied them on demand once they were married. She never understood why some women took lovers, because it seemed the cost could outweigh any potential benefit, even if her lover were someone important.

Ogden made love to her on the floor of the study, a first in their marriage. He never behaved with so much impropriety before, and Lorelei was disturbed. This was not the way things were supposed to be, and he was violating his own rigid standards. At least the children were in bed so there was no worry they would hear. She lay silent on the floor underneath him and waited for him to be through.

18

He rolled off her with a grunt and lay beside her on the floor, his naked manhood glistening in the light. Lorelei jumped up to turn off the lamp but he held her, preventing her from leaving his side.

"But...the light..." Lorelei stammered. They never had marital duties with the light on before.

"Leave it. I like it." Ogden pushed himself up on his elbow and stared at his wife with a strange look. "I like...looking at you. You look very beautiful tonight."

Lorelei stared. Ogden had not called her beautiful since the day they met, that odd day in his father's living room when she was introduced for the first time to the man her parents had promised her hand. He was young and awkward and seemed to be trying to please. He took her hand and stroked her palm, staring into her eyes as if trying to read her soul. He mumbled that she was too beautiful, and darted out of the room. He didn't come out of his closet until she was gone, and she didn't see him again for two weeks. By that time, the deal was complete and she was his official fiancée.

"You are beautiful, you know." Ogden was practically purring now, and he stroked her face as he spoke. His touch was gentle, not the usual efficient moves he used when he made love to his wife. He leaned forward and kissed her, his right hand stroking her hair and his left arm snaked around her waist in an embrace. Lorelei felt uncomfortable, not sure what she was supposed to do in this odd moment, not sure if she should touch him or speak or just lie there.

Ogden took her arm and wrapped it around his waist. He squeezed closer to her, bringing their chests into contact and wrapping his legs around hers. She sensed he was planning to make love again and she remained close to him, not trying to escape. That would be insulting, and she didn't want to make any false moves. She felt his manhood soft against her leg, and she knew he would not be able to make love again while it remained soft.

The two of them remained in the embrace for what seemed like forever, then Ogden released her, slowly and reluctantly. He sat beside her and stroked her thigh, his eyes closed and his head tilted back. She felt a jolt of electricity as he stroked a particular spot, and felt the jolt again when he ran his hand over that spot a second time. It felt good and it confused her. What was happening between them? It didn't make sense and she didn't like being in this state. She kept her eyes closed, willing him to be done with her so she could make her escape. She was conscious of being naked, and of him staring at her, even though his eyes were still closed.

It was past their usual bedtime when he stood and pulled his clothes on, finally covering his nakedness. He pulled Lorelei to her feet and helped her get dressed, tenderly buttoning the buttons on her dress. She didn't move to help him, in shock at his manner, ready to bolt if he made a sudden move. When they were both dressed, he spun her to face him. She braced herself for retribution, though for what she wasn't sure. He stared into her face and touched her cheek. She stifled the scream she felt well up and remained limp, allowing him to move her as he pleased. He pulled her into his arms, claimed her lips for a long, slow kiss, and then released her.

"Go", he said, but it was less a command than permission. "It's bedtime. You must be tired."

Lorelei stumbled out of the study, shaken and afraid. Yes, something was changing. Something was definitely wrong. Ogden had never been concerned with whether she was tired before. And he never looked at her, or touched her, in that way.

When he came up to bed a few minutes later, she pretended to be asleep. It was best to avoid contact with her husband, at least until she could figure out what was wrong with him.

5

Ogden was not in bed when Lorelei woke in the morning. She stared in horror at time monster, its hands clearly indicating she was an hour later than her usual rising. She forgot to set the alarm last night in her rush to get into bed and now she would pay a heavy penalty. Ogden went to work without his breakfast. No, he must be waiting downstairs. It was only just time for him to get up, and he would be furious, sitting at the dining table without any food.

Lorelei stumbled downstairs, not even taking time to brush her hair. That in itself was a transgression, as her husband believed women should not be seen in an unkept state. She decided it was more important to get breakfast started. She poked her head into the dining room to let him know it would only be a few minutes, but Ogden was not there. She knocked lightly on his study, unwilling to announce her presence in the face of her sin but knowing she had to make things good. There was no answer.

Lorelei pushed the door open. The room was empty. The drapes were still closed and the room looked exactly as it did when they left it last night. The jacket was still on the floor and Lorelei picked it up in an automatic motion as she pulled the drapes to let the sun in. Ogden never left the drapes in his study closed. All drapes were to be opened upon rising, and closed upon retiring.

She moved through the house in a panic, trying to figure out where Ogden was. She watched over her shoulder as though expecting him to jump out at her any moment and wrap his hands around her neck. Her hand went instinctively to her neck as she trudged up the stairs, hoping she would find him in the library. He was not there, either. The only rooms she had not checked were the children's rooms, and there was no reason for him to be in there.

She cracked the door to Molton's room. Molton was still asleep, his left leg hanging off the bed and his arms wrapped around his pillow. She called his name and instructed him to get washed and dressed for breakfast. He mumbled something she couldn't hear, and she smiled. Molton never liked to get up in the morning and she hated to disturb him. He looked darling lying there, but he needed to get to school on time.

Micra was already awake, playing breakfast with her dolls. Micra never overslept and rarely stayed in bed as long as she was supposed to, but she was well trained and would not come out of her room until she was given permission. Lorelei gave her the same instructions, though it was likely the girl was already washed since she was dressed in a pretty pink dress that brought out the sparkling green in her eyes. Lorelei nodded with pride. The child would turn out to be a very good wife someday. And Molton is shaping up to be a traditional husband, she thought.

The door to cold box was creaking, swinging back and forth, and Lorelei rushed to close it. Don't waste energy, don't waste money, she repeated to herself over and over, the words Ogden would use if he saw her doing anything he deemed inefficient. She basked in the warmth of the house, then jumped to realize that Ogden had not turned the heat down when he left. She struggled with the thermostat, unsure how the thing worked, and was still trying to reset the heat when Molton erupted into the kitchen, wailing for his breakfast.

"You're doing it wrong."

Molton at seven was already well versed in the proper way to talk to women, even older women, and Lorelei growled at the smug, bossy tone in his voice. She stood aside and let him adjust the thermostat, bringing it back down to a temperature only slightly above the temperature outside. Today was going to be a cold day and she would have enjoyed more heat, but rules were rules and she did not break rules.

"Thank you, Molton. Your father forgot to turn it down this morning for some reason."

A memory of the night before flashed before her eyes, disturbing her again at the violation of strongly enforced rules, and this violation by the man who established the rules. Last night was disturbing enough without the strange disappearance this morning.

Molton rushed to the dining table, eager for his breakfast. He lost his traction on the tile floor and slid into his place at the table. He threw a guilty look at the head of the table, an apology quivering on his lips, a look of fear marring his cute face.

"MOMMY!"

Lorelei heard Molton's shout from the kitchen. They probably heard it at the end of the block. She rushed into the dining room to find out what was hurting him but there was no evidence of danger.

"What?"

"Where's Daddy?" Molton pointed to the empty place at the head of the table as though Lorelei could not understand his verbal question.

"I don't know. He had to leave early."

"Is he going out of town again?"

"No. At least, not that I know of. It's possible he got called out, but I didn't hear voice monster beep."

Molon lost interest in his father's absence and settled at the table, happy in his realization that this would be a meal only with their mother. The children enjoyed the more informal setting when their father wasn't present, because Mommy let them talk and laugh at the table, and sometimes served them fun food.

"Can we have pancakes today?" Whenever Ogden wasn't home for breakfast, Molton wanted pancakes, a food his father would not permit.

"Sure. You want them shaped like?"

"I want mine shaped like a gun."

Molton had a fascination with guns and wanted everything gun shaped right now. Lorelei hoped he would outgrow that phase soon, not only because gun shaped pancakes were difficult to make. She mixed the batter and was pouring it on the griddle when Micra descended the stairs with more dignity and grace than her brother had demonstrated. Lorelei smiled to see her little daughter so fastidious, one might even say prissy, at the age of five. What will she be like when she's my age, Lorelei wondered. For the first time, the thought made her shudder.

"Mommy, can I have my pancake shaped like dolly?" Micra thrust the doll toward her mother so Lorelei could see which doll she wanted her pancake to resemble.

"Sure, I can do that. Leave her here, on the windowsill, so I have a model."

Lorelei didn't need a model since all her doll shaped pancakes came out looking the same, and Micra never minded. She could always see her current favorite in the familiar shape and would use the syrup to create eyes, nose, mouth, and hair. The children had good imaginations, anyway. She started to hum as she turned the pancakes, the strange events of the past few days put to one side in her joy at sharing breakfast alone with her children.

6

The children kept her occupied, rumbling around the house looking for lost homework, shoes, or other items too important to leave behind. Lorelei fetched and carried for them until they were ready, and they tumbled out the door just as child mover pulled up to the curb. They chattered continually until they disappeared into the huge yellow machine that would transport them to low school. Child mover would return later for the students at high school, but Lorelei would pay it little mind as her children were not yet old enough.

Her list of chores beckoned and she moved into a feverish dance through the house, washing dishes, sorting laundry, and making beds. Lunch would be just her, and that was nice. She enjoyed these moments to herself. When she was first married she hated them, because her mind kept filling with thoughts of other things, things forbidden to her, as to all women, and disturbing her peace. Now she welcomed the thoughts. It was fun to dream of a different world, even though her dreams were forbidden and weird. I mean, who ever heard of a woman sailing on the ocean all by herself? Or riding a bicycle along a country lane without an escort? What woman ever…well, the dreams were big and impossible, and they were a great escape from a boring morning.

Lorelei lingered over lunch, taking time to prepare it more lovingly than usual and eating each bite slowly and deliberately. She decided not to rush to her afternoon chores until she felt ready. She chastised herself for her subversive attitude but did not accelerate her pace until her daydreams turned into nightmares, reminding her that these dreams, if ever discovered, could cause her not only loss of status in the community but could lead to one of the painful beatings Ogden inflicted only occasionally in their marriage. Her status as a good wife protected her better than some of her friends, but mostly because they were married to men who beat them for no reason. Merris beat Amity nearly every day, and there was little Amity could do to prevent his anger.

She washed her dishes and grabbed the dust rag. Ogden's study was the most important. If anything was out of place or dirty, it was cause for anger. If he dropped something where it didn't belong, it could lie there as long as he liked, but if Lorelei so much as entered the room, it must be returned to its rightful place by the time she left. When he came home in the evening, the room must be immaculate.

Lorelei dusted, swept, and mopped. There was little to pick up today, since Ogden hadn't spent much time in his study last night. Well, actually, he did, she thought, and felt her face grow hot and red at the memory. She wanted to say something to him about it, to let him understand how uncomfortable it made her, but it wasn't her place to decide when and where to have marital duties. That was the domain of the husband.

She paused with her duster as she realized that all parts of life, even when, where, and how she cooked and cleaned, were the domain of the husband. Well, that's only right, she thought. That's how it's supposed to be. She pushed back the memory of her time in college, her thoughts reminding her that she hadn't always felt that way, and her treacherous daydreams suggesting she didn't really believe that now.

She ran the duster lightly over Ogden's safe, surprised to see it was not closed all the way. The door was slightly ajar, not sealed. She knelt in front of the large steel box, intending to push it closed, but her curiosity got the better of her. What were the men so worried about? Maybe there would be a clue in here.

She swung the door open and gazed in wonder at the pile of papers nestled inside. This was a huge document...or, she realized, the papers, though old and yellowed, didn't seem to be a single document. There were many different ages of paper, different styles of writing, and different looks of the documents. She picked up the one on the top of the stack, a sheaf of documents held together by a single staple. She settled on the sofa to read a document stranger and more disturbing than anything she'd ever seen.

7

The document she pulled out of the safe bore a strange title: Declaration of Sentiments and Resolutions, Woman's Rights Convention, Held at Seneca Falls, 19-20 July 1848. This document was more than a thousand years old! Lorelei held it with caution, not wanting to tear the delicate paper or leave any sign she ever held it in her hands. She set the old paper back in the safe and sat down with the translation, recorded in Ogden's painstaking penmanship. The words on the paper leaped at her, startling in their bold strangeness.

Resolved: That such laws as conflict, in any way, with the true and substantial happiness of woman, are contrary to the great precept of nature, and of no validity; for this is superior in obligation to any other.

Resolved: That all laws which prevent woman from occupying such a station in society as her conscience shall dictate, or which place her in a position inferior to that of man, are contrary to the great precept of nature, and therefore of no force or authority.

Resolved: That woman is man's equal—was intended to be so by the Creator, and the highest good of the race demands that she should be recognized as such.

Resolved: That the women of this country ought to be enlightened in regard to the laws under which they live, that they may no longer publish their degradation, by declaring themselves satisfied with their present position, nor their ignorance, by asserting that they have all the rights they want.

Resolved: That inasmuch as man, while claiming for himself intellectual superiority, does accord to woman moral superiority, it is pre-eminently his duty to encourage her to speak, and teach, as she has an opportunity, in all religious assemblies.

Resolved: That the same amount of virtue, delicacy, and refinement of behavior, that is required of woman in the social state, should also be required of man, and the same transgressions should be visited with equal severity on both man and woman.

Resolved: That the objection of indelicacy and impropriety, which is so often brought against woman when she addresses a public audience, comes with a very ill grace from those who encourage, by their attendance, her appearance on the stage, in the concert, or in the feats of the circus.

Resolved: That woman has too long rested satisfied in the circumscribed limits which corrupt customs and a perverted application of the Scriptures have marked out for her, and that it is time she should move in the enlarged sphere which her great Creator has assigned her.

Resolved: That it is the duty of the women of this country to secure to themselves their sacred right to the elective franchise.

Resolved: That the equality of human rights results necessarily from the fact of the identity of the race in capabilities and responsibilities.

Lorelei dropped the page and stared at it as though it might bite. She started to return the document to the safe and go about her business, but the words kept drawing her back. She continued to read.

The history of mankind is a history of repeated injuries and usurpations on the part of man toward woman, having in direct object the establishment of an absolute tyranny over her. To prove this, let facts be submitted to a candid world.

He has never permitted her to exercise her inalienable right to the elective franchise.

He has compelled her to submit to laws, in the formation of which she had no voice.

He has withheld from her rights which are given to the most ignorant and degraded men—both natives and foreigners.

Having deprived her of this first right of a citizen, the elective franchise, thereby leaving her without representation in the halls of legislation, he has oppressed her on all sides.

He has made her, if married, in the eye of the law, civilly dead.

He has taken from her all right in property, even to the wages she earns.

He has made her, morally, an irresponsible being, as she can commit many crimes with impunity, provided they be done in the presence of her husband. In the covenant of marriage, she is compelled to promise obedience to her husband, he becoming, to all intents and purposes, her master—the law giving him power to deprive her of her liberty, and to administer chastisement.

He has so framed the laws of divorce, as to what shall be the proper causes of divorce; in case of separation, to whom the guardianship of the children shall be given; as to be wholly regardless of the happiness of women—the law, in all cases, going upon the false supposition of the supremacy of man, and giving all power into his hands.

After depriving her of all rights as a married woman, if single and the owner of property, he has taxed her to support a government which recognizes her only when her property can be made profitable to it.

He has monopolized nearly all the profitable employments, and from those she is permitted to follow, she receives but a scanty remuneration.

He closes against her all the avenues to wealth and distinction, which he considers most honorable to himself. As a teacher of theology, medicine, or law, she is not known.

He has denied her the facilities for obtaining a thorough education—all colleges being closed against her.

He allows her in Church as well as State, but a subordinate position, claiming Apostolic authority for her exclusion from the ministry, and, with some exceptions, from any public participation in the affairs of the Church.

He has created a false public sentiment, by giving to the world a different code of morals for men and women, by which moral delinquencies which exclude women from society, are not only tolerated but deemed of little account in man.

He has usurped the prerogative of Jehovah himself, claiming it as his right to assign for her a sphere of

*action, when that belongs to her conscience and her
God.*

*He has endeavored, in every way that he could to
destroy her confidence in her own powers, to lessen
her self-respect, and to make her willing to lead a
dependent and abject life.*

The words blurred on the page as her mind struggled to
comprehend what she read. This was subversive stuff indeed. No
woman in the history of the world would have dared write something
so bold, so demanding. Maybe…that's why it was hidden, Lorelei
thought. The woman who thought such things had to be scared; to
write them down must have terrified her.

She wondered what happened to the author. What did the men do
when they found out she wrote this? Lorelei was certain men found
out. Women were never able to hide their basest instincts from men.
Men always found out. The penalty for writing such things must have
been great indeed, considering the severe punishment women faced
for having dinner on the table a few minutes late.

The outer door slammed and Lorelei thrust the paper back into the
safe. She pushed the door closed, hearing the click with satisfaction.
She would not be found out. The safe was locked and she did not have
the combination.

Ogden was still in a strange mood and Lorelei kept a close eye on him as she finished her afternoon chores. He didn't say why he came home early. He headed straight for the study. She was dusting and felt his presence as she swept the cloth over each surface, most of them already clean, aware of his every movement. She worried he would be able to see, be able to tell from her face or her body language that she trespassed. It wasn't the first time she'd read his papers while he was gone, but it was the first time she worried he would find out. But then, none of the documents she'd ever looked at were so…strange. So…foreign. So…dangerous.

She heard the tumblers as Ogden swung the lock of the safe through the combination. For the first time, she wished she could tell from the clicks what the numbers were. She wanted to read more, to find out what else was in those odd papers. She suspected he wouldn't leave these lying on his desk, trusting her to be a good wife and not snoop into his work. None of the things she'd read before had been so disturbing, so…exciting.

She felt electricity shoot from her toes all the way to the top of her head as she dusted, the words of the document running over and over in her head. Resolved: that woman is man's equal. That phrase became a chorus, sung by an entire choir, humming in her head and her heart. She would never be able to forget the phrase. It was something the like of which she had never heard.

She felt Ogden behind her, following her steps as she cleaned. She didn't turn around. It wasn't her place to question her husband, even when he behaved strangely. She acted as though she wasn't aware of his presence, but it was impossible to be unaware. He was so close she felt his breath on her neck. She worried she hadn't taken enough care with the papers. What if she put them back in a position different than he left them? What if he figured out?

His hand snaked around her waist and she stopped, her duster hovering in the air waiting to be assigned to another spot, a spot where no dust resided because she never allowed that to happen. She remained still as he nuzzled her neck and tickled her ear. What was going on? Ogden never acted like this before. First last night, now today…and he hadn't said a word about her oversleeping and missing his breakfast.

"You smell nice." Ogden's words tickled her neck.

"I…it's…lemon." Lorelei stammered, not sure what to say.

"You always smell nice. I should tell you that more often." Ogden nibbled her ear. "I brought you something."

Lorelei went numb with shock. Brought her something? What could he have brought her? She didn't have any needs right now. The house was stocked, the yard was tended, and the children didn't need any clothes. Had she forgotten something and he was trying to remind her subtly? That wasn't his style. But then, nothing else he'd done over the past two days was his style, either. It was like some other man with her husband's face had taken over the house.

Ogden breezed out the door and was back before she could move, bearing a bouquet of flowers in a pretty pink vase. The flowers – she didn't know their name, they were a kind she'd never seen – were delicate shades of pinks and purples, and she buried her face in them. The smell was exquisite.

"What kind are they?" Lorelei couldn't think of anything else to say in such a strange moment.

"Orchids."

"I've never heard of those."

"Most people haven't. Most orchids went extinct hundreds and hundreds of years ago. We found them in a deserted area in that place we visited two years ago. You remember, they used to call it China?"

Lorelei didn't point out to him that he never shared with her where he was going. She never heard of China, but these were gorgeous flowers. "Thank you." It seemed the most appropriate thing to say, and was a lot more polite than "Why did you do this all of a sudden?"

"China. That's right, you don't know about China. We're about ready to publish our discoveries, so people don't know about it yet. It was a really ancient culture, but the land became so polluted and over used that the civilization collapsed about…oh, let me see…about a thousand years ago, I think. Too many people, not enough food, a dangerous combination. These were growing wild all over the place, and we brought some back to see if they would grow here."

Ogden lost interest in China and wandered around the study running his finger along the surface of the windowsills, the furniture, and the woodwork. Lorelei tensed. She hadn't finished her dusting. He was sure to find a speck of something somewhere.

"You do such a wonderful job keeping the house clean. You're a treasure, Lorelei. You know how much I appreciate you, right?"

Lorelei nodded, unable to speak for fear she would choke on the lie. No, she had no idea he appreciated her. He certainly never acted like it, just took what she offered as his due. And it is his due, she reminded herself. He is the man, the head of the household, and it is my duty to make sure he is comfortable without him having to think about the house. It was hard to repeat the familiar mantra with "Resolved: that woman is man's equal" running through her head. She shoved on the phrase mentally, hoping it would retreat back into the ancient past where it belonged. It had no place in her household. She was a good wife. She was trained well.

Ogden was restless. She stood near the corner, afraid he was going to undress her again and have marital duties in his study. She didn't want another weird episode. It was too much for her mind, for her heart, to bear. He watched her as he paced but didn't make any moves toward her, and she started to relax.

"I think…" Ogden started, then stopped, a strange look in his eyes. "I think…I'll take a mist before dinner."

Lorelei gaped at him as he exited, heading for the bathroom and the mister he never went near except in the morning. Taking a mist at this time of day? She'd never heard of such a thing. No one misted in the afternoon. Men misted in the morning and women at night, right before bed. It was the standard schedule. Everyone followed it because it worked. Now here was Ogden, shedding his shirt before he was even out the door as though he couldn't wait to get in the mister.

She picked up the shirt and draped it over the back of his chair. He wouldn't want it wrinkled when he got out. He would expect her to make sure nothing went amiss. She frowned. She was doing her best, but it was difficult when what was going amiss was Ogden himself. She stared at the safe. It was standing open, the forbidden papers calling to her. She shrugged off the intense desire and headed for the kitchen. Ogden had never been so careless with his papers. Maybe she'd get lucky and he would leave the safe open again. Meanwhile she'd better get dinner ready. Just because he was acting unnatural didn't mean she could.

9

The children were home by the time Ogden came downstairs. Lorelei heard him in the hallway and shooed them outside to play. Ogden hated noise and the children tended to be noisy when they first got home, burning off the energy that had been building up all day. She piled a couple of small treats and a cup of hot beverage on a tray and headed toward the study. She decided if he could behave out of character, she could, too.

"I brought you something." Lorelei stood at the door, tray in hand, waiting to be invited to enter. She only entered his study unasked during the day when he wasn't there, and only to clean.

"Come in. My, that looks appetizing. I'm not sure I should eat before dinner, though. I know you spend a lot of time cooking, and I wouldn't want you to think I didn't like the food." Ogden spoke in a cheerful tone but with a note that sounded more like…fear?

It was Lorelei's turn to watch him as he returned to the safe and added something to the pile of paperwork already resting there. She wanted to see what it was but he was between her and the safe, and she was afraid if she craned her neck to see he would catch her snooping. She forced herself to keep a stoic and disinterested look on her face while he placed the paper in the safe and shut the door. The click of the door closing felt like her heart and brain being closed. The treasures inside were once more hidden from her view.

Ogden turned and realized Lorelei was still holding the tray. He came to her side and relieved her of the load, placing it on his desk before taking her in his arms for a kiss. She stood passive, accepting the kiss he bestowed, not returning his affection. She was well trained that a passionate woman would make a man unsettled, worrying about where else she might be spreading her affection while he was gone. She submitted to his embraces until he released her and moved toward the window.

"The weather is lovely today." Ogden was trying to make small talk but he didn't really know how, and his words sounded choppy.

"It's going to get cold again tomorrow. Amity said Merris told her it might snow."

"We'll need to turn up the heat if it snows. I wouldn't want you to be cold."

Lorelei didn't speak. There was no possible answer to such a strange statement, no way she could reply to something she never heard before. Ogden was diligent about turning down the heat when he left in the morning so no energy was wasted warming a house he wasn't in, and she never complained about being cold. She was used to it, and planned her baking for cold days. Hot box did a good job of warming the kitchen, at least, and if she stayed busy, her own motion could help her keep warm.

"I had a great idea this morning while I was at the office. I thought…maybe you and the children would like to take a little vacation this summer? We could go…I don't know, where does one go on vacation?"

Lorelei thought. She didn't know either. They'd never taken a vacation. "I could ask Amity. She and Merris took a vacation once."

"That's a good idea. Merris has a good head on his shoulders. He wouldn't waste money on an overly extravagant vacation. He'd take a sensible vacation, one you could enjoy without worrying about how much it costs."

Lorelei relaxed. That sounded more like Ogden. Okay, so vacation didn't sound like him, but inexpensive vacation was the only kind of vacation she would expect him to take. She nodded, again not trusting herself to speak in this strange situation. She found her voice finally, and was able to escape.

"I need to…call the children in for dinner. They'll need to…wash up", she stammered. "They've been playing…outside. They'll be…dirty."

She raced out of the room toward the kitchen. Hot box was chirping, telling her it was time to stir the vegetables. She flew between kitchen and dining room, wanting to make sure she got the plates on the table before Ogden emerged from his study. Molton and Micra came in, presented their hands for inspection, and trotted upstairs obediently to wash. Although their father rarely punished the children – that was her job – they feared his anger almost as much as she did.

10

The next morning, Saturday, a box arrived for Ogden. It was one of his artifact boxes, and Lorelei held it longer than normal before depositing it in his study. He was out for his morning round-a-bout, so it would wait until he returned. She lingered near his desk eyeing the box, wishing she knew what it contained. This was not papers. The papers arrived in a different sort of box. Ogden came up with the system of different boxes. That way he would know even before he opened it what sort of treasure to expect. He hated surprises.

Lorelei's mother arrived to pick up the children. She was taking them to the seashore for the day, an opportunity to teach them about starfish and jellyfish and other strange creatures that once lived in the ocean. The nearest coast was thirty minutes away by people mover, so her mother brought mini transit, hoping to shorten the journey by a few minutes.

"Have you heard?" Mom was breathless, an unusual condition for her.

"No, I haven't heard anything. We've been busy and I haven't really had a chance to…" Lorelei stopped at the look on Mom's face. This was not the typical news of a scandalous nature her mother usually preferred. This was something different…or was Lorelei imagining it, because of all the strange goings on at her own house lately?

"The men are going to announce something soon." Mom watched the door, probably with the same thought running through Lorelei's head. It would not do to have Ogden hear them talking about…whatever. "The announcement is…not normal. It's…scary. Some people are saying it will be the end of civilization."

"Oh, come on, Mom, you always exaggerate." Lorelei mouthed the familiar words, but she didn't feel them. She was willing to believe Mom might be right today. Things were definitely not normal.

"No, it's no exaggeration, at least not according to my sources." Mom always referred to the ladies she gossiped with as 'sources'. "The men discovered something…something that may lead to clues about why the former civilization collapsed. Something they worry might happen to us if they don't prevent it."

Lorelei remembered Amity's words: Disaster. Catastrophe. Women. She didn't share her own information with her mother, because nothing Mom ever heard would stay between them. Within seconds of its telling, the word would be on the street. Lorelei didn't understand her hesitation. After all, Amity was the one who told her, and Amity was only slightly more discreet than Mom. Still, Lorelei didn't want to be the responsible party for alerting the men to what the women knew.

"Mom, you might want to be careful who you say that to."

"It's not like I go blabbing everything I know to everyone." Mom was on the defensive.

Lorelei stifled a smile. It actually was like Mom went blabbing everything she knew to everyone, but she would try to placate her. "It's just…the walls have ears, you know. We have to be careful they don't find out we know. The men, I mean."

Mom nodded. "Of course, dear, you think I don't know that? Okay, so I tell things to women friends, I'll admit that. I'm not ashamed of it. But you think any man out there has any idea how much I know, and when I knew it? Not one…not even your father."

Lorelei relaxed. Of course she didn't tell the men. She knew Mom had a large network of sources, and she never got in trouble for finding out things she wasn't supposed to know. That meant only one thing: the men did not know how much she knew.

"Sorry, Mom. I've just been a bit…tense…lately."

"Really? Why? Is something happening?"

Lorelei tried to frame an answer that wouldn't be embarrassing or give away painful household secrets. Hot box rescued her by chirping with its insistent chirp, and she raced to the kitchen to stir the lunch. When she returned, Mom moved on to the next subject of interest.

"Okay, so I'm keeping the children all day. Can I have them overnight, too? I thought it might be fun for your father to visit with the children."

Ogden thrust open the door and entered just as Mom finished her thought. Lorelei invited him to join them. She could not give permission for an overnight without him. Mom filled him in on the outing, and that she wanted to keep them for the night. Lorelei watched Ogden's face. He nodded, so slightly it was barely noticeable, but it was noticed by the two women who watched with intent concentration. Lorelei agreed to the overnight and left to pack a small bag for the children.

When she returned, neither Ogden nor Mom had moved from their positions. Men tended not to interact with women unless they were related or married to them, and in-laws were to be tolerated. It annoyed Lorelei because her parents were so nice to Ogden, and he ignored her mother whenever they were in a room together. Today she felt less annoyance than relief, because she wasn't sure if Mom could contain herself with such momentous news. This was news Ogden must be familiar with; the only thing he didn't know was that the women had some inkling. Lorelei intended to keep him in the dark.

"Bye, Mom. Don't let the children eat candy before dinner. And make sure they wash their hands." Lorelei hugged her mother and the two women walked together to the door, leaving Ogden in the living room like a marble statue.

"I'm glad the children are going to be away" Ogden said as she returned. "I have a lot of work to do today, and it'll give them a chance to play without worrying about bothering me."

Lorelei stared. That was not the sort of sentiment she expected to hear. Why was Ogden worried about the children being able to play? He hardly noticed the children unless one of them spoke out of turn at dinner, and she was sure he had no idea what they played, or if they played. She added it to her growing list of weird behaviors. If the list got much longer, she might need to see about sending him to the medic.

Ogden disappeared into his study and Lorelei turned her attention to lunch. Soon she would have to call him out for their silent meal, but she decided to wait a few extra minutes. She was enjoying an unusual moment of peaceful silence. Well, not totally peaceful. Every time silence fell, all she could hear was "Resolved: that woman is man's equal."

11

Ogden appeared for lunch before Lorelei called him. He really was so peculiar lately. She moved between kitchen and dining room, rushing to make up for the fact that his plate was not on the table when he sat down. Of course, it was his fault for coming out early, but men were not expected to take that into consideration. A wife should know her husband's needs before he did, and she failed to anticipate his out of character appearance.

She felt Ogden watching her as she moved between hot box and table, cold box and sink, and back again. She snapped out the table cloth and covered the table; he stood aside to be out of her way, but did not offer to help. She breathed a sigh of relief. That would have been more weird than she could have handled in a week full of weird. She felt him watching her as she laid the plates and silver on the table, and got so flustered she gave him the wrong silverware and forgot his glass. Now he would think she was inefficient and messed up a lot, because he wasn't watching when she did her usual daily routine that was smooth and efficient.

When lunch was on the table, Lorelei started to settle into her place at the foot of the table. Ogden motioned for her to sit beside him, where Micra usually sat. She picked up her plate to move and tripped over her own feet, or something, landing with a graceless thud on her knees. She struggled to get up, and was as grateful as she was surprised when Ogden stood and offered a hand to help her to her feet.

The orchids graced the center of the table and their odor filled the room with a sweet, sad smell. Lorelei paused. Sad? What was sad about a smell? She shook her head, confused by her own thoughts, and brushed off the constant refrain that threatened to tip her world upside down. She settled on the edge of Micra's chair, not able to get comfortable in this unfamiliar configuration. Ogden watched her with an amused smile, and picked up his fork. Now she could pick up her own fork and eat the food that tasted like ashes in her mouth. It was like she wasn't even real anymore, like she died and was in some perverted purgatory. She didn't even believe in purgatory. Her parents did, but she assumed Ogden's religion when they married and she no longer believed in anything he didn't believe.

Lunch was silent, but it was not the heavy, suffocating silence she was used to. The mood between them was charged with electricity, not just sexual electricity, which was strange enough, but some other sort of electricity, some sort of excitement and danger. Lorelei tried to concentrate on her food but she kept watching Ogden. Because she was watching him, she was aware that he spent most of the lunch watching her. She scraped her fork along the plate to satisfy him she was eating and not wasting her lunch, but she wasn't sure she managed to get much of it into her mouth. When he put down his fork and pushed back his chair, she laid down her own fork with a sigh of relief.

"You don't have to quit eating if you're not finished. We don't have to be so formal today. Relax and enjoy your lunch." Ogden was staring out the window and not looking at Lorelei as he spoke.

Lorelei pushed back her own chair and picked up the plates. "I'm full", she announced. "I really don't think I could eat another bite."

"You seem...nervous." Ogden turned and watched her clear the table.

"It's just...I don't know, maybe there's some sort of bug going around. I don't feel quite myself today." Lorelei shrugged, hoping to divert the conversation away from her.

"You should rest. Sit down, don't worry about the chores for one day. You don't want to get sick." Ogden took the plates out of her hand and carried them to the kitchen.

Lorelei watched his retreating back. She nearly fell when he took the plates. That never happened before. Men didn't clear tables. Men didn't wash dishes. And men didn't tell their wives to rest and not worry about chores, even if the wives were sick. It was a violation of nature's laws...and God's laws, which was even worse. Lorelei mumbled, and followed him to the kitchen.

"Really, I'll be fine. I can't leave the house in the state it's in. What if someone were to drop by?" Lorelei took the plates he was still holding and deposited them in the sink.

"The house is clean. There isn't a speck of dust or dirt anywhere. And the children are with your mother, so you don't have to worry about them. Relax. Just one day, then you'll feel better and you'll get back to your regular routine. You don't want to get sick."

Lorelei started to protest that she could not possibly feel better when things were so strange and out of order, but before she could say anything, Ogden lifted her, carried her to the living room, and deposited her on the sofa. He pulled a blanket over her and brought her a pillow from the bedroom. As if that wasn't enough to make any woman worry, he adjusted the pillow behind her head with a concern she had never seen before. She waved him away to get him to stop fussing over her.

"I'll be all right. You don't need to do all this."

"I want to do it. I want to…take care of you. I want you to…be happy." Ogden had a strange look on his face, and his voice cracked as he spoke.

Lorelei assured him she was happy and she didn't need to be taken care of. She promised him she would sit for at least an hour and rest before she washed the dishes. Satisfied, he retreated into the study and closed the door, alone with his box full of artifacts and his safe full of papers. Lorelei wished she could find a reason to go in there, to interrupt him ever so briefly, to get a look at what was in the box, but she knew if he told her to sit on the sofa, she'd better sit until the hour was up. Then she'd get up, wash the dishes, sort the laundry, and try to get the world to turn right side up before dinner.

12

Lorelei didn't realize she fell asleep until she woke to the sound of dishes breaking. She flew to her feet in a fit of guilt and fear. The sky was turning dark and she hadn't started dinner. The kitchen door was half open and the light was on, so someone must be in there.

Ogden had his head in cold box and didn't hear her enter. She surveyed the mess in the kitchen. A broken plate on the floor, dirty dishes in the sink, and boxes and cans of food scattered over the counter. Whatever he was looking for, it seemed he hadn't found it.

"Ogden?" Lorelei approached with caution, watching nervously to sense his mood.

He stood and bumped his head on the top of cold box. Swearing softly, he rubbed his head and turned toward her. "I have no idea how to find anything in here", he confessed.

"What are you looking for? I'll help you find it."

"I thought I would just have cheese and crackers for dinner, so I didn't disturb you. I thought that would be easy. But I can't find the cheese, and I can't find the crackers."

Lorelei stepped over the broken glass and rummaged in the mess on the counter. She pulled out the box of crackers and handed them to him as she passed him on her way to cold box. The cheese was in its usual spot, and cold box managed to maintain at least a semblance of its usual order. Ogden hadn't managed to create nearly the destruction he had with the cupboards.

"I'm sorry. I made a big mess, and I was trying to help so you wouldn't have to work so hard tonight. Now you have a lot more work because of me." Ogden looked and sounded almost like Molton when he misbehaved and was trying to wheedle her into being lenient.

"Don't worry about it. I can get it back in order." Lorelei shooed him to the table with his food and got him a plate and a knife. "I just need you out of the way so I can move around."

Ogden patted her on the fanny as he passed and she jumped. She heard of men who did that with their wives – Merris used to pat Amity when they were first married – but Ogden had never been physical. Any minor shows of affection were saved for the routine marriage bed times and not expressed out of proper order. At least, until this week, Lorelei thought, her cheeks reddening with shame at the memory.

She started to clean the kitchen, but Ogden called and she had to tend to him. He was at the table cutting cheese and laying it on crackers. His brow wrinkled in concentration. This was not a normal role for him, and he was cutting the cheese much as he would carve a hunk of meat.

"Bring a plate. You should eat."

Lorelei didn't answer. She retreated into the kitchen and returned with a plate for herself. She automatically assumed when Ogden told her she should do something it was an order, and she did not question his authority. As she settled into her chair, her traitorous brain reminded her of the new refrain: Resolved: that woman is man's equal. She pushed it aside, snapping at the thought to go away and stay away, telling it how stupid anyone could be to think such a thing, and scolding her brain for refusing to forget the one thing it must never remember.

She settled in for dinner, accepting several crackers with cheese that looked like it had been hacked rather than sliced, and ate in silence, watching Ogden watching her. They both raised crackers to their mouths and chewed, never taking their eyes off the other. It was like a game, but she didn't understand the rules. She bit her finger and yelped, but when Ogden asked after her she told him she was fine.

And she was. She was fine, whatever it took to get there. She would not let this odd behavior of her husband, nor the odd declaration from a long-silent voice, disturb her. She fought hard against her baser instincts so she could become a good, obedient wife, and she was not going to lose all that hard work and have to start again. She was going to get over whatever disturbed her, and accept that Ogden decided to be odd for his own reasons. If he felt it was appropriate to pat her fanny, she would assume it must be so. If he felt having marital duties in the study was right and proper, she would assume it must be so. Perhaps it was a test, and if so, she intended to pass. She would show him she was as good a wife as ever, no matter what sort of strange things he threw her way.

Dinner finished, Ogden told her to leave the cleaning. She shook her head. No, this was one order she could not follow. Leaving the kitchen in such a mess would disturb her so much she would be unable to sleep. She picked up the dishes and took them to the sink, then began the tedious process of putting her kitchen back in order. Ogden watched for a minute, then to her surprise he moved to her side and began helping. Holding up cans of food and beverage, he asked her where they went, and installed them in their proper place on her instruction. She moved around him in silence, not protesting his presence, but not comfortable either.

They worked side by side until everything was back where it belonged and the kitchen once again sparkled. She laughed to watch Ogden try to figure out how to use tidy box and brush to clean up the glass, but stepped forward to help him, having him hold tidy box while she brushed the glass. She dumped the broken pieces and the kitchen was once again normal. She wished she could clean up her life so quickly and easily, but she had a feeling the pieces were too scattered for easy access.

It was time for her misting, and she headed to the bathroom. This was the one time of day she could truly call her own and she cherished it. Standing under the faucet with water running over her tired back, she allowed herself to relax. The water was warm and the steam rose around her, enveloping her in a soft cloud. She decided to take a slightly longer than normal mist tonight to ease the tiredness from her troubled sleep.

She tensed when the door to the bathroom opened. It was Ogden, of course. He was the only other person in the house. No one ever disturbed her while she was misting before, and she didn't know what to expect in this odd new world he had plunged her into. She closed her eyes and pretended not to notice she wasn't alone, so she didn't realize he undressed until he stepped into the mister with her. She stepped back, her instinct to keep distance between herself and the interloper who violated her territory. She reached behind her and moved the water from warm to hot so he would not have to experience a less than ideal mist.

He stepped toward her and she was trapped. She could not move any further. Her back was pressed against the tile of the mister. He wrapped his arms around her, and she could feel his manhood hard and firm against her thigh. He kissed her and put his hands against her chest. She kept her eyes closed, disturbed by yet another act of impropriety, another improper location for marital duties, but did not refuse him. That would not be in the playbook of a good wife, and she had long since gotten past the urge to push him away and tell him no. She stood in the mist, her hair dripping, water running off her nose and into her mouth, as he pressed against her and made love to her with a strange heat and passion that threatened to suffocate her.

They remained in the mister until the water turned cold. Ogden held her and rocked back and forth, saying her name over and over, even after his manhood went soft. She remained passive until he moved her arms around his waist and asked her to hold him. She held him as he wished until he released her, the water now making him shiver as he searched for an extra towel. He wrapped the towel around his dripping hair and held out her towel as she stepped out of the mister. He wrapped the towel around her and rubbed her dry, lingering over her private parts, moaning with pleasure as he dried her chest, and touching her face with an affection that felt almost real.

He helped her dress, slipping her nightgown over her head and helping her get her arms into the sleeves. He knelt in front of her and put her slippers on her feet with such serious attention that she didn't have the heart to point out he put them on the wrong feet. When he turned to leave, she slipped her feet out and reversed the slippers. She slid out of the bathroom behind him and followed him to the bedroom. It was clear he intended to perform marital routines tonight, in spite of the strange interlude in the bathroom. She slipped into the bedroom and was about to turn off the light when he stopped her.

"Please. Leave it on. I want to look at you."

Lorelei left the light on. She slipped her gown over her head and slid under the covers beside her husband...or was it her husband? This man was acting very unlike her husband and she debated refusing him as he reached for her. Her training got the better of her, and she allowed him to take her in his arms. When he was done she turned off the light and rolled over to go to sleep, hoping nightmares would not trouble her tonight.

13

Lorelei tossed and turned, and woke up tangled in the covers. She struggled to get free, but the covers were wrapped so tightly she couldn't figure out how to get out of them. A hand reached down, removing the end of the blanket from the knot and rolling her over and over until the covers released her. Ogden lifted her off the bed and stood her on her feet.

"Better?" His look teased her, but it was not the mocking look she was accustomed to seeing when she needed help with a simple chore. It was almost like he…understood…or something.

She nodded, indicating she didn't need any further help, and wrapped her robe against the cold air while he fiddled with the thermostat.

"It seems to be broken", he announced. "I'd better go downstairs and check on it."

Lorelei thrust her feet into her warm slippers and padded to the kitchen. Even on Sunday Ogden wanted his breakfast at the usual time, and she went to work with the pan and hot box. By the time Ogden returned, the heater now restored and warmth creeping into the household, she had a hot breakfast ready. His plate and silver were on the table, and he settled in with his morning paper and his hot beverage, waiting until Lorelei brought his food fresh off hot box.

She settled in her own place at the end of the table. Ogden nodded as she sat but didn't insist she move closer this morning. She breathed a sigh of relief. At least he wasn't going to be weird this morning…she didn't think she could handle much after another troubled night. Her dreams were frightening and outlandish, but fortunately she couldn't remember the details. All she could remember was being scared.

Ogden retreated to his study after breakfast. Lorelei peeked in to ask if he needed anything, her regular weekend routine giving her the hope of catching a glimpse of what was in the artifact box. It was no use. Ogden stood between her and any interesting things he might have left lying about, and she was sure he would have them put away by the time she entered his study to clean. On Sundays, he took his round-a-bout late and she would not have a chance to clean until late afternoon.

Lorelei was dressed and waiting when Ogden appeared for church. He told her he planned to accompany her that morning, so she didn't head out the door when she heard first bell ring. She waited until he was ready, worried they would be late. Pastor hated it when you walked in late, and she hated the look he gave them. They left the house just in time to reach church by final bell.

Pastor preached a majestic sermon that morning, but it was difficult for Lorelei to listen. The sermon was about the good wife, a popular theme, but particularly potent today. He worked up to a rousing finale, his booming voice filling the church with the glories of the obedient woman and the terrors that awaited a woman who did not know her place. Lorelei slouched in her pew, unable to forget the strange declaration and the refrain that continued to pass through her head on a continuous loop. It was as though he was preaching the sermon just for her. It was probably her imagination, but she thought she saw Ogden nod to Pastor and Pastor nod back as though there were some grand project they had just completed.

The walk home was chilly, and Lorelei pulled her thin coat up to her ears trying to keep warm. She jumped with surprise when Ogden put his arm around her, sharing his thick warm coat and warming her thin body with his own. She pressed against him, grateful for the warmth, and he held her lightly but firmly as they moved toward home. She forced herself not to think about what a strange move this was for the man she had known for almost a decade, and tried to comfort herself with the knowledge that it was not strange behavior for the man she had known for the past three days.

14

Mom planned to keep the children until just before dinner. Lunch was uneventful, and Lorelei proceeded with her chores once church was over. She was the good wife, she told herself, the good, obedient wife who anticipated her husband's every need before he needed it, and took care of her house and children. She didn't expect more from life.

She had not had a chance to clean the study before the children came home. Ogden remained sequestered all day and didn't venture on his usual routine. Whatever was in that box must be fascinating because he seemed unable to tear himself away. The absence of the children made the house quiet, and in light of the strange occurrences, somewhat spooky. She was glad to see Molton rush up the steps and burst into the door, sliding to a stop and landing on his bottom when she put her finger to her lips.

"Daddy's working."

Molton nodded and tiptoed the rest of the way through the house to the backyard. Lorelei grabbed him and hugged him but he wriggled out of her grasp and headed toward the swing, silent for nearly two days and waiting for him to pump it as high as he could go. Micra followed him into the house, no warning needed. She was always lady-like, at least until she got outdoors where she could whoop it up with the best of them, and would keep up with Molton until she sensed someone watching.

Mom settled on the sofa and Lorelei brought them both hot beverages. As they wrapped cold fingers around the warm cups, the two women let out a simultaneous sigh, a sigh which would have emphasized to any observer just how alike they were. The women sat in silence as they sipped, and Lorelei threw nervous glances toward the study.

"He's home." It wasn't so much a question as an announcement.

"Yes. He hasn't gone out all day, except for church."

Mom watched as Lorelei collected the cups and headed toward the kitchen. She wished people would quit watching her. It was making her uncomfortable. When she returned, her mother continued to keep her eyes on her daughter's face as the two fell into silence again.

"Are you all right?" Mom's voice held a trace of panic, and Lorelei winced.

"I'm…fine. I've just been…tired and maybe a bit…I don't know, feverish?" Lorelei regretted the question mark the moment the statement came out.

Mom nodded. "I thought so. Something is going on. Give."

"I don't think…no, it's not something…it's not something I can talk about."

Mom bent closer, her voice lowered to a conspiratorial whisper. They both glanced at the study door as she spoke, but the door remained closed and there was no evidence Ogden heard.

"Is it Ogden?" Lorelei nodded, and Mom leaned closer. "Let me guess. He's acting strange."

"Yes. Very strange."

"How?"

Lorelei hesitated. She had a close relationship with her mother, but she wasn't prepared to share the shame she felt the last few days, not even with the woman who had borne and raised her.

"He wants to…have marriage duties…in strange places, at strange times, right?"

Lorelei stared. "How did you know?"

Mom looked around. Satisfied no one else was listening, she lowered her voice further. "It's happening to me, too…your father. He's behaving strangely. He's never asked to have the children overnight before."

"I thought that was strange. I thought…maybe you were just saying that so we'd let you have them for your own pleasure."

"Since when do I do things for my own pleasure that would annoy your father? What sort of woman do you think I am?" Mom reared back, insulted by the innocent suggestion.

Lorelei apologized, and launched into an explanation of the strange happenings. The strange passionate encounters. The affection. The orchids…Mom nodded. She received orchids, too. The kitchen, where he tried to help out…the…Lorelei paused, blushed, and plunged on…the study. Then the walk home from church and his attempts to help her keep warm.

"You know what I think?" Mom was fond of the phrase and Lorelei humored her by shaking her head, so Mom could continue with her opinion in the one place where her opinion would be heard and respected. "I think…the men have all gone crazy. Like, maybe something…you know, something in the water…or the air…but not at home, because we're not crazy. Something, maybe, at that new site…maybe they caught something from those old…things…they look at."

Lorelei nodded. It made sense. She wasn't sure it was in the water or the air, though. She thought it might be in the papers, maybe even in the artifacts. What could possibly make the men behave like that, though? The one paper she read didn't seem like enough to account for the strange behaviors. The men would laugh it off, see it as the insane ramblings of some long dead woman who probably got what she deserved from the men of her time. No, this was bigger than one document, one piece of paper. This was huge. So big…

"Mom, I think…I think…they found something there. I don't think they caught something." Lorelei paced, unable to sit still now she knew it infected her father, too. "It must have…Ogden…and Dad... must think it's really…important."

"And Merris." Mom crossed her hands with a smirk, knowing she was imparting information her daughter should have, and didn't. "All the men…every one of them…they are all acting this way."

"Merris? How come Amity didn't say anything?"

"Probably for the same reason you didn't say anything until I put you in a corner…the same reason I almost didn't say anything. It's embarrassing. It's shameful. How can we talk about something like that?"

"So…Amity told you?"

"She came by yesterday morning. She was in tears and didn't know who to turn to. She needed to talk to someone, and her mother…well, you know her mother…"

Lorelei nodded. Yes, she knew Amity's mother. Amity's mother was a good wife, an obedient wife, but she was not a good mother. She made Amity's life so much hell that Amity was relieved when they promised her to Merris. She didn't like Merris, but she thought things would be better once she got away from her mother. But they weren't.

"Anyway, Amity was all upset because she didn't know what was happening. She was angry when I laughed, because she didn't know…"

50

"Didn't know what?" Lorelei hated it when Mom stopped a story without getting to the end. It was even worse today, when the story was so important.

"She didn't know that...well, her story helped me. It released me from my own shame, my own horror. I realized it wasn't just your dad going crazy, you see. All the men...from what I found out, every single man who was on that trip has just gone totally insane."

Lorelei frowned. "Found out how?"

"You know me. I have a lot of friends. They tell me things, but only if I know what to ask. Just like you...I had to ask the right question to find out what was wrong. You weren't going to tell me, were you?"

Lorelei agreed she hadn't intended to say anything. "So the women just...told you? Stuff like...*this*?"

"Not...well, yes...but...I had to tell them first. I had to say it, then they would just say yes or no. They all said yes."

Lorelei heard the study door creak before Mom did. She was on her feet headed toward the hallway before Ogden could even get his head out.

"Do you need anything?"

Ogden shook his head. "No. I thought I heard voices, but I guess it's just your mother."

"Yes, it's...*just*...my mother." Lorelei tried to keep the anger out of her voice at his dismissal of her mother yet again, but she heard it creep in and started to stammer something. Ogden stopped her.

"I didn't mean that, you know. I just meant...it wasn't someone with...you know...a package...or something...for me." Ogden stammered in his rush to reassure Lorelei, another odd incident in a man who a few days ago would simply have shrugged and returned to his study.

"Do you...want to join us...for a hot beverage?" Lorelei offered the olive branch.

"That...would be...nice. But...oh, look at the time. I haven't had my round-a-bout yet." Ogden grabbed his coat and rushed outside, escaping from an uncomfortable situation. He wouldn't be back until dinner, leaving this late.

"That's good. Now we can talk for real." Mom didn't seem perturbed that her son-in-law preferred to avoid her company.

"I have to cook dinner."

"I'll help. We can talk while we work." Mom's voice didn't brook any argument, and Lorelei stood aside to allow her mother to enter the kitchen first. "You sit. Let me cook tonight. You look tired."

Lorelei shook her head. She handed Mom some vegetables to prepare while she spiced the meat. The two women chatted about inconsequential things while they moved around the kitchen, two women perfectly in tune with each other who understood what the other was going to do next and managed not to be in her way. Lorelei felt comfort seep back as the old familiar routines of her childhood spent learning how to be a woman made her feel like the world might be all right after all.

15

Lorelei invited Mom to dinner but Mom refused. She needed to get home and fix dinner for Dad, and she was running late already. Lorelei saw her out, relieved when she turned down the invitation. Things were difficult enough with Ogden acting so strange; having her mother at dinner would only make it worse.

The children didn't respond when she called them for dinner. It was starting to get dark and she couldn't see the corners of the yard, so she assumed they were playing hide and find. She turned on the light and called again. Neither of them answered. The yard appeared to be empty. Lorelei searched every possible hiding place, but the children were not in the yard. Micra's doll was face down on the grass, the only sign anyone was in the yard that day.

She rushed upstairs to see if they'd come into the house without her seeing and gone to wash. It wasn't like them – they liked to play outside as long as possible – but since their father wasn't acting like himself lately, why should she expect the children to act like themselves?

They were not upstairs. They were not in the living room or in the bathroom. The house was empty. The only other living thing was the vase of orchids on the table, mocking her with their beauty at this time that was so frightening.

She turned toward the door, trying to decide if she should go look for them but not sure where to go. She didn't even know how long they'd been gone. She should have checked on them but having Mom here altered her routine, and now she was paying the price. How could she have been talking about herself, thinking about herself? It was her failure to be eternally vigilant, the way she learned, that led to the disappearance of her children.

Lorelei made up her mind and snatched her coat off the rack. She noticed the children's coats were gone. At least wherever they are, they'll be warm, she thought as she headed for the door.

The door opened just as she reached it, banging her in the head and causing her to lose her balance. She dropped to the floor, hurting her wrist as she put her hand down to break her fall. She crawled to her knees and grabbed the legs of the intruder. As her arms wrapped around his knees, she realized it was Ogden. He helped her to her feet.

53

Two little faces peeked out from behind his knees, surprised to see their mother sitting on the floor, but Lorelei didn't notice.

"Are you okay? Oh, you were going out."

"I was just...I need to...find the children. They're not...in the back yard."

Ogden tried to help Lorelei off with her coat but she resisted. "No, I need to find the children!"

"The children are here. They went with me. I thought they could use an outing."

Lorelei nearly fell to the floor again, this time in shock, but Ogden's arm around her waist prevented her from falling. She leaned against him for support, her breath coming in short, sharp gasps. "They went with you?" Things could not get stranger.

"Yes. I thought...it might be nice to have company. They might enjoy the exercise. And we could...get to know each other." Ogden sounded defensive as he explained himself.

Lorelei nodded. There was nothing she could say. He was right, of course. Ogden was always right. It wasn't her place to argue. Still...he'd never taken the children anywhere. That was her job.

"Something smells good." Ogden dropped a hint, a gentle reminder that she was being remiss in her duties.

"Oh! Yes, it's time for dinner. Children, show me your hands."

Molton and Micra moved finally, now that their mother was acting like their mother again. They stuck out their hands, filthy from playing, and Lorelei shooed them upstairs to wash. "And under your fingernails!"

Ogden settled at the table, his usual post, but he had to wait tonight because the children were not ready. Lorelei hoped he wouldn't be upset, because after all, it was sort of his fault the children weren't washed yet. If they had been home, they'd have been sitting at the table waiting for him.

Hot box had given up on her, and the chirping sound that told her dinner was ready was silent. She rushed to the kitchen, hoping the dinner had not burned while they played out their little drama. She opened hot box and found the food was done to a turn, perfect as usual. She pulled it out and dipped up the plates as the children clattered down the stairs, slowing to a quiet tiptoe when they remembered their father was in the dining room. Children were not meant to be hooligans, he always admonished them.

Dinner was strange and surreal. Ogden made pleasant conversation about their outing, and even allowed Molton to interject his own opinions. Lorelei frowned. Children were not supposed to speak at the table. This was unprecedented. This was weird, strange, frightening. The world tipped further off center as Lorelei listened to the banter between her son and his father, two men who barely knew each other this morning, and probably hadn't spoken this many words to each other in Molton's entire life.

Micra remained silent, along with her mother, both of them silenced by years of training about the proper role of women. Lorelei was jolted by the realization that her daughter already internalized the role of the good wife, the obedient wife, and practiced it daily with her good daughter, obedient daughter attitude. The girl could be quite lively, jumping and running without restraint when it was just her and her brother playing together, but when her father was around she fell silent and bowed her head, just as she saw her mother do when men were present.

Lorelei tried to stop the surge of resentment that welled up inside her, but it wasn't possible. Why did her little daughter have to be a woman before she finished being a child? Her brother was allowed to play without thinking about being an adult. Why couldn't Micra have fun, play, and not think about the world of men and their expectations? Had Lorelei been like that as a child? She couldn't remember. She made a mental note to ask her mother when she saw her next.

Dinner finally ended and the dishes were washed. Lorelei escorted her children to their rooms. They would be allowed to play quietly until bedtime, but after dinner was adult time, and children were expected to be neither seen nor heard. She helped them get toys from the top shelf of the closet beyond their reach, told them not to destroy the room, and retreated downstairs to read. She didn't know why this had to be adult time, since she and Ogden never spent it together, but rules were rules. She would read while he worked in his study.

16

Ogden settled beside her on the sofa, his own book open on his lap. He put one arm around her shoulders and turned the pages with the other. Lorelei sat stiff and still beside him, her book unopened, the bookmark still on the page where she stopped reading. Ogden scooted closer until they touched, and pulled her head down to rest on his shoulder.

"You don't feel like reading?"

Lorelei shook her head. She didn't know what to say. They had not read together even once in their marriage. His presence disturbed her and she didn't think it was possible to read in this state.

Ogden put down his book. "You're upset."

Lorelei shook her head again, unable to speak.

"I've done something. You're...angry?" Ogden stared into her face.

"No. I'm...fine. It's just...I assumed you'd work tonight."

"I need a break. I've been working too hard lately. I need to spend time with my family. You know, enjoy life a little."

Ogden stumbled over the unfamiliar words. He sounded almost as though he were rehearsing a script. Lorelei shot a furtive glance toward his face but she was unable to read what he was thinking. He looked as stoic as ever, but his words held just the slightest trace of affection. She struggled to get free but he held her shoulders in an embrace that felt more like bondage. It was useless to resist. She opened her book.

"I think...it's a really good book. I do want to read." Lorelei couldn't remember what book she was reading. She stared at the words on the page. They looked like so much gibberish.

Ogden relaxed and returned to his reading. The couple sat on the sofa for their usual evening adult time, for the first time spending an evening together, and read their separate books, but he never took his arm from around her shoulder. Lorelei felt compelled to remain beside him, but she got the feeling he intended something different. Something...pleasant, perhaps? Something...loving? No, not possible. They married because they were told to marry. Love was not required.

Lorelei slipped off to put the children to bed and when she returned to the sofa, Ogden was gone. She breathed for what felt like the first time all evening and settled onto the sofa to read. She heard noises in the study, and realized his determination not to work was an act put on for her benefit. In the end, he could not spend an evening in domestic bliss anymore than she could. Work was his life, and her rare moments of solitude were hers.

Ogden appeared again just as she was getting ready for her mist. She tensed, afraid there would be a repeat of last night, but Ogden just wanted to tell her good night, and he was going to bed. He told her to enjoy her mist, and don't forget to turn out the lights before she came to bed. He headed upstairs and she relaxed when she heard the bedroom door close. This was as close to normal as he had behaved all week…still disturbing, telling her to enjoy her mist, but…not as disturbing as his other recent behaviors.

Lorelei decided this was a great time to be the obedient wife. She would enjoy her mist. She stepped into the warm water and arched her back as it ran down her body, soothing and warming her cold, tired muscles. She closed her eyes and stretched her arms. She felt good for the first time in days. She started to slip into a reverie, but was jolted back to reality by the recurring refrain that bothered her so much: Resolved: that woman is man's equal.

If I really am Ogden's equal, she thought, I am as entitled to hot water as he is. She reached for the faucet and started to turn the warm water to hot, but her years of training stopped her. No. Just because some stupid piece of paper from a long ago time claimed for women the rights that belong to men, it did not mean she got to have a hot mist. She stepped into the warm water and scrubbed herself clean.

She dried herself and pulled on her night clothes. She stared at herself in the mirror. Ogden called her beautiful. Was she? She examined her face from every angle and decided she was not. She was not ugly, no, not at all, but she certainly wasn't beautiful. She had a nice face, a decent face, a face most women would not be ashamed to have, but she could not, would not, call herself beautiful.

She clicked off the light and checked the other lights in the house. She made sure the front door was locked, and set the pot on hot box to be ready for hot beverage in the morning. She climbed the stairs and slid into bed beside her husband. She clicked off the light as he turned toward her and took her in his arms. He didn't attempt to make love to her, just held her and stroked her hair as she fell asleep. He whispered something as she drifted off, something she couldn't quite hear, but it sounded like he said "Don't leave me."

17

Lorelei struggled awake. Her dreams were strange, tormenting, dreams of women dressed as men while men cooked dinner. She even had a dream where men bore children right along with women. The strange, upside down world was getting to her, causing even her dreams to torture her, teasing her with sights no woman should ever, or would ever, see.

She fell back into a disturbed slumber where professors wrote math equations on the board while a young woman huddled in the back, hunched down wearing a man's coat to hide from prying eyes. The dream, and her sleep, ended when she was discovered, a young man who looked suspiciously like Ogden grabbing the cap that covered her long hair, exposing her to the ridicule of the entire group. She woke up in a cold sweat and shivered in the chill morning.

Her robe and slippers were beside the bed and she slipped into their warmth, wrapping her arms around her against the cold. She sat on the edge of the bed for what seemed like an eternity, listening to the regular breathing that told her Ogden was still asleep. That wouldn't last long, if time monster was correct. Lorelei needed to get up and make breakfast.

Hot box warmed the cold kitchen quickly and she fell into her morning routine. It was Monday. Ogden would go to work, the children would go to school, and nothing would disturb her regular day. Things would not be weird when it was just her in the house. She could cook and clean. Today was laundry day, and she always enjoyed the laundry. It smelled so fresh when it came out that she looked forward to folding.

Ogden came downstairs, fresh from his mist, just as she placed the last plate on the table. Perfectly synchronized, as usual. Perhaps the world was normal after all. She called for the children and heard them clatter around as they got dressed. She was able to forget how strange things had been all week. When the children came down and presented their hands for inspection, the last trace of tension lifted at the normality of the morning. She passed them on their hands and sent them to the table. Breakfast was at the peak of perfection when she spooned it onto their plates.

Ogden stopped at the door as he was leaving for work, and the tension started again. He turned toward her and she got the impression he was about to kiss her goodbye. Instead, he told her there was a staff function that evening and wives were expected to attend. She should wear her best dress…oh, and she would need to be ready when he got home. It was a dinner function and they wouldn't have any time to waste. She nodded. It was a familiar situation, and as usual, delivered at the last possible moment. He assumed she would obey.

The children followed their father out the door, eager for a moment of attention. She frowned. His outing with them yesterday could lead to expectations he would not be able or willing to fulfill. She tried to prevent them from bothering him but he brushed her off and walked them to the curb, his hands resting lightly on their shoulders. The normal morning tipped slightly in the direction of weird, but she caught hold of herself and righted the world before it could turn her upside down.

The rest of the day passed without incident. There was nothing in her chores to disturb her, and no one came or called to deliver strange information. She put off calling Mom. There was something she wanted to ask her but she couldn't recall what it was. She was relieved to put off the talk that would almost certainly turn to the strange events of the past week. With both the men at work, the women would feel free to speak.

Her chores completed, she pulled her best dress out of the closet. A brilliant shade of blue, it was the perfect complement for her fair skin and her brown hair. She put curlers in her hair as soon as Ogden left, and now her hair fell in a cascade of curls all the way down her back. Like all women, she had not cut her hair since she was seven, though she clipped a few ends when they got broken or shaggy. She applied just the right touch of makeup and lingered over her jewelry box, trying to select the right pair of earrings.

Her hand lingered over a pair of bright blue hoops she wore when she was seventeen, but her sense of propriety won out and she settled for a pair of decorous pearls. Fastening the matching pearl necklace around her neck, she surveyed her image in the mirror and declared herself satisfied. Ogden would have no cause to be ashamed of her tonight.

Ogden arrived at the exact moment he said he would be home. His sense of timing was impeccable and she was glad of that. She spent no time worrying about him because of tardiness, unlike some of her friends. She knew what to expect from him every minute…well, almost. Scenes from the past week flashed through her mind but she pushed them aside and turned for inspection. If Ogden was not satisfied, they would not leave until he was.

Lorelei held her breath until Ogden pronounced her fit…in fact, he pronounced her perfect, a word he never used. There was always something…a small flaw, unnoticeable to anyone else, that would eat at him all evening if it was not remedied. Tonight she managed to be flawless, though she couldn't see anything different from the many other nights he insisted something be changed.

Ogden pulled his hand from behind his back and presented her with an orchid. She pulled it out of the box and started to add it to the ones on the table, but he insisted she pin it on her dress. She struggled with the pin and he stepped closer to help her. As his hand brushed against her bodice, she felt him draw in his breath. She stood stiff and still, partially so he would not accidentally stick the pin into her flesh, but also hoping he would be focused on the staff function so he would not decide to behave inappropriately right here in the hallway. He stepped back, examined the effect, and held out his arm to escort her out the door.

Molton and Micra wiggled in the back seat of the micro-transit, squeezed between their parents and full of energy that threatened to burst them out of their seat belts. The vehicle pulled to a stop in front of the home where all the children were being tended for the evening while their parents were at the function. Seeing their friends peering at them through the window, the children were no longer able to contain themselves and erupted out the door. By the time the vehicle started again, the children were being greeted by friends they had been with at school only two hours before as though they had not seen each other in years.

The function was at the downtown office, the only place with a room large enough to hold all the employees and their spouses. Ogden's smaller office building was closer to home, and they passed it as they threaded through the busy streets. Lorelei watched it as they passed, wondering as she had so many times what they actually did behind those walls. The world of work seemed so mysterious. Her only real experience with his work was the strange packages of artifacts and the large envelopes of papers that were regularly delivered and which she placed on his desk without being able to satisfy her curiosity.

The meeting room was bright and noisy when they arrived. They were neither late nor early, and the early arrivals were already in party mood as the function officially commenced. Lorelei knew that dinner, and any announcements, would be planned for later because of the expectation that close to half the people would arrive late. Ogden usually fumed about that, berating his sluggish colleagues for their tardiness. If something was scheduled for a particular time, it was their job to be there at that time. Lorelei nodded whenever he started his rant; it seemed a small enough thing to ask, but she didn't think he needed to get quite so upset.

Tonight he didn't even notice the room was half empty. He moved around the circle of his friends and colleagues, holding onto Lorelei and dragging her along with him as he greeted each of them in turn. She did her part, nodding and smiling, murmuring a polite word as needed, and showing everyone she was a good wife. She knew Ogden was proud of her, still attractive and having kept her figure, and also knew he was proud of her ability to say and do all the right things. She also knew he took full credit for her talents as a good wife. She pushed the thought to the back of her mind as she greeted a few of the wives who were her particular friends with warmth and hugs.

As they moved around the room, Lorelei noticed several of the women wore orchids. All of them were married to men on Ogden's team. One of the other women noticed her looking at the orchid pinned to her bosom, and shrugged. Her look said "Who knows?", a testimony Lorelei could share. Who knows why Ogden…and the other husbands…were acting out of character? Who knows anything?

Once everyone was greeted – Ogden didn't feel compelled to greet people who couldn't be bothered to show up on time – Lorelei was released from the circuit and allowed to congregate with the other women. A small group clustered near the hot beverage table and she headed toward the circle. Amity waved at her from across the room and she changed direction to join that group of women. She noticed Corinne and Grenata in the group, so their Thursday group would be complete.

"You don't know what they're going to announce?" Corinne was quizzing Amity when Lorelei reached them.

"No. Merris has been...silent...about intentions lately. Nobody has been by, and he certainly isn't going to say anything to me."

"Hi, Lorelei." Grenata pulled on Lorelei's sleeve to bring her in closer.

The group was whispering, but no one would see anything suspicious about their whispers. The men expected the women to gossip whenever they got together, so they could whisper about anything and no one would suspect any subversive ideas. Not that they talked about anything particularly subversive, Lorelei reminded herself. This was a group of good wives...well, maybe not Grenata. Lorelei smiled at her friend as though to take the sting out of the thought Grenata would not even have heard.

"Have you heard anything? I know Ogden is lead investigator on this project..."

All heads turned toward Lorelei. She shook her head. Ogden was behaving strangely, but not strangely enough to actually confide anything in her.

"Maybe it's not about that project. Maybe it's..." Lorelei paused, trying to remember something Ogden had said. "Maybe it's...China."

"China? What's that?" Amity breathed directly into Lorelei's ear, and it tickled.

"I don't really know. Ogden said something about it last week...that's where they got these flowers." Lorelei pointed to the orchids on each woman's chest.

"China. I haven't heard about that." Corinne stuck out her chin. "Are you sure you heard correctly?"

"He said they haven't announced it yet. They were going to make an announcement soon."

Amity shook her head. "I don't think this is about... China...but...well, I haven't heard about China, either. Maybe Ogden was trying to...lead you the wrong way?"

Lorelei shook her head. "No, I wasn't asking him anything, other than about the flowers. He brought me a bunch and I'd never seen them before. He sort of said it without thinking, like, it just came out. He acted like I already knew. So probably not a secret. That might be their announcement."

Amity jumped on her mention of the bunch of flowers. Merris brought orchids to Amity. One by one, each woman in the group verified that she, too, received flowers from her husband. Even Grenata, who spent most of her time dodging her irate husband, Lymon, received flowers from a husband who usually only gave her criticisms about how poorly she managed the household. Something was definitely going on.

A bell sounded and the group trooped in to dinner. Wives were placed next to their husbands, and the next wife would be next to her so no man would be sitting next to a woman other than his own wife. Lorelei marveled at the skill that went into coordinating such a seating arrangement for so many people, but there were never mistakes. Men should not be sitting next to a woman other than their own wife, and the company was determined to make sure they didn't violate any social restrictions.

Lorelei found herself seated next to Amity, a rare treat, and they took advantage of the coincidence to whisper to each other. The proximity of their husbands on either side meant they couldn't whisper anything of real interest, but gossiping among the women was expected so they amused themselves by whispering nonsense phrases back and forth, playing a game they devised years ago to see who could come up with the most outlandish collection of words. Lorelei usually won, but she was not at her best tonight and Amity ended up taking the prize.

The dinner was far below the standard Lorelei set in her own kitchen. The meat was dry and the vegetables were soggy, but she choked down enough food to be polite to her hosts. She struggled with eating through the lump in her throat; even if the food was the best she'd ever eaten, she would have found it difficult to eat much. The women watched their husbands carefully and made sure that they did not put another bite in their mouth once their husband laid down his fork...except Grenata, who loved to eat and never managed to notice when Lymon was done. All eyes on her, no one else eating, Grenata ate until she cleaned her plate. A disapproving silence fell over the crowd.

The man at the head of the table stood. Lorelei craned to see if she could recognize him, but the table was long and they were at the other end. Surely that wouldn't be the case if this were about Ogden's

64

project. He would be near the head, where he could reach the podium quickly after being introduced.

The man was a stranger to her. It was not Ogden's supervisor or even the head of the agency. This man was someone else, someone with a job title that was long and important sounding. He spoke for several minutes, explaining who he was and what he did, and giving a long list of credentials. Then he introduced Ogden. Every head turned in their direction.

Ogden stood, slow and deliberate, and held out his hand. An aide rushed to thrust a voice amplifier into his outstretched hand, and his fingers curled around it as though around the hilt of a sword. Lorelei shivered. This was too theatrical. It didn't fit with the normal routine of the staid group. It didn't fit with the normal routine of her husband. Ogden held the voice amplifier to his mouth, but did not speak.

The tension grew. Ogden paused, waiting for it to reach maximum peak before he began to speak. He spoke for less than a minute and when he finished and sat down, the room sat in stunned silence. There was no applause, not even polite applause, for the announcement.

The grand announcement this function was called to deliver was …that there was no grand announcement. Yes, a site had been found, and there were a lot of materials. These were collected and brought home, and were currently in the process of being evaluated. But…and this was the point that astonished Lorelei…the language was so obscure, so primitive, they had not yet been able to decipher a single word. The artifacts were mysterious, strange, and perplexing, mostly just small fragments. This particular site would likely be a long time in the unraveling. Meanwhile, he was going to turn the floor over to Merris, who would fill them in on the China dig. Most of the husbands lost interest, and the wives weren't interested in China to begin with since none of them ever heard a single word about the place until tonight.

Lorelei thought about the paper, the declaration, translated in Ogden's own hand, lying in the safe at home. She thought about the phrase that haunted her – Resolved: that woman is man's equal – and realized Ogden had not told the truth. He was buying himself some time…time to…what? What was he afraid of? Lorelei realized there was a lot more involved in the documents than what she had seen. Something so dreadful, so frightening, something that wasn't about women being equal with men, since everyone knew they were not, something that could change everything they knew. Only something earth shattering, Lorelei realized, could make Ogden, the most conscientious of men, lie to his colleagues.

18

Lorelei submitted to marital duties, then fell into a troubled sleep.
Nothing Ogden said made sense. Her mind kept turning it over and
over, preventing her from falling into a restful slumber. Shortly before
dawn, her mind shut down enough to allow her to catch a short nap
before it was time to wake.

Ogden was already awake when time monster chirped and
reached for her as soon as she stirred. She stiffened. Not in the
morning…please, not in the morning. It was useless. Ogden leapt
totally over the deep end. When he wrapped his mouth around her
nipples, she knew nothing would ever be the same again. But that did
not prepare her for what came next.

Ogden began exploring her body, tracing circles on her stomach
with his tongue and moving lower, lower, until his lips reached…that.
Her most private parts, intended only to receive the manhood, and
now his tongue was slipping into her. She tensed, not sure how to deal
with this new indignity, but her husband didn't appear to notice her
discomfort. He continued to explore with his tongue and his fingers,
and she tried to relax her body into her usual passivity. She was
shocked when an electric sensation, a pleasant sensation, shot through
her body as he touched parts of her anatomy. This was the worst, the
absolute worst…how could a woman possibly enjoy this? Women
aren't supposed to enjoy marital duties, and this…this…it was too
much.

When he was done, Lorelei tried to roll out of the bed to escape
to the kitchen, but Ogden continued to hold her. He wrapped his arms
around her and stroked her back, starting a chain reaction in her brain
that sent paroxysms of pleasure through her body. Shocked and
horrified, she lay in his arms, allowing him to do as he pleased, and
tried not to let him see she enjoyed what he was doing.

"Do you like that?" Ogden whispered in her ear as he stroked her
at the bottom of her spine.

Now she understood. He was testing her. Lorelei didn't answer.
The only honest answer she could possibly give was yes, and that
would be the most certain way to fail the test. He would know, and
her shame would be complete. Then the punishment would begin,
because her humiliation could never be punishment enough for this
transgression.

He continued to stroke her for several minutes, then released her after a deep kiss. She climbed out of bed, acutely aware of him watching her as she pulled on her robe, finally covering the nakedness that was so unnatural at this time of day.

She didn't look at him as she fled the room, and could not look at him over the breakfast table. He had shamed her, and she kept her head down for fear the children could see her shame. Molton was busy with his breakfast and didn't pay attention to his mother, but Micra watched her with eyes that rarely missed anything. She was going to be a smart one, that girl, not like her brother who seemed only interested in playing and breaking things.

Ogden escorted the children to the curb where they would wait for child mover to carry them to school. He waved at Lorelei as he disappeared into the micro-transit, something he had never done before. She stared at the disappearing vehicle and wondered what happened to the man she married, a man steeped in tradition and order, a man who would never behave with impropriety.

She remembered the night before, when her conscientious and honest husband told a lie to his colleagues, and she wondered how many other people in the room knew it was a lie. She recognized the two men who came to the house last week, and was sure they knew. She thought probably Merris and Lymon knew, and any other man who's wife was wearing an orchid. She decided the strange behavior was related to whatever was in those papers.

Voice monster beeped and she raced to answer. Mom was checking on her. "I was worried by how pale you were the other day, dear."

Lorelei murmured some answer, vague and intended to soothe, but Mom didn't accept her story. Under her mother's gentle questioning, Lorelei broke down and confessed all the things that happened since they last saw each other. She told her about the children. She told her about the comment to enjoy her mist. She told her about the meeting, even though Mom was there. After all, Dad was part of this project and would be expected to attend, though he was only working as Ogden's assistant this time and did not speak. And Mom had been wearing an orchid. Still, Mom didn't know what she knew…that Ogden lied.

Then she told her about the morning marital duties. She heard Mom draw in her breath on the other line, sharp and disturbing. "You too?" she asked. Mom affirmed that Dad was, indeed, expecting marital duties at odd times and in odd places.

"Even in the mister!" Mom exclaimed, so indignant her voice quivered.

Lorelei verified that Ogden, too, violated her time in the mister, and went on to describe the oddities of the morning. "He...he...did...things...", she stammered, "that were not designed for reproduction. They were just...I don't know, he just...did them." Lorelei decided she would not tell her mother she felt pleasure when he touched her. That would be to confess something so unacceptable her reputation would never recover.

Mom offered words of condolence, and tried to reassure Lorelei the shame was not hers, but Ogden's, and she was doing the right thing by submitting. If the men thought it was proper, who were they to question? The tone of Mom's voice led Lorelei to believe Mom wasn't so sure the men always knew what was right. She asked Mom if it was time to call the medic, but Mom suggested they wait. Perhaps this was a momentary aberration. Perhaps they would get over it, and things would return to normal. Just...humor him for now, and wait to see what happens.

"I knew a woman once, and her husband went crazy. Then, one day, he just...got sane again. The crazy went away."

Lorelei doubted it, but Mom knew a lot of people, so maybe it had happened. She'd try to hold onto the hope. It might help her get through these strange days.

They turned the conversation to more ordinary things, routine trivial things that would not disturb them, but their hearts were not in it. After a few more pleasantries, they ended the conversation. Lorelei stared at voice monster and frowned. It was difficult enough to think Ogden was losing his mind, but Dad? Dad was the sanest, most solid man she had ever known, much like Ogden, and now both of them were going crazy together.

19

Today was shopping day, and the market buzzed with busy women moving up and down the aisles with brisk efficiency. She pushed her cart around the aisles, greeting one friend and another, each of them asking her about Ogden and how he was doing. This was an unusual question, and she realized they were hoping she had more information on the project since he was the lead. It seemed all the women reached the same conclusion – the strange behavior of their husbands was related to the material from their latest site.

Lorelei responded to all queries with the same answer. "Ogden doesn't confide in me", she would say, and the women would nod. None of their husbands told them anything, either. She flushed with guilt every time she said it, remembering the papers she read. It wasn't really a lie, though. Ogden had not confided in her, she had snooped. Snooping was okay among the women. It was the only way to get information. They would not report on her transgression or shame her in any way for doing something that came naturally in a world where they were kept in the dark. Still, she didn't want to reveal what she knew until she really knew...something. She could not admit Ogden lied, even to her friends, until she had some idea why. It might be something so terrible that keeping it secret was the only way to survive.

Amity shoved her cart into Lorelei, breaking her out of a reverie. She hugged her best friend and they pushed their carts together, selecting items off the shelves in an automatic manner that comes from long practice. They didn't say much until they reached an aisle where they were alone.

"So what gives?" Amity watched her friend's face closely, studying it for any clues to the strange behaviors of the men.

"I...don't know." Lorelei didn't want to lie to Amity. After all, this was the woman who knew her better than anyone, who knew she sneaked into the men's classes in college, and who knew every other secret she ever had.

"Ogden was lying." Amity wasn't asking, she was stating something as though she knew.

"What makes you think that?" Lorelei hedged as she tried to think about what she should do, or say, in this situation.

"I know. I know something is in the material that they are able to read. I *know*...remember? I told you last week. They're scared. Disaster. Catastrophe."

Lorelei remembered. She was not able to forget the conversation, though it competed in her head with another phrase, a nonsense phrase about equality between men and women. She shook her head. "I don't know."

Amity stared into her eyes and Lorelei tried to hold her friend's gaze, the honest blue eyes boring into her own. She shuddered.

"I think you know something", Amity announced. "I think you heard something."

"I haven't...heard...anything", Lorelei mumbled. "No...but..."

The pause hung in the air between them, saying as much as any words could have said. It told Amity that Lorelei did know something, something she hadn't heard but had learned. Amity grabbed her arm and pulled her to cold box aisle just as another woman, a loud and gossipy woman, entered their aisle.

"Give." Amity commanded her friend, standing with her hands on her hips, making it obvious she would not take no for an answer.

"I can't. Not here. Not yet."

"Why not?"

"I don't know enough yet. I need...time. I have to...make sure. Can you...give me until Thursday? I'll tell you at group."

"I'll hold you to that...do you want me to tell Corinne and Grenata a different time, so we can have time together before?" Amity was hosting group that week.

"No. I want them to be there. I think...I think...we may need to talk."

Amity nodded, and the conversation ended as the loud, gossipy woman entered cold box aisle.

"Amity! Lorelei!" Resenta gushed as she noticed the two women, rushing toward them and grabbing them in hugs.

Lorelei submitted to the hug from a woman who usually avoided them as diligently as they avoided her. Clearly Resenta believed Lorelei or Amity had some idea what was going on. None of the other women would give her information, because anything she heard was immediately broadcast through the entire city, magnified by the magnificent sound amplifier of Resenta's booming voice.

71

"Hello, Resenta." Amity spoke in the most dismissive tone possible, her hello having all the ring of a good-bye.

Resenta ignored the message. She cornered the two women so it was impossible to make an escape without harming either her or themselves. Since she was a large woman, it would be difficult to move her. They turned their attention to cold box, examining meat selections as if this was the most important decision in the universe.

"I hear you were at the big do last night." Resenta would not be put off. Her husband was one of the few men in the neighborhood who did not work in archaeology and she felt left out.

"Yes. It was just one of those boring staff functions we all have to endure. You know, the guys talk, they bring their wives so everyone can see how pretty and how obedient their wife is, they make some dull speeches, and we all go home." Lorelei dismissed the meeting with a casual wave.

"I heard something big is happening."

"Well, I can assure you, nothing big was announced last night." Amity pushed her cart back and forth, back and forth, trying to persuade Resenta to move from their path. The larger woman stood her ground.

"I heard…something big is happening." Resenta repeated her statement, her face close enough to Lorelei's that her breath blew warm on Lorelei's cheek.

"Nothing big. Nothing much at all." Lorelei dismissed the woman and this time Resenta responded by moving back a step. "All they said was that nothing could be deciphered. It was nothing."

Resenta peered into the faces of the two women, first Lorelei, then Amity, then back to Lorelei. Lorelei tried to hold her stoic face as much as possible. After all, she wasn't lying. That was exactly what they announced. The buzz among the women suggested no one else believed it any more than she did, but she was going to stick to her story.

"Well, I never! All this buzz over nothing? Someone is lying." With that pronouncement, Resenta flounced down the aisle, delivering her parting words over her shoulder. "I'll find out who."

Amity and Lorelei watched her go in silence, then broke down in giggles. The fears of the past few days dissolved into hysteria as they held onto each other and giggled like schoolgirls. Resenta brought a much needed moment of comic normality into their upside down lives, and they felt refreshed and stronger.

"Someone is lying." Amity repeated Resenta's comment.

"Yes. And we know who." Lorelei stifled a giggle that threatened to start the hysteria again.

"Thursday." Amity whispered in her ear as they stood together in line to have their groceries inventoried and their account marked by the bored young man behind the counter.

"Thursday", Lorelei whispered back, her heart in her shoes. "Thursday."

20

Lorelei knelt in front of the safe. She ran her hands over the cold steel as if the feel would give her a clue to its contents. She glared at the combination lock, willing it to give up its secrets. She needed to get inside. She had to have more information before she could tell the group anything. What she had was so little, and did little to elucidate the odd behavior of the men in their lives.

She absently twirled the dial as she had seen Ogden do. She had no idea how to find a combination, though she read about men who were able to do that by listening to the dial and the clicks. She wasn't sure what it would sound like if it were clicking to a correct sequence. She turned the dial first one way, then the other, as though that would give her inspiration.

She turned it to the right and stopped at 5. To the left, she stopped at 28. When she turned it to the right again, and stopped at 13, to her surprise the door swung open. She was just playing and she hit on the right combination. Trust Ogden to use his birthday as his combination. For the first time, she was glad to have an unimaginative husband.

The safe was crammed full of papers and artifacts. These were probably the artifacts that were delivered over the weekend. Lorelei pulled out the top artifact and examined it with interest. It was an old item, ragged and torn, but still able to be identified. It was a yellow sash, bright yellow once but now faded, with letters in glitter stretching across the face. The letters said 'Votes for Women'.

Lorelei rocked back on her heels, stunned by yet another unimaginable idea. Votes? For women? Where in the world could anyone possibly have gotten such a peculiar idea? And to put it on a sash, meant to be worn over a dress where everyone could see it? This was mutiny, pure and simple.

Nothing could have surprised Lorelei more, not even if she found an extinct alligator residing in the safe. Lorelei read about extinct alligators in another of Ogden's papers and looked for weeks hoping there would be something more. She wouldn't recognize an extinct alligator if she saw one, because there were no pictures in his papers, but she would love to see what one looked like.

Lorelei laid the sash beside her with care. The fabric was old and fragile and she didn't want to risk tearing it, especially since that would alert Ogden someone had been in his safe. She would be the only possibility. As soon as he finished whatever punishment he deemed appropriate for such behavior, he would change the combination on his lock. She could handle the punishment, but could not bear the idea of not being able to get back into this treasure trove.

She turned her attention to the stack of documents. There were more papers here than the last time she saw them and she lifted the one on the top of the pile, taking as much care as she would take lifting a dish out of hot box. She carried it to the table where the light was better and started to read. It was an astonishing document, a letter from Ogden.

"To the Honorable Patterson J. Framje, Archaeologist General of the Continental Imperium" the letter began. Lorelei realized this was important. It was going to the highest official in Ogden's field, the person who reported directly to the Imperial Consul, who reported directly to the Imperial Leader.

The contents of the letter were as astounding as the sash, and they confirmed what she suspected – Ogden lied last night. And he had been instructed to lie from the highest level of government.

The letter described the cache of materials they found, preserved in a safe zone he referred to as a vault. The location was known in its own time as *The National Museum and Library of Women's History*, and was located in a place known as Berkeley. It was on the other side of the land mass and was destroyed in the various wars, fires, and rioting that followed the collapse of the world's natural systems in the early 22nd century, more than a thousand years before.

Lorelei was familiar with the history of the collapse, but never heard of anything like a museum of women's history. Women's history was straightforward, right? History was made by men. Women only made the men, and took care of them. There were no women mentioned in any of the history books.

The letter described the materials in a much different way than Ogden did last night. The documents and artifacts, he explained, were obviously left behind by a highly civilized culture that built enormous cities and connected them with thousands of miles of a substance he called asphalt, once used for making roads. The papers were written in a language identical to their own, but with strange idioms and phrases common in other documents of the time. Ogden believed these people might be direct ancestors of the people living today, but was not prepared to guarantee that, and preferred to keep it to himself until he had more evidence. A comment in a different hand – perhaps that of the Imperial Leader himself – indicated agreement with this proposal.

The rest of the document unfolded the story of why Ogden lied. The documents were dangerous, he explained. They needed to stall for time until they had a chance to defuse the contents and minimize their negative impact on society. These items, he warned, could bring about confusion and anarchy, and perhaps end the world. Here were those words again. Disaster. Catastrophe. Women. Wives.

Lorelei finished reading the letter, taking in the contents as though it were a novel. The documents showed that, at some point in the past, women demanded their rights. The declaration she read was only the beginning. Women followed up this document with meetings and speeches. They wrote books and pamphlets. They marched down the street wearing these sashes, in broad daylight. They left their homes and their families to attend marches and demonstrations. The most amazing thing, the thing that startled Lorelei the most, is that they won.

The women won. They won the right to vote. They won the right to work at a job of their choice. They won the right to choose not to have children, or even to get married. They even won the right to say no to their husbands when they demanded marital duties, usually referred to in these documents simply as "sex". The women fought for decades…even a couple of centuries…but they won the right to be treated as equals to men, at least in theory. The documents indicated they were still struggling for their complete equality, for recognition of their full worth (here Ogden inserted a rude comment), when the collapse happened.

Is it possible, Ogden speculated, we were wrong about the cause of the collapse? It wasn't because the natural resources were decimated, and the human population was too large to support? The real reason was the acceptance of women into the political and economic sphere, not to mention the academic sphere, into roles for which they were not suited by intellect or temperament, that caused the collapse?

It seemed plausible to Ogden, and on first reading to Lorelei, that women doing the same things as men would lead to societal collapse, but as she read further, she realized women were still having children and men were still being fed, it was just that the roles shifted and men shared the duties, as well as more services provided from outside the home, helping the wives…and husbands…manage in a busier world. Lorelei remembered the other papers she read in the past, the descriptions of what happened right before the collapse, and she came to the conclusion that Ogden was wrong. The collapse was caused by the overuse of resources as they always thought. The women getting rights did not appear to have destroyed anything, to judge from his own letter.

The letter concluded by asking permission to delay revealing the contents of this find. We need time, he warned, to gather the men and instruct them how to keep this from happening again. If word of this gets out, it will unsettle the women, perhaps make a few of them want more, want to have what their ancestors had, and that would destroy everything we worked so hard to preserve. Once we've figured it out, Ogden claimed, we can put safeguards in place. They were already working on some documents they found from the time that could give them ideas how to keep the women from wanting anything different, from wanting something they were clearly unsuited for, and from insisting on bringing the world to an end by working for themselves. The men involved on the project were conducting experiments with their own wives to see how successful some of these ideas would be. He referenced a pamphlet they found in the museum, a pamphlet written to help husbands keep their wives at home.

Lorelei realized this pamphlet, wherever it was, probably explained the strange behavior of their husbands in recent days. They were implementing suggestions they found in the pamphlet. But why would they think any of that would be pleasing to their wives? Their wives were finding it horrifying, disturbing, and definitely shameful.

There was more writing in two or three different hands following Ogden's signature. Whoever answered the correspondence agreed with Ogden about the desirability of keeping these documents under cover. The deadline for first announcement was next week (and this was dated last week), so they would have to make some sort of announcement. They approved Ogden's idea – apparently in a different communication because it was not here – that he announce difficulty in translation, obscurity of language, primitive culture, etc etc etc...

Lorelei returned the document to the safe and laid the yellow sash back where she found it, arranging everything so things looked precisely like before she disturbed them. She stared at the cache of papers underneath the letter and realized she needed to read these documents herself. She would need to set aside time from her housework each day to come into the study and read one document every day. It would take her a long time to work through the stack at that rate, but it was probably the only safe rate she could manage. She needed to find out why… when… *how*…the women succeeded.

21

The day crawled after she put the items back in the safe. She wandered the house in an aimless daze, her world disrupted by what she read and by what she was thinking. She shook off the ideas that insisted on presenting themselves to her worried brain and focused on cleaning an already immaculate house. She dusted Ogden's study with a ferocity that would have scared any dust away, if there had been any dust present. She straightened his desk, secure touching his things because there were no papers on his desk today. She hung his clothes and sorted the children's socks with no awareness of what she was doing. She was on automatic, her brain engaged with her own thoughts as her hands were engaged with her duties.

The evening was close to normal, with Ogden disappearing into his study the moment dinner was over and the children begging to be allowed to play just ten more minutes. The only departure from normal was when Lorelei agreed to their request and allowed them to remain up a few minutes past their bedtime.

Her eyes followed Micra as the little girl cleaned the playroom, putting away toys and brushing the floor with her tiny toy brush and tidy box. After Micra wiped down every surface with her own personal dust cloth, the children scrambled to bed. Lorelei tucked them in and kissed them good night, lingering over Micra's bed, wanting to tell her it's okay, you can relax and be a child, but knowing she would not, at least not yet. She needed to process things first.

Oh, that was what she wanted to ask Mom! She started to head for voice monster, but realized it would be a bad idea tonight with both Ogden and her father at home. They would not be able to speak about anything but "girl chatter", as husbands called conversations between the women. Lorelei hated "girl chatter", and she and Amity dreamed up codes that allowed them to speak of other things without being caught, but she and Mom had no such code…not yet, Lorelei thought. We need a code.

Too restless to read, Lorelei took her mist early and retired. Perhaps if she was asleep when Ogden came to bed, there would be no marital duties tonight. She was exhausted and would rather not participate, but she did not have the right of refusal. Her nervous tension prevented her from sleeping, but when Ogden came upstairs she forced herself to breathe evenly and lie still, at least until she heard his regular breathing and knew he was asleep.

She slipped out of the bed into the cold house. If she stayed in bed, she would disturb Ogden and he would realize something was the matter. It was difficult to hide her mood at night when she would toss and turn. She settled into the living room for only seconds before she took flight again, landing in the kitchen. She spent the next hour cleaning out cold box but her mind was elsewhere, on a cold steel safe that held treasures she craved. She stood twice to go to the study and read, but common sense forced her back to her knees in front of cold box. Ogden was home. Even though he was asleep, there was no guarantee he would remain in bed. It wasn't unusual for him to get up and work in the middle of the night if he was on an interesting project. She suspected this project was as interesting to him as it was to her.

She finally slipped back into bed, her cold legs shivering until the blankets restored some warmth, and fell asleep from sheer exhaustion. It was a trick she learned early in her marriage when the new routines were upsetting and disorienting. Get up and clean cold box, and do housework until she was so exhausted she simply couldn't stand any longer. Time monster told her she could sleep for four hours.

Ogden reached for her in the morning before time monster beeped. She stiffened, but he only wanted to give her a hug before they got up. She lay beside him while he stroked her arm and her hair and whispered endearments in her ear, endearments he previously used only when other people were around and a number of endearments he had never used. When he released her, she rose and headed to the kitchen to start breakfast.

As soon as Ogden left for work, once again with his hands on his children's shoulders, Lorelei headed to the study. She wanted to get into the safe first thing today, because there was little cleaning to be done after her sleepless night. She did need to take out the waste, but that would only take a few minutes. She would have time this morning to investigate the past.

She settled in front of the safe, her hand on the knob, and hesitated. The messages in her head this morning were the old familiar refrains, the mantras she learned in college about her proper role, not snooping, and allowing the husband to maintain his secrets while not keeping any secrets of her own. She was not following her good wife training and would be considered in full rebellion, but it felt good. It felt right. It felt like the secrets he was keeping concerned her at least as much as they concerned him.

The door to the safe creaked open and she stared at the papers inside. Had she spun the combination? Had her own unconscious mind instructed her hand to do that, or had her hand done it on its own? No matter. The safe was open, so she might as well read. She pulled out the letter and the next document down. This was the declaration she already read. She skimmed it, memorizing a couple of key phrases, but put it aside. There would be time for re-reading at a later date. She wanted to delve into the remaining papers, and there appeared to be hundreds.

The next item in the stack was a picture, and she held it in her hands as though it were a precious gem. The picture was in shades of gray and white and appeared to be extremely old. A date on the bottom indicated it was taken in 1917. It was a group of women, all dressed in white, wearing sashes just like the one in the safe. Votes for Women. Many of the women held signs, all of them saying something about the rights of women, and she touched the signs in the picture with reverence, as though she were touching the delicate pages of the Bible.

She stared into the faces of the women, expecting them to look like some sort of unfeminine mutants, but they looked like ordinary women. One of them looked a lot like her, and she stared at the face wondering if that woman might be some distant ancestor. Had some woman in the deep dark past marched for rights and borne children that eventually led to her? She touched the face as though contact might impart some secret wisdom.

Lorelei jumped at the jolt that shot through her body. As she touched the picture she felt herself tingle with a new emotion, one she never felt before. She felt desire surge through her, desire to find out what men knew, to discover a world long closed to her.

She let the feeling fill her and realized she was wrong. She had felt this before. When she was in college, when she crept into the classes where the men learned things the women were not permitted to know, she felt this same surge of desire, this same tingling sensation. She had no word for what she felt...until now. The word was on one of the signs in the picture and she adopted it as her new motto. Liberty. The feeling was one of being herself rather than a well trained robot who did the bidding of other people.

Liberty. Lorelei repeated the word and stared at the picture until she memorized every face. She put it aside with reluctance, and plunged into the remaining items in the safe. She wanted to learn everything about women's history, and she realized she wanted what these women wanted…the right to self-determination. The right to choose her own path. The right to say no. She wanted liberty.

22

Thursday, and the group headed toward Amity's house. Lorelei closed the door to her own home with a feeling of excitement she had never felt for such a mundane activity, and headed down the street to the home where her best friend lived with her brute of a husband. Lorelei wanted to free herself, but even more, she wanted to free Amity, who suffered so much more than she did. Ogden could be cruel, but he was only cruel when he believed Lorelei transgressed her role. Merris was brutal for no reason, without warning, and often.

Amity was waiting for her and pulled her into the house as soon as she knocked. Corinne and Grenata were already there, both of them uncharacteristically early. Amity must have told them Lorelei was going to bring information. All the women were silent as Lorelei shed her coat, poured a cup of hot beverage, and accepted a snack from Amity. As soon as she was settled, they erupted in questions.

"Wait! Let her have a second to talk." Amity shushed the group, and all three women sat forward in anticipation.

"Well...you know Ogden lied, right?" The three women nodded as a group, and Lorelei continued. "I know why."

She stopped. She took a sip of hot beverage. She nibbled on her snack. She waited, and was not disappointed. The women watched her, unable to curb their impatience, and tried not to push her. Grenata was the first to break.

"Tell us!"

Lorelei plunged into the story of the safe, the sash, the letter, the picture, and, of course, the declaration. She told them about a pamphlet she found in the stack of papers, a pamphlet written in the middle of the 21st century, advising men on how to keep their wives at home. Some of the advice was to bring them flowers, to offer to help around the house from time to time, to show them affection and do things together. And, of course, to be romantic. To have marital duties – Lorelei decided not to use the "sex" that was the most common description in all the papers of the 21st century – at unusual times and in unusual places, keeping the marriage spontaneous and exciting.

The women sat in stunned silence when she finished. Whatever they expected, they didn't expect this. They thought there was something perhaps about bombs and weapons, something that could physically destroy civilization. They didn't believe their ears. It was about women…about women who wanted more than being wives and looking after men.

It was a strange idea, but…oh, it was exciting. It was tempting. None of them were happy in their marriages but they were brought up to believe happiness was not the goal of a woman. Now here were women of long ago demanding they be allowed to at least search for happiness…and evidence that they succeeded, at least in part.

"Do you think…" Amity started, and stopped.

"I…" Corinne similarly had difficulty getting her thought out.

Grenata looked from face to face, examining each of her friends as though she had never seen them before. She had certainly never seen them so unable to express their thoughts. This was a well read, literate group, trained to be the wives of well read, literate men who didn't want their wives to be an embarrassment. Grenata whooped. This was her sort of news.

Grenata's whoop brought the other women out of their daze. The three women began chattering at once, talking so fast and furious that Lorelei couldn't understand what any of them were saying. She was on the verge of getting a headache when Amity put up her hand.

"Stop!"

The voices stopped as abruptly as they started. All eyes turned to Amity as though she was the group leader and in a way, she was, since they were in her house and that was their unofficial rule.

"Look, we can't all talk at once. We sound like the hens our husbands accuse us of being. Let's…calm down and…talk sense."

"You start." Corinne yielded the floor with grace that was surprising from the most gossipy member of the group.

"All right. I was thinking…Lorelei, you said the women succeeded only part way."

"Yes. At one time, they won a lot. They had jobs, and were paid, and got to choose their own husbands. They got to choose how many children they had, and could even choose not to marry or have children at all."

Grenata sat forward, her eyes shining. "Not marry?"

Lorelei nodded, and her friends stared in disbelief. They could not comprehend a world where no one forced women to get married. Choosing their own husbands was more than they could imagine, but not marrying at all?

Lorelei continued. "They started to lose in the early 21ˢᵗ century, but they fought back and held the line on the men who kept trying to take things away. They never did win equal pay, or get men to stop treating them like objects, but they were still fighting."

"Do you think…" Amity paused, then picked up her thought again. "Do you think, if the collapse hadn't happened, they might have…finished the job?"

Lorelei shrugged. The fight continued for a long time, several centuries, and it seemed like most of the forward movement stalled. "I don't know."

"Do you think…" Now Corinne wanted her turn. "Do you think…they caused the collapse?"

"No." Lorelei was firm. "There wasn't anything that suggested the collapse was because of women. Everything looks like it's what we've always been taught it was – too many people, too much exploitation, too many extinctions, and too many wars."

"So you don't think it would lead to the collapse of society if…" Corinne didn't finish her thought.

Lorelei finished it for her. "If we try to gain our rights, you mean?"

Corinne nodded, unable to speak, perhaps for the first time in her life. Amity let out an audible gasp, though Lorelei suspected she was thinking the same thing. Grenata wriggled and bounced in her chair but didn't say anything.

"I've already thought of that." Lorelei watched her friends. All of them hung on her words. She was well regarded by this group, and they often looked to her for advice. "I think…we should try."

"But…" Amity didn't finish her thought. She didn't need to; all of them were thinking the same thing.

"Yes. I think…it's weird, you know, because when I first read that declaration, when I first saw what was in the safe, I thought how stupid it was. How unnatural. But when I saw the picture, all I could feel was…liberty. I want to be free."

"Free?"

"Free from hot box and cold box. Free from time monster and voice monster. Free from…Ogden." Lorelei dropped her voice as she said the last word, aware she was committing a serious crime by voicing such a thought.

"Free from Lymon." Grenata spoke for the first time.

"Free from Merris." Amity added her own voice.

They looked at Corinne expectantly. Of the four, she was the most cautious, the least likely to depart from orthodox behavior. She was also the only one with a husband who never laid a hand on her in anger, and she had a lot more to lose...or, maybe, Lorelei thought, it was a lot less to win.

"Free from...Corydon." Corinne spoke in a near whisper, and there were tears in her eyes. "Free from a man who barely knows I exist and has marital duties with other women instead of me."

For the first time, Lorelei realized why her friend had never been a mother, though she was eager to get pregnant. She fell into depression each time one of them announced a new child on the way, and now her cheeks glistened with tears as she confessed a shame none of them knew. Grenata, also cursed with a roving husband, reached out and put her hand on Corinne's arm in silent solidarity.

The four women sat in silence as they digested all the information, and thought about how they could put it to use to free themselves from the deadly routines they despised, even if this was the first time they admitted out loud that they despised their routines. Plans for the charity bazaar were forgotten even though the time was growing short. There would be time for that later. They had more important discussions today.

23

Lorelei stopped by her mother's house on the way home, the excited voices of her friends ringing in her ears. She was worried about what she started, and worried she would not be able to finish. But she did want to talk to Mom and perhaps…maybe…bring her up to date. Lorelei was cautious, and Mom did tend to tell what she knew, even if only to the other women. Even that much could be dangerous at this point.

Mom was waiting for her. She saw her coming up the street and had the door open before Lorelei got up the steps. All the women were full of nervous energy today, and it made Lorelei more nervous. Mom swept her into the house and sat her on the sofa. Lorelei had a hot beverage in her hand before she could stop to catch her breath.

"Okay, now, tell." Mom sat forward, her eyes shining.

"Tell? What?" Lorelei wasn't feigning ignorance. She really didn't know if Mom was asking about what she told group, or if something else was on her mind. How could Mom have found out?

"Tell me what you know. Yes, I know you know. You can't keep secrets from me, and every time I call you, I feel it. Excitement. Fear. Tension. Anticipation. You brush me off so quickly, I almost begin to believe I am unloved."

"Oh, Mom, of course you're loved. It's just…things have been…weird…lately. But you know that."

Mom nodded. "Of course I know that. They've been weird for everyone…or at least, all the wives in Ogden's group. Some of the women are…well, normal. But they're starting to notice we're not."

Lorelei filled Mom in on her meeting with Resenta at the supermarket. "I think she suspects something, but she doesn't know what she suspects."

"Yes, dear, that's my feeling, too. And not just Resenta. Ornata pumped me at the library yesterday. I had trouble getting away, but my goodness, I'm not going to talk about…you know."

Lorelei knew. Mom…her…Amity…Grenata…even Corinne confessed that Corydon was performing marital duties with her now. He grabbed her in the back of people mover the other day, with all the other passengers around and able to watch. Fortunately, he realized where he was before he did anything too embarrassing, but he insisted on marital duties as soon as they got home, the door barely closed behind them. And she was sporting a large orchid at the staff function, even though Corydon rarely looked at her.

"Amity told me…you…know something." Mom whispered, even though Dad was at work and no one could hear.

Damn it, Amity, why did you have to blab? Lorelei thought as she tried to decide how much to tell her mother. "Mom, I…can't …unless you promise…swear…that you won't say a word to anyone else in the whole world."

Mom looked hurt. Lorelei kept her face stern and stony. This was too important to be passed among women like Resenta and Ornata who were in good position to spoil everything just for kicks.

"Honey, do you think I would? I know, I know, I'm considered a go-to girl for gossip, but I would never…I only tell things that aren't important, mostly things everyone else already knows. It gives me something to talk about when no one wants to listen to old women." Mom looked like she was about to cry.

Lorelei put her arm around her mother's shoulders. "Mom, I'm sorry, but…if this gets out…well, if anyone finds out what I've done…you know…"

Mom nodded. She knew. She hadn't been alive in the world all these years living in a daze, she informed her daughter. She had experienced a lot, and expected to experience a lot more before she was done, but she never sold out another woman when the chips were down, and she certainly would not sell out her own daughter.

Lorelei hesitated, then plunged forward, sharing her story once again. She paused, not sure if she should share the plans they were making at Amity's house earlier. That was…dangerous.

Mom picked up the thread. "You know what I think?" Lorelei shook her head. For once, she really did not know what Mom thought. "I think…we should finish the job. We should…get those rights back, and take it the next step. Finish what they started. We should really become the equal of men. We are, you know. I've always known it, but never had anyone I could tell it to. Now I get to share it with my own daughter."

Mom sat back, finished and exhausted. Lorelei told her Amity said the exact same thing…well, not in the exact words, of course, but basically the same thing.

"And?"

The word hovered in the air. Mom waited, expectant, while Lorelei struggled with her inner demons. She tried to push the good wife forward but it was obvious the good wife was dead. She couldn't bring her back. She had to admit, she didn't want to bring her back.

"I have been thinking the same thing, ever since last week when I read that declaration. I haven't been able to sleep. It runs through my head all the time, that damned refrain. Resolved: that woman is man's equal. At first...it was...I said, no. But I think...you know, I think...I could do this. I could...be someone different."

Mom nodded. "You can, dear. I believe in you."

Lorelei remembered what she wanted to ask her mother. "Mom, I've noticed that Micra...well, she's already a 'good wife' in her play, in her behavior with her father and everyone else except Molton and me...she's already learned her role."

"I've noticed that, too. She's obedient."

"Well, I was wondering...I don't remember...was I like that? The 'good wife' from such a young age?"

"Heavens, no, Lorelei, you were a spitfire." Mom laughed, but it wasn't a cruel laugh. It was a laugh of genuine pleasure, something Lorelei hadn't heard from her mother in many years. "We had to work...your grandmother and I...to turn you into any sort of wife at all. I didn't want to. I liked you the way you were. I wanted my daughter...I wanted you...not to have to be...you know, the same as I was. Submissive. Obedient. I didn't want you married to someone who only wanted you to take care of him and look good at staff functions. But in the end it was no use. There simply was no place for you in the world if you weren't a wife. I hoped...when we met Ogden, he seemed...shy. Dreamy. I hoped he'd be a good husband, not a normal husband. Instead, he's...well, I'm sorry. I just can't say it too often, Lorelei, I'm sorry. I should have fought. I should have waited. I should have insisted we find a better man, one who would appreciate you, love you, and allow you some room to breathe. Can you forgive me?"

Lorelei took her mother in her arms. She felt warm tears against her cheek, and realized her mother was crying. "Mom, it isn't your fault. None of it is your fault. I don't even blame Grandmother, though I bet she was the one who put pressure on you."

She felt her mother nod. "Grandmother...was a true believer. She knew women were made to be just what we are. It made her angry when I didn't agree. I can't agree. I can't. I can't feel it in my heart."

"I don't need to forgive you, Mom, because you didn't do anything wrong. Besides, look at it this way. If I hadn't married Ogden...would we know anything about those papers now?"

Mom sat up, cheered by the thought. She leaned toward her daughter and began to whisper all sort of plans, big plans, the result of big dreams she had been nursing for years. Like Lorelei, Mom wanted liberty. Mom wanted to be free.

24

Lorelei had dinner ready when Ogden got home. The children rushed in for a hug and their father gave them an awkward embrace before they raced upstairs. He handed Lorelei another vase of flowers and she put it on the table, taking the place of the dead ones she threw away that morning. He touched her on the shoulder and pulled her close for a quick kiss, but jerked away as soon as the children raced to the table, their hands clean and their faces shining.

Ogden retired to his study after dinner, as he did most nights, but asked her to come in and talk to him as soon as she got the children to bed. She nodded, not trusting herself to speak. He kissed Micra good night and shook Molton's hand. The little boy threw out his chest, puffed up with pride that his father now regarded him as a man, important enough to be noticed. The children started to shout good night at their father but at his wince, they turned their voices down to a whisper and he nodded in acknowledgment. The family headed their separate directions, Ogden to his study, the children to the playroom, and Lorelei to the kitchen where dirty dishes waited.

When the children were in bed, she gave a timid knock on the study door. She was tense and acutely aware he might intend something…inappropriate, but he said to come, and while her good wife was dead, it was in her best interests not to let him know yet. She would continue to play the role for as long as was needed. All the women in the group agreed they must not appear any different to their husbands.

Ogden pulled her into the room. He flung his arms around her and kissed her. She stood stiff and straight and he pulled back. "Don't you like it when I kiss you?"

Lorelei answered slowly. "It's not…that. It's just…it's strange. It's not usual. Why here?"

Ogden shrugged. "I'm here. You're here. Why not here?...I want to make you happy, Lorelei. I want you to feel you belong here and you want to be here."

Lorelei didn't answer. This was not a safe conversation, especially since she knew why he was doing what he was doing, and had some idea of things he might do in the future. She read and re-read the pamphlet, and filled in her friends so they could be prepared.

Ogden stroked her arm. She waited, not sure what he would do next. His touch was light, and it felt almost like he meant it to be loving. She relaxed and leaned into him, allowing him to stroke her hair and tickle her ear with his tongue. That actually felt...good, she had to admit. What a strange thing to enjoy. She leaned on him, allowing him to hold her up, giving him confidence that his plan was working. It would throw him off guard.

The love making continued as he stroked other parts of her body. She submitted to his attention, and discovered some of the moves he was making were pleasurable. She tried to notice what he was doing when she enjoyed it...they were all things he'd never done before. She directed his hand back to a particular spot, to see if she still enjoyed it when he touched her there again. She did.

She tried not to let the strange behavior bother her. It actually was less disturbing now that she knew the reason. If the husbands weren't going crazy, then maybe there wasn't anything to worry about except embarrassment. She responded when he did something pleasurable, and in most cases he repeated the motion. She decided to enjoy the marital duties as much as possible. One thing she learned from the ancient documents was that women did, in fact, enjoy sex. Many women of the time actively sought out sex and sometimes even initiated it before the men made their move. Where had women lost that? She realized as electricity shot through her body again that they might have lost something of great worth when they were condemned to submit to marital duties without pleasure.

When Ogden finished making love on the floor of the study, he picked her up in his arms and carried her upstairs to the bedroom. She protested she was naked; he brushed it away. No one was there but them. The children, she said. The children were in bed. Who would see? She reminded him she hadn't had her mist yet. He told her she could have her mist when they finished. She fell back in his arms and allowed him to carry her to the bedroom and deposit her on the bed. She closed her eyes, expecting him to get in beside her, but she didn't feel the bed move. She opened her eyes to find him on the opposite side of the room, struggling with something she couldn't see.

"Do you need help?"

"Where is the damned cord hole?" Ogden was so unfamiliar with his own home outside of his study, he did not know where to put the cord to get electricity.

Lorelei directed him to the cord hole, and he concentrated until the thing he was working with flowed with electricity and hummed, an ominous sound. What was he going to do to her? It sounded like an electric saw and she instinctively put her hands down to protect her legs.

"Don't worry, it's a new thing. I just got it today...saw a description of it in...a...well, a trade...paper. Said it's something women love. I had one made and thought I'd try it."

Ogden thrust the thing at her and she stared in amazement. It didn't look like anything she'd seen before, and it shook in his hand. He started to put it between her legs but she shrieked and jumped away.

"What are you doing?"

"It's perfectly safe. It comes with a guarantee." Ogden was practical, as usual, even when trying to please her.

"I don't know...it looks strange. It's scary." Lorelei glared at the offending object.

"Just...give it a try. It's supposed to be...very pleasant."

"Have you tried it?"

"It's not for men. It's for women." Ogden was using his patient voice now, like when he had to explain something to Molton.

"What does it do?"

"It...feels good." Ogden stared at the object as though suddenly unsure about what it was. He put it against his hand. "It feels good when I do this. It's...here, try."

Lorelei held out her hand with caution. He laid the thing against her palm. She jumped. It was electric. It vibrated and caused her hand to shake and quiver. It was not unpleasant. She still shook her head. "I don't want it...down there."

"It's your decision, of course." Ogden started to unplug the thing. "I don't want to force you to do something that would scare you."

Lorelei stared at Ogden. This was a new Ogden. He sounded sincere, as though he weren't just trying out things to keep her tied to him. She moved toward him, for the first time since she'd met him feeling a surge of feeling for his needs, something more than her automatic, robotic care of him. She touched his hand and jerked away. It was electric. It was odd. It was…exhilarating.

"You can…try it", she announced. "But…if I don't like it…if it hurts…you have to promise to stop."

Ogden nodded. "I don't want to hurt you. You believe me, don't you?" His voice sounded plaintive, like a small child, and Lorelei felt a sudden urge to comfort him.

"I…believe you." Lorelei heard the slight quaver in her voice but she didn't think Ogden noticed. She didn't believe him, she couldn't, but she had to convince him, at least for now.

She lay down on the bed and Ogden moved toward her with the…thing…in his hand. She stared at it in fascination, unable to believe she was going to allow him to do…what he was about to do. She closed her eyes as he came closer and clenched her fists around the bedpost, determined not to scream as he touched her with the strange electric thing.

She was not prepared for the sensation as the electric object made contact with her flesh. It felt like it had on her hand, but oh, so much more. Pleasure shot through her like a wave and she allowed herself to respond. Ogden placed his hand on her chest, rubbing her nipples as he used his other hand to operate the thing. She moaned and gave herself over to pleasure. For the first time, men were allowing women to experience something more than submission, and she decided she was going to enjoy it while it lasted.

25

Lorelei stared at the paper in her hand. It was a diagram of the thing Ogden used last night, complete with instructions on use. In the margin, Ogden had written "Order one for every man on the team". This was not something they just invented, it was something from long ago they decided to build for themselves. She found it in the pamphlet on how to keep your wives at home, but it wasn't actually part of the pamphlet. It was stuck inside, a loose paper sticking out at the edge. She was sure it had not been there yesterday.

The set of papers continued to grow and new artifacts appeared every day. A statue of a woman pointing outward, titled "Forward". A strange, plastic-like device in a package that contained the word "diaphragm". Lorelei read the instructions for use and realized the device was intended to prevent pregnancy. What an idea! Women could just insert this and not get pregnant. It never occurred to her before, although she often thought about all the women who suffered through multiple pregnancies and wore out in exhaustion. What if they didn't get pregnant so often? Would they live longer? Now here was something that suggested women not only thought about that in the past, they took actions to make it happen.

Another artifact looked much like the device in the diagram, the one Ogden had last night. She turned it over and over in her hands. It was ancient and probably didn't work anymore, but it definitely looked the same. The drawing identified the device as a "vibrator", and she thought that was a good name for it. Apparently these were commonplace at one time. She found an ad for a medic from the late 1800s that advertised these devices for women who suffered from "hysteria". The women came to his office and the medic used this to relieve their tension. Lorelei thought it sounded very inappropriate. Her medic should never be doing anything so intimate. She was glad that stopped, at least.

Someone was at the door. She gathered the papers and artifacts, and replaced them with care in the exact order they were when she opened the safe. She dusted off her apron, smudged from kneeling on the floor, and raced to find out who was at the door.

Amity tiptoed into the hallway, putting her fingers to her lips and looking around with fear.

"He's at work." Lorelei stood aside to let her friend come into the house.

"Are you sure?" Amity had a look of terror that Lorelei had never seen on her usually well balanced friend. "He hasn't snuck home?"

Lorelei shook her head. "I've been here all morning, and no one has come through that door, or any other door."

"Would he enter through a window?"

"Ogden? Come on, you know better than that." Lorelei remembered the strange behaviors of the past few days and shivered. This was not the Ogden she knew so well.

Amity asked for hot beverage and Lorelei disappeared into the kitchen, keeping a close eye on her friend as she went. Something happened; it disturbed Amity in a way that none of the other strange events bothered her. This was something new, something frightening. She returned with hot beverage and pressed it into Amity's hands.

Amity took a few sips and stopped trembling. Lorelei realized her trembling was a combination of cold and fear, and hot beverage could do a lot about both of those states. She led the other woman to the living room, Amity moving as though in a daze. Lorelei inspected her visible skin for any sign of new bruises, but there were none. Merris stopped hitting her when the strange behaviors began. Lorelei suspected he was instructed that hitting your wife was not considered a good way to make her want to stay with you. In fact, that was one of the first pieces of advice in that stupid pamphlet, and the only one that made sense – Don't hit your wife.

Amity settled on the edge of the chair and wrapped her arms around her knees, which were pulled up under her chin. Her tension worried Lorelei, who was usually the tense one but had been feeling strangely relaxed all morning.

"What is it? Talk to me."

"It's…Grenata. Lymon came home early from work. She was not…well, she was being Grenata, so the house was still a mess, and nothing was where it belonged. He…flew into a rage. He threw her out in the yard and locked her out of the house. She…tried to get back in, but he just shouted and cursed. He said he had been doing everything they told him to and she still wouldn't clean the damn house, so why shouldn't he lock her out? He called her horrible names and told her to go away and never come back."

"Where is she?" Lorelei looked outside, but didn't see any sign that Grenata was with Amity.

"She's at Corinne's. She came to my house. She didn't know where to go, and I was closer than you, so she came to me. She had to crawl all the way. I think he may have broken her leg. She looks awful. I took her to Corinne while I came here to talk to you. I'm hoping Merris doesn't come home and find I went out."

Lorelei nodded. It was Friday, and Friday was for home and hearth...it was even listed as Home and Hearth Day on the woman's calendar (it was just listed as Friday on the man's calendar). Amity leaving the house to come visit Lorelei on Friday was a serious infraction indeed. Merris would destroy her for this.

"What can I do? What does she need?" Lorelei mentally went through the steps that were taken when a woman was abandoned by her husband, but wasn't sure if it was the proper protocol, since it specifically addressed abandonment for another woman. There was nothing about a woman being locked out of the house or thrown away for not being a good wife.

"I don't know. We can't take her in. Our husbands wouldn't allow it. But I think...I think...we should do something. If we're going to be true to our new mission, we can't just...shun her." Amity lifted her chin and stared defiantly at Lorelei as though daring her to disagree.

"I agree. We need to help. I just...how? What happens in a situation like this? Where can she go?"

Amity shook her head. She had no idea either. Grenata couldn't come into their homes without permission from their husbands, who had final say on all household decisions. There wasn't any place for her to go besides their homes. She didn't have money to go to a hotel because Lymon controlled all the money and refused to give her anything, not even her own clothes. He claimed they belonged to him, since he paid for them. Grenata, in a final act of defiance, shot back that she expected to see him wearing them next time she saw him in town. That was when he beat her.

"I have an idea." Lorelei stopped, her idea only half formulated, teasing at her brain. Amity didn't press her, but gave her time for the idea to ripen. "Yes, I have an idea. I don't know if it's a good idea, but..."

Amity nodded. It was the only idea they had.

"Miss Clavelle. You know, over on Center Street?"

Amity frowned. "I don't know. She's crazy, right? She might not be so good for Grenata right now."

"She's the only woman in town that doesn't have a husband. She's the only one who could possibly help. Since her parents died, she's all alone there. She doesn't have to ask anyone."

Amity paced and thought. She started to ask Lorelei something, then stopped. She tried again. Finally she came to a stop directly in front of Lorelei. "How can we get her there? She's too messed up to go by herself, and we can't take her. We're not allowed out of the house."

Lorelei nodded. Amity already risked everything to come over here; it would be too much to ask her to take Grenata to Center Street. It was only three blocks, but still…if anyone saw them.

"I'll take her." Lorelei sounded defiant, as though Amity was going to try to stop her.

"That's…brave." Amity made no attempt to stop her. "I…I'll go with you."

"No. You've already done too much, and Merris is a lot more brutal than Ogden. If I get caught, I only have to deal with his anger until the punishment is over, then he moves on. Merris will hurt you for weeks."

Amity nodded. That thought was clearly in her mind, as well, and she had no death wish, nor did she like pain. She accepted Lorelei's decision without fuss, knowing Lorelei was in a better position to ride out the storm.

"I'll go right now. There's still two hours before Ogden is expected home. I can have her over there and be back without anyone knowing. And my house is already clean." Lorelei thought about dinner. "Could you put the meat in hot box for me? I've already spiced it."

Amity agreed. Lorelei slipped on her thin coat and started toward the door. She needed to get this done before rationality stepped in and made her change her mind.

26

Lorelei shivered on the porch waiting for Miss Clavelle to answer. She was afraid the woman might not be home. She was known to leave her home for hours at a time, even on Fridays. Grenata leaned against her, struggling to stand on her leg. Lorelei was sure it was broken because it was bent at an odd angle. She practically carried Grenata the three blocks, which was a challenge because Grenata was larger than Lorelei.

The door opened a crack, then a little more. A face peeked out, a face not friendly but not unfriendly, either. The woman stared at Lorelei and Grenata; Grenata stared back, curious about this unusual woman, but Lorelei managed to remain polite in spite of her curiosity.

"Yes?" Her voice was low and pleasant, a musical voice, a voice that belonged somewhere else, somewhere in a deep dark past when women were allowed to be…people.

"We…have a problem. None of us knew where to go. We thought…maybe you could help." Lorelei came straight to the point. It was obvious Grenata had been beaten, so there wasn't much reason to be delicate. "She…her husband…locked her out. Our husbands won't let us take her in…please, we need help."

The door closed, and Lorelei drew in her breath. They had failed. She heard noises on the inside of the door and realized the woman was locking a chain against them…or…did she dare to hope the woman was unlocking the chain? The door swung open and a tall woman about their age, dressed in a warm yellow shirt and a pair of gray pants…pants, Lorelei thought, a woman in pants…motioned them to enter.

The house was warm, warmer than any of their houses, as warm as her house would be tonight when Ogden came home. Lorelei detected the unmistakable smell of dinner cooking and hot beverage brewing. The woman knew how to do woman things, at least.

"Bring her in here." Miss Clavelle bustled toward the inner room, a room decorated beautifully with elegant paintings and odd sculptures.

Lorelei laid Grenata on a large sofa and sat in the chair near by. She hovered on the edge of her chair, ready to take flight if the other woman acted crazy. She held Grenata's hand and stroked her hair.

Her friend was in pain and she didn't know what to do to make her feel better.

"It looks like the leg is broken." The other woman neared the sofa and Lorelei felt Grenata stiffen. None of them knew this woman, and had no idea if she was friend, foe, or something in between. "I won't hurt you. But I do know how to set a broken leg, so if you'll let me…"

Grenata submitted to having her leg manipulated. She let out a stifled scream as the woman moved her leg back into shape, then she settled on the sofa pillows. "That feels better."

"What would you like from me?" Miss Clavelle stood over the two women, a tall, formidable figure. "You must have something in mind to come to the house of the unmarried woman."

"Miss Clavelle…" Lorelei stammered.

"Linolin."

"Linolin. Yes. Of course. We want to take Grenata in, but there is no way. Our husbands will not give permission to take in a discarded woman who was abandoned for not being a good wife. We don't want to shun her or desert her, but…we don't know where to take her. This is the only place we could think of."

"Very good. You've done the right thing. I approve. Too many women being shunned for stupid things, ridiculous things. I can take her in, at least for a few days, and we'll see what can happen from there. I presume he didn't let her have any money?"

"No. If you need payment…I can…probably find something in my household…"

Linolin stopped Lorelei. "No, I'm not asking for that reason. It's just…it would be easier to help her if she had money to make a new start. I have a place…but…no, it's not time for that yet. I'll let her stay here at least until she heals. Then we'll see what we can do."

Lorelei wanted to hug the other woman but she wasn't sure how it would be received. Linolin held out her arms as if reading her mind, and Lorelei moved toward her, wrapping her in a grateful embrace.

"I don't know how to thank you."

"I do." Linolin stood back and stared into Lorelei's face. "Your husband. He's the chief on that mysterious project, right?"

Lorelei stiffened. She wasn't prepared to give away Ogden's secrets to someone she didn't know. "Yes."

"Don't worry, I'm not asking you to betray him. I know he lied, and I know why. For now, just...trying to be sure who I'm dealing with, that's all."

Lorelei stared at her host. How did this woman know Ogden lied? What was she going to do with the information? Lorelei thought about the stack of papers and artifacts in his safe, carefully translated from a language almost like their own, and shivered.

"I'm not planning blackmail. Don't worry. I have...other ideas...in mind. For now, let's just get your friend...what is her name?"

"Grenata." It was the first time Grenata spoke since they left Corinne's house.

"Grenata. That's a nice name. I think we'll be good friends. And you are the top priority right now. We'll get you better...but...I think..." Linolin looked at Lorelei, struggling to remember if she had given her name.

"Lorelei?" She put it as a question because she wasn't sure what the other woman's look meant.

"Lorelei. I think...we need to visit again. Is that possible?"

Lorelei thought. "It's...difficult. This is the last place my husband would give me permission to visit. I think he'd let me go to a brothel first."

Linolin flung her head back and laughed, a deep laugh that rumbled in the back of her throat. "You're funny, you know? Yes, I know. I'm a pariah. It doesn't bother me, except...well, I want to...want to...move forward."

Lorelei thought about the statue, the one with "Forward" as the inscription. Looking at that statue excited her. She wanted to move forward, too. "What's that have to do with me?" She decided to maintain suspicion for now. It was safer.

"Maybe...nothing. But I think...I think...you have...ideas. I want to talk to you, find out what you're like, get to know you, and your friends. I want to...join."

The two women locked eyes, each looking deep into the other woman's soul. Could they trust each other? Lorelei made up her mind and stuck out her hand to take the other.

"I want you to join."

"Good. Then I think...we need to make plans. But...you can't let...what's his name...your husband...know. I think we should have code names for each other. I could call you Elizabeth. You could call me Susan."

"Why?"

"Elizabeth. For Elizabeth Cady Stanton. Susan. For Susan B. Anthony." Linolin looked hard at Lorelei, who flinched when she heard the names from Ogden's papers. "Yes. You understand. All right. You'd probably better go home before your husband misses you...Elizabeth."

"Good-bye...Susan. I'll see you soon."

Lorelei said her goodbyes to Grenata, who had a scared, don't leave me yet look on her face, and reassured her she would visit as soon as possible. She hugged her friend and Grenata held on as if she would never let go. Lorelei held her as long as she dared, then slipped out of her grasp, shook Linolin's hand, and headed back home. She still had enough time to finish dinner before Ogden got home.

27

Ogden came home late, with a look of fury that would have scared the sun. Lorelei rushed to call the children and put the finishing touches on a dinner she managed to get cooked in record time. Hot box performed well, and she gave it a pat as she pulled the meat out and basted it one last time. Hot box was on her side.

Ogden was washing his hands but he would be down soon. She steeled herself. What exactly did he know? Or was it something else? She would find out soon enough, she told herself, and tried to look casual as she placed the orchids in the middle of the table.

Ogden hadn't said a word to her or the children by the time she put his dinner in front of him. That wasn't unusual, at least not for normal Ogden, but over the past few days weird Ogden was much more talkative. She settled at the end of the table and watched to make sure neither of the children accidentally picked up their fork before their father.

He placed his hands palms down on the table and looked across at her. The children fidgeted, knowing they could not begin eating until their father did, and he appeared to have no intention of picking up his fork. He stared at their mother with an intense concentration that made her shudder. This did not bode well.

"Have you seen Grenata lately?" Ogden's voice was casual, too casual for the question to be anything but deadly serious.

"I saw her yesterday. At Thursday group." Lorelei assured herself she was telling the truth, but knew that would be no defense if Ogden discovered her omission.

"I just came from Lymon's. He says she left him, and he wants her back. He's in quite a state. They had a fight and he said some mean things, and she just…walked out." Ogden watched Lorelei closely as he spoke.

"Really? I can't imagine. That's not like Grenata." Lorelei matched his casual tone, and was horrified to find out how easy it was to lie when so much was at stake.

"If you see her…" Ogden finally picked up his fork, and the children erupted in a frenzy of eating in case he should put it down again. "If you see her, would you tell her…Lymon is sorry, and would like her to come home?"

That was it. Nothing was said about Lymon locking her out of the house, or breaking her leg, or being tired of her not being a good wife. Lorelei watched Ogden and realized he was watching her. She forced herself not to look at him, to pay attention to her food, though she didn't want anything to eat. Her throat felt closed and tight, and she was sure it would choke her.

Ogden scraped the last of his food off his plate but did not put down his fork. He kept his eyes on her as she continued to try to eat. Molton was on his second helping and Micra was picking at her food, as usual, even though she knew she only had a short time to eat. It was difficult to get enough food into the child with the dainty way she ate. Lorelei got the impression he was holding onto his fork to give them time to finish. She pushed the food around on her plate a little longer, but she still couldn't eat. Molton cleaned his plate, the first time since he'd been old enough to feed himself, and burped in satisfaction. He threw a guilty look at his father but Ogden didn't notice. He was watching Lorelei.

Lorelei looked at him, trying to signal him she was done and he could put his fork down. Micra finished what she wanted and put her fork down with a ladylike clatter beside her plate. Ogden continued to watch Lorelei. She dropped her fork on her plate and he finally put his fork down, allowing the children to be released from the table to tumble upstairs to the playroom.

"If anyone comes by, bring them to the study." Ogden pushed back his chair and disappeared into his own world.

Lorelei cleared the dishes and scrubbed the kitchen. She feared she would have another sleepless night but at least it allowed her free time during the day, since her housework would be done already when she got up in the morning.

She stumbled around the kitchen dropping things and stumbling over nothing, her usual efficiency blunted by fear. What did they want with Grenata? What would happen to her if they found her? And what would happen to Lorelei and Amity if they were discovered to have helped her?

Lorelei was sure Ogden knew what happened and was making up the story about Grenata leaving and Lymon wanting her back. Why? He'd never seen fit to play games like that before. She wished she could get into the safe and find out if there was anything about that in the pamphlet. Ogden was playing a script someone else had written, and if she could get her hands on the script, she might be better able to prepare for whatever was coming next.

28

When the knock came, she almost missed it. This was not the loud, authoritative knock customary to Ogden's visitors. It was almost timid, a quiet, unassuming knock. Lorelei opened the door to the visitors. They didn't speak; they assumed she knew they were here for Ogden and there was no need to announce their purpose to a mere woman. She led them to the study without a word, and they disappeared into the warm room where her husband waited.

She hesitated, overcome by curiosity, the kind of curiosity driven by fear and self preservation. She knelt, placing her ear to the keyhole. The voices were low as though the men were whispering, but her ears acclimated and she was able to hear their conversation.

They were talking about Lymon. It seems Lymon endangered everything by his actions and he was at risk of being thrown off the project. The problem was, he knew too much, so they had to keep him around if they wanted to make sure no one heard until it was time.

Ogden was late getting home because he, and these men, were at Lymon's house doing something they called an "intervention". Lorelei knew what intervention meant, but she had no idea how it would apply to this situation. She listened, hoping they would explain, but all they talked about was Grenata.

Grenata was a problem. That was plain from their conversation. None of them would defend her. She was not a good wife, and there appeared to be no hope she would ever become a good wife. They were sympathetic with Lymon but it was not possible for him to discard her at this time. The idea of a woman without a man...that was dangerous, more dangerous than ever. Grenata had to return.

"Where is she? Did your wife give you *anything*?"

Ogden demurred. "She doesn't know. I'm convinced of that. Lorelei has never lied to me, and she wasn't lying today."

"Are you sure?"

"Yes. She was as calm and cool as ever. There was no sign of nervousness, her eyes never flickered, and she ate a normal dinner. Nothing to indicate guilt or worry."

Lorelei almost snorted. Surely he didn't think that was eating a normal dinner...but then, he never paid much attention to her at the table, and since she never got to finish her dinner before he put his fork down, perhaps he assumed she didn't want to eat more. Sometimes there were benefits to their life routines.

"If you say so. I never trust women, myself. They're all stupid, and lazy, and they lie for fun."

Ogden started to say something but apparently changed his mind. Lorelei hoped he was about to defend her, and all women, but his courage departed him at the moment of truth. She marked it against him in a mental notebook she was starting to keep. She never lied to him before tonight, and Amity did not lie to Merris. She knew Corydon lied to Corinne all the time, but she didn't think Corinne lied to Corydon. Grenata lacked the guile to lie. She was innocent and simple, dreamy and mischievous, but she was as honest as the rest of them. It was men, Lorelei thought, men who lied. Men who cheated.

"My wife doesn't lie to me." Ogden was speaking again, and this time he was defending her. "She is the opposite of lazy. She keeps this house spotless, and raises the children, and does all sorts of things for me. And she certainly isn't stupid, though I doubt she has any idea how smart she is."

Lorelei mentally erased the black mark beside Ogden's name. She realized he didn't have to say any of that for their project. He had no idea she was listening. He said it by choice, and some of the things he said…smart?...could actually get him in hot water with his friends.

The other man, who had not spoken so far, snorted. "Smart?" He echoed Lorelei's thoughts. "She's a woman." Obviously he felt nothing more needed to be said.

The sound of scraping chairs indicated the men were getting up. Lorelei moved quickly, slipping silently back to the kitchen. When Ogden called for her, she came out of the kitchen wiping her hands on a dish towel as though she had been cleaning up the already sparkling kitchen.

"Yes, dear?" The endearment was obligatory when other people were around. She suspected most other men knew there wasn't any love in their marriage, or most other marriages, but everybody insisted on playing the game.

"My guests would like hot beverage. Is there any ready?"

Lorelei nodded and slipped into the kitchen. When she returned to the study with the tray, they were bent over the table, which was adorned with the yellow sash and a couple of the other artifacts. She noticed the diaphragm lying in the middle of the table and one of the men was tapping it with his pencil. He appeared disturbed by its presence. She was elated. It was a sign of freedom for women.

She didn't speak as she served the men, moving between them with brisk efficiency that belied the nervous tension in her shoulders and neck. None of the men looked at her until she served Ogden. Then she felt three pairs of eyes stare at her as she poured him a cup of hot beverage and placed two cookies on his plate.

"Thank you, darling."

Ogden gave her a peck on the cheek as she bent over him. She suspected that was what the men were watching for, the peck that was not a normal behavior but was probably one of the things they were doing as part of their "project". She nodded and moved out of the room. She didn't relax until she was alone in the kitchen. She collapsed against the table and might have slid down onto the floor in relief if Molton hadn't called for her. She glanced at time monster, and realized it was time for the children to go to bed.

When she returned downstairs, the men were gone. Ogden had set the tray on the floor by the study door for her. She picked it up and took it to the kitchen, where she would spend another hour scrubbing an already clean floor in an effort to tire herself out before bed.

29

The next day was a blur of activity. Ogden was doing many things, secret things, and Lorelei was kept running supplying him and his many visitors with hot beverage and snacks. The children were at their most energetic, and she raced between study, backyard, and playroom trying to keep up with the three of them. She hoped to have a little time to slip over to Linolin's – Susan's, she reminded herself with a smile – on her Saturday free hour, but it didn't look like she was going to be able to take her free hour.

A few minutes before time for free hour, Amity appeared on her doorstep. Lorelei rushed to let her in, and rushed back to the study to pick up one tray of cups left behind by the just departed guests and deliver another tray of cups for the newly arrived guests. Out of breath, she leaned against the wall in the hallway, wondering what was happening to her normal, placid life.

Ogden stuck his head out of the study. "Lorelei? Isn't it time for your free hour?"

Lorelei nodded. "But you have guests."

"We can take care of ourselves. Just…bring me the pot of hot beverage, and we'll pour if we need more. You go. Have fun with Amity. I did hear Amity, didn't I?"

Lorelei nodded and raced to the kitchen. She delivered the hot beverage pot and a tray of clean cups, and was rewarded with a peck on the cheek and a pat on the fanny. She glared at Ogden, let him know he embarrassed her, and slipped out of the room. She dropped her apron on the chair in the kitchen, patted her hair, and joined Amity in the living room.

"I thought we could go see Grenata", Amity whispered.

Lorelei pulled her out of the house so they could speak in private without worrying about the men hearing. "We shouldn't. They might be watching. They want to know where she is."

"I know. I expected that when I heard about the intervention."

Amity knew about the intervention! Perhaps she even knew what it was. "Intervention?"

"I really need to teach you to listen at keyholes. You need to be more informed." Amity brushed an imaginary crumb off her coat.

"I did listen. I heard about the intervention. But they didn't say what it was."

"Well, apparently Lymon wasn't supposed to behave like he did. The men went by the house yesterday afternoon. They spent two or three hours there...they must have been there while I was over here." Amity scowled, the reality of the risk she took finally sinking in. "They talked to him, and threatened him, and made him promise he would stick to the script. He promised, but I don't think he's happy about it. Now he has to pretend Grenata left him, and that he wants her back. He's sulking."

Lorelei smiled. The image of Lymon sulking, that great hulking brute of a man who no more deserved Grenata than Merris deserved Amity, was delicious. Having someone force him to be someone he wasn't for a few days was almost worth everything they were going through.

"So how can we go see Grenata?"

Amity didn't answer. She took Lorelei by the hand and they headed in the direction of book room, a favorite destination during free hour. Lorelei wasn't prepared for the sudden sharp turn Amity made as soon as they were out of sight, heading toward the other end of town, the forbidden zone where women were not allowed.

"We can't go that way." Lorelei panted trying to keep up with her friend. "It's not allowed."

"I know. Isn't it grand?" Amity was having an adventure.

"Stop. We...can't."

Amity stopped and stared at Lorelei. "Where are you?"

"I'm here...right here. See me?"

"No, I mean...where are you, the woman that used to sneak into men's classes, that used to take every risk to learn, to be more than just a woman?"

Lorelei stopped to think. Where was that woman? What had she done with her? Had Ogden managed to beat that woman out of her? No, he hadn't beat her nearly enough for that. He was sparing with the beatings and stopped short of breaking her spirit, perhaps because he wasn't aware she had a spirit to break. "I'm still here."

"Then come." Amity didn't pause any longer. She moved briskly forward, clearly expecting Lorelei to follow.

Lorelei followed. She hesitated, and almost lost sight of Amity. Her long legged friend was moving at top speed, and Lorelei broke into a run to catch up with her. Amity laughed as Lorelei pulled up next to her and grabbed her hand.

"I knew you'd come. I knew you weren't buried that deep."

The two didn't speak again until they arrived at their destination, a gray building that looked like a factory. The sign identified it as Acme Manufacturing. A large doorway presented an efficient face to the world, but there was no sign of anyone coming or going. The only sign that someone might be there was a small light by an almost unnoticeable door in the west wall. Amity pushed on the door and it opened. They entered a world neither of them ever dreamed existed.

30

The world inside the gray wall was nothing like the exterior. The walls were a warm yellow, a color much like the shirt Linolin was wearing yesterday. The artwork was…unusual…the only word Lorelei could think of to describe it. She stood in front of a picture of a time monster that looked like it was melting, and it felt so real she thought it might drip onto the floor. All the pictures had the same, not quite right look to them. Even the ones that looked right at first had something odd when you looked close.

Amity wasn't interested in the artwork. She acted like there was nothing different about this place, and moved as though she had been here before. She grabbed Lorelei and pulled her along a corridor until they reached a door at the end of the hall. The door was marked Linolin Clavelle. Amity knocked, and a warm voice, a familiar voice, said Enter.

The two women entered the room, tiptoeing over the soft carpet. They crept toward the woman behind the desk, standing to offer them her hand. Lorelei saw Grenata behind a wall, the large window offering her a view of her friend that apparently did not allow her friend to see her. She shook Linolin's hand absently, her eyes on Grenata.

"Good afternoon, Elizabeth. It's good to see you again." Linolin smiled, and the smile seemed to radiate genuine warmth.

"Good afternoon, Lin…Susan." Lorelei faltered, and changed the name at the look on the other woman's face. Clearly she took the code names seriously. What was going on here that could make her afraid even to speak her name, a name written on the door to this room?

"This must be 'Lucretia Mott'." Linolin assigned Amity her own code name.

Lorelei frowned. She wasn't familiar with that name. Was she being given information? Or expected to know something she didn't? She shook her head, not to disagree but to indicate she had no familiarity.

"Oh, well, you'll know soon enough." Linolin smiled. "I imagine you're here to see…'Matilda'?" She gestured toward Grenata as she spoke.

Amity nodded. She was willing to accept her new name without any clue what it meant or why. If the woman who helped Grenata wanted to call her 'Lucretia', 'Lucretia' she would be. Lorelei hesitated, then nodded in agreement with Amity.

"Gren…'Matilda'…" Amity stumbled over the unfamiliar name. "Voice monster…she asked me to come here. Is she…all right?"

"She's having a wonderful time. I brought her here this morning because I want to see how she fits in. I think she's going to do well here." Linolin beamed as though she were personally responsible for Grenata's success.

Linolin pushed on the wall and an unseen door opened. The three women moved into the next room. Grenata looked up as they entered, and squealed with delight when she saw her friends. She tried to stand, but her leg was too weak. Linolin helped her back to her seat and told her not to rush things, she'd heal sooner if she rested. Grenata nodded, a look of adoration on her face as she watched her new friend.

"How are you doing, Grenata?" Lorelei winced at her banal comment, but couldn't think of how else to start the conversation. This was not a normal situation, and the usual gossip was not in order.

"I'm doing better than I've ever done. Look."

Grenata waved her arm at a project she was working on. Lorelei and Amity stepped over to investigate. Grenata was painting. The painting was strange, in the way the ones in the hallway were strange. It looked normal at first glance – just some children playing in a yard – but a closer look caused Lorelei to shudder as she realized the trees that surrounded the children were actually mysterious cloaked figures carrying knives.

"Grenata! That's amazing. You have real talent." Linolin knelt in front of the painting and inspected it like an expert. "You told me you hadn't painted before."

"Well, I painted some little stuff when I was a kid, but just the sort of things children paint. I guess it was okay. Mom used to hang it on cold box and people would pretend I was a genius. But I knew, because Mom told me, that I was just a girl." Grenata had a wistful tone as she remembered.

"Just a girl. Damn, I hate that phrase. Let's not say it here, okay?" Linolin held out her hand in a fist. The other three women stared at it. She indicated they needed to make fists, too. When

Lorelei and her friends held out their fists, Linolin bumped their fists with hers. "There. An oath."

"What is this place?" Lorelei noticed for the first time that there were other women in the room, about a half dozen, women doing various things. Some were painting, some were writing, some were reading, but none of them were sewing or cleaning or washing or knitting.

"It's a shelter. For battered women."

"Battered women? What's that?" Amity leaned closer as though expecting to hear the wisdom of the ages from a woman none of them had been willing to speak to until yesterday.

"Women who have been beaten by their husbands. Some of them were abandoned, some of them walked out."

"Walked out?" Lorelei was stunned. "Just...left? They can do that?"

"Of course they can. So can you." Linolin watched Lorelei as she spoke. She seemed genuinely interested in the impact her words had on the other woman.

"I can't. It isn't done. Women don't do that."

Linolin nodded. "I hear that all the time. Women don't do that. Usually from women, which makes me sad. When I hear it from men, it makes me angry. But for women to accept that, for women to teach it to their daughters so their daughters grow up to believe it...that's sad."

Lorelei thought about the conversation with her mother, and how upset Mom was when Grandma made her teach Lorelei to be a good wife. "My mother didn't want to teach me that."

Amity stared. "What do you mean? Your mother is a very good wife."

"She told me. Thursday. My grandmother made her teach me how to be a good wife."

"And you still snuck into men's classes every chance you got. She must have had a tough time."

Linolin threw back her head and roared. "You snuck into men's classes? Good for you! I hope you remember some of what you learned. You may need it."

Lorelei nodded. She remembered a lot...and she continued to read Ogden's papers when he left them lying around. "Why?"

"I thought…didn't you…aren't you planning some sort of…mission? Aren't you planning to free women?"

Lorelei hesitated. Could she trust this woman? She didn't know her well enough to be sure. She could trust Amity…Corinne…even Grenata…and, apparently, Mom…but this woman was asking a lot of her on such a short acquaintance. She made up her mind. "Yes."

"Good. I'd begun to think I'd joined something other than what I planned."

"Why me?"

"That's the question we always ask, isn't it? Whenever something happens, it's why me? Why me, God? Why me? Because you happen to be married to the chief on that project…and fortunately, you have a spirit that can't be easily broken."

"How do you know that?"

"If it could, you'd be broken already. If it could, you wouldn't be here."

"Who is Lucretia Mott?" Amity broke in, finally curious about her new name.

The next twenty minutes were spent with Linolin catching them up to date on the history of women. Some of it Lorelei already learned from Ogden's papers, but quite a bit of it was new to her. Lucretia Mott. Matilda Joslyn Gage. And many others, thousands of women through the ages fighting against men who insisted they were inferior, even childlike. Women fought back, and won. Kept on winning. Never quite getting the blue ribbon of full equality, but inching ever closer.

Then things started to shift. Women started to lose. They grew complacent, thought they didn't need to fight anymore, but men kept fighting. They pushed women back toward the corner, but women refused to go. Every push the men made, the women rose up and pushed back. They were on the verge…they were close…so close…they would have won.

Linolin stopped. She had tears in her eyes. Clearly this part of the story upset her. Lorelei urged her to go on…what happened? If women had so much, why did they have so little now? Linolin continued. Women were winning again. They were moving forward, and were gaining so much ground nothing could stop them. They would have won…they would have achieved the ultimate goal…but then…Linolin paused, wiped a tear from her eye, and finished. The collapse.

31

Linolin stopped. Time monster showed it was time for Amity and Lorelei to leave if they wanted to get home by the end of free hour. Linolin was well versed in the routines married women followed, even though she didn't follow them herself. She knew the cost for violating one's schedule could be painful – even deadly in some cases. No one could spend their life working in this shelter and not know the consequences for misbehavior.

They returned by a route that led toward book room, so when they appeared in the sight line of their husbands they would appear to be coming from book room. Amity left Lorelei at her door and headed three doors down to where her own husband waited for her return. Lorelei entered cautiously, as though Ogden could see where she had gone.

The study door was closed and a tray of cups was on the floor outside. Lorelei picked them up and carted them to the sink. She wondered about that as she washed dishes. Ogden's usual habit was to leave them in his study and she would collect them when she cleaned in there. He didn't usually go to the trouble of leaving them outside the door for her.

She didn't hear Ogden come into the kitchen until he spoke.

"Did you enjoy your free hour?"

Lorelei nodded. "Amity and I spent the time in book room. It was quiet and no one bothered us." Lorelei knew Ogden would not check her story, since book room was a woman only space and no man would venture in there.

"I'm glad. You're looking tired. You need some time for yourself."

Ogden came up behind Lorelei but did not put his arms around her. He stood behind her looking out the window into the backyard where Micra was climbing a tree, secure in the knowledge that if she couldn't see her parents, they couldn't see her either. Molton was digging a hole, a favorite game of his. Lorelei hoped he remembered to fill in the hole before he came in. Ogden did not like him leaving open holes, even though he did dig them only in his assigned space.

Lorelei was aware of Ogden in a way she had never been aware of him in the past. She steeled herself, not knowing if he was going to grab her or leave her alone. He stood behind her, leaning slightly toward her, his breath on her neck as she finished the last of the dirty cups. He stepped back so she could move from sink to hot box, where the meat was cooking on a slow heat. He watched her as she moved between hot box and cold box, cold box and cupboard, and back to hot box.

"You're very good at that." His voice held a trace of wonder.

"What?"

"Cooking. You make it look like...dancing."

Lorelei laughed. There was very little that dancing had in common with cooking, and she didn't think she did it much different from other women. Still, he probably never watched a woman cook before. It was unlikely he ever watched his mother prepare dinner.

"It looks...easy." Ogden hesitated, possibly remembering his difficulty even finding the cheese and crackers the other night. "I don't mean it like...you don't work. It's just...you make it *look* like you don't work."

Lorelei didn't speak. She wasn't sure where this conversation was headed and didn't want to create problems for either of them.

"Maybe that's why so many men think their wives don't actually do much? Because it comes so natural to them, it's so embedded in their nature, they make it look like...I don't know, but not work?"

Lorelei frowned. The main gist of the comment she caught was that housework comes natural to women. She knew it had not to her. She spent many hours and years being trained how to be a good wife, and she fought long and hard against the enforcement of this routine. Surely she wouldn't have fought so hard if it was part of her nature, just part of being a woman. She paused at the thought which never occurred to her before.

"Maybe." Lorelei struggled to sound non-committal, disinterested. This conversation could be a land mine.

"I just wanted to...thank you...for everything you do for me...us." Ogden gave a vague wave in the direction of the back yard as he added the last word, indicating that he realized she worked for the children, too.

"It's nothing. That's...what I do. It's...what women do." Lorelei repeated the mantras she learned and internalized during her indoctrination in college. She forced herself to suppress her rage.

"Why do you think it's so hard for Grenata?"

Oops. The land mine was about to explode. Ogden wanted information and he suspected Lorelei knew things he didn't know. Lorelei didn't know; she wondered that often herself.

"I don't know. Maybe...maybe...she has...bad..." Lorelei stopped, not sure what word she wanted.

"Bad heredity? No, because her mother was a very good wife. It must be something else. Something you have, and Amity has, and Corinne has, but Grenata doesn't. Maybe...maybe...she was dropped on her head as a baby. Yes, I'll bet that's it." Ogden smiled at the brilliance he displayed, sure he had solved the riddle. "I was wondering...you didn't happen to see Grenata in book room, did you?"

Lorelei shook her head. "No. Grenata doesn't go to book room very often. I didn't expect I would see her there."

Ogden paced. "It's very important, you understand. Very important we find out where she is. Lymon is going crazy with worry and grief. He doesn't know how to live without her."

Lorelei wanted to say he'd manage. She wanted to say he didn't deserve Grenata. She wanted to say a lot of things but the time hadn't come yet, and she wasn't sure what she would do if she found herself in the same spot as her friend.

"I'm going on round-a-bout", Ogden announced. "I didn't get a chance this morning, with all those visitors. Can I take the children?"

Lorelei went numb. Not only did he want to take the children, now he was asking her permission.

"I know you were worried when I took them before. Do you have any objections? We'll be back in time for dinner."

Lorelei nodded, afraid her voice would shake if she tried to speak. Satisfied, he grabbed his coat and left through the back door. She watched as he and the children disappeared into the twilight. Hot box chirped and she turned her attention back to her normal routines. There would be time to think later.

32

Ogden came into the kitchen again as she was washing dinner dishes. This was more times than he had been in the kitchen in their entire marriage. In fact, the first time he came in was probably more times than he'd been in there. He didn't even check the kitchen when he bought the house, because he wouldn't know what to look for, and it never occurred to him to ask his wife's opinion. She hadn't seen the house until the day they moved in.

He stood to one side as she worked, which she appreciated. It was difficult to work with him standing behind her. She wiped and put away the dishes, then scrubbed the counter with a more vigorous stroke than she usually used, more for Ogden's sake than for the cleanliness of the counter. She felt his eyes follow her as she took the dishrag to the laundry and started to remove her apron.

She stiffened when he took the strings of her apron and finished the untying. Not here, she whispered. Not the kitchen. Not with the children still in the playroom. She began to wonder if all of this "making the wives happy" was really more about receiving extra marital duties for themselves. It seemed he was enjoying it more than she was. She remembered the other night, when she let herself go and enjoyed it, and blushed.

Ogden noticed her blush and slid his arms down her shoulders. He pulled her close and whispered in her ear. "Don't worry. Nothing while the children are up. But...once they're in bed...join me." He turned and left the kitchen.

Lorelei stared at his retreating back. He was still behaving strangely, but the odd thing was, she was beginning to enjoy it. She felt a tingle when he stroked her shoulders and electricity shot through her when he told her to join him. What was wrong with her? Were a few papers in a safe enough to turn her into...what? What was the name for a woman who enjoyed marital duties? She wanted to ask someone, but the only person she could think of that might be able to answer something like that was...

Voice monster jolted her out of her thoughts. That's strange, she thought. Who would call at this time of night? No civilized person would use voice monster after dinner...unless it was an emergency. She dried her hands and hurried to the living room. She knew Ogden would not answer voice monster – that was women's work - but she rushed to get there before he could. It might be Grenata.

"Elizabeth?"

Lorelei's heart dropped at the familiar tone. "Susan?"

"Look, I hate to ask you this, but…is there any way you could get to book room tomorrow? Meet me there?"

"Maybe. If…if Ogden doesn't go to church with me, I might be able to…but I'd have the children." Lorelei tried to think about the rest of her day, if there was a single open spot, but the half hour after church was the only time she could imagine.

"Can you leave them with anyone?"

"Is…'Lucretia'…" Lorelei struggled with the unfamiliar name. "…coming too?"

"No. Just you and me."

Lorelei nodded, then remembered she was on voice monster and Linolin couldn't see her. "I can have Amity take them for a few minutes. But I won't have long."

"I don't need long. Right after church, then." Linolin rang off.

Lorelei stared at voice monster as though she hadn't seen it before. She went over and over the conversation in her head, but there were no clues as to what Linolin might want her for. She hoped there was nothing wrong with Grenata. If so, would Linolin wait until tomorrow? She shook her head and noticed she was still holding voice monster.

A voice from the playroom reminded her it was time to put the children to bed. She felt a strange excitement as she climbed the stairs. Once the children were in bed…she wondered what Ogden had in mind tonight. Her heart beat faster and her brain seemed to flutter at the thought. She began to wonder if she really knew herself.

Who was this strange woman who was climbing the stairs to get her children to bed in a rush to have marital duties with her husband …perhaps in some strange and embarrassing place? Who was this woman who had a code name, and made friends with the most unacceptable woman in town? Who was this woman who was going to leave her children with another woman to have a meeting with a woman she wasn't allowed to see? Lorelei paused on the top stair, the questions without answers running through her head, challenging her, accusing her, and, in the end, exciting her.

The children went to bed without fuss. When they were tucked in, their blankets pulled over their chins, Lorelei blew each of them a kiss and closed the door behind her. As the door shut on Molton, always the second one down, she paused to allow a surge of excitement to fill her, then she headed with a light step toward the study where she could see a thin sliver of light under the door.

Her hand poised near the door, not ready to knock. She straightened her hair and arranged her skirt, which had ridden up in the back while she was helping Molton get into his night clothes. She looked in the hall mirror and decided she needed to refresh her lipstick. As her hand poised near her lips, she almost lost her nerve. She wasn't going on a date, or to a function, she scolded herself. She was just going to meet her husband in his study. Her hand operated as if on its own and applied a fresh coat of lipstick.

Satisfied with her appearance, she returned to the study and knocked, a gentle knock that surely couldn't be heard through the door. Ogden called out to come in, and she turned the knob and entered. Ogden stood with his back to her, watching out the window. She moved toward him and could see her reflection in the window. She came up beside him and he put his arm around her waist as he closed the drapes. She shuddered as he turned to kiss her, but not a shudder of disgust or fear. For the first time, she entered her husband's embrace with anticipation.

33

Church was nearly empty on Sunday morning, an unusual situation which made it difficult to daydream. Lorelei wanted to think about the night before, figure out what it said about her that she enjoyed marital duties, and about her meeting with Linolin, but Pastor stared directly at her and she had to look absorbed in the service.

Molton squirmed beside her and because of all the empty pews, there was no one to block the view of his energetic little body from Pastor, who spent the entire sermon glaring at Molton, at Lorelei, and, for good measure, at Micra, who sat on the other side of her mother with her hands in her lap not making a sound or squirming. Lorelei wondered if she was asleep but when she looked at her, the child's eyes were open and she was staring at Pastor with the intensity of a mesmerist.

Lorelei made her escape immediately after church, not staying to chat with the ladies. She always cultivated that time of day, so on days when she wanted some time to herself she could duck out for a few minutes without Ogden suspecting. She was never doing anything wrong on her outings, mostly going to book room or just walking slowly and counting some aspect of the world as she enjoyed a beautiful day. Today, however, she was doing something no good wife would dream of doing.

Book room was deserted when she arrived. A head stuck above one of the reading chairs, the comfortable ones in the middle of the room that tempted you to overstay your allowed time and got Grenata and Corinne in trouble more than once. Amity and Lorelei had a better developed sense of discipline than either of their friends, and managed to vacate the wonderful chairs just in time to get home at their assigned time.

Lorelei peeked around the chair, not sure if she should look further for Linolin if someone else was there. A bright yellow arm shot up to a forehead as her new friend greeted her with a sharp salute.

"Mornin', Elizabeth."

"Susan! What a wonderful surprise to see you here." Lorelei decided not to shout to the world that she came here specifically to see someone. No one here would tell on her, but it was always better to be safe.

Linolin motioned her to the other chair and moved the reading table so she could scoot her chair closer. She watched her book and pretended to read as she spoke to Lorelei. "A meeting."

"Where? When?"

"Thursday. Amity's house. Group."

Lorelei forgot the charade and looked at her new friend in amazement. This was a woman who thought of everything. No safer place to have a meeting than Thursday group. Then she remembered.

"Wait a minute. It isn't Amity's week. We were at her house last week. This week, we're supposed to be hosted by…" Lorelei stopped.

"Grenata. Not possible. Amity can step in, can't she? Or…should we come to your house?"

Linolin did not look at her. Lorelei nodded. "Yes. My house. Thursday."

"I'll bring the recruits. Your job is to inspire them."

"Recruits?" Lorelei wasn't sure she liked the sound of where this was going. "Are we going to war?"

Linolin didn't speak at first. She traced her finger along the lines of the book as though she was reading but Lorelei was sure she heard, and that she was not reading. When she spoke again, her voice was lower than before.

"Yes. We are going to war."

Lorelei started to ask for more information, but one look at Linolin's face told her the other woman had said all she would…or could. She stood to leave.

"I have to go…I'll prepare. How many will there be?"

"Eight."

"Eight? I've never prepared group for so many…plus Amity and Corinne?"

"Of course. I'm looking forward to meeting Corinne. Is she with us?"

Lorelei nodded. One thing she was sure of was that all the friends were together on this. "Is Grenata coming?"

"No. Not this time. While the men are looking for her, it isn't safe."

"Tell her…tell Grenata…I'm going to do what I can to help her."

Linolin stood. She held out her arms and Lorelei accepted the embrace. "She knows."

Lorelei pulled out of the embrace and headed for the door. She looked back just once, feeling like Lot's wife, but all she could see was the top of a head. The chairs were once more apart, the reading table between them. "She really works fast", was all Lorelei thought as she pushed open the door and left.

34

Ogden was in the living room when they returned from church. He had made a snack, having apparently figured out how the kitchen worked. Lorelei pushed open the door to the kitchen and frowned. He still had a lot to learn. The mess in the kitchen would take a long time to clean.

"I'll help. I'm sorry, I didn't intend to leave a mess." Ogden was behind her, his hands wrapped around her fanny, his breath on her neck.

Lorelei moved away, afraid proximity would lead to indiscretions in front of the children. Ogden was having trouble controlling himself lately. She moved around the kitchen with typical efficiency, Ogden blundering around in her way until she shooed him out and finished the job on her own. Lunch was ready in hot box, and she called her husband and children to the table with relief. What could happen over the lunch table?

Ogden was his usual quiet self at the table and the children didn't say a word as they ate. It was like the old days, before the project. Lorelei stared at her plate, her fork poised over her vegetables. She wasn't hungry. She needed to eat, having hardly eaten anything for three days. She plunged her fork into the meat and forced herself to swallow her food until Ogden put his fork down. She was relieved when he finished eating and she didn't have to choke down any more food.

The rest of the day was quiet, and Lorelei followed her usual routine. Ogden remained in his study all afternoon, only coming out to ask for hot beverage. The children were next door with a friend and she had the house essentially to herself. She cleaned with a ferocity she never felt before, a warrior-like approach to any dirt and dust that might dare to hide in some dark corner.

The metaphor pulled her up. Warrior – war – recruits. The conversation with Linolin disturbed her, and she was behaving as though she were already at war. At war with whom, she thought. Ogden? Maybe...but that seemed silly. He was not a warrior sort. He was more of a...Lorelei frowned. What was Ogden? When he was punishing her, she could see a warrior, the way his eyes would blaze with anger. But when they had marital duties last night, that was not a warrior. That was a…well, not a lover, not exactly. More like a timid boy trying to please his girl…now where had that image come from? She remembered a little boy on the playground in low school, blushing as he rushed over to steal a kiss from her before rushing off again, leaving her surprised and amused at the same time. That was how Ogden appeared last night.

Her cleaning completed, she checked the dinner in hot box and settled in with her book for an hour of reading. She opened it to the bookmark, but found she could not concentrate. War images flew before her eyes, images of women in tanks charging hapless men armed only with vibrators, trying desperately to prevent disaster. Disaster…there was that word again. Catastrophe. Women. Wives. Well, at least they now knew what the disaster was. The men were afraid the women would ask for freedom. It appeared the men were right.

The sun was dropping in the west and the sky was growing dark. She could no longer see the pages of her book, but time monster told her she had another hour before she could turn on the light. Ogden was determined she not waste any energy. She glanced down the hallway and spotted the sliver of light coming from under his door. For the first time in her married life, she didn't stomp down the surge of resentment. She allowed herself to feel all the small slights and remember all the large indignities – and the pain, she thought, rubbing her fanny where Ogden placed his hands earlier. She stiffened every time he came near her fanny, remembering all the painful punishments he administered for real or imagined transgressions of her role as a good wife. All of those transgressions, she thought, were things so minor no one should even consider themselves wronged over them. In fact, most of them shouldn't be considered transgressions at all.

The resentment grew and began to fester, so when hot box chirped she considered leaving the meat inside to burn. She headed to the kitchen to turn it up to a high enough heat to burn it before dinner, but settled for basting. Her fanny hurt as she reached for the knob, so she let prudence win out for today. Besides, it was too early to tip her hand. They needed to plan properly before any of them acted out of their usual manner.

By the time Ogden came out for dinner, she had teased and argued herself out of her bad humor. Once she turned on the light, she forgot why she was mad and allowed herself to think about things unrelated to lights, or war, or husbands, or fannies. She managed to read a few chapters before being summoned again by hot box and surrounded by her family. The children clattered into the hallway with a muted racket and skidded to a halt when they saw their father already seated at the table. Micra dropped her face with a demure apology, but Molton held his chin up with a defiant glare.

Ogden laughed and Lorelei sent them upstairs to wash their hands. She watched her husband closely. It seemed strange their 'project' had taken hold of him so easily. There was no sign of ill humor or even mild annoyance when the children clattered in, no sign that he was forcing himself to act in a manner to which he was unaccustomed. Could it be he was starting to like his new role?

Lorelei dished up dinner in silence and they all settled down to eat. By the time Lorelei was in her chair at the foot of the table, Ogden was half finished with his dinner. She was able to eat a few bites, and no one noticed she had not gotten much food by the time he laid down his fork. She planned it just right.

35

Monday was a quiet day. Lorelei maintained her normal routine, determined to wait until Thursday to think about her plans, her mission. She moved from room to room, her dust rag flying, until she reached Ogden's study. She had been up half the night, unable to sleep, and his study needed no cleaning today. She knelt in front of his safe and swung the dial. She dug into the treasure inside eagerly.

She managed to work through several documents by the time disaster struck. She heard the door close and got everything returned to its place just in time. By the time Ogden entered the study, she was finishing up the final touches on a job well done.

"Looks nice." Ogden grunted. "I need you to leave."

Ah, it looked like the old Ogden had returned. Well, all except the looks nice comment, something he never said in the past. She brushed past him and swept out the door. She heard the door close and lock behind her. Whatever was happening, it was serious. He rarely locked the door because he trusted his family to respect his privacy.

Lorelei lifted the receiver on voice monster. She heard him dial before the door closed, and she wanted to know what was happening. She suspected it had to do with her, or at least with her friends.

"She won't come." Ogden spoke without greeting to the man on the other end.

"Make her."

"I can't make her without force. We all agreed it has to look as though she came back on her own."

A heavy sigh from the other end. "I never agreed with that. I think it is more powerful if we show we can bring back any woman who leaves. Letting her come back on her own is giving the woman too much power."

"I agree, but I think for the moment we need to be…gentle. We can't give the women any reason to *want* to leave."

"What about your wife? Is she all right?"

"She's good. She's always been a good wife, never like Grenata. I have punished her a few times, but for the most part she didn't deserve it. I felt I had to punish her to make sure she understood who was in charge."

Lorelei stifled the angry cry that tried to escape. So he knew she didn't deserve being hit and he hit her anyway? And here she had thought he was at least a little better than that brute, Merris. Calming down, she reminded herself he was better than Merris. He only hit her a few times, and didn't hit her as a matter of course every time he walked in the door.

"Bring her home. I don't care what means you have to use, that woman needs to be in her husband's home by morning. Or else."

The man slammed down his voice monster. She waited for the telltale click that would let her know it was safe for her to hang up without Ogden hearing. The click didn't come. She imagined him standing in his study, voice monster in hand, staring at the receiver. She forced herself not to breathe, knowing he could hear her now that the conversation was over. It seemed like an eternity, but time monster only moved one tick by the time she heard him hang up. She laid the receiver gently on the cradle and was in the kitchen by the time Ogden reappeared.

"I have to go back out. I only came home for...some papers I forgot."

Lorelei nodded, pretending not to notice he was empty handed. He came home to make the call, perhaps, because home was closer than the office to wherever he was. He pulled his coat around his shoulders and hunched back out into the cold outdoor air. Lorelei watched him go, then grabbed voice monster and dialed.

"Susan?" She breathed heavily into the phone, the lump in her chest choking off any speech. "Susan, is that you?"

"Calm down, Elizabeth. Just...take it slow. What's happening?" Linolin sounded tense.

"They're coming for her." Lorelei didn't feel any further explanation was needed.

"I know. They already came by. They've figured out she's here...but she wasn't. She was at the shelter when they came. I...might have to leave her there for a couple of days. I hate to, with her leg not healed, but..."

"Don't. Please, don't leave her there."

"Slow down, Elizabeth, take a few deep breaths. Breathe. Okay, now, slowly, calmly, don't get worked up. I need to understand what you're saying."

"She has to go somewhere else. She can't stay at the shelter. They'll find her, and they'll find the shelter, and everything will be ruined."

"Of course they won't find the shelter. Oh, men are always looking for their runaway wives, but no man has ever found the shelter. It really doesn't look like much, but you know that."

Lorelei gasped. It was still difficult to speak and she gulped a couple of times. "This is different. This isn't some man looking for his runaway wife. Lymon doesn't want her. He's being forced to take her back. This is...this is all of them. This is big. They are willing to do whatever it takes...that's the words he used, whatever it takes."

"Who? Who used those words? Ogden?"

"No. The man."

"What man? You have to work with me here. I have no idea what you're talking about."

"The man...on voice monster. He was talking to Ogden. He told him to do whatever it takes to bring her back."

Linolin was silent. Lorelei began to worry she had hung up, but she heard the other woman breathe and realized she was just thinking. "I'll...I'll go over there and...think of something. Maybe we can...move her...put her somewhere they can't find her."

Lorelei realized Linolin was taking her seriously now. She understood the implications of the situation and she would help. Lorelei wanted to protect her friend, but she knew they also needed to protect the shelter. The work Linolin was doing was too important to be sacrificed for the sake of one woman.

"I'll call you."

Linolin rang off and Lorelei hung up. She dropped to the floor, too exhausted and scared to stand.

36

The men found Grenata. She was not at Linolin's, but she was not at the shelter, either. Lorelei heard Ogden stomp in the front door and remained in the kitchen. He stood in the doorway and watched her, her nervous fluttering silenced to a normal pattern only by the sheer force of her will.

"Grenata is home." Ogden didn't move from the doorway as Lorelei poured him a cup of hot beverage. He accepted the beverage gratefully and wrapped his cold fingers around the warm cup.

"When did she return?" Lorelei held onto the pretense.

"This morning. She showed up on the front porch and begged Lymon to take her back. She was very contrite about running away, and promised she would do her best to be a good wife for the rest of her life."

The final words fell on Lorelei's brain with an ominous thud. Rest of her life? That should be a long time for a young woman, but for the first time, she felt the tentacles of mortality wrap around her and squeeze. It was the first time she realized the enormity of the step they were about to take. She suppressed a shudder. It appeared Ogden didn't notice. He was staring into his hot beverage as though it held the secrets of the universe.

"I think she's glad to be home." Ogden sounded his final note as the kitchen door closed on his retreating figure.

Lorelei leaned against the counter, her legs too weak to hold her. This was serious. This was frightening. She began to wonder if she embarked on something in a fit of enthusiasm that she would be unable to carry through in the face of deadly reality. Her nerves were on fire and her hands were shaking.

It was another quiet dinner. Ogden was preoccupied, seeming to be a thousand miles away. The children were not home. He told her he intercepted them as they got off child mover and delivered them to her mother. She nodded, a horrifying weight dropping down and weighing her every move, so she could barely drag herself from kitchen to table. Ogden noticed.

"You're tired."

132

"I'm all right. I've just been working hard. Thursday group is going to be here. I need to be prepared." Lorelei did her best to sound casual.

"Again? Weren't they just here?"

"Yes, but it is Grenata's turn, and we thought…since she wasn't there…we should move it. I told them I could get ready in time, so we decided to meet here."

"Good idea. You women really know how to organize things. I'm in awe of you."

Lorelei shot him a sharp glance, but he appeared to be sincere. Nothing in his tone or on his face suggested he was mocking her, or that he was playing a script. He should have been an actor, she thought. He's good at this. The thought of her husband being so good at lying brought her up short. What else might he be lying about?

"I took the children off for a reason", Ogden was saying.

Lorelei forced herself to pay attention. This could be important.

"I thought…I wanted…to spend the evening together. Alone. It was…pleasant…the other night." Ogden stammered, like a shy boy trying to get a girl to notice him.

"That would be…nice." Lorelei stood. Ogden was done eating, and she started to clear the table.

"Don't."

Lorelei stopped. Her instincts told her to obey her husband, no matter how much her brain was telling her she shouldn't have to. He stood up, came around the table, and took her by the hands.

"Let's…" Ogden stopped. He looked at his wife, and she looked at him.

Lorelei understood what he wanted. He wanted marital duties. Here? She wasn't sure. He pulled the drapes. She started to unbutton her dress. He helped her, his hands fumbling with the buttons in his eagerness. She leaned into him, ready to allow herself to experience pleasure at his hands again. She was not going to believe the lies anymore. Marital duties were fun.

37

Lorelei was up before Ogden as usual in the morning. She rushed through her morning routine, running upstairs to get the children out of bed before she remembered they were with her parents. She set out Ogden's clothes and his plate, and pulled on her own clothes with haste, not stopping to check if she was straight or crooked. Her shoes disappeared in the heat of passion last night, and she was on her knees searching under the table when Ogden came down.

"Looking for these?" He had her shoes dangling off his fingers.

"Yes! Where were they?"

"Under the bed. I thought you might need them." He looked amused.

Lorelei snatched her shoes and started toward the kitchen to get breakfast. He grabbed her as she went by and swept her into a passionate embrace, ending in a moist kiss.

"Do you think this is what it feels like to be a newlywed?" His eyes twinkled with mischief.

Lorelei glared at him and pulled out of his arms to head to the kitchen. She couldn't let herself get swept up in excitement this morning. She had a lot to do, a lot of places to go, and she needed to get him out of the house.

When she finally got him out the door, after three more embraces and a couple of grabs at her that missed their mark, she started to collapse. Then she remembered what she needed to do and headed out the door. She received a message last night from Linolin while Ogden was asleep. She was glad he had not heard voice monster beep.

Linolin sounded scared and desperate. She wanted Lorelei to meet her as soon as she could and they arranged to meet at book room. Any day of the week, except Friday or Sunday, wives were allowed, even encouraged, to spend an hour or two in book room, and Lorelei didn't worry as she headed out. Today was safe.

Amity was already at book room when she arrived but Linolin was nowhere in sight. Amity grabbed Lorelei and pulled her into a corner where no one would see them.

"Are you all right?" Amity was breathless.

"I'm fine. What about you?"

"Merris...sent the children to Mom last night. He spent the entire evening..." Amity stopped and blushed.

Lorelei nodded. "Ogden too." She remained casual, not intending to let Amity know she enjoyed it. She felt like a traitor...or worse.

"He told me...Grenata came home. I know she didn't. She wanted to stay with Linolin. She was happy there." Amity watched the door as she spoke. Lorelei nodded to let her know she heard the same news. "Do you think she can be trusted?"

"Who? Grenata? Of course she can."

"No, I mean...Linolin. Do you think...it isn't possible she told them where to find Grenata is it?"

Amity gave voice to a fear that plagued Lorelei all morning. She spoke as much to reassure herself as to reassure her friend. "No, I think she's straight. But...we should be careful. Don't...shhh."

Linolin appeared in the doorway, her tall figure filling the room. She spotted the two women and headed their way.

"Elizabeth! Lucretia!" She embraced both of her new friends, then stood back and examined them with eagle eyes. "How are you?"

Lorelei spoke first. "I'm scared. What happened?"

"I took her to a friend, someone who has taken in women before - a widow, so she doesn't have to ask. She didn't want to go. Grenata...'Matilda'...wanted to stay with me. I loved having her, but it wasn't possible once they knew she was there."

"Did they find the shelter?"

"No. They found her when I went over to take her some clothes. They must have been hiding at my house. I looked around...poked the bushes...I never saw them. But they followed me and took her."

"Was she hurt?"

"They need her not to be hurt. That's the best thing. They are trying to send a message, that they can find you and bring you home no matter where you go, but they didn't want to hurt her because they are still on their project."

"We know." Amity met Lorelei's eyes, and the two women blushed.

Linolin pulled them to the comfortable chairs, the only chairs tall enough for them to talk without being seen from outside. The top of Linolin's head showed, because she was so tall, but other than that, they were invisible.

"I'm sorry. I promised you, and I've let you down."

"You couldn't have helped it." Lorelei surprised herself with her vehemence. "They mean business and they hold all the cards...at least for now."

"For now. Yes. We shall overcome."

"That sounds like a slogan. Is that our motto?" Amity looked from Linolin to Lorelei, convinced her two smart friends had all the answers.

"It's a song. From a long, long time ago. A song for people who fight for their freedom, for their equality. It's just a song, though. It's not magic." Linolin looked sad. Lorelei understood. She'd like to have a little magic right now.

The three women huddled in whispered conversation as long as they dared. Linolin told them everything about the raid, as they decided to term the mission that brought Grenata home to Lymon. Ogden was in charge. Lorelei said she thought that was good. She explained the conversation on voice monster yesterday, and how the other voice was willing, even eager it seemed, to do Grenata harm, but Ogden insisted they needed to make sure she wasn't hurt.

There were seven men against the three women...Grenata wasn't much use in a pitched battle with her leg broken, so it was just the two women who stood their ground against the determination of the men. The women stood in front of Grenata and refused to move. They locked their arms together so they would be harder to move by force but eventually the men succeeded. One of the men proved too much for them, a large brute of a man who seemed to delight in punishing women.

Amity and Lorelei shared a look. Merris. He managed to move the women from in front of the sofa where Grenata was lying. He picked her up in his arms without any help and carried her, screaming, outside and down the stairs. Linolin thought he probably carried her all the way home.

"It's only about three blocks." Lorelei volunteered the information absently.

"She wasn't at my house. She was at a friend. This woman lives on the other side of town."

"Oh. I forgot." Lorelei realized they meant business if they were willing to carry a woman, a tall woman with a full figure, for such a distance.

136

"If he put her down, she would have run. I'm glad she didn't. Her leg might never heal if she runs."

"I imagine it won't heal." Amity hadn't said much until now. "There is no way Lymon will let her rest. He's determined to make a good wife out of her if he has to take her back."

Linolin nodded. "That's my impression, too. We've got to get her out of there."

"That won't be easy." Lorelei had some ideas, but she didn't think they'd actually work.

"We'll have to take a lot of chances."

"One thing I have to know." Amity wasn't going to let go. "Did you…did you…tell them…we brought her to you?"

Linolin shook her head. "I would never do that. I told them…and Grenata backed me up…that I found her lying in the street and helped her to my house. I took her to my friend until she could recover. That's all they know. I think they believed it."

Amity breathed audibly and Lorelei realized she had been holding her breath ever since Linolin arrived. She tensed when Linolin described Merris, and Lorelei massaged her shoulders trying to get her to relax. She felt the tension ease out of the other woman as she realized their role was still secret.

"We'll never be allowed to do Thursday group if they know we brought her to you. We'll be on solitary for the rest of our lives." Amity smiled, but the smile was a grim one. She wasn't joking or exaggerating.

"Are we still on for Thursday, then? I presume we'll be expected to go to Grenata's house now?"

Lorelei shook her head. "No, I told Ogden we planned to do Thursday group at my house after Grenata…ran away…" She paused, looking to see if Linolin understood that was the story the men were putting out. Linolin nodded, and she continued. "He thought it was a good idea, and that we should do it there even now that she's back. He thought…it would do her some good to be able to rest."

"Good. Since Ogden seems to be in charge of this…mission…maybe he'll make Lymon allow her to recover." Linolin sounded almost normal, the first time since she'd talked to Lorelei on voice monster last night.

The women made small talk. Lorelei asked them what sort of refreshments they preferred for Thursday, and they left book room.

Amity and Lorelei left together, chatting with animation as though they were having a nice gossip session. They didn't wait to see Linolin leave, several minutes later, swinging down the street to her house. They were already closed into their own homes, safe from any prying eyes that might wonder had the three women left together.

38

The next two days were quiet. Lorelei threw herself into her housework and her preparations for Thursday group. Ogden stayed at work late and worked in his study until dinner. After dinner, they would sit together in the living room until the children went to bed, and then go upstairs to the bedroom for marital duties. It as almost like normal, except the together time after dinner and the every night marital duties. Lorelei even enjoyed it on Wednesday night when Ogden joined her in the mister. She welcomed him and participated in a way she never had until recently. And she got to have a hot mist, because Ogden would never tolerate only a warm mist.

Thursday was cloudy and cold. There was a smell of impending snow in the air and Lorelei shivered as she helped the children with their warm clothes. She kept an extra pot of hot beverage brewing, expecting she would need it to keep warm. She stood back and inspected Micra, than Molton, pronouncing them bundled up enough to go out and wait for child mover.

Ogden fiddled with the thermostat. Lorelei watched him, trying to understand what he did to make the dials move. It didn't look mysterious, but she had never been able to manipulate the thing. She always had to wait for him to adjust the temperature.

"I'm putting it higher today. It's supposed to be cold. You'll need more heat than we have right now when the temperature drops."

Lorelei stared but didn't speak. Ogden always turned it down when he left. No use wasting money keeping the house warm when no one was there, he always said. She never pointed out to him that she was someone. Like him, she always assumed she wasn't. Now they were both thinking of her as a person.

Ogden kissed her lightly on the cheek and left for work. He didn't escort the children today, because they already left on child mover. He waved at her from the curb, and she waved back and blew him a kiss. She felt silly as soon as she'd done it but he blew her a kiss in return, to her surprise.

She fidgeted all day, unable to concentrate. Every time she tried to settle, she envisioned a group of armed women warriors appearing on her porch for Thursday group. She burned her hand pouring hot beverage without a pad, and stood at the sink running cold water until it stopped stinging. She skipped lunch, too nervous to eat, and flitted from one room to the other, settling in first one spot, then another, then another.

She was glad for the sleepless night that allowed her to clean her house to her usual standard. She would not have been able to clean today even if the house was filthy, even knowing all those people were showing up. She couldn't stay in one place long enough.

Snow began to fall around lunch time and she finally settled, her face pressed against the window watching the grey parched world turn sparkling white. It was the first snow in three years. Was it an omen? Lorelei built a snowball in the front yard and stuck some small candies on it to make a face with a smile. She perched the snowball on the front of the porch to welcome her guests. There wasn't enough snow for a snowman, at least not yet, but she could make the world a bit cheerier anyway.

Linolin was the first to arrive. She blew up the street like a battleship, her tall slender frame wrapped in a man's black coat and hood designed to conceal her identity as a woman. She could not be seen going into Lorelei's house so she moved past with a determined step. Lorelei watched her disappear from view, her heart in her throat. She jumped when a knock at the back door announced her visitor. She had almost forgotten Linolin in the fascination of watching the snow.

Linolin shook off her coat in the kitchen and thrust her hands over hot box, where Lorelei had a pot of hot beverage brewing. She offered her guest a cup, and Linolin wrapped her long fingers around it with a grace Lorelei could only envy. In spite of Linolin's height, Lorelei always felt like a huge monstrosity when the elegant and graceful woman was near.

"This is a lovely house." Linolin walked around the kitchen opening cupboards and drawers as though she belonged there. She caught sight of Lorelei watching her. "Sorry. Old habit. I just love kitchens."

Lorelei nodded and invited her guest to continue exploring. She showed the woman around the house and led her into Ogden's study, where they stood in front of the safe that held their history, secret and mysterious, but for the first time accessible to those whom it most concerned.

"Do you want me to open it?"

"Not now. We might do that later, if we need, but we should wait in the living room for the rest of the group."

Amity arrived next. She was usually early, because she wanted to help her friends with preparations. She felt bad that Lorelei hosted two so close together, but it would have been the same for her. Corinne could not host today because Corydon's parents were staying while their house was being remodeled, but she promised she would be able to host at her normal time next Thursday.

Amity and Linolin perched on the seats clutching hot beverage. There was nothing for them to do to help Lorelei. The house was spotless, the food was prepared, everything was ready. All that was needed now was the women…recruits, Lorelei whispered, afraid of the coming war.

Women began to trickle in, one or two at a time, never more. Corinne arrived with Grenata, helping her friend navigate the snowy sidewalk and tricky stairs and settle on the couch. Amity fussed over her, getting her a blanket and a pillow, until Grenata shooed her away. "I have a broken leg, not a terminal illness."

Other women arrived, women who seemed as normal as the four Thursday friends, women who were identified by Linolin with the names of early feminist leaders, and all of them given the title "former good wife".

One of the women, who Linolin introduced as 'Carrie Catt', informed Lorelei that, technically, she was still a good wife. She was here today in hopes of earning that title of 'former', and perhaps taking a few other women into the light with her. Several of the other women nodded.

"We are all still good wives", 'Sojourner Truth' informed Lorelei. She stuck out in the group, the only dark face in a sea of pale white faces. Lorelei was nervous when she arrived. She had some black friends as a child, but as a good wife she was not allowed to socialize with darker skinned women. "We are still good wives, because to be anything else would give away our plans…and it would be a damn shame to give away our plans before we know what they are."

The group laughed. It was clear that Lorelei and Linolin were the only ones with a clear idea of why they women were here, other than to throw off their "good wife" role. Lorelei wasn't sure she even had a clear idea, but she knew it was bigger, much bigger. They were here to rescue all women.

Linolin took charge of the meeting. She had a long history of working and running things, and Lorelei had no problem turning the meeting over to her. The women gathered close and waited. Linolin paused for dramatic effect before she plunged into the story, the same story she told Lorelei and Amity the other day at the shelter. That time, she ended with the collapse, but today, they had more time.

39

Until the collapse, the story was the same as what Lorelei already knew with a few details added. She allowed her mind to wander, and watched the faces of the other women as they took in information grander than they ever imagined. She watched emotions flicker across faces that belonged to good wives from all over town, some of whom she had seen around but most of them unfamiliar.

The emotions were familiar, the same emotions she felt since Ogden came back from the dig. Fear was a prominent feature, but excitement, anticipation, and worry also played across the faces. Anger burst out in all eyes at crucial points in the story, anger that they never knew any of this, and that a coordinated effort was being made to keep it from them.

When Linolin reached the collapse, Lorelei sat forward. She learned about the collapse in school, they all did, but Linolin appeared to know a great deal more. What Lorelei was most curious to learn was how the collapse stopped the rapidly moving force that was women. What happened all those years ago, more than a thousand years in the past?

The collapse was sudden, although it had been coming for many years. The archaeologists believed the actual period of the collapse took over a century, perhaps as long as two centuries, but no one noticed until the final moment. Well, that wasn't quite correct, Linolin inserted. There were people warning of the collapse for a long time, but most people chose to believe everything would be all right. They believed until it wasn't possible to believe anymore.

The collapse began in the ocean. First coral reefs, then fish. Then dolphins. Eventually the ocean itself collapsed, unable to cope with the demands of enormous human populations. Desalinization for drinking water, nasty things (petroleum? What was that? Lorelei asked Linolin, but Linolin shrugged. No one was sure. That's one of those untranslatable words was all she said), and overfishing. Acids from the atmosphere...Lorelei interrupted again. How could they survive so long if there was acid in the atmosphere? Linolin shrugged again. She only knew what was known; it isn't possible to know what isn't known. Lorelei glared at the philosophical non-answer, and Linolin grinned.

Wars broke out over dwindling resources, and massive weaponry was deployed by all sides in an effort to secure for themselves the things that were needed to ensure survival. Before it was over, enormous busy human civilizations were reduced to a handful of hungry, half naked tribes all over the world. Stuff remained behind, traces of what they once were, and a few civilizations, such as theirs, managed to hold onto some of the life they once lived. They had to fight constantly to protect it, and many of the remaining tribes died in the wars that followed the collapse. Now there were little areas...civilization islands, Linolin called them...scattered at long distances from each other. They didn't interact much but some of the men traveled, as Lorelei and the rest knew, and were in contact with these civilizations. Sometimes individuals from one civilization moved into another civilization. Lorelei thought about the foreigners that drove the mini-transits, the foreigners that outraged Ogden so much.

Their civilization was once known as New York City. It was a thriving city, one of the largest in the world, and housed many more people than existed in the entire world today. These houses, the people movers, the mini-transit, and all their things were built from records left behind by their ancestors. Some of the things had incomplete plans, in some cases, fragments that they had to piece together, and they did not know what they were called – hot box, for instance. Cold box. Washing machine. Other names, such as sink and bed, had come down from antiquity intact.

Occasionally the men would find intact collections of treasures, like what they found in China. Linolin only learned about China when the announcement was made the night of the staff function; the news was full of China the next day to make up for the anticlimactic announcement on Ogden's project. She was now fascinated by China and hoping to hear more about what appeared to be one of the most ancient civilizations, and possibly one of the biggest. Lorelei shared what Ogden told her, and what Merris said at the function. China got too big to survive and fell apart almost overnight, at least according to what they could figure out from the records and the ruins.

Linolin continued the story. When the collapse came, men began to fight back against the growing equality of the women. Instead of working to prevent collapse, some of the men took advantage of the chaos to return women to positions of subservience. It didn't look like it would work at first, but in time, they were able to restore women to what the men considered their rightful place – the kitchen and the bedroom. Lorelei and Amity looked at each other and blushed.

In the millennium since the collapse, much was rebuilt by the small remnant civilizations, but there were a lot of things lost. These were the things the archaeologists were looking for. What treasures might wait for them, what new things might they be able to build? Lorelei thought that was stupid. It seemed the men hadn't learned anything from the collapse if they wanted to rebuild the same world that led to the collapse. Linolin agreed.

"Now we come together because the archaeologists may have opened one vault too many for their own comfort." Linolin waxed dramatic, flinging her arms skyward in a grand gesture. "They opened a vault that contained items considered so dangerous the men have to lie to protect themselves."

"Protect themselves from what?" Corinne hadn't been privy to the conversations the other friends had been part of, except last Thursday's group.

Linolin paused. She cleared her throat. She stood up. She lowered her voice. She cast her eyes to the sky and spoke in a low whisper that rumbled through the room. "From women."

40

Now it was Lorelei's turn. Linolin turned the floor over to her new friend, and Lorelei stood. She hesitated. All the eyes were on her, and she felt the enormity of what they were about to embark upon. She cleared her throat. She moved from foot to foot and looked at Linolin. What was she was going to say?

Linolin gave her a smile of encouragement and Amity raised a fist in the air. Lorelei stared. Where did Amity learn that gesture, one Lorelei saw frequently in Ogden's papers? She remembered the motion Linolin made the other day right before she bumped their fists. Lorelei raised her fist in the air and motioned for the other women to do the same. Slowly, hesitantly, ten more fists flew skyward.

The motion worked. Energy surged through Lorelei, energy driven by desire, anger, and rebelliousness. Perhaps that was why the women of the ancient past were always making that motion…it helped them stay on task and gave them energy to keep going when times got hard. From what she read in Ogden's papers, sometimes times got very hard indeed. Women suffered for their determination to be free.

She opened her mouth and the words started to flow. She explained how she found Ogden's safe open and about the Declaration. Resolved: that woman is man's equal. A collective gasp rose from the group as she said the words. They knew they were here to gain freedom, but it never occurred to them they might actually be equal to their husbands, only that they might have more say in the affairs of the home. It was the first time they realized they were here for something much larger than not having to spend all day slaving over hot box.

Lorelei ran through the history of women as far as she had learned it, much of it echoing what Linolin said but with more detail. Linolin listened in fascination; much of this was new to her, as well. She was having holes in her knowledge filled in by this wonderful cache from the museum. Lorelei had prepared another treat for the women. She whipped out the yellow sash she secreted nearby and slipped it over her dress. She paraded around the group, allowing each woman to touch the sash.

She passed around pictures of women marching, of women protesting, of women winning. Her women were transfixed. The faces of long ago women, not odd looking women, not mutated unnatural woman, but faces much like their own, held them in thrall. One woman would have to practically pry the picture out of the hands of the woman before her because no one wanted to pass it on. They wanted to stare at each picture, to touch it, to make contact with women who were brave enough to risk everything for freedom.

Once the pictures came back around, mercifully unharmed (Lorelei had a few nervous moments), she removed the sash and led the group to Ogden's study. The women, all good wives, knew the risks she was taking. They touched nothing and took off their shoes before they entered. Lorelei opened the safe and pulled out the declaration. She read it in a ringing voice and the women bowed their heads as she read. This was history, but it was history no one ever taught them. It was the history of women, and they were women.

The final thing was for Lorelei to read the letter from Ogden to the Archaeologist General in which the plan for lying to the women and tricking them was laid out in detail. She finished with the handwritten comments of the Archaeologist General, or whoever wrote the answer, and then returned the document to the safe. As the door closed with a reassuring click, sealing the records back inside, the mood changed. The entire group let out a large sigh, largely because no one would know they had been there. There was a rush to dust and clean the surfaces in the study before the group returned to the living room.

As soon as the women settled, voices broke out in an enormous clamor, all of them talking at once. Lorelei tried to sort out the chains of conversation, but it was just so much noise. Amity stood, raised her fist, and waited. The women stopped talking, raised their fists, and waited.

"We need to talk one at a time." Amity lowered her fist. "If you want to say something, raise your fist in our gesture and let Lorelei recognize you."

The women lowered their fists and waited for Lorelei to acknowledge the silence. Lorelei nodded at one woman who had been eagerly speaking loudly, trying to be heard over everyone else.

"I think we should let the men know what we know. Then they will realize they can't just trick us back into submission."

Another woman waved her fist. Lorelei nodded in her direction. "I think that would be a bad idea. I think we need to make plans, and study, and catch them by surprise just when they think they've fooled us."

Voices broke out again in a jumble of noise. Lorelei raised her fist and the voices quieted. "Sorry" was heard from several corners of the group, then someone giggled, but the mood turned serious.

Lorelei spoke for the first time since closing the safe. "I think we need to make plans. If we do speak up now, we will be defeated. They have more men than we have women, they have the advantage over us of knowledge and skills we haven't yet learned, and they are willing to do whatever it takes." She flinched as she remembered Ogden's conversation on voice monster, the cruel delight at the idea of hurting women in the unknown man's voice, and the very words she just spoke.

Grenata nodded. "They will kill us."

All eyes turned to Grenata, breaking her silence for the first time. Her broken leg was propped on the table in front of the sofa, and the bruises on her face were mute testimony that she spoke from experience. Her words carried weight.

Amity agreed with her friends. "Nothing can be done today. It must be carefully organized. But we're good at that. We've organized many events and all of us manage the complexities of a home and family. We are all intelligent and motivated."

'Carrie Catt' spoke, then blushed and raised her fist. As soon as Lorelei nodded, she began again. "Intelligent? We're just women."

"What are you saying, friend? Just women? We're people!" 'Sojourner Truth' burst out, her fist thrust in the air after she spoke.

"People? Since when are women people?" Several voices spoke at once. "We are only half of men."

Linolin stood, speaking for the first time since she turned the floor over to Lorelei. "We are people. We are fully people, not half people. We are as complete as any man, and we have skills they don't dream of. Think of this, women. How many of your husbands would be able to survive in the world if you weren't taking care of him?"

The question startled the women, even Lorelei, who thought about a lot of things in the past two weeks but had not thought about the possibility that Ogden would be helpless without her. Now she

148

thought about the mess in the kitchen, his inability even to turn on hot box, and his lack of knowledge of how to make hot beverage, or meat, or vegetables. No, without her, Ogden would not even eat.

Grenata raised her fist and was recognized. "Lymon thinks I am not a good wife because I don't do as much housework as other women. He thinks I dream too much and sit too much and read too much. He's probably right. But while I was gone, he wasn't able to fix a single meal. He had to bring his mother over to take care of him. I do a lot, and the fact that he eats and has clean clothes to wear to work is testimony to that. I just…well, if there are a few magazines on the floor and a couple of socks hanging on the lamp where *he* threw them, it doesn't bother me. But if he is left to do his own work, his home would be a mess that would go beyond anything I could ever create. He doesn't even know where I keep tidy box, and he's never been in the kitchen."

Grenata sat back, exhausted by her outburst. Lorelei stared at her friend. She never heard her express so much before. She realized she had underestimated her. Grenata was a good wife, but Lymon was not a good husband. She said it out loud and the group gasped. The idea of a good husband never occurred to any of them.

"How many of you are experiencing strange things from your husbands?" Corinne spoke for the first time.

About half the hands went up. Lorelei did a quick poll and determined that the women with their hands up were all wives of archaeologists, though not all of them were on Ogden's team. The project spread beyond the immediate team, but was still apparently limited to the archaeology wives. The other wives wanted to know what sort of strange behaviors, and the archaeology wives filled them in, haltingly at first, embarrassed, but urged on by Linolin who apparently had no shame about such things. Lorelei assured them that any shame was that of their husbands, and they were able to speak.

Most of them reported the same behaviors Lorelei and Amity noticed. Corinne and Grenata nodded. Before her exile, Lymon was demanding marital duties on a daily basis, like the other husbands. Since she returned, he had increased his demands.

One wife, a shy young woman who stayed in the back of the group, stuck up her fist and was acknowledged. "I probably shouldn't say this", she started, "but…when my husband demands marital duties…I…sort of…enjoy it." She turned red and sat back down, clapping her hand over her traitorous mouth.

One by one other voices chimed in. Yes, they were liking marital duties. Their husbands were doing new things, things they hadn't done before, things that felt good. They felt electricity. They felt tingles. They didn't understand what was happening. Once again, voices began to overlap and coalesce, and once again Lorelei raised her fist.

"I've been thinking about that", she said as soon as the room was quiet. "I…yes, I've enjoyed it, too. But you know what? In the papers I've been reading, the ones from the museum, I've discovered something…women of the past enjoyed marital duties…they called it sex. They had to fight men for the right to enjoy the experience, but…they did. They even sought it out themselves at times, not waiting for the man to initiate. And sometimes…they said no, even to their husbands."

Lorelei paused to allow the information to sink in, then continued, explaining many of the things, including the diaphragm, that she discovered. Marital duties…sex…was a natural process, and women often enjoyed it as much as men, if the men did it right. Thanks to the pamphlet, which Lorelei originally thought was stupid, the men were learning how to do it right. And the women were learning to enjoy it.

"Don't feel embarrassed, or shamed", Lorelei added. "You have a right to enjoy your own orgasm."

The group erupted again, unsure about the new word Lorelei dropped on them. Fortunately, this did not need translation by Ogden because there was a lot of information in some of the papers explaining the concept and why it was normal for women. The group settled, disturbed and trying to digest all the new information. Linolin thrust her fist in the air and Lorelei bumped her own fist with Linolin's. She realized her new friend was expressing her approval.

They only had a little time left before the group needed to head back to duties, and they still had a lot to do. With Linolin's help, Lorelei organized the women into study groups with various duties. She realized the women who joined them today were two other Thursday groups, and she set each Thursday group to a different task. The groups would meet as a whole again in two weeks, when it would be time for Lorelei's house. Grenata offered to take over since she hadn't done this week but Lorelei said she thought her house was probably safer. Amity and Grenata nodded; both of them had a lot more risk than Lorelei if they stepped out of the routine. Plus, the papers were here and it was not safe to take anything out of the house if they needed something.

The meeting over, the group broke up. Amity helped Grenata back to her house, and the other women left in the same groupings they arrived. Only 'Sojourner Truth' held back, waiting until the group was gone and it was only Lorelei and Linolin.

"I just wanted to say…thank you. You've given me a lot of hope."

She grabbed Lorelei in a big hug before the other woman could protest. Oh, well, she was getting used to being hugged, because Linolin hugged her every time she saw her. And now Ogden was hugging her, too. It was a strange sensation.

"I was wondering…could I bring some of my friends to the next meeting?" 'Sojourner' searched Lorelei's eyes anxiously. "They are all…black like me…but…we can wear make up, or cover our faces, if you're worried."

Lorelei nodded. "Bring them. The more women, the better. We need to hear what all women need, not just my group. And…well, we need to be stronger than the men."

"My friends are very strong." 'Sojourner' hugged Lorelei and Linolin again, and she was gone.

"We might need to find somewhere else to meet." Linolin was watching the door. "This will be dangerous if the group gets too large."

"For now, I can tell Ogden we are having other women join us to learn how we plan our bazaars. But…we won't be able to do that for long." Lorelei jumped. "Oh no! The bazaar! We haven't finished planning it yet."

Linolin grinned. "What do you need done? I have three dozen women who will be willing to take on the job, and right now they don't have a lot to do. Some of them will be thrilled to plan and organize again."

Lorelei dug the planning notes out of her drawer. "We've got most of it done. But there are still some details…"

Linolin took the paper and promised the bazaar would be the best one they ever planned. With all the women to help, it would go off smoothly. All Lorelei and her friends needed to do was show up. She hugged Lorelei and whispered to her to be brave. Then she pulled her man's black coat over her woman's figure and swept out the back door to return to her own house by a route designed to confuse anyone who might try to follow.

41

Everything went quiet for the next week. Ogden and Lorelei continued to explore their new relationship, and the children enjoyed the growing relationship with their father. On Saturday, Lorelei bustled into the living room to call the children for lunch and was surprised to find Ogden rolling on the floor wrestling with his children. On Sunday, he knelt in the backyard to show Molton how to dig his holes deeper and wider using a slightly different technique. Micra climbed the tree behind them, not worrying her father might see.

Amity dropped by every day on some excuse and they would head to book room where Linolin waited, often with friends. Some of the friends were new recruits, others were familiar faces who were present at the first meeting of the rebels. Corinne joined them when she could, and Grenata limped over on Wednesday to join the women, leaning on a cane Linolin provided. Lymon was being solicitous, for the first time being a good husband, and Lorelei suspected it was on the orders of Ogden. She only wished he had done that because he thought it was the right thing to do, not because he was trying to prevent the women from asking for freedom.

Lorelei's duties for the mission were to continue reviewing the material in the safe, learning all she could learn about methods, techniques, what worked, and what didn't. She stopped obsessing over the house, no longer taking time to clean already immaculate surfaces, so she could spend more time in Ogden's study. She developed a system to review the papers without getting them out of order. She was enjoying herself.

Thursday group was about the mission. The women could think of little else. They worked as usual, keeping their duties done, but most of it was so automatic they could think while they worked. Day dream, that's what Grenata always called it. They were daydreaming.

Lorelei, Amity, and Corinne took turns helping Grenata with her housework. They wanted her to have time to rest so her leg would heal but it was necessary to keep Lymon happy so there were no more incidents, at least until they were ready to step out in their protest march...or whatever technique they decided on. Lorelei was worried a march wouldn't have the effect it had in the past, when there were so many more women in the world than there were people now.

Amity pointed out they were still half the population, and that should be effective enough. Thursday group was lively as they discussed and debated, four friends tied together by the bonds of submission, and now tied together by the bonds of rebellion.

Another week…and it was time for the big group. Lorelei was horrified to hear from Linolin that she could expect 25 women. So many. How would she manage to feed them all, and find places for them all to sit? She sat at the kitchen table and planned the logistics of the meeting, and when they all showed up, they all fit.

'Sojourner' was true to her word. She brought her friends, ten women who were good wives, but were tired from childbearing and housework and being expected to take care of husbands who needed more care than babies. They had their own Thursday groups, and this was the first time they met in the home of a white woman. They arrived with hoods pulled over their faces and their hands thrust deep in their pockets. The cold weather allowed them to hide their dark skin from prying neighbors. Most of them hesitated to come in, not sure of their welcome. Lorelei hugged each of them and put them at ease. They entered her house with a casual air none of the women, including Lorelei, really felt. If they were caught mingling, the punishments would be severe.

Other women brought friends, friends who weren't sure but wanted to hear. They wanted to hear for themselves, see for themselves, these documents from ancient women. Lorelei obliged, and they all trooped to the safe, careful to remove any possible smudges in Ogden's study that would give Lorelei reason to fear discovery and punishment, and trooped back out to the living room, ready to join a group that a week ago they never dreamed could exist.

Lorelei stared at the group, wondering how so many women could be so tired of their role, and none of them knew. Most the women went through life thinking they were the only one who wanted more, bowing to the pressure of their husbands, their mothers, and their friends, all acting the part of a good wife for the benefit of other women who were also acting the part of a good wife. They all participated in the training of girls to be good wives, and took on unofficial enforcement duties.

She began to realize how many ways women managed to be agents of their own oppression – a phrase she picked up from some of the papers she read that week, and which she managed to drop into the conversation during group. She was proud of that phrase, and of her own recognition of what it meant.

The women all completed their tasks, and reported on what they found or did. Lorelei was impressed at the amount of work these women managed to do around their own household duties, and they were all able to continue to act the part of the good wife so well their husbands never suspected a thing. She was amazed at her own ability to perform all her roles, and she realized they had acted a part for each other for so long, it came naturally.

Since the tasks were completed, new committees were formed and new tasks assigned. Women were excited and willing to do anything. Lorelei suspected that wouldn't last for all of them, that many women would remain supportive of their efforts but would themselves drop off the face of the earth as far as work was concerned. She also realized, looking at the eager faces, there would be more to take their places. Her goal was to get as many women in the city involved as possible.

Amity reported on her work recruiting. Resenta bumped into her in the grocery store – here she stopped to recount the literal bumping into, as Resenta rammed her cart into Amity's – and tried to get information about what the women were up to. Amity played dumb, pretending she had no idea what Resenta was talking about. Resenta hinted she and Ornata would like to join group, but Amity said Thursday group was about to wrap up the bazaar plans, and weren't looking for more help right now. All the women agreed it would be dangerous to have Resenta and Ornata in on the plans. Neither of them could keep a secret for seven seconds.

The group decided to meet again in two weeks. For now, they were going to keep to that schedule. Linolin suggested they should not meet at any of the women's houses anymore. The group was too big. It was dangerous. She volunteered use of the conference room at her shelter, and the motion was voted and approved. Lorelei sighed with relief. Two weeks would be Grenata's week, and there was no way it would be safe to have this group at her home. It was risky enough to have them here, though Ogden accepted her story that they were having some other groups over to train them in organizing. He said if she couldn't teach them to organize, no one could. She accepted the compliment and the kiss he followed up with.

Lorelei read the declaration, pausing at her favorite phrase for effect, and the women shouted and bumped fists. She reported on the information she was collecting about the earlier movement and the women took copious notes, writing them in a code Linolin devised, which looked like cooking cards. The men would never bother with them.

The meeting adjourned and Lorelei collapsed with exhaustion. Linolin and Amity both offered to stay and help clean up. Lorelei sent Amity home so she wouldn't get into trouble by overstaying her time, but accepted Linolin's offer. She realized there were benefits to having no husband as the two of them washed dishes, brushed floors, rearranged furniture that was out of place, and talked, joked, and laughed. When Linolin left, her black raincoat hiding her identity, the house felt empty.

42

On Friday, Mom stopped by. Lorelei pulled her into the house, horrified to see her on the porch on Home and Hearth day. She was expecting Ogden home early, and was afraid of what he would do if he found her mother there on Friday. Mom said not to worry, she wasn't going to stay long.

"I want in." Mom announced.

"In?" Lorelei stammered. She had an idea what her mother meant, but did not want to fill anyone in by accident.

"I know you are doing something. I have some idea what it is. I hear whispers. And I want to be part of it, if you're going to do something to free women. I want to be free. I want you to be free. I want everyone to be free."

Lorelei covered her mother's mouth and pulled her into the kitchen where there was no worry anyone would hear. She told her mother in nervous whispers what they were doing. She quoted the Declaration by heart, unwilling to take the risk of going into the study to show her mother, not when she knew Ogden would be home early but didn't know how early.

Mom's eyes glistened with tears. Lorelei wasn't sure what to expect. Why was Mom crying? Was she upset at what her daughter was doing? To her surprise, Mom grabbed her and held her in a tight embrace as though afraid to let her go.

"I definitely want in. But...I want you to be careful. I couldn't stand to lose you."

Lorelei realized what the tears meant. Mom was excited, happy, and scared. She understood. Those were her constantly seesawing emotions, too. This was a new time and none of them knew what to expect from their upcoming adventures. The men had been in charge a long time, and they weren't going to give up easily.

They heard the door open at the same time. Mom froze. Lorelei sprang into action, ushering Mom out the back door and helping her get the back gate open. She was back in the kitchen pouring hot beverage just in time. Ogden pushed open the door to the kitchen and moved toward his wife. Lorelei thrust a cup in his direction. He accepted it but kept his eyes on Lorelei. She was used to him watching her, and she moved easily around the kitchen without her earlier nervousness.

Ogden perched on the edge of the table and sipped his beverage. He apparently planned to stay. She had no idea why he came home early, but she assumed he'd tell her when he was ready. She moved quickly around the kitchen, not missing a beat even when he patted her fanny as she passed.

He put down his hot beverage and reached inside his coat. She tensed but kept moving, not wanting him to see her nervous. When he pulled his hand out, he was holding something she couldn't see, a small box of some sort. He stared at it for a minute as though he wasn't sure it was what he wanted and wondered how it had gotten into his hand. Lorelei ignored him. He was in her space, and she felt more at home here than he did.

He thrust the box in her direction. She took it with caution as though it were a snake.

"Happy anniversary."

Lorelei stared at the box. She didn't realize it was their anniversary. She had no reason to remember. They never celebrated. When you make a marriage because you're told to, there is little reason to celebrate another year in a loveless relationship. Now Ogden was giving her a gift, and she didn't know what to say.

"Open it."

Lorelei took his request as an order. It was difficult to tell the difference sometimes. She put down the plates she was holding and unwrapped the small package. Ogden watched every move. She opened it with care, as she always did her Christmas presents, because Ogden hated it when anyone tore into a present. He thought it showed an extreme lack of discipline. Even the children opened gifts neatly.

The small stone nestled in the box was unfamiliar. She had a few pieces of jewelry Ogden provided her, the sort of jewelry that was proper for a good wife, and she had a couple of exuberant pieces she wore as a teen, but she had never seen anything like this. It was soft and pink, and flashed with a fire that was simultaneously daring and soothing.

"What is it?"

"It's a..." Ogden checked the paper in his pocket. "...an opal."

"I never heard of that."

"We found a lot of them on a dig a few years ago. The stones haven't been released for general use yet. A couple weeks ago, they offered up three stones for purchase to the team. I bid for one, and I got it. I thought it would look good on you."

Lorelei touched the stone. It flashed in her hands and she couldn't take her eyes off the crystal fire. "It's the most beautiful thing I've ever seen."

"I know. It's the only stone that's beautiful enough for you."

Ogden looked away, embarrassed by such an extravagant compliment. If he was playing a part, he was doing it well, Lorelei thought. He sounded sincere. She moved toward him and bent his face to hers for a kiss.

"Thank you. I love it."

"I thought…you might like to…go somewhere for dinner tonight. I thought…maybe that new food center that just opened? You said once you'd like to try it. I thought…you could use a break from cooking."

Lorelei nodded. It was exactly what she would like. They hadn't eaten in a food center in several years. Ogden preferred not to waste money, and he claimed her cooking was better than any food center. She was sure that wasn't true but she liked that he said it. He said that even before the project, when he didn't have to say nice things to her.

"Go put your prettiest dress on. Amity's going to get the children from child mover, we're going to go just the two of us."

Lorelei dashed upstairs and rummaged in her closet to find the dress she hadn't worn in so long she wasn't sure it would still fit. It was a shocking shade of blue with a plunging neckline, and she only wore it once, the night she and Ogden got married. It was not her choice, since she didn't like the man she was marrying, but his mother gave it to her and she felt she had to wear the dress that one time. Tonight she pulled it out for the first time in nine years and looked at it with new eyes.

The dress still fit; since she was eating so little lately, it was almost too big. She opened her jewel box to find a pair of earrings to go with the dress and the new necklace. Her fingers hovered over the staid blue studs she would normally wear, but she gave into temptation. When she went downstairs, her ears were festooned with a pair of large blue hoops she wore when she was in high school.

"Can you help me fasten this?"

Ogden obliged by fastening the opal around her neck, his hands lingering on her shoulders, left bare by the off the shoulder dress. She shivered and he wrapped his arms around her.

"You're cold."

"No, I'm not. I'm just..." Lorelei stopped. Could she possibly admit to this man that she was excited by his touch? No. Instead, she asked him a question that puzzled her for years. "Ogden, when we met...that first day...what did you mean when you said I was too beautiful?"

Ogden hesitated so long she thought he wasn't going to answer. He kept his arms around her and rocked back and forth slightly while he formed his answer. "I...well, I thought...you were too good for me. You were too beautiful for someone like me, and I could never possibly deserve you. It took three men and four women to talk me into going through with the marriage. I couldn't believe my luck. This beautiful woman was going to be my wife, and you were nice, too. I think I loved you already."

"You...loved me?"

"I loved you...and I love you. You mean everything to me."

Lorelei moved out of his embrace and turned to face him. "I never knew. You never acted like you cared."

"Because...well, I know you don't like me, and it was...hard. I couldn't say it. I knew they made you marry me. I knew you wanted something else. I knew I couldn't give you what you wanted."

Lorelei struggled to deal with this new information. If Ogden was telling her the truth...this could mean...maybe the project was his idea, but maybe...no, she was being vain to assume he would go to this much trouble just to get her to be closer to him. The project was for real, and it was for the reasons they said. Ogden may or may not be lying to her. Maybe the project gave him the chance to express what he really felt...maybe he was just taking advantage of a youthful moment of fear to press his project. She decided to take him at his word, at least for now.

"I...don't dislike you. I...it's tough being married when you don't know someone, and we never really got to know each other. We...had Molton so soon after the marriage, and we never had time to...learn to love...to trust...each other."

Lorelei stumbled over the words, because she wasn't sure what to say. It was half true, at least, probably more true than not true, but she didn't want to lay it on too thick. She had no idea where things were headed, but she was sure when the women made their move Ogden wouldn't love her…he wouldn't even like her.

"So let's get to know each other. Let's…spend time together. We'll start tonight. Let's…go to…a moving show…no, you can't talk in a moving show…let's go to the park. We'll walk, hold hands maybe, sit on the park bench…you look too good to stay inside. I love those earrings, by the way. How come I've never seen them before?"

"I haven't worn them since I was seventeen. They were a youthful exuberance that I sort of…got over. I outgrew them."

"Exuberance. I like that. Yes, that's what they are. Exuberant. You should wear them often."

Ogden left abruptly and came back with another gift. He bought her a new coat, a warm coat that cost much more than the thin one she had been wearing for years. It was a lovely coat, not the simple utilitarian one to which she was accustomed. As he slipped it over her shoulders, he kissed her neck. "That kiss will have to hold us until later", he whispered, and he escorted her out the door.

43

Mom left her Thursday group and joined Lorelei's. One by one, all her group moved with her and Thursday group doubled in size. They now had eight women and could spread the work thinner, giving each of them a respite as they alternated households. The big group continued to meet at the shelter and were now meeting every day. Any woman who could manage would attend. The meetings were large, loud, and energetic, as women all talked at once in their excitement until someone raised a fist to quiet them.

Lorelei was elected leader of the group. She protested that they were all equals, but accepted once she realized without a leader they were going to head in all directions at once and not get anything done. Mom's group, women with children no longer in the home, volunteered to help her with her household duties as needed to free up some of her time. She accepted, and soon had a group of four women puttering around her house, instructing her to call them "Mom", and managing to be helpful without getting in the way. They were well trained good wives and knew how things worked.

November bled into December, and Christmas was on the way. She moved through her usual routine, making clothes for the children's presents, baking special treats for Ogden to take to the office, and finding nice little things to do for her friends, who were finding nice little things to do for her. In spite of the extra holiday load, she spent as much time as possible with the safe and working on the plans for the big event. The group was very hush-hush, not speaking out loud about their plans, using coded words and phrases, and she respected that, though she thought the codes were probably not needed, and within the shelter the whispers definitely weren't needed. The sense of secrecy excited the women, made them feel like they were in a novel, and energized the group.

Christmas always started Lorelei thinking about meanings. The holiday was handed down from the ancients and apparently meant a great deal to them, but no one now knew what it meant. It had apparently been a time of joy and giving, and there were a lot of documents and artifacts that urged people to remember "the reason for the season" but most of the ancients must have assumed everyone knew what that was, because it was never explained. The artifacts were even more confusing. At some point, Christmas apparently had something to do with fat men, babies, stars, and a number of animals with antlers.

This year, Ogden gathered the family together and shared what was known about the season. He told them the animals were known as rain deer. The baby was a mystery, though it seemed to have a lot to do with the star and the reason for the season. The fat man was apparently the main reason for the season, since there were more of the fat man artifacts than any other, but they had no idea who he was, or what he meant. Ogden suggested they should just enjoy it and not worry about what it meant.

Some people thought it might be a religious holiday, but Pastor insisted there was nothing religious about Christmas. "It isn't in the Bible", he said firmly, crossing his arms across his chest every time someone claimed it was based in religion. "Nothing in the Bible about Christmas or fat men." Lorelei heard that sermon every year she could remember. "Don't pretend Christmas is about religion. It is a time for fun, not prayer."

The day before Christmas, Mom stopped by to bring the children their gifts. Even though it was Friday, Lorelei didn't protest. It as the one Friday of the year wives were allowed out of the house, because visiting was expected the day before the big day. If it was on Friday, Home and Hearth rules moved to Thursday. That was unfortunate, because it meant Thursday group was cancelled, but Lorelei and her friends were so busy they barely noticed.

Lorelei pulled Mom into the kitchen. "Come look", she breathed in a barely audible whisper.

She had the things for making hot beverage spread out on the counter. Mom started to pick them up and put them away but Lorelei stopped her. She had something she wanted to show her mother.

"I found…in my papers…hot beverage…only…it's different." Lorelei no longer called them Ogden's papers; they were her papers now. "They had hot beverages, but not just one. Look."

Lorelei moved the ingredients for hot beverage around on the counter until she found the one she wanted. "This? This was a beverage they called coffee." She measured out the proper amount and put it in the pot. She moved through the other ingredients one at a time, showing her mother, then adding them to the pot. "And this they called tea. This was…" she searched her memory banks for the name.

"...hot chocolate. Here? This was known as bouillon. And a bay leaf to finish." Lorelei stood back with a flourish, waiting for her mother to compliment her on her new knowledge.

"You mean they drank them all *separately?*" Mom grimaced, the sort of look you give someone when you've just found out they're a barbarian...or at least, that's what Lorelei thought the look meant. She'd never actually known anyone who found out someone was a barbarian.

Mom picked up the little packet of yellow powder, the last ingredient in hot beverage, the one you added just a trace right before you set the pot to boil. "This?"

Lorelei took the package and added a touch of the powder to the hot beverage she was mixing. "This they called lemonade."

Mom shook her head. "Well, I never. Such a strange custom. Drinking them one at a time...they did drink them all at the same time, at least?"

"I don't think so. Usually when I see references to them in the materials, it is one or another, never all at one time, though sometimes coffee and tea seemed to be served together on the same tray. People usually chose one, though."

Mom made a face. "I don't think I'll try that. I can't even imagine."

Lorelei laughed. "I did. They were...strange. But...I think...I might serve them as refreshments at our next meeting...not Thursday group", she added hastily at the look on her mother's face. "At the shelter...and only a choice, you understand. I'll make sure there's plenty of hot beverage for everyone. I just thought...it might be fun to try. Since we're taking so much inspiration from them, we might as well try a couple of other things they did."

"Yes, well, I hear they didn't even mist, but just went around all the time in their dirt." Mom snorted, clearly disapproving.

"They did, though. They called it a shower."

"Shower? What were they showing?"

"I don't know. None of the literature says. It just says a shower."

Mom accepted the hot beverage from the pot that was ready and added a touch more yellow powder to the pot Lorelei just started. "You never put enough yellow stuff in."

164

The two women moved to the living room for a chat. Ogden wouldn't be home for at least two hours, and the children were playing outside. The snow that fell at Thursday group was long gone and it was parched earth again. It was the first snow the children could remember and Lorelei wished it lasted longer, because they enjoyed it so much. She knew from her own childhood they wouldn't likely see another one for several years. The material she was reading suggested there was much more snow before the collapse.

Mom left shortly before Ogden came home. She wasn't ready to leave but Lorelei didn't think she could stand seeing her husband insult her mother again so she urged her to go. She promised to come over and say hi to Dad next Saturday during free hour, and they could visit. Lorelei knew she would see her mother frequently between now and then, since Mom was able to make shelter meeting often, and Lorelei, as the leader, did her best to be there every day. Sometimes, of course, it wasn't possible. On those days, Linolin ran the meeting for her. And, of course, Mom would be over helping with her chores.

Christmas day was clear, without a hint of cloud in the sky. The children were up early, as usual, ready for the one day a year they didn't have to follow the usual routines. Ogden promised them yesterday he would permit them to be noisy if they needed, and even told them they could tear open one of their packages if they liked. Lorelei couldn't believe it. Was Ogden turning into someone else before her eyes?

Lorelei woke late on Christmas. Time monster told her she was an hour past her normal time. Horrified, she rolled over in bed to wake Ogden, but her husband was gone. In a panic, she pulled on her clothes and rushed downstairs. The family was seated in the living room waiting for her. Ogden was reading and the children were playing quietly at his feet. When she entered the room they rushed to her, welcoming her with an enthusiasm they didn't usually show when their father was around. Ogden watched with amusement, then rose and came toward her himself.

Lorelei flinched as her husband approached. Sleeping in was one of the deadliest sins a wife could commit. This was sure to be punished. She stood stiff as a board when he wrapped his arms around her, waiting for the inevitable pain.

"Aren't you going to hug me? I thought we were getting along now." Ogden whispered in her ear, and it tickled.

"I…got up late." Lorelei stammered, not knowing what to say.

"I know. I turned off time monster and told the children to let you sleep, we could eat late. I thought you needed the rest."

Lorelei wrapped her arms around her husband and returned his hug. Impossible as it seemed, she was not going to be punished for sleeping late. She rested her head against his chest while he stroked her hair and she decided not to question everything today. She would just accept her good fortune.

Ogden followed her into the kitchen and shooed the children into the backyard. "You look tired. You haven't been sleeping well."

"I'll get better sleep now that Charity Bazaar is over." Lorelei clicked on hot box and shoved Ogden out of the way so she could get to cold box. She marveled at how bold she had gotten.

"I wanted to mention…I got a lot of compliments about the Charity Bazaar. Everyone said it went smoothly, and was marvelous. They congratulated me on what a clever and hard working wife I have. And I heard you looked beautiful, too. I wish I could have been there, but…well…." Ogden stopped, apparently unwilling to point out that Charity Bazaar was for women and no man would want to be there unless he was an invited speaker brought in for the day to lecture women on something they probably knew more about than he did.

"I…wore the opal necklace." Lorelei decided to respond to the comment about her being beautiful, because she felt uncomfortable taking compliments for work done by the shelter women. She needed to keep up the act, because if he found out she hadn't done all the arrangements…well, with Amity, Corinne, and Grenata…he would wonder what she *had* been doing every Thursday afternoon.

Lorelei pushed him out of the kitchen so she could get breakfast in peace. She put their breakfast on the table and the children and their father sat down to eat while she put lunch in hot box. Ogden put down his fork shortly after she was settled at her place, only two bites into her own breakfast. She lay down her fork and started to rise to clean the table.

"Stop. Eat. I'll take the dishes to the kitchen…the children will help me…and you can finish eating before you wash the dishes." Ogden started toward the kitchen with a precarious stack of plates and cups.

"Don't break anything!" Lorelei was too late. She heard the crash just after the door closed behind them. She started to get up, then shrugged and returned to her breakfast. For the first time in a long time, she was actually hungry.

"Sorry!" Molton's voice rang out from behind the kitchen door. Apparently it was his plate that broke. Lorelei winced. His plate was one she lovingly painted with a small train engine, and he had been eating off it since he was old enough to hold a fork.

Ogden poked his head out the door. "Don't worry, it wasn't his plate. He dropped a hot beverage cup." His head disappeared, to reappear a moment later. "Do you know where tidy box is kept?"

Lorelei attended to the mess in the kitchen, with her husband and children trying to help and mostly getting in the way. Micra stayed behind when her mother shooed the men out so she could get the kitchen cleaned. Now that Micra was six, she would be spending Christmas Day in the kitchen with her mother, learning how to be a good wife. Ogden already selected her future husband, though he had not shared the identity with Lorelei yet. Lorelei watched her daughter, so tiny, standing on a stool beside her mother wiping the dishes her mother washed. Her heart ached.

The rest of the day went smoothly. Nothing more was broken, and no one transgressed any major rules. It was much like Christmases past, except Lorelei and Ogden were smiling at each other, sharing joy for the first time since they'd met. Molton and Micra didn't appear to notice anything different, but they did bounce onto Ogden's lap when the gift exchange was done, wrap their small arms around his neck, and tell him how wonderful he was. That was definitely *not* like Christmases past, and Lorelei welcomed it as a good thing. She almost lost her resolve to succeed and considered staying in this world that was becoming so much better. She remembered Micra on the stool, and her determination returned. Surely Micra was worth all the danger of what they were doing.

44

Early in January, Corinne told Lorelei she was going to have to drop out of the mission. "Not out of Thursday Group", she said, "but…I can't be part of anything that will risk my marriage right now. I'm pregnant."

Corinne glowed with happiness. She waited many years for this day, but Corydon hardly touched her from the day they were married. He preferred to get his marital duties outside of the marriage bed. Now, instructed by his team leader that he would do his part to keep the women at home, he began coming to her bed at night and reaching for her at odd times, just like the other men. The result was the fulfillment of Corinne's dream.

Lorelei congratulated her with a heavy heart. Corinne was a great organizer, and she had a talent for getting people to complete tasks. She would be sorely missed. Lorelei was happy for her friend, but she also realized for the first time how the men's project could succeed. She finally understood what she read in the material about men using child bearing to keep women in the home. No, her children weren't part of the problem, they were just her children, or so she had insisted to herself.

She now realized that women became so tied to children, and were led to believe they weren't full women without them, that the very presence of children in a household gave a man more authority and presence when he ordered his wife to stay home. Still, her papers showed that women were once able to have children, and have their freedom and do exciting, stimulating things, even working outside the home. She decided to explore ways to make that succeed again.

Work moved forward, and the great day grew closer. The women chose the day for their project, and the excitement built as the women modified the shelter to suit the needs of their mission. They were building new rooms, and as they took shape, the women felt a glow of accomplishment and a sense of danger as the mission became more real.

They would be ready, Lorelei had no doubt. They would probably be ready if something happened and they needed to do it today. The women were organized, efficient, and newly radicalized to work for themselves on something they wanted for a change. Everything was taking shape.

Linolin supervised the design and construction of yellow sashes for all the women. Lorelei looked over the growing stack of sashes sewn by shelter women and glowed. This would be a grand moment. Nearly all the women in town were part of the project now, as good wives poured into their Thursday groups and their shelter group and added their voices, their time, and their talents to making this a reality. The Declaration hung on the wall of the shelter, printed with care in a beautiful script by Grenata, who added her own touches in the form of paintings to surround it. The paintings depicted women in their ordinary roles, seemingly ordinary paintings, but all of them with a twist if you looked closer.

Lorelei particularly liked the painting of the woman who was stirring hot beverage. The kitchen was clean and shiny, the sun came in the window, and it looked like a peaceful, ordinary day. If you looked closer, you could see the woman was chained to hot box, with a chain that extended out the door and around the hall, to a tiny figure Grenata placed in the corner of the painting, the figure of a man standing with a whip in his hand and a cruel look on his face. It made Lorelei shudder whenever she saw it, but she loved the painting because it was exquisite in its detail. Clearly Grenata had some real talent.

Two days after Corinne dropped out, Lorelei came home from Thursday group at Amity's house to find Ogden home early. She wasn't worried, because she was home on time from a routine activity, and the house was spotless. So it surprised her to find him blocking her path to the kitchen, an enigmatic look on his face.

"You want to tell me about it?" Ogden didn't sound angry. His voice was calm and steady, but without the flirty teasing tone he'd adopted with her lately.

"I'm sorry, but I don't know what you're asking." Lorelei hesitated, wanting to shove him aside as she now did when he got in her way, but realizing he was not new Ogden right now. This was old Ogden, the Ogden who insisted on respect on his terms and was prepared to enforce it.

"I have been hearing rumors…some woman, loud, obnoxious, large….in the supermarket…" Ogden began.

"Resenta?"

"I don't know her name. She's not one of the archaeology wives. I've never met her. But she is going around telling women you have some information from me, some sort of...inside dope? She said you told her all sorts of things, secret things, things the wives aren't supposed to know."

"Did she say what that was?" Lorelei held her breath. Had someone filled Resenta in on the project? She and Ornata were left out because neither of them could keep a secret.

"No. When...my...source...tried to get more information, she clammed up. Wouldn't say a thing. I haven't told you anything...how would you find out things to tell?"

Lorelei relaxed. Resenta was blowing off steam, angry at not being given the information she wanted. She didn't know anything.

"I haven't told her anything. She's...well, Resenta is...she makes things up."

"You're saying she was lying?"

"Yes. She's angry with Amity, because Amity wouldn't go to the moving show with her because she always talks through the show. She's angry with me, because I told her I don't know anything about your project. You don't give me information, I'm just your wife. Why would she think I would know?" Lorelei held her head up and her eyes steady. She hoped her habit of always being straight with Ogden would hold her in good stead now.

"I...wasn't sure. For a minute...I wondered. I'm sorry, Lorelei, I know you...it's just...well, we have to, you know, check it out."

"Is something wrong with the project?" Lorelei put on her most innocent look. Wouldn't it be funny if he trusted her enough now to tell her something?

"Nothing I can talk about...not yet. We're still... assimilating... all the information. We plan to announce as soon as possible, but it's a very difficult project. The material is fragile, old, and hard to read."

Lorelei suppressed her anger at Ogden lying to her. Of course he lied to her, that was the project. It didn't mean all the other things they were doing together were meaningless, it just meant he was...well, he was...a man. And a man who was trained to think of women as lesser beings. She also realized she needed to continue acting her part, particularly now. She touched his face.

"I understand. You couldn't risk someone else getting the information and publishing it before you had a chance. You needed to check it out. I'm not angry."

Ogden relaxed. "Yes, of course. Mine is a very competitive field."

He believed her. He trusted her and was willing to accept her explanation for why he was so worried about what would be, for all she knew, a normal project. In fact, Lorelei got the impression he jumped at her offered explanation, having plainly not come up with one himself yet. He patted her on the fanny and headed to the study, where he locked himself in to work until dinner. Lorelei wasn't going to get any time to read her papers today.

She knocked on the study door after about an hour and he called to her to enter. She brought the tray of hot beverage and sat it on his desk. He didn't turn around or move toward her; he was immersed in a document Lorelei recognized, one that gave her a great deal of inspiration and hope. It appeared from the set of his back and shoulders it was giving him a great deal of anxiety.

She turned at the door. "Corinne is pregnant."

Ogden turned. "Yes, I heard. She's happy?"

"Very. She's wanted this for so long."

"I'm glad for her. It must be difficult for a woman to be without a child. She'll finally be a complete woman."

Lorelei murmured something she hoped sounded like agreement and escaped the study before she lost the battle against her urge to hit him. Corinne was every bit as much woman as her, with her two children, Amity with her four, or Grenata with her three. Corinne was an unhappy woman, yes, but it was about much more than just not having children. There was so much in her life to be unhappy about, and Lorelei doubted life would be much happier for her now that she was going to be a mother. It would just be…busier. She leaned against the door and brought her temper back into control. There would be time for anger later. She'd need it soon. For now… housework waited.

45

Throughout February, Lorelei and Ogden continued to get to know each other. It was almost as though her husband was courting her…except, she thought, if he was courting, we wouldn't be having marital duties. That would not be allowed. She continued to enjoy marital duties, but felt guilty about her blooming relationship with her husband while she was plotting to turn his world upside down and use his own documents against him and all other men.

He got in the habit of taking the children on his round-a-bout on weekends and he and Lorelei spent many evenings in the park, counting the stars, watching the lone tree, and listening to each other. She would rest her head on his shoulder and he would stroke her hair, and they grew closer. Life was easier now that Ogden was kinder, but the routines continued. She was not freed from the ordered, regimented life, and was still a good wife. It was just…well, now she had heat during the day, and a warm coat she could wear to church and the store, and a husband who actually interacted with her as if she were a person…well, only half a person, she reminded herself. She was not under any illusions that Ogden saw her as his equal. Nor was she under any illusions that transgressions of her good wife role would be allowed without punishment.

The children enjoyed the new Ogden as well. Every evening after dinner, he wrestled with them on the floor, the three of them rolling around and shrieking, having fun together. She stepped in from the kitchen frequently to watch, glad to see her family having fun and relaxing. She persuaded Ogden to allow Micra to be released from kitchen duties early so she could join the fun.

"It won't be for long, though. She's six now, and she needs to put away childish things and start learning how to be a good wife." Ogden wasn't letting go of his world so easily.

"Just…for now. She won't be young long, and I want her to remember her childhood…and her father…with joy."

"Remember her father with joy. I like the sound of that." Ogden stroked Lorelei on her bare thigh and ran his lips down her arm. "I like that."

The children watched out the window every day at lunch time, hoping for the snow that didn't come. When the afternoon dawned clear, they raced outside to climb trees and dig holes. Lorelei promised she would accelerate Micra's teaching if her father wouldn't make her quit climbing trees yet.

"Honestly, Ogden, a girl doesn't need so much training. She learns quickly, and then it just becomes dull repetition. By the time she gets married, she's done all the chores so many thousands of times it isn't even interesting to do in her own kitchen."

Ogden grunted and Lorelei took that for yes. She continued to allow Micra to be a child, and did everything she could to subvert the girl's growing good wife tendencies. Soon, she told herself. Soon Micra will be free.

The group continued to meet every day, and the pile of sashes grew larger. Lorelei protested to Linolin that they didn't need so many. There were already enough to give three to every woman in town, and still the women sewed.

"Let them", Linolin shrugged. "It makes them happy. They like this so much better than doing the kind of crafts we did when they first came. They need this, too."

Lorelei watched the faces of the sewing women and realized her friend was right. These were women with precious little to live for, and this project gave them hope. The possibility of being able to free themselves from the men who threatened them, the men they still feared even locked away in this gray building the men couldn't see in front of their face, was giving them all hope for a better future.

"You're the cause of all that, you know." Linolin was watching Lorelei watch the women.

"Me? No, it's you. You're the one who took them in."

"I took them in, but I couldn't give them a new life. You're leading them home."

Lorelei winced. This was not something she liked to hear. "Yes, but…we're not likely to succeed, not all at once. It might take…years. Most of the early women…Elizabeth…Susan…didn't live to see the results of their work."

"I know. I wish I could promise them that. But they understand. Just…working for it…just…hoping for it…gives them a reason to get out of bed in the morning. It gives them something to fight for, and we need that. We need women with fight."

Lorelei decided to change the subject. This was something that bothered her, the promises the women made themselves and each other, and she wanted to think about something else for now.

"Linolin? All that stuff you told me...all about the early...what were they called?"

"Suffragists?"

"Yes. Elizabeth...and Susan...and Lucretia...and Matilda...how did you know all that? I watched you when I explained about the papers. There was a lot you didn't know, but you knew so much."

Linolin turned to the bookcase behind her desk and brought out a book large enough to be at least four books. Then she brought out another of equal size and laid it on top of the other. Lorelei leaned over to look at the title.

"The Decline and Fall of the American Empire? I've never heard of that."

"This is the only copy. It was written by one of my ancestors, a long distant ancestor, who lived about a century after the collapse, when the original records were still somewhat available. He set out to write a history of the collapse, and ended up including a lot of other history that was already getting lost. This second book, Volume II..." Linolin picked up the volume on top. "This is a history of women. The women in the American Empire, from the beginning to the end. It's...fascinating. But it doesn't go into nearly the detail that Ogden's papers do."

"American? What's that?" Lorelei turned the unfamiliar word over on her tongue to see if she liked the feel. She wasn't sure. It felt strange.

"That's us, honey. At least, until the collapse. This was once a giant country called the United States of America."

"Oh! I've seen that phrase in my papers a lot. I didn't know what it was."

"Where we live was known as New York City. It was considered one of the most amazing cities in the world. People loved it or hated it, but no one could remain unaware of it, not if they lived in the United States."

"And Berkeley? Where Ogden found my papers?"

"I don't know...let me check." Linolin opened the bottom book and turned to a detailed map. "Oh, here it is."

Linolin pointed to a dot near the ocean, along a jagged coast she said belonged to a place called California.

"And where are we?"

Linolin moved her finger across the map, all the way to the other side of the land mass. The map said "New York City". They were also on the sea coast, but they were apparently not the same coast.

Lorelei ran her hand over the map as she had the picture of the women. She felt none of the charge from the map that she got from the photograph, and she decided there was no magic in this thing called… "America?"

"Yes. That's what people called it for short. It had fifty different states, all with different ideas and customs, and all wanting to have things run their own way. It couldn't have lasted much longer, because it seemed like everyone hated everyone else, at least reading Uncle Edward's history."

"Uncle Edward?"

"I call him that, but he's probably not really my uncle. The relationships sort of get twisted up when you go that far back. After the collapse, no one kept good records for at least three hundred years, so we aren't sure. We just know he's a relative, because he left this book to his son, and it got passed down over and over, until finally it reached me."

"It looks almost new…the cover, I mean. The pages are really old, though."

"The binding is new. No one was publishing or printing at the time he wrote this, because resources were so scarce, even scarcer than they are now. He kept it in a box. My parents had it bound and gave it to me for my 20th birthday. I couldn't have asked for a better present."

Linolin ran her hand over the book, a look on her face as if she was somewhere far away. Lorelei began to believe the book might have magic, it was just a personal magic she couldn't feel.

"I'll let you borrow it if you like. I know you like to read…but you can't take it home."

Lorelei nodded. Ogden would never understand. "We can leave it in my locker at book room."

"Good idea. Now let's get back to work. I'd hate for the women to do all this work and have it fail because the two coordinators fell down on the job."

46

February was almost over. Things were tense at the shelter as the great day approached. No one was sure what would happen, but they had enough imagination to make up their own scenarios. 'What if' ran around the group like wildfire and when it got back to the beginning, started over again. No one could eat or sleep properly because they were all nervous. Meanwhile they needed to maintain their cover as 'good wives', which meant hours of cleaning and cooking, shopping and taking care of their husbands. For the wives of the archaeologists, it also meant frequent marital duties, which the men were clearly enjoying and demanding often. Many of the women discovered pleasure in marital duties, but still found the experience exhausting when they were not getting enough food or rest.

Lorelei paced whenever she was at the shelter. She stayed on her toes at home, always careful with the safe when she was done. She doubled her caution after Ogden grilled her over Resenta. There was no evidence he doubted her word, but she felt the need to be on a heightened state of alert. Resenta was spreading rumors all over town, and from what Lorelei could tell, they were based on nothing other than her desire to know more than she did, and her assumption that Ogden would tell his wife something.

That raised questions for the rest of the women. Did Resenta's husband tell her things? Lorelei doubted it, but even if he did, he didn't have much to tell. He worked as a cleaner of the waste, delivering waste from each house to the waste pile every week. Lorelei suspected there were few, if any, of the archaeologists that were putting secrets in their waste, if only because none of them trusted each other, let alone the men who picked up their waste. Oh, Resenta's husband might know who drank too much, and who was throwing away expensive items, but that sort of information was common knowledge. It traveled rapidly on the gossip grapevine.

That was one of the things that amazed Lorelei most about the shelter group. All of these women were born and bred in a society where women were expected, and even encouraged, to gossip, but none of them breathed a word of the mission, or any of the information they had, outside the group. The gossiping stopped at the door of the shelter and not a word made it outside. Some of the women, the ones who had serious problems with gossip, would 'zip their lip' as they crossed the door of the shelter and the ritual seemed to help them remember what not to talk about.

The women coordinated all their activities for the great day down to the minute. They set their time monsters over and over as the day approached, to make sure they were all set exactly the same. They peeked into closets and around doors even when they were just doing their housework, acting as if they expected someone to be listening to them. They shot furtive glances at each other when they met in the grocery store. They established elaborate codes for talking about forbidden things in public places and giggled like school girls. Fortunately, the men expected women to giggle – even though most of them usually didn't – so that didn't give them away.

Lorelei maintained her usual routine and kept her house even cleaner than usual. No one would have suspected anything in her behavior but a good wife. Ogden continued to flirt with her and tease her, and want marital duties in strange places at strange times. So far they had done marital duties not just in the mister and the dining room, but in the kitchen and the laundry room. Lorelei got over her embarrassment at the odd times and places, and participated with an eagerness that surprised her even after three months.

She watched the calendar move by, simultaneously nervous and eager for the great day and wanting to postpone the great day until she figured out what to do about Ogden. At times she began to imagine she was falling in love with him but she insisted that could not happen. No, Ogden would not make her love him. She could enjoy his company, even enjoy marital duties, but love? That was too much, and she wouldn't do it.

The only one she felt she could talk to was Amity, who was going through some of the same struggles. Amity, always afraid of Merris and wishing he would take a mistress and stay away from home like Corydon, now looked forward to him coming in the door, because he always brought her something new. Little gifts, mostly, not expensive, not fancy, but at least he was thinking about her. And she was enjoying marital duties, as well, especially now that Merris wasn't hitting her anymore. Still, she could not forget Linolin's description of his part in bringing Grenata back to Lymon, even when Grenata had no desire to go. Amity and Lorelei spent hours trying to sort out the ambiguities of their relationships.

Mom was having the time of her life. She was here, there, everywhere, helping to coordinate, to sew, to cook, to clean, wherever she was needed. She seemed to have an unending supply of energy, and Lorelei envied her ability to keep going even in the face of long hours of housework interspersed with long hours of planning and meetings, plus helping Lorelei with her housework whenever she could.

Grenata was mostly absent from meetings. Lymon was keeping a close eye on her and rarely let her out of the house. He told her if he had to take her back, he was going to make sure she stayed. They mostly saw her at Thursday group, since Lymon was ordered to keep up appearances. Mom and her Thursday group stopped by regularly to help Grenata with her housework. Even though her leg was mostly healed, she still had difficulty getting serious about keeping the house free of clutter. She cried a lot and had trouble explaining why she was crying. She wanted to stay with Linolin, that was clear, but beyond that, she didn't know why she was so much more miserable than she had been when she lived with Lymon before, even though he wasn't hitting her now.

They didn't see Corinne. She only came to Thursday group when it was in her house. She seemed to move away from the world as she began to deal with being pregnant. She wasn't showing yet but she probably would be soon, and she confided in Lorelei that she was sick every morning. Not that she was complaining, she hastened to add. She waited for this a long time and she cherished every moment, even those moments when she was losing her breakfast. She was losing weight, and her gauntness frightened Lorelei. Lorelei was sick during her own pregnancies but managed to maintain an appropriate weight.

Although Corinne's organizing skills were missed by shelter group, other women discovered a hidden talent for organizing and moved into the duties Corinne left behind. They were delighted with their newfound abilities, having been told by their husbands for years they were good for nothing.

New women continued to arrive at the shelter, women in various states of disarray and ill health from neglect and violence. Lorelei was getting lessons from Linolin on the issue Linolin called "domestic violence", which was one of the big items of concern she found in the papers in Ogden's safe – her papers, she thought. He might consider them his, but they weren't his. He was not a woman and was not entitled to them. They were hers, and she would share them with every woman in the world. Well, maybe not Resenta or Ornata, but every other woman.

Sojourner Truth, whose real name Lorelei finally learned was Montoya, continued to bring new women to the shelter group. Lorelei was learning that the issues faced by darker skinned women had a great deal of overlap with the white women, but there were other issues they had to deal with that the white women had trouble understanding. She added items to the agenda of every meeting based on suggestions by Montoya – excuse me, Sojourner – and the new friends kept arriving. It was the first place in their life they had been listened to or felt like anyone cared.

The group that surprised Lorelei the most was the working women. She had no idea there were such women. She was told all her life that men went out to work and women stayed home and took care of their husbands. These women were all married, but they were working at paying jobs. Their husbands were unable to make enough money to support the family, and the women went out every day to clean houses or cook food for strangers who paid them. Many women worked in service, washing clothes or cooking food in the businesses that lined the streets of downtown. Some of them sewed in a factory, some of them picked up waste alongside the men, and several of them worked down in the sewers, spending their day in human waste. Construction, building streets, making products - it seemed there were few hard labor jobs that women could not do.

When these women got their pay every month, they were required to take it home and hand it to their husbands. If they didn't, it wouldn't make any difference, since the checks were made out to the husbands. Women were not allowed to have bank accounts or receive money for services, though a few women who walked the streets performing marital duties for lonely men confessed that some of the men would give them money direct if they would do 'special' things, things the men wouldn't ask their wives to do.

Lorelei was horrified when the first of 'those' women showed up, but she soon got to know her, and the friends she brought along later, and realized they were women just like the rest of them, but because of the difficulties of being a woman in the working world, they took up the only profession they could as a means to keep alive. Their lives were rough, and they frequently died of exposure or abuse, but they were strong and determined and joined in with glee and hard work.

The working women brought along a whole new set of problems that Lorelei tried to incorporate into the agenda. They weren't paid as much as men who did the same job, or even men who did much less, and they were given the least desirable jobs. Their bosses frequently demanded marital duties and they could lose their job for saying no. If they lost their jobs, their husbands would beat them. If their husbands found out they were having marital duties with the boss, they would turn them out to starve. When they got home, they were still required to be good wives, no matter how exhausted they were from working all day. There was no answer to their dilemmas. Most of them confessed they wanted nothing to do with either their boss or their husband, but they had no place else to go. Lorelei hugged each and every one, and vowed to do whatever was in her power to make things better. The women joined the mission with ferocity the good wives had trouble matching.

The shelter group was so large now it threatened to outgrow the commodious area of the shelter. Lorelei decided to split the group up so women would only come some of the time, being assigned to a group based on the duties they were interested in or capable of performing. This allowed all the work to get done without overwhelming the shelter or prohibiting Linolin from fulfilling the mission for which she opened the shelter. Mom was a member of at least three groups, and Lorelei, as leader, was an unofficial member of them all. She attended as often as possible, to give pep talks and rally the troops, or help with a particular thorny problem they were unraveling.

The work on the shelter, converting it for their mission, was moving forward rapidly. The new wings would be ready by the time the great day arrived. Women bustled from one side of the building to the other, helping out where they were needed, carrying hot beverage to other women who were working elsewhere, and having the time of their lives. The women looked at their handiwork in amazement. They did this. It was a monument to women.

Now that the event was coordinated, plans were made, and things were ready, the groups continued to meet, mostly as gab sessions and support for each other. No one wanted to stay home or go to book room anymore. They wanted to be with their new friends. Lorelei felt a sense of pride. She had done this. That's what Linolin said – and kept saying. She had done this. Now she hoped she didn't let anyone down.

47

The big day finally arrived. Tomorrow, all the women would put their plan into action. All of them. Nearly every woman in their little "island of civilization", as Linolin called it, joined. Those that hadn't either had too much to lose, or had not been invited. Resenta and Ornata continued to spew vitriol to everyone who would listen, insisting Lorelei knew something, but when the men finally got her to talk she told them such nonsense it was obvious she didn't know anything. Ogden told his colleagues what Lorelei told him, and they decided he was probably right. Nobody pursued the matter further, and Lorelei relaxed.

Lorelei was at the shelter, her last trip before the great day, her only free hour. Tomorrow was the final stage of their plan. Linolin was somewhere else in the shelter tending to a crisis that arose during the night. Lorelei hadn't seen her since she got there, but had a beeper to page her if necessary.

She was so engrossed in the final plans she didn't notice when Corinne stumbled into the office Lorelei and Linolin shared. Her friend dropped into the chair across from her and only then did Lorelei look up. Corinne, the tidy, neatly dressed, and always perfectly turned out Corinne, was a mess. Her hair straggled out of the neat arrangement she pinned up that morning. Her dress was torn and covered with blood. One of her shoes was missing its heel, and the other shoe was missing. Lorelei rushed around the desk and threw her arms around the sobbing woman.

"What happened?"

"Corydon..." Corinne gasped. She stopped to get her breath, and tried again. "Corydon...he...threw me down the stairs. And kicked me."

Lorelei could only stare at her in incomprehension. Corydon never struck Corinne. He hardly touched her at all before the project began. Now she was in as bad a shape as any of the women in the shelter.

"What? Why?"

"He...he...didn't want a baby. He wanted...me to lose it. He...said to tell everyone...I fell."

Lorelei tried to take it all in, but she was stunned. A husband who didn't want a baby? Most men demanded them. If a wife didn't deliver a baby within a specified period of time, he felt justified in setting her aside and finding a new wife. How could Corydon not want a baby?

"He says he never wanted a baby, that's one reason he never touched me. They made him...he had to. And then it happened, and he's been angry ever since. Today...he couldn't take it anymore. He said..." Corinne gasped again, her breath giving out.

Lorelei rushed to get her friend hot beverage. When she returned, Corinne was in tears again. She knelt in front of the sobbing woman. "You don't have to tell me if it's too hard."

"I need to. You're...the only one...the only one that never loses her head...that knows what to do...everyone wants you for a friend, because you're...well, you're..." Corinne gave out again. She took a sip of hot beverage and got her strength back. "Corydon says...when a woman has a baby...she becomes worthless as a wife. He says...he wants me to take care of him, not some screaming brat. He...said...I would appreciate it later."

Corinne stopped. She couldn't go on any longer. Lorelei grabbed a blanket from the stash in Linolin's closet and wrapped it around Corinne's shoulders, hoping to at least help the shivering. She stood in the middle of the floor watching her friend cry, not knowing what to do. This wasn't like with Grenata...this was...more. This was...she didn't know what it was, but a man trying to kill a baby was...she could only gasp at the thought.

She remembered the beeper and pushed the button to call Linolin. She paced, not wanting to alarm Corinne but unable to sit still. Linolin rushed in, breathless, knowing Lorelei would not beep her if it wasn't an emergency. She skidded to a stop at the sight of Corinne.

Lorelei filled Linolin in on the situation, her voice hushed to an urgent whisper. Linolin didn't say anything, but her muscles grew tense with anger. She picked Corinne up and told Lorelei to follow her. They moved down the hallway to an examination room, where Linolin deposited the other woman on the table. The medic in the room looked up, neither surprise nor fear showing on his face. Lorelei stared. It was the first male she had seen in the shelter.

The two women filled the medic in on the situation. Linolin tersely introduced him to Corinne as Dr. Maestro and he began the examination. Corinne flinched when he touched her, but Lorelei grabbed her hand and stroked it, whispering calming words as the medic worked. Corinne remained tense, but allowed him to complete the examination.

When he was done, the medic stripped off his gloves and motioned the two women to the hallway. He spoke for the first time since Lorelei met him, his voice low and pleasant, a kind voice. He told them Corinne miscarried…not surprising considering the circumstances, he growled. He wanted to admit her to the hospital for the night, but he couldn't do that without her husband's permission.

"Corydon won't give permission." Lorelei kept her voice low, and glanced into the room to make sure her friend wasn't hearing. She didn't need to be upset any more right now.

"Are you sure?"

Lorelei told the other two what Corinne told her about Corydon not wanting a baby. The medic, after an initial look of surprise, nodded.

"We see that from time to time. Men who can't cope with the idea of sharing their wife with anyone else, not even their own child. It never ends well. She needs out of there."

"If we take her to the hospital, she won't be able to be admitted."

"I can't treat her properly here. She needs to get to the hospital, at least overnight."

Lorelei broke in. "Is it possible for another man to sign? Act as her guardian?"

"If he's willing to accept responsibility for her. And I can tell you, if you intend to spirit her out of there back to here, no man will take that responsibility. They will be standing right there at the hospital when she is released so they can deliver her back to her husband."

Linolin and Lorelei looked at each other. Lorelei shook her head. "I was going to ask Ogden, but he'll never agree to let her escape."

Linolin agreed. "We'll have to treat her here."

"I'll do the best I can, but I can't promise anything. She's lost a lot of blood, and I can't bring blood from the blood bank without someone finding the shelter."

"How do you get blood?" Lorelei was amazed. The idea of blood lying around in a bank was new to her.

"We take it from other people."

"Like, after they're dead?"

"No. Living people." Linolin stared at her friend. She was amazed Lorelei was naïve enough not to know that.

"Doesn't that kill them?"

Dr. Maestro laughed, not a mocking laugh, but a gentle one. "No, my dear, it doesn't. We can stick a needle into a living person, withdraw blood, and they'll be just fine. Their body will make more."

Lorelei thought about it. The image was a strange one, and not pleasant, but she wanted to help her friend. "Can you get blood from me?"

"It depends. What's your blood type?"

"I...don't know?"

Dr. Maestro led Lorelei to a small examining room next to the one where Corinne was struggling to remain conscious. He told her to stick out her finger and close her eyes. She felt a cold wash on her finger and then a small stick.

"Ow!"

"It's over. I've got enough."

Lorelei stared at the tiny drops of blood in the needle. "That's all the blood Corinne needs?"

"Oh, dear, no. She'll need much more than that. That's enough to test for your blood type. I've gotten a small sample of hers, and I'll see if you're compatible."

The medic busied himself with some scary looking equipment on the other side of the room while Lorelei watched. She rarely went to the medic. She was healthy and didn't need care, except for the normal two visits for each of her pregnancies. She took the children to the medic, but mothers were instructed to wait in the waiting room. Having a mother in the room when children go to the medic was believed to make them soft.

"You'll do." That's all Dr. Maestro said but he was coming toward her with more equipment, and this time he had a needle that looked like it could take a lot of blood. It was attached to a large bag.

"That...you're going to use...that?" Lorelei stammered.

"Yes. You don't have to if you don't want to."

Lorelei stuck out her arm and closed her eyes. She was going to help Corinne if she could, even if it meant giving blood for her, and apparently it did. Linolin entered the room and watched the procedure, making comments from time to time. Lorelei wished she wouldn't. It made her more nervous.

The procedure didn't last as long as she feared. While the medic bandaged the spot where he took the blood, he gave her instructions on taking care of it. Lorelei didn't imagine she'd be able to follow the instructions not to do any heavy lifting or to rest. She was a good wife, and violating her duties on this day of all days would be a dangerous risk to the mission. Linolin could tell what Lorelei was thinking.

"Call your mother."

Lorelei nodded. Linolin knew Mom would come over and help with hot box and dusting, as well as whatever other chores might be needed. Linolin had become a good friend of Lorelei's mother. Mom was suspicious of the other woman at first, her lifetime habit of avoiding unmarried women – and as far as Lorelei knew, Linolin was the only unmarried woman either of them ever met - keeping her at arm's length. Once she ventured closer and began to talk to her, they discovered many mutual interests, and the two women shared an energy that brought them together.

"You'd better go. You've been here longer than an hour already." Linolin pushed a book into Lorelei's hand.

"What's this?"

"If anyone asks, you were at book room. This…you checked this out."

Lorelei nodded and slipped out the hidden doorway group women used to access the shelter without being seen. She headed off on a circuitous path that led past book room, and soon was back in her own home.

Mom was waiting for her. "Linolin called" was all Mom said. Well, that's all she said after "You rest."

Mom blew through the house like a tornado, cleaning, dusting, and spicing meat. Lorelei sat on the chair in the kitchen and instructed her mother on what spices Ogden preferred, and what temperature on hot box to get the meat to his preferred doneness at just the right time. Mom was an excellent cook, but all the men had their own specific tastes and it was up to their wives to know how to provide those tastes. Even though there were only five spices, there were many different ways to combine them, and Lorelei knew from painful experience that mixing the wrong spices was not acceptable.

When everything was done, Mom leaned over and embraced Lorelei. "You took good care of Corinne. I'm proud of you. You're a better woman than any I've ever known."

After Mom left, Lorelei put her head on her hands and cried. All the nervous tension, all the fear that was bottled up from the intense day flowed in hot tears over her cheeks, over her arms, and down the table. She cried until she was empty, then she stood, wiped the table, and went upstairs to change. She looked like she had gone through the sort of day she had gone through, and she didn't want to give Ogden any reason to ask questions.

48

By the time Ogden arrived home, Lorelei had changed and fixed her makeup so there was no evidence she had been crying. He came into the kitchen as she prepared his dinner and put his arms around her. He didn't say anything, just rested his cheek against her head and rocked back and forth. He seemed tense, maybe even scared, and Lorelei turned and took him in her arms. She heard him whisper something as they held each other, but she couldn't hear the words.

She wondered if Ogden knew about Corinne. She could not bring it up if he didn't, because under the circumstances she would not be expected to know. If he thought Corinne disappeared, he might think she would come here, but if she had Lorelei would have told him by now. She decided to wait and see if he would mention the 'accident'. It was possible Corydon might not say anything to the other men because he would have to admit his culpability. He might be hoping Corinne would show up at the hospital and say she fell. It was what a good wife would do.

Ogden still hadn't spoken. He released her and looked at her with an enigmatic look in his eyes. She thought she read fear, but the look passed and was replaced with something she couldn't understand. He watched her work, as he had become accustomed to do since they had become closer, but didn't offer to help tonight. He turned and left the kitchen just before the children burst in, ready to be examined and sent upstairs to wash before dinner. For the first time, Lorelei wondered why they bothered presenting their hands for examination when they always ended up having to wash. Even the children were bound by ritual, apparently. Well, tomorrow…ritual was going to be shattered.

As the evening wore on, Ogden relaxed. He played with the children in the living room after dinner while Lorelei washed the dishes, and she was glad he didn't insist on Micra joining her in the kitchen. He had done a good job sticking to his word. When she was done washing dishes, he invited her to join them. The four of them tumbled around in various games of chase and leap until bedtime. The children were exhausted, and their parents each picked up one child and carried them to their bedroom. After tucking in their own little charge, Ogden and Lorelei crossed in the hallway on their way to say goodnight to the other child. As they passed, Ogden gave Lorelei a peck on the cheek.

The children safely in bed and dropping off to sleep, the parents headed back to the living room for a quiet evening together. They opened their books to the bookmarks, scooted close to each other on the sofa, and Lorelei rested her head on Ogden's lap. He stroked her hair while they read, and told her little stories about his day, nothing work related, of course, because her woman's brain wasn't up to that, but at least he was starting to share little anecdotes of his life outside the house. It made him seem more real, more human.

It was now Lorelei's turn. For the past several weeks, he had shown an interest in what she did during the day and she began to share little stories of the home and market with him. Today was difficult, since her day was not the appropriate kind of stories she could tell him, but her routines were so familiar she could adapt stories from two years ago and tell them as if they happened today. They passed a pleasant evening in their new project of getting to know each other, but neither of them got much reading done. When the evening was over, they replaced their bookmarks in nearly the same place as they were before and closed their books.

Ogden followed Lorelei upstairs and joined her in the mister. They did not have marital duties in the mister tonight; he held her and massaged her tired shoulders and rubbed her with soap, but the marital duties waited for the bedroom. He toweled her off and lifted her nightgown over her head, not giving an inch when she protested she could do it herself.

"I want to do it for you", he insisted. "You do so many things for me, I should do something for you sometimes." He poked at the tiny bruise in the crook of her arm. "You hurt yourself."

"It's nothing. Just a can that fell out of the cupboard." Lorelei and Mom planned what story she would use if Ogden noticed the bruise, since he spent so much time examining her these days. She practiced it several times, and it rolled off her tongue easily.

"You should be careful. You are much too valuable to be hurt." He bent and kissed the bruise, then ran his kisses down her arm. It tickled, and she giggled.

Ogden had gotten in the habit of performing marital duties with the light on because he liked to look at her. She was embarrassed at first when he stared at her nakedness with eager appreciation. She got used to it and was now comfortable with his gaze even when, like tonight, he pulled her on top to sit on him. They struggled at first when he wanted to do that position but they figured it out weeks ago. She thought again about how different he was than the man she married, and realized that he…and the other men…were wrong. When men believed women were their equal, things would be better. They were getting better already, and men were only afraid women might demand to be equal.

They dropped off with their arms wrapped around each other, two strangers who had learned to be lovers and were in the process of learning to be friends. Just before she dropped off to sleep, Lorelei felt a tinge of sadness that she was leaving her role as a good wife even as Ogden was just starting to learn to be a good husband.

49

March 8. They selected the date carefully, to coincide with a day once known as International Woman's Day. It seemed appropriate. Lorelei slipped out of bed long before her usual time. She padded downstairs and pulled on her clothes in the dark living room. Before Ogden and the children got out of bed, she was out of the house and headed for the shelter via the circuitous route that was her normal path. She arrived just as Linolin unlocked the door.

Lorelei and Linolin were the first to arrive. She timed it that way so she could be there to check off all the other women as they showed. Amity was next, slipping in the door two minutes behind Lorelei, according to time monster. She asked what she could do to help, but most of the work was finished. It was now just a matter of waiting. And the waiting was almost over.

Corinne appeared around the corner, wrapped in a soft robe over her nightgown. She looked much better than when Lorelei last saw her, but the women rushed to their friend and urged her into a chair. She protested that she could stand, but accepted the chair with grace and dignity. She told them she had come to march. She couldn't sit on the sidelines anymore.

Lorelei protested and argued and growled at her friend, but Corinne wouldn't budge. Linolin called Dr. Maestro, and he gave his permission for her to march as long as she was careful and as long as another woman marched with her to help her so she didn't overexert. Corinne glowed with victory, and gave a fist bump to Amity as Grenata stumbled in, her eyes bleary with lack of sleep. Lymon paced until late into the night, and Grenata whispered to Lorelei that she thought he was upset about Corinne, because it was disturbing all the plans. Lorelei told her Ogden seemed quite all right last night, but perhaps it was all an act.

Before the women started to arrive, Lorelei pulled Linolin aside to quiz her about Dr. Maestro. "Are you sure we can trust him? After all, he's a man."

Linolin laughed. "Don't worry, Elizabeth, he's the real thing. He's been on our side since birth, and I would trust him as much as I trust you."

"Who is he? Where did he come from? Why would a man help women?" Lorelei persevered, not willing to put their mission at risk for the sake of a man.

"Whoa, one question at a time! He's my brother…I guess I never told you my last name was my mother's name. My father's name was Maestro. Manx came from the same place I came from. He helps us because not all men believe in the mantra that women are inferior. Some men…not many right now, unfortunately…are able to see women as they are." Linolin hugged her friend and whispered to her not to worry. "It isn't Manx we have to worry about. It's Ogden…and his friends."

Lorelei realized her friend was right. One man in the compound was less risk to them than hundreds of men outside, men who were ready to commit violence to maintain their world in the way they knew and understood. She asked a couple more questions about Maestro, but trusted Linolin enough to let it go.

The other women arrived, sneaking through the darkened streets, darting behind trees and around voice monster poles like they were in a spy novel. They were having the time of their lives. Linolin and Lorelei checked each name against the sign up sheet. Only a half dozen women in the entire town were not signed up, and the job was a big one.

They were startled by the turnout at meetings, especially after reading in Ogden's – Lorelei's – papers about the number of women that sided with the men in the ancient movement. Lorelei suspected that surprise was on their side; the men didn't know what was happening, so they hadn't worked to turn the women to their side. They didn't even realize lots had been drawn for sides. The women's ability to keep the secret had given them an edge.

Each woman gathered the white dress made especially for her from the pictures of the earliest marchers. Every woman had selected her own dress, and was eager to don the unfamiliar clothing like that once worn by their new heroines. Each woman selected a bright yellow sash from the stack of sashes that reached nearly to the ceiling. The sashes bore slogans in bright, glittery colors, slogans that said 'Freedom' 'Liberty' 'Equality' and other slogans Lorelei found in the women's literature. Lorelei picked up her dress, made in the pattern of a dress she saw Elizabeth Cady Stanton wear in one of the pictures.

She selected her own bright yellow sash, with the slogan 'Forward'. She picked up a sign she had carefully hand-lettered that read 'Resolved: Woman is man's equal'.

She moved to the door at the head of the line of women and waited, her heart fluttering in her chest and her stomach knotted with tension. The women waited with her. There was no chatter, no gossip, no cheery noise as they waited. This was to be a quiet group until the signal was given. That wouldn't be until the group reassembled in their selected meeting place, the park near book room. They planned to be in place by the time the men rose and found their houses empty.

It was time. Lorelei gave the signal and slipped out the door. She headed toward the park, not making a sound and not holding her sign high, not yet. She heard the door close behind her. So far she was the only one out. If anything happened now, it would only happen to her. She had insisted on that. The others would follow one by one, Linolin giving the signal for each woman to slip out and head in a different direction toward the park. The routes were carefully worked out over the past several months, and each woman walked her route frequently until she could do it in the dark. Now it was time. They would be crossing town in the dark.

Lorelei reached the park and stood near the tree. She kept her sign down and tried to look casual, but anyone passing by would not be fooled. The bright yellow sash would be a give away. Fortunately, it was early and no one was passing.

Amity arrived one minute later, out of breath not from rushing, but from nervousness. She stood next to Lorelei, their free hands clenched together, their shoulders touching, but not speaking. No one would speak until it was time. Grenata joined the group, and the three women stood in a quiet embrace waiting for Corinne. Lorelei wanted Corinne to go last, but she insisted on remaining with her friends.

Next to arrive was Mom. Now their group was five, but it still wasn't large enough to prevail against all the manpower that would likely mobilize as soon as the men realized the women were gone. Mom's Thursday group arrived one by one, doubling the numbers of the small group and swelling their confidence with each safe arrival.

Now women were arriving in rapid succession. No more one minute intervals. Once the first women were safely out the door, the procession sped up. Women departed in groups, slipping through the town on separate routes, so all the women could arrive at the park on

193

time. The groups continued to surge toward the park, and finally the last woman slipped out the door. Linolin was on her way. Once she arrived, the group would be complete.

Linolin burst into view with her fast lope, her long legs covering the distance quicker than the other women, who crept cautiously through the quiet streets. She removed her black man's raincoat to reveal her own white dress and yellow sash. She had chosen a sash that said "Break our chains". It was the first time Lorelei saw her in a dress, and she realized her friend was truly beautiful.

Lorelei raised her fist and the march began. The women held up their signs and started down the street behind Lorelei and Linolin. They remained quiet as they passed through residential areas. They moved rapidly toward downtown and surged onto the main street, where the city was just beginning to come to life. The men heading for work were going to see a strange sight this morning. The women they couldn't find at home would greet them on the street, waving signs and shouting for their freedom. The working women held their empty pay envelopes high above their heads, and when the signal went up would demand to know where their money went. One of the workers wrote a song especially for the occasion, and the working women were going to sing:

Why is my pay envelope empty
The minute I come home?
Why is my pay envelope so light
When I work my fingers to the bone?
Why is my pay envelope yours
When your pay envelope is not mine?
Why must I work for nothing all the time?

Grenata took a shine to the song, and worked for three days to compose a tune for the ditty. The women practiced for weeks and the combined sound of their voices was something to hear.

Lorelei raised her fist again, and the group burst out in the agreed upon order. The working women went first, their song filling the morning air with a plaintive tune. The battered women went next, their cries for justice pitiful enough to move the hardest heart. The good wives finished up the chorus, reciting a litany of duties they were expected to perform for men who didn't appreciate their work. Then the chorus started again, working women to good wives, over

194

and over until the air rang with the sound of women's voices in a part of town where women's voices were rarely heard.

Traffic came to a standstill as micro-transit drivers honked and booed at the women, and their passengers screamed orders to go back home. Men in people movers shouted and screamed at the singing, chanting women, and Lorelei heard several men shout "Hey, that's my wife!"

Men poured out of every vehicle and attempted to silence the women. The women locked arms, rocked, and continued to chant. The men backed off, startled by this unfamiliar site of good wives refusing to do what they were told. Unwilling to beat other men's wives, they settled for shouting and throwing things. Lorelei was hit on the temple with a shoe that one man lobbed, but it didn't hit hard. It glanced off her head and landed in the gutter. The man who threw it growled and glared as he rushed up to collect it, but didn't make any move on the women. Everyone seemed too surprised to have any idea what they should do.

Men tried to grab their own wives, but every time a man approached his wife, other women formed a circle around her and held off the men. They had practiced this for hours, each of them taking turns attacking a woman while other women protected her, and their practice made them strong. None of the men were able to break the circle that surrounded their wives unless they were willing to violate protocol and beat another man's wife. Bound by rigid tradition, they fell back defeated. The women shifted and flowed, moving to protect first one woman, then another, as men surged forward and fell back.

The women continued to march, stopping frequently to sing and chant to passing men. They moved through the downtown retail area, past the recreational area, and headed toward their final destination, the business district. They surged forward, not stopping as men clutched at them, pushing aside men who tried to get in their way, and continued moving by the sheer force of their numbers. Not a single woman broke ranks, not one interrupted the march.

Lorelei felt someone pull on her arm and tried to brush them off. No one was taking her easily. She felt the tug again and looked toward the source of annoyance. Resenta was grabbing her and crying, Ornata by her side.

"Let me march! Please, let me march! I want to be free, too!"

Lorelei searched her face for any sign of duplicity. Too much had happened to trust easily, but Resenta appeared to be sincere. She was sobbing and insisting she wanted to be one of the women. She screamed apologies at all of the women for the gossip that nearly got them in hot water. She dropped on her knees and held Lorelei by the legs as she insisted she wanted to help.

Linolin looked at Lorelei. Lorelei nodded. Some of the women held two signs, and she motioned to them to give Resenta and Ornata each a sign. The two women joined the march, singing and chanting out of tune and at the wrong time, but with loud, angry voices that made up with enthusiasm what they lacked in preparation. They made quite a sight in the army of white-clad, yellow-sashed women, Resenta in bright red and Ornata in purple. They would be hard to miss in the multitude.

The group reached their final destination, the office where Ogden and the other archaeologists worked. The building looked strangely empty. The men should be here at this time of day, but there was no sign of movement anywhere. Linolin tried the door; it was locked. The women weren't interested in going inside, but they did want the men to know they were there. It was a disappointment that the men had not arrived and would not likely arrive now that the march was public.

The women marched in a circle through the business district. There were plenty of men to notice their march, and the voices calling from office windows told them their presence was making a stir. Heads popped out of windows and doors, and even a couple through skylights. Women were the most interesting thing in town today. Lorelei swelled with pride. They had done it. People were noticing.

The march continued, with plaintive chanting and mournful singing, until nearly ten. Men occasionally approached as if to stop them, but one encounter with the united force of all the women caused them to back off. For two hours, no one was able to stop the women or quiet their voices. The city was stunned. No one had ever seen anything like this group of marching, singing women. No one expected the women to leave their kitchens and demand to be free. Linolin realized Ogden's secrecy was the men's undoing. Without the other men aware of the danger, no one was prepared.

The police arrived and the group began to tighten the circles. The police spilled out of their uni-transit machines and tried to surround the women, but there were more women than there were police. The police were not trained for this sort of situation, and they stood helplessly for several minutes watching the women march and sing. One policeman got tired of waiting and smacked one of the women with his club. The woman fell, and the policeman grabbed her and threw her in his uni-transit. The other policemen began to move, clubs held high.

The women dispersed on Lorelei's order. Linolin moved for Grenata and Corinne, determined to protect the two fragile women. On cue, other women surrounded the battered women and acted as body shields as Lorelei, Amity, and Mom locked arms and faced down the police. The officers tried to pull them apart, but the women had practiced and knew they could last long enough to allow some of the other women to get away. Other female chains joined with them, working women and good wives facing down groups of policemen, gathered to the front of the group to protect the more fragile women to the rear. One by one, policemen clubbed women and flung them into cars, while other women ran down pre-arranged routes toward the shelter.

Now only the three women remained. One policeman for each woman faced the group and worked to pry their arms apart. The women knew they wouldn't be able to last much longer, and it was time to run. They turned together, arms still locked, and set off at a fast pace until they could no longer run together. They separated and headed in three different directions, hoping the policemen could not follow all of them at once. Lorelei made about ten steps before she was felled by a policeman who made a giant leap and landed on her. In seconds, she was locked in the back of a uni-transit on her way to her husband's house.

50

Ogden was on voice monster when she arrived. The policeman thrust her into the house with a barked order to stay home, and she fell on her knees in the hallway. When she stood, Ogden was in front of her, his face warped with fury.

He grabbed her by the arm and twisted it behind her back. With his other arm, he grabbed a handful of her hair and yanked her head backwards. He shoved her toward his study and she decided not to fight, at least not while he had her in this helpless position.

The door to the safe was open and the familiar papers and artifacts were visible, not in their usual neat order but in a jumble as though someone ransacked them. Lorelei realized Ogden was the ransacker, looking for something in particular, and in his anger unable to do it neatly.

He threw her on the floor and shoved her head nearly into the safe. Lorelei tensed, wondering if he intended to slam the door on her head. That would kill her for sure. She expected consequences, but she needed to live if she was going to finish the plan.

"Have you been snooping in my safe?" Ogden yanked her head once, twice, three times, watching her face as if looking for duplicity. "Have you been reading my papers?"

Lorelei didn't answer. She and Linolin decided the best course of action would be silence for as long as possible in the face of such a contingency, because once you started talking it would be hard to stop. Her main goal was to protect the shelter, protect the other women who were now making their way to the shelter, or, she hoped, were safe inside. Her silence appeared to make Ogden angrier.

"Answer me! That's a direct order…answer." Ogden had none of the flirty loving tone he adopted most of the time recently. This was the old Ogden, cold, hard, and angry.

Lorelei winced as he yanked her head back again. She left her hair loose today, and it proved a good handle for Ogden's use. He thumped her head against the safe, not enough to hurt her but enough to let her know he could, and would, hurt her if he chose. He was in the power position, and he had no intention of letting a mere woman get the better of him.

"See this picture?" Ogden thrust a picture her direction. "This...this...is the exact dress you are wearing. This...is the sash."

He thrust a picture of Elizabeth Cady Stanton in her direction, forcing her to look at the picture. He pulled out the sash, a faded, fragile yellow sash saying "Votes for Women". She looked at them but still did not speak.

"I guess your silence says it all." Ogden sneered.

He released Lorelei's hair and she tumbled out of the nook onto the main floor of the study. She started to rise, but his foot on her head prevented her from getting out of the vulnerable position she occupied. He removed his belt and forced her to her knees. Lorelei knew that this time, he wasn't planning to ask for marital duties. She steeled herself.

The first blow hit her back and she fell. He yanked her back onto her knees and swung again. Two blows. Three. Four. The belt kept swinging high and connecting. She was bleeding, and her white dress was torn. Whenever she fell, he yanked her back to her knees. More blows, and still more. Lorelei counted twenty blows, but started to swoon. More blows landed but she didn't know how many. Just when she thought she was going to lose consciousness, the blows stopped.

Ogden jerked her to her feet and held her, staring into her face with a new look, a look she hadn't seen before. This look was not so much angry as it was sad. He touched her face and his look hardened. He thrust her away from him, and she landed in a heap on the floor at his feet.

"I trusted you. I thought...I thought maybe you were learning to love me. I thought we might be able to...build something worthwhile. But you were only being nice to me so you could keep reading my papers...*my* papers..."

Lorelei started to protest, to tell him that wasn't true, to say she almost stopped because...but she didn't. She wasn't sure herself how much was true and how much was an act, and besides, why should she give any comfort to a man who just demonstrated a level of violence and hatred she had never experienced in her life. She had never seen her father beat her mother, and wasn't sure he ever punished her. He never punished Lorelei, and the scattered punishments Ogden administered had not prepared her for the severity of his rage.

"I told all the men…told them my wife was wonderful. Told them she was a good wife, she could be trusted. She would never betray me, and she was never unkind. They told me to wait. No woman could be a good wife for long, they said. No woman could keep her promises. No woman could be trusted. I insisted. I knew they were wrong. I knew. But…they were right. You are no better than the rest."

Lorelei stumbled to her feet but wasn't able to stand on her own. She held onto the side of the desk, hoping she could get her balance so she could get out of there. She saw blood stains on the carpet, and the sight of her own blood was almost enough to send her back to the floor. She closed her eyes and leaned on the hard surface, finding relief in being able to contact something solid and unchanging.

Ogden grabbed her arm and thrust her toward the door. She fought and pulled against him, but at her best she wasn't as strong as he was, and his assault weakened her. There was no hope she could break free of his grip. She let go of the desk and allowed him to shove her down the hallway. She needed to get treatment for her wounds. She was losing blood. She would get to the bathroom as soon as possible and then find her way out of the house. She needed to get to the shelter.

Ogden thrust her into the kitchen and told her she was not going to leave the house again for a long time, perhaps never. He could no longer trust her and he was going to keep her secured. There would be no more fun times, he said, no more loving moments. She was back on routines, and don't expect any more indulgence from him. He slammed the door, and her heart sank as she heard the key turn in the lock.

The door to the laundry room was unlocked. Ogden didn't put a lock on that door because he needed her to be able to get from kitchen to laundry room to do her work even when she was being punished. She stumbled into the laundry room, her bloody hands leaving marks wherever she put her hands on the wall to steady herself. She headed toward the back door without much hope. Ogden would almost certainly have locked that before she got home, knowing they would be bringing her back.

The door was locked, as she expected. She examined the windows. They were big enough for an adult female to fit through, but in her condition, she wasn't sure it was possible. She looked for Ogden, searching the visible portion of the backyard and checking his study window to see if he was watching. Not seeing him, she decided to take the risk even though she knew he could be hiding, lying in wait for her to try something that would require more punishment.

She pushed the window gently. It moved easily in her hands. She breathed a small thanks to her fastidious husband for insisting everything in the house be in working order. She found the small stool she used for reaching the top cupboards in the kitchen and set it beneath the open window. Scanning the yard again, she satisfied herself it was as safe as it was going to be, and she stepped up on the stool and over the window sill. A surge of energy moved through her, a self-preservation instinct kicking in and giving her just enough strength to climb out the window and drop onto the grass below.

The yard was as empty as it looked from the laundry room, and Ogden apparently was not in his study. The drapes were drawn, and he did not allow the drapes to be drawn when he was in there. Even while he was beating her, the drapes were open. She blushed as she remembered the only times the drapes in the study were drawn while Ogden was in the room. She berated herself for remembering that now. This was no time for tender hearted memories. This was time for escape.

She dropped to her knees, already bruised and bleeding from the rough treatment they had received, and inched toward the back gate. When she got near the study window, she flattened to her stomach and crawled the rest of the way toward the gate, her one and only chance for freedom. The backyard was not large, but it felt like she was crawling across a continent. She moved slowly, partially from fear of being seen by Ogden, and partially from her own weakness.

Her hand slipped into one of Molton's holes he had not filled in properly. She tugged on her arm, but it was stuck. She lay on her stomach, gasping for breath. It was over. She couldn't go any further. She glanced at the study window; the drapes were still closed. She could lie there for hours and no one would find her. Her strength was slipping away. She had lost.

A sound startled her, but it was just the wind blowing through the space between their house and the one next door. She gritted her teeth and pulled again on her arm. It was still stuck, but it seemed looser than before. She turned it one way, then another, and felt it move more freely. She watched the study window as she twisted back and forth to free her arm. The drapes remained closed. Ogden didn't show at the window; there was no sign of life in the house. When her arm was free, she resumed her escape, inching across the yard until she felt another surge of energy from some unknown source deep inside her.

She gained the back gate without further incident. She fumbled for the latch, trying to open it without standing, but she couldn't reach. Rising to her knees, she managed to unhook the latch and slip out of the yard into the alley behind. Her plan was to stand and walk once she was out of the yard, since she was shorter than the fence, but she was too weak to stand. She continued to crawl, sometimes on her knees, dropping to her belly whenever her knees were unable to hold her.

She moved instinctively toward book room, the selected site for rendezvous for any woman who could not make it back to the shelter. She followed the familiar route as long as she could, but collapsed shortly after it came in sight. Looking up to plead with the heavens for help, she realized it was a good thing she hadn't made her goal. Book room was surrounded by police who were hauling off any woman who showed at the rendezvous. Book room would no longer be a safe place for women.

Linolin moved through the city looking for fallen warriors. She was worried about Lorelei. No one had seen what happened, and they had no idea where she was. Amity made it back, dodging policemen and managing not to be caught, heading to the shelter once she lost the police. She thought Lorelei was right behind her. Lorelei had not been seen at book room before or after the police cordoned it off, and she hadn't shown at the shelter. Linolin feared the worst for her friend.

When she was in sight of book room, she dropped to her knees and crawled, even though she was wearing the black raincoat that hid her feminine figure and made the men believe she was one of them. She couldn't afford to get into a conversation right now, especially without enough information about what they knew to avoid being trapped. It turned out to be a fortunate choice because she found Lorelei without stepping on her.

Linolin tried to wake her fallen friend, but Lorelei was too weak and lost too much blood to regain consciousness. Linolin swore when she saw the shredded state of her dress and the skin on her back. Blood seeped through her clothes and stained the ground underneath. Throwing caution to the winds, she stood and lifted the other woman in her arms, bearing her quickly toward the shelter where Manx would do his best to keep her alive. If any of the men saw her, she would just say she was taking this woman back to her husband.

The men surrounding book room paid no attention to the man who appeared from behind the row of houses carrying a woman. He would be one of them, because he was a man. Linolin didn't even look in their direction as she headed toward the residences as though to deposit the misbehaving woman in the proper home. As soon as she was out of their sight, she switched directions and headed toward the shelter. She ran as fast as her long legs would carry her, taking the most direct route, not worrying about whether anyone would follow. Lorelei was losing blood, and there wasn't any time to spare.

The door of the shelter opened as Linolin approached and she was safe inside with her precious cargo. She didn't stop moving until she reached the room where Manx was examining the superficial wounds of a woman who fell and was kicked by the fleeing crowd.

"Hurry!" she breathed.

Her brother took in the situation at one glance and wasted no time. He cleared another exam table, and Linolin laid Lorelei on the table face down. Manx swore as he looked at the damage Ogden inflicted. "These damn men", was all he said.

51

Lorelei needed blood, and fast. Manx knew the hospital was out of the question. The moment they showed up there, Ogden would claim his wife and he would be free to inflict as much pain as he wished short of killing her. Hell, he swore, they might even allow the men to kill the women today. No, he needed to find a donor at the shelter. The trouble is, no one had been typed. He cursed himself for not arranging that small detail during the months of preparation, knowing the women were at risk for serious consequences from their daring actions. He knew Corinne was the same blood type, but she couldn't give blood so soon.

Linolin swept through the building rounding up all the women who managed to get back to the shelter without injuries. As soon as the women heard Lorelei needed blood, there was a line outside the clinic stretching down the hallway and wrapping around the large entry hall. Every woman who was in good enough shape was ready to help. Every woman hoped she would be the one with the right blood type. None of them knew what blood type meant, and the idea of a needle removing their blood made them woozy, but they would brave anything to help their fallen friend.

Manx showed Linolin how to test the blood, so she could take care of that detail while he tried to stop the bleeding and bandage the wounds. Linolin tested herself first, and cursed when she found her blood type was not a match. She called to the first woman in line; one by one they presented their arms and Linolin took their blood. Manx suggested she keep a record of every woman so in another emergency they would not have this problem, and she handed each of them cards to record their name and cot number. When she was done with the test, she added their blood type and set the cards aside for Corinne to create a database.

When Linolin found the first match, she sent the woman to Manx and kept testing the line of women. Manx wanted her to find several potential matches in case Lorelei needed more than one pint, and she lined up six women who could match Lorelei in a reasonably short length of time. She kept on testing the line of women, knowing Lorelei might not be the last woman who would need blood.

204

Corinne came in to check on her friend and offered her blood at once. Linolin explained she could not give blood when she received blood herself only yesterday. She was still too weak, and her wounds were not healed. Linolin told her she could fill out a card so they would have her information on file later, and of course, she could use her organizing skills to create the necessary database for the shelter women. The two women worked side by side until all the women were tested, filed, and organized.

Manx continued to work on Lorelei, who was regaining consciousness and was in a lot of pain. He motioned to Linolin and she collected a vial of the pain killer he slipped out of the hospital in small batches over the past several months. Thanks to Manx, and the failure of the hospital to keep good inventories on medicines, they had a large supply of the drugs they would need to deal with the sorts of injuries the women were likely to receive. She stood by his side and handed him instruments as he stitched up the gaping wounds on her back.

"What did he do to her?" Linolin stared with horror as he stitched up a wound that gaped enough to reveal the muscles inside Lorelei's back.

"I suspect he beat her. Probably with a belt. Some of these look like the buckle might have hit her at least a few times. He must have hit her hard, over and over. This is one of the worst I've seen in a long time." Manx cursed again, and consigned Ogden to eternal flames. "He should be arrested."

"He won't be. He didn't do anything illegal." Linolin cursed a justice system that would allow a man to nearly kill a woman. As long as she didn't die from her wounds, and as long as she was his wife, he could do as he pleased.

"There. That's all I can do. We need to find a bed for her. She can't sleep on a cot until she's recovered."

"Then she will recover?" Linolin tried to find reassurance in the smallest things.

Manx shrugged. "It's too soon to tell. People have died from lesser wounds. She's strong, she's healthy…but…"

His voice trailed off, the but hanging in the air like an invisible sword, ready to slice her friend in half. Linolin rushed out to find a bed. There were no free beds right now. So many battered women arrived at the shelter last week they were full up. She struggled to figure out how to rearrange everything to accommodate Lorelei, but there were no spare rooms. Lorelei was so good at logistics she probably could have found a solution, but Lorelei wasn't able to do anything right now.

A knock announced a visitor, and at her response a small face peeked in the door. Cannata asked if she was free. Linolin nodded and motioned the woman inside. Cannata had been at the shelter for six weeks. She arrived in a mess from a brutal beating, and spent two weeks in Manx's makeshift ICU at the shelter after the hospital turned her away for lack of permission from her husband. Linolin had found her in the street, unconscious and bleeding. Now she was recovering, but still weak and scared. She stayed in the back row of women today, a position where she was able to get back to the shelter without incident, thanks to the diligence of the good wives who took care to protect the battered women.

Cannata perched on the edge of the chair. Something was on her mind, but she didn't want to speak until permission was given. Linolin sighed. It was so hard to get these women to break out of good wife mode, so hard to get them to understand that in here, they were all equal. They didn't have to defer to her, other than to follow the basic rules of the shelter, which were necessary to keep peace among a group of people living together in close quarters.

"Yes?" Linolin tried not to let annoyance creep into her voice. Six weeks was not enough to undo the training of a lifetime, and it wasn't Cannata's fault.

"I heard…" Cannata started, then choked. She started again. "I heard…Lorelei needs help."

"I'm sorry, but the battered women aren't allowed to give blood until Dr. Maestro clears them. We found several women who have been able to donate. I'd be glad to test you in case someone else needs help in the future."

"Oh, I wasn't talking about that….I wouldn't mind, you know", she hurried to add. "I meant…I heard she needs a bed."

"Yes. But we don't have any beds right now."

"She can…she can have mine."

Linolin looked at the woman with admiration. Here was a woman who was still struggling with fear, and she was volunteering to sleep in one of the big rooms they built for the project with rows upon rows of cots. She was willing to give up the private room that gave her so much peace of mind to help another.

"I appreciate that, Cannata. You're sure?"

"I'm sure. I think…it's probably time for me to start making friends, anyway. I need to get over being scared. I need courage."

Linolin hugged the tiny woman. "You have courage, my dear. Just making the offer took more courage than most people could drum up. I promise, we'll get you a private room again as soon as possible."

Cannata nodded. She was too choked up to speak. She wanted desperately to be part of the march, and fought and argued when Manx said she wasn't ready. She convinced him to allow her to go out, and now she was taking another courageous step by giving up the one security she possessed. Normally Linolin would have turned down the offer and told her they would find something, because her need was so great. But there was nothing. Linolin tried everything, and there was no way to rearrange the shelter without one of the women voluntarily giving up their room.

The shelter buzzed as more women arrived from all parts of the city. Many of the women were beaten. Some of them, like Lorelei, literally crawled out of their captivity and headed toward the shelter. Many of them needed blood. Linolin sent troops all over the city looking for fallen women, troops dressed in men's clothing with their long hair tucked under hats, troops that brought anyone they found back to the shelter for help. Manx would be busy all night getting the women stitched up and bandaged.

The women who managed to get back to the shelter without being taken or injured were settling in on the cots that were assigned to them before the march began. Linolin looked around the large sleeping room, filled from wall to wall and from floor to ceiling with double and triple-decked cots, each cot with a small bag of personal items the women brought with them this morning. All these women realized at the beginning that when it was over, they were not going to go back home. The march was only the beginning, the announcement of intent. The walk out was the main event.

52

Lorelei remained in her room for three days, but refused to rest any longer. Mom sat by her bed, holding her hand and stroking her head, her tears watering Lorelei's face and hair. She refused to move even to sleep until Amity led her out of the room and back to her small cot, promising to wake her in a few hours. Mom and Amity slept only in short shifts, preferring to tend to Lorelei as much as possible. Both women were assigned duties elsewhere, but Linolin released them from all other duties as long as Lorelei needed them. The group needed Lorelei, and Lorelei needed her mother and her best friend.

Grenata moved her painting supplies into the room and used her newly discovered talent to create a record of the brutality the women experienced. She mixed the paint with her own tears, feeling it would be more authentic.

Linolin stayed by Lorelei's side the first night, not going home until she knew her friend was out of the woods. Manx visited as often as he could, but many women were showing up with minor to serious wounds and he was their only medic, at least for the first two days. The third day, the day Lorelei was starting to sit up and take a little food, a young man showed up at the door, an intern who worked with Manx at the hospital. He suspected Manx was up to something, and followed him to the shelter the night before the march. He watched Corinne stumble into the building and knew she had not come back out. He drew some incorrect conclusions, assuming the woman was coming for an illegal termination of an unwanted pregnancy.

When the march began the young man, whose name was Raulston Klax, watched from the hospital windows, fear nearly choking him. He recognized his mother in the group, waving a sign like she meant it, and his sister was there. He noticed other women he knew, including a girl he had a crush on in high school but who was promised to another man. At first he was as horrified as the other men, but he listened to what the women said and watched their faces.

He was surprised when he started hoping, silently of course, that they would succeed. He cheered them on in his heart, and nearly cried when he saw a policeman chase his mother and knock her to the ground. He knew his mother was a good woman, a kind woman, and an intelligent woman. If she believed something, it was probably true.

His mother was carried home to his father, who beat her and locked her in the kitchen. As soon as his father went to work, Raulston let her out. He offered to take her wherever she wanted to go, but she insisted on going herself. She would not tell him where she was going, or let him help her, for fear of revealing the location and endangering her friends. As soon as she left, limping a long and circuitous route to the shelter, he slipped out and followed her.

Once he knew where she was, he hung around for a couple of days, trying to gather the courage to knock, to offer his help, to do something for the women he had learned to admire. He was sure his sister, who left her husband and son at home, was in the shelter, too. Perhaps even the girl he realized he still had a crush on…maybe all the missing women were there. He hid whenever search parties went by, afraid they would see him and demand to know what he was doing. He didn't want to give away the women's location. He paced and circled and hid in the bushes, wanting to help but scared to act. It meant the end of the life he knew.

Now he was a member of the team, and Manx could manage to do more than just stick bandages on wounds. Raulston handled the minor injuries, freeing up the more experienced older man to tend to serious wounds. The women realized they needed to make plans for where to house the men. Clearly Raulston could not move in with Linolin and Manx. They would need to find a place for him, since he could not return home from the moment he freed his mother. They rigged up a cot in Manx's office until they could prepare a more permanent solution.

Amity helped Lorelei to a soft armchair where she could watch the women who were not injured as they went about the work of managing the shelter that would be their home as long as they were on walk out. Most of the women were sure they would not be able to go home again, but others were confident the men would see the light as soon as they tried to take care of themselves for a few days. Amity decided she didn't care if Merris saw the light; she didn't want to go home. She wanted to go back to school and learn everything she was prevented from learning in her youth. She wanted to study under Manx and learn how to be a medic. She wanted to be free.

Lorelei felt pride surge at the efficiency and comfort of the home the women prepared for themselves under her guidance. They did this – mere women, not believed to have a big enough brain to do more than cook and clean. They built this room, and were now building another one to house Raulston and any other men who might decide to join them. It was likely more men would come. Many were hanging around the streets following women when they snuck out to look for fallen friends, asking how to join. None would be admitted until they were vouched for by a reliable source and passed a series of tests. Corinne and Mom were working on the appropriate tests, and soon men would be able to prove they were trustworthy.

Linolin settled by Lorelei's chair. "How are you feeling?"

"Better. I'm still very tired…and sore."

"I imagine. I've never seen such a devastating beating. That must have been…." Linolin stopped. She realized from the look on Lorelei's face that she was being insensitive.

"Ogden has hit me before…never like that. He would give me several swats, but not so hard, not so vicious…and never so many. His face…it almost didn't look like him, he was so angry."

"I was afraid…we shouldn't have let you be in front. You had so much to lose, because it was going to be obvious where we got the idea…and the information. Only Ogden had access to most of those papers, right?"

Lorelei nodded. "I knew. I knew it was a risk. But I had to…and I'm still here, right?"

The sadness in her eyes touched Linolin. "Someone wants to see you."

"Oh? Who?" Lorelei's tone was tired and disinterested. She was saying what was expected, but she didn't really care.

Linolin made a motion behind her. Lorelei didn't look around. She hurt too badly to move, and she didn't want visitors right now. When a small, soft hand touched hers, she knew at once who it was and her spirits lifted. She grabbed her daughter in her arms, ignoring the pain in her back and all other parts of her, and held her in a tight embrace. Molton stood beside the chair, shy and silent, his boisterous energy curbed by seeing his mother in such a state.

"Mama?" His voice was a whisper, and she reached for him and wrapped her arm around his shoulders. He moved the wrong way and she cried out in pain. "Sorry, Mama!" He moved back, but she pulled him close.

"Don't be sorry about hurting me, Molton. I needed you…and Micra…more than anything right now."

Micra was staring into her mother's eyes, still scared from all the disruption of the past few days, and not sure what to make of her mother looking so worn out and tired even after having been in bed for so long. "Did you fall down, Mommy?"

Molton clenched his fists. "I bet some bully beat her up. I'm gonna find him and…and…"

Lorelei released Micra and brought Molton to her lap. "No, Molton, you're going to…let it go."

"But, Mama…"

"Violence is no way to solve your problems. Haven't I been telling you that all your life?"

Molton whined. He hadn't had much chance to work off his energy since they'd been at the shelter, because of the need to keep the location secret, and he was anxious for a fight or anything. "Yes, but Daddy says…"

Linolin took the boy and led him out of the room. She could see tears well up in Lorelei's eyes at the mention of Daddy. "We'll let Mamma rest now. We'll let you play with Manx" she told him as she led the children out of the room.

"How?"

Amity perched on the arm of Lorelei's chair, careful not to bump her or hurt her in any way. "I picked them up off child mover. I thought I wouldn't get them. Ogden was on his way, and I got out of there just before he saw me. He's been looking all over for them, threatening everyone that if he doesn't get his children back, he'll…" Amity stopped. They both knew what Ogden was capable of.

Mom hovered nearby, waiting for Lorelei to be finished with the children. Now she moved forward and settled beside her daughter, holding her hand and filling her in on all the things that happened at the shelter while she was out of action. The women moved easily into their new roles, and the cooking and cleaning schedule Lorelei worked so hard on was operating splendidly. Now they were cooking and cleaning for themselves, and the women sang as they did chores they once hated.

"That was a smart idea, to have alternates. I wouldn't have thought about that, even though I knew a lot of the women would likely be...damaged." Mom paused, looking at her daughter with a searching glance that saw more than Lorelei wished. "There have been a few grumbles, of course, and some slacking here and there, but not much."

Lorelei closed her eyes. "I knew putting you in charge of complaints was the right thing" was all she managed before she fell asleep.

53

Lorelei was able to rest now that she had her children back. She had worried about them, not sure whether Ogden in his anger would be able to restrain himself from hurting them, and knowing he didn't have the knowledge to care for them. They would be well taken care of here, settled into the children's wing Amity and Corinne set up when women began to rescue their children.

She slept and rested for the next couple of weeks, getting her strength back while the women warriors, as they now called themselves, ran their new home just as she and they had arranged. Mom flitted in and out, dividing her time between her management duties and her daughter, and taking Lorelei's place as de facto leader until Lorelei was recovered enough to do it herself. Lorelei watched her mother and wondered how she managed to escape the brutal beatings that were inflicted on so many of the women.

"Oh, I just stared your father in the face, said I was leaving, and walked out", Mom told her with a breezy wave. "He was so shocked he wasn't able to move until after I was out the door. He never could run as fast as I can."

There were a few anxious moments when a man known to be hostile would wander near the shelter and look their way with a knowing look, or when men would snoop too close to the building while looking for their wives. A couple of times there were knocks on the door by men who knocked on all the doors to see if their wives had been seen. Raulston and Manx handled most of the men, unless it was someone who knew them and who would know they disappeared at the same time the women did. Then they would turn it over to someone else, holding their breath with worry that it would go badly. It never did. The responses Linolin scripted in advance worked every time, and the factory façade convinced the visitors that this was a world of men.

Some of the knocks were other men who also knocked on every door hoping to offer their services to the women. These were vetted carefully. The possibility of spies infiltrating the fortress – their new name, since shelter was a place for helpless women, and none of them considered herself helpless anymore – was a real possibility, and they took care with any man who suggested he was on their side. The men of the fortress were masters at playing dumb when someone asked to be allowed to join. Until the new recruit proved himself trustworthy, he would not be let in. If he did prove sincere, he would be welcomed and given a cot in the new Men's Wing that was in the process of being built. It was rough, but in time they would have it looking as good as the big halls where the women lived.

Linolin spent most of her time at the fortress. Manx bunked at her house after the great day, but now moved to the fortress with the other men. It was safer that way, he said. He wanted to protect his sister, and was worried she would be immediately suspected of conspiring with the women. So far, no men had come to her door looking for their wives, so it was possible they had not yet connected her with the rebellion. He sent two of his most trustworthy men to guard her house every night. He knew if she found out she would be angry at him, so he urged them to be discreet.

Lorelei was getting stronger and started taking on some light duties by the end of the second week. She looked forward to getting to the office she shared with Linolin, because she finally felt useful. She took on some of the duties of schooling the children who were rescued by their mothers or other women and were now in the new children's wing of the fortress.

Many women were able to pick up their children off child mover the first day, catching their husbands off guard because they knew the routine and the men didn't. Women who escaped without injury took great risks to collect as many of the children of the injured women as they could. Others collected their children from various places as the days passed, and there was now a large gathering of children that needed to live as normal a life as possible. The women took turns tending to the children and schooling them. Corinne fell into the role with zest, making up for never having a child of her own by being of assistance to other women's children.

Lorelei returned to as normal a routine as possible. At first she contented herself with making hot beverage in the great dining room, and folding sheets and towels while she rested in her armchair, but now she was buzzing about with some of her old energy. The walk out would be a success, she was determined. Oh, they wouldn't win everything at once, she knew that, but the big plan had always been the walk out. Start with the march, then the women return to the fortress. Let the men try to survive in a world without women. Since almost all the women in the city participated, and even the few who hadn't marched had come to the fortress since the great day, there was little other choice for the men.

Lorelei saw a red dress pass and thought she recognized Resenta. She called to the other woman, and winced as she was wrapped into a bear hug. Resenta realized she was hurting Lorelei, and released her with a whispered apology. She appeared to be a very changed woman.

"What happened? Why did you join us? I thought you were happy as a good wife."

Resenta paused, then plunged into her story. Her life had been truly horrifying, and Lorelei was in tears when she finished. She was beaten badly and nearly died. When she recovered, she decided to hide her pain behind loudness and flashy clothes. Her husband liked bright colors, and she adopted the persona Lorelei knew from the grocery store. At home, she kept her head bowed and her voice quiet, as quiet as all the other good wives. Her husband beat her frequently, in spite of her subservience and attention to household routines.

She voiced her anger with the other women because it was the only place she was safe. As a result, the only people who could have understood and sympathized avoided her, and she had nowhere to turn. Everyone else had friends, but she had none. Thursday groups shut her out all over town. When Ornata moved into the neighborhood, she found a kindred soul, another beaten woman who managed her pain the same way, and they started hanging around together. Then everyone started whispering about something new, something exciting.

"I...I...you were doing something. You were making something happen. I wanted to be part of it, but I didn't know how. You kept turning me away. I know, I know, I can't keep a secret...I can't. It's my fault. But once you started...once I saw you on the street...I thought...they can take me now. It isn't secret any more."

Resenta had been doing some amazing things since arriving at the shelter. Somehow managing to escape injury during the march, even though she was in the front and stuck out like a sore thumb in her red dress, even though she was knocked down three times and stepped on twice, she made it to the fortress, helped by another woman who directed her where to go. Since her arrival, in between her regular assigned duties, she had been collecting women's stories and was writing them down. "I'm not much of a writer, but I can get the details. Maybe someday…someone who can write better than me…maybe the stories could be collected into a book. So other people will know why we're doing this. So other women in other places can get courage themselves."

Lorelei nodded. She thought it was a wonderful idea, and sent her to talk to Amity. If you wanted something written, Amity would be the best resource, at least the best she knew. There were probably other women here who could write, and perhaps the project would bring them together and help them find something to do to keep themselves from despair whenever things seemed to be taking too long.

The hallway seemed very long with all the aches Lorelei still suffered. She was looking forward to getting into the office and settling into her small stuffed desk chair. She could work just fine once she got settled, but while she was walking down the hall it seemed impossible that she would be able to work once she got there.

She pushed open the door and entered, but stopped before she could get to her desk. Linolin was in the office, which wasn't unusual, but Grenata was also there. The two women were locked in a passionate kiss, and it was evident more was coming than kissing. It was the first time Lorelei had seen such a thing, and she stood frozen in shock for nearly a minute. The other women didn't notice her, and when she was able to move, she slipped back out and headed toward the great hall. She could work from her armchair this morning, she thought. It was more comfortable anyway.

54

Linolin perched on the arm of Lorelei's chair, blocking the light. Lorelei looked up into the bluest eyes on the planet. She put her hand on Linolin's arm, but didn't say anything. She was busy with calculations that would tell them how long they would be able to continue the walk out. Money was an issue, even though they had received a large donation from an anonymous donor. They needed to plan every expenditure.

"You saw us." Linolin came straight to the point, blunt as usual.

"I wasn't going to say anything." Lorelei didn't look at her friend.

"You're shocked."

"No...yes. Maybe." Lorelei didn't know what to say. She was shocked, but not as much as she would have expected. Somehow it made sense.

"Grenata should never have married a man. It wasn't right to force her into that marriage."

"None of us should have been forced into marriage." Lorelei didn't want to sound testy, but Grenata was not the only one who suffered.

"I know. I agree wholeheartedly. I didn't get into this for Grenata, though...it was obvious to me from the beginning she was not like the rest of the good wives. I got into this for you...and Amity...your mother...Micra...and every woman everywhere. I mean, you know I started this shelter. Can you doubt my sincerity?"

Lorelei didn't say anything. She was still trying to collect her thoughts. When she did speak, it was with hesitation. "I know. I just don't...understand."

Linolin started to say something, but was interrupted by the alert bell. The women leapt into action. That meant only one thing – an intruder breached their security. There was only one other instance of the bell going off since they arrived. That had been a false alarm.

"Probably another false alarm." Linolin tried to reassure Lorelei, but the look on her face gave her away. She was worried for real.

Cannata rushed into the room, terror on her face. "There's a man here!"

"Who?" Linolin grabbed the woman by the shoulders. "Did you get his name?"

"I don't know. He's one of them. The enemy."

Cannata was trembling. Lorelei threw a blanket around her shoulders and urged her into one of the armchairs.

"I'll go." Linolin was out the door before Lorelei could stop her.

The alarm continued to ring, and women scurried. The fortress looked like it was in motion as all the women moved, securing doors and cabinets, locking down the rooms where women were still recovering from injuries, protecting the most fragile among them, and going into lockdown themselves. The sleeping halls would soon be full of women, huddled in their beds, the doors locked against a possible invasion. They practiced it frequently and now it was in action. This was not a drill.

Linolin returned. "It's Ogden", she announced.

Fear shot through Lorelei, and she shuddered. Her back began to ache in places she hadn't ached for days. He'd found her. He would drag her out of here and take her back to that house, take her back to...she shuddered again.

"He won't." Linolin spoke as if reading her mind. "I will not let him remove you from here. They will need an army to get you out."

"And if he brought one?"

"We'll all go down together." Resenta spoke from behind the women, causing them both to jump. "They have no right. We will protect you if it costs our own lives."

"Why aren't you in lockdown?" Linolin gave her most fierce glare to the other woman.

Resenta stood firm. "Lorelei needs me. I'm staying with her."

Lorelei struggled to her feet, her knees almost too weak to hold her. She leaned against Linolin, using her for support. "I can't let him see me like this. He can't see my weakness."

Linolin massaged her shoulders. "Relax. Your strength will return if you relax. The anxiety is sapping you."

Lorelei nodded. She took several deep breaths and a few tentative steps. Her knees did not let her down, and she started to stomp. She needed to be able to stride into the room, strong and sure, and face down the man who tried to kill her.

"You can't go out there." Resenta pulled on her arm, trying to prevent her new friend from walking into a trap.

"I have to. If I don't, he *will* bring an army."

218

Lorelei marched out the door and down the hall. She forgot she was weak. She forgot she was tired. She summoned every ounce of strength, and drew strength from the two women who flanked her on her journey. With grim determination they remained by her side as she entered the dining room where Linolin left Ogden. Linolin nodded at the security detail guarding the door, and they moved aside to let the women pass; as soon as the women entered, the guards returned to their posts.

Ogden stood as Lorelei entered and held out his hand. She moved away, holding on to the two women by her side as lifelines. He put his hand by his side and stayed where he was, making no move to rush her or to take her away.

Lorelei noticed with glee he was rumpled; his clothes had not been pressed since she left. She wasn't surprised, since his mother was also at the fortress. Lorelei was shocked when she first showed up to shelter group and avoided her at first, convinced she was a spy for Ogden. After all, this was the woman who rarely spoke to her whenever they met for holidays or obligatory meals with the parents.

One day when Lorelei was alone in the great room, Malletta surprised her by sneaking up behind her and wrapping her in an enormous embrace. The older woman had tears in her eyes as she begged Lorelei to let her be part of the movement. She convinced her daughter-in-law to trust her, and she proved to be a great addition to the fortress. With effort, Lorelei thrust those memories away and turned her attention back to Ogden.

"Can we speak alone?" He looked first to Linolin and then to Resenta.

"Are you armed?" Resenta glared at him.

"You can have…" Ogden removed his belt and handed it to Linolin. He kept his eyes on Lorelei; he must have noticed her wince as he reached for his belt.

The two women moved aside and consulted in whispers. Ogden and Lorelei watched, neither of them sure what they wanted the answer to be. When the women finished their consultation, they nodded.

"You may speak with her alone if she agrees…and we will be nearby. We will be in here at the first false sound." Linolin spoke in a voice that could have frightened an army of gods, let alone a single man.

"Lorelei?" Resenta presented her with the final decision.

Lorelei wished they hadn't left it up to her. She was scared and tired, and she wanted someone to tell her what to do today. She wasn't in shape to make such momentous decisions herself and she was afraid whatever she did, it would be the wrong thing. She looked at Ogden; he remained stoic, not giving her any guidance. She shuddered with fear remembering the look of anger and hate when she last saw him. She looked at Resenta, who gave her a quizzical look that didn't help. She looked at Linolin; Linolin nodded.

"I...I'm willing."

Lorelei cursed herself for stammering. She needed to be strong, and here she was stuttering like a weakling. Ogden would think he had her for sure. He would be confident and brutal. She wanted to rescind her decision as she watched her friends move toward the door, but she hated the thought of looking scared more than she hated the thought of being alone with Ogden. The door closed behind the two women, and they were alone.

"I...I'm sorry." Ogden looked at his shoes rather than at her as he spoke.

"Sorry?" Lorelei tried to make her voice drip sarcasm, but she was afraid it came out sad.

"I...in the heat...all I could think was...how could she do this to me? How? When we were getting so good together? I thought...I had begun to think...you were learning to love me. And then...you walked out with the women, and I thought...she was using me."

Lorelei didn't say anything. It wasn't what she expected. She expected him to come in blustering like a bully and demanding she go home, demanding she come back to face her punishment. She expected him to bring an army of men and drag all the women back to their prisons. This might be harder to deal with. She could face his anger – she had faced his anger – but his remorse threatened to sap her strength.

"I've thought a lot since you've been gone. Life isn't the same...of course. I mean, how could it be? But...I kept looking for you. The bloody handprints in the laundry room...the blood in the alleyway...leading to book room...I knew it was you because I followed the trail. The police said...you didn't show at book room…no one had seen you…I was afraid you were…dead. I was afraid I had…killed you. The blood trail just…ended."

"Linolin found me. She brought me back here."

"I know. She told me."

That surprised Lorelei. She didn't know they had talked. "She did? When?"

"A week ago. I caught her at her house. She wouldn't tell me where you were, but she told me you were alive. She told me it was no thanks to me. She told me you would be fine as long as you stayed away from me. That hurt. But…I knew she was right. I don't deserve you."

Ogden turned away. She thought she heard him sob but she found it hard to believe. Was she reading into his attitude what she wanted to see? She didn't want him to be the monster he was that last day. She was letting her guard down and she knew that was dangerous. She steeled herself and was cold as ice when he turned back around.

"I brought you something."

Ogden reached inside his coat and Lorelei stiffened. She heard movement outside the door and realized her friends were close…but were they close enough? He brought his hand back out of his coat and motioned to her to hold out her hand. She did, and he dropped something in her palm. She closed her hand over it, not able to look.

"Look at it."

Training took over and Lorelei obeyed his request as if it were an order. She opened her hand to reveal the small opal he gave her what seemed a lifetime ago. She held it back to him.

"I can't take this."

"It's yours. It's been yours since the moment I bought it. If you can't bring yourself to wear it, you could sell it. It's quite valuable, and this place could probably use the money."

"Thank you." Lorelei kept her voice devoid of any emotion.

"I've thought a lot since that day. I've thought about the things I said, the things I did. It was terrible. I…I made it all about me. It wasn't about me, was it? It was about you…and Amity…and Corinne…and Grenata."

"And Micra…and Mom…and Linolin…and all the battered wives and working women and good wives. All the women. And you lied to them, lied to me, lied to the world to keep us from being free."

"I know. I don't feel good about that. I didn't realize."

"How could you not realize? How could you not see women being beaten and held captive in their own home, forced to marry men they don't love and bear children they don't want, and think that was okay? Would you think that was okay if it was happening to men?"

Ogden winced. She had hit home. "I know you never liked me, and I'm sorry you had to marry me. I should have tried to stop it, but...I wanted to be the sort of man I was supposed to be. And I ...wanted...you."

Lorelei turned away. Her eyes filled with tears remembering the moments when she thought it might actually work, that they might actually find something together. It was over, and she knew it was over, but there were still those moments.

"Lorelei, why didn't you say something? Why didn't you tell me you wanted to be free?"

Lorelei faced him, her eyes flashing. "Would it have made a difference? Would you have understood?"

Ogden shook his head. "Probably not. I didn't understand when I saw the march. I didn't understand when I saw the signs."

"You saw? No one was at the office."

"I was on the way. We were all running late because of Corinne. No one knew what happened to her. It was threatening the project to have her gone. Corydon told us she ran away, and we were trying to find her."

"He threw her down the stairs. He made her lose the baby."

Ogden drew in his breath. "I had no idea. He just told us he came home and she was gone. And then...all the women were gone. You. Amity. My mother. Your mother. And when we saw the march...all the women...we realized why she left. Or, I guess, we thought we realized."

"She almost died. Fortunately, she knew to come here. She knew this place helped beaten women. There is a medic here who saved her life. She needed blood, and he couldn't get it for her because there was no man who would have admitted her to the hospital without taking her back to Corydon when she was released. I was going to ask you...I thought...you'd been...maybe you'd help. But then I realized you would not let her return here. You'd force her back to the husband who...who..." Lorelei choked on her anger, and couldn't speak.

"It can be really difficult to see yourself through someone else's eyes." Ogden moved toward Lorelei and put his hand on her shoulder. She didn't respond, but she didn't push it off.

They stood silent for so long that Linolin put her head in the door to check on her. "Are you all right?" Lorelei nodded, and her head disappeared.

Ogden moved back and the moment ended. "Can you...show me around the place? Or is that forbidden?"

"How did you find us?"

"I...I looked everywhere. I went to every building in town. This was the only building I hadn't been in. I just...took a chance. When I found the hidden door, it seemed...It's much bigger than it looks from outside, isn't it?"

Lorelei watched closely to see if he was lying. He stared back at her, holding her gaze with no sign of nervousness or duplicity. She decided he was telling the truth.

"I'd really love to see the place, if it's allowed."

"I'll need to get the agreement of the women." Lorelei didn't move.

"Please. I'd love to see."

Lorelei asked Linolin and Resenta to come back. Mom had joined them, and the three women flanked Lorelei as though they were her bodyguards. She presented Ogden's request to them. It was an unusual request. They had no protocol. It seemed dangerous. "Can we trust him?" Linolin whispered. Lorelei shrugged. She had no idea.

They consulted for more than five minutes, arguing over every possibility. They finally agreed to let Ogden see the facility. After all, the real danger had already happened. He knew where it was. Nothing worse could happen from him seeing the inside. He would not be allowed inside the sleeping halls where the women were on lockdown.

It was agreed that Lorelei would lead him around the facility. Linolin would remain close in case she was needed. Mom hovered, but didn't move toward either Lorelei or Ogden. Resenta was sent off to alert security to be on standby. Only when she reported back did the tour begin. Security details were deployed in every room and every hallway, ready to rush Ogden if the need arose.

Lorelei started in the dining hall, since they were already there. This was where the women took their meals. They took turns cooking, and she showed him the assignment sheet for the teams of women that prepared each meal. He seemed amazed at the elaborate arrangements, and that they worked without a hitch, except occasionally when a woman got sick and someone had to fill in. The women were still in the excited phase of their project, and there were always plenty of volunteers.

Ogden asked if he could have hot beverage. Lorelei told him to help himself. He poured himself a cup from the long line of pots on the table and took a sip. Lorelei put on her most innocent look and pretended to be surprised when he reacted with disgust.

"What…is…that?" he sputtered.

"Coffee."

"What?"

Lorelei grinned and showed him the line of pots and what each contained. Some of the women discovered they really liked coffee, so they kept pots of it around. The same for tea. Hot chocolate. She moved through the beverages one by one, giving him a taste of each. He reacted even more strongly against the tea than the coffee, but seemed to like the hot chocolate. The bouillon generated a puzzled look, and the lemonade he spit out immediately. After he sampled all the unfamiliar beverages, she explained that these were the ingredients of hot beverage.

"What made you think you could drink them separately?" Ogden had a look of astonishment that made Lorelei laugh.

"There was a lot more in your papers than the woman's museum." She stopped there, and didn't elaborate.

He waited for her to explain. His curiosity got too strong, and he asked her what she meant. She explained how she worked out the dynamics of the beverages from the contents of the papers in his safe. She went to her desk and got the calculations she did to figure out the right mixtures and what broke down into what. He examined the paper with shock.

"You figured all this out from the papers?" She nodded. "You are…amazing. I hadn't been able to sort out what half that stuff was yet. I've been puzzled for a long time about certain references, and you got right to the heart of the matter."

"You don't know the ingredients of hot beverage. You've never made it for yourself."

He stared at the paper again, and nodded. "Can I…see the rest of the place?"

Lorelei led him around the fortress, explaining the set up and how they built the great halls where the women bunked. He asked more questions than he had ever asked her, and expressed astonishment at what they had built. She showed him the plans for the march and the walk out, the months of planning and logistics that went into getting everything just right, and the continued planning required to keep it moving smoothly.

"We clearly underestimated the women. What you pulled off here…you put a committee of men on this, and they'd botch it up. They'd all want to be boss, and they'd all have suggestions, and most of the suggestions wouldn't work."

"Most of our suggestions didn't work, either." Lorelei paused. "But…we were planning for something so important to us that we figured out how to overcome the desire to be in charge, to have things our way, to be the boss. We were planning for our freedom."

"You deserve it." That was all Ogden said. Then he was gone, out the door and down the street before Lorelei could answer.

55

The next day, another man showed up. The alarm once again went off, and the women once again went into lockdown. Lorelei, Resenta, and Linolin moved in step with each other as they strode down the hall to the dining room where security was holding the intruder. He asked for Lorelei's mother, but she was not bringing her mother into danger.

Amity joined them halfway down the hallway and the four women marched in grim silence toward the other end of the facility. Scared faces peered at them as they passed, women supposed to be in lockdown but too curious to stay behind. Surely there could not be two men arriving in two days and neither of them with evil intent. This one must be the real thing, the moment of truth. There was a buzz of excitement overlying the fear. Would their plans be able to withstand an onslaught?

Lorelei thought about the meeting in Sleeping Hall Anthony last night, the women crouched several per bunk as she explained the situation. One of the men knew where they were. He seemed not to be planning to turn them in, but there was no certainty because the men demonstrated over and over again that they were able to be duplicitous. Everything would be on red alert until further notice. Security would be stationed in every hallway until they knew things were clear. The women nodded, their faces pale, their voices silent until Lorelei raised her fist.

"We will not go back to our chains!"

The room was silent, so silent you could have heard a snowflake fall. Then Sojourner – now able to be called Montoya again – raised her fist and shouted in her loudest voice. "We will not go back to our chains!"

The room erupted. Angry voices mingled with fearful ones, but through it all, Lorelei sensed an element that had been lacking since Ogden showed – optimism. They faced their first intruder, and were still intact. One of the women shouted that Lorelei was magic. Lorelei frowned and shook her head. She didn't want them becoming overconfident.

Now she faced the same walk that so frightened her the day before. She felt Linolin's fear and Resenta's optimism. Between the two of them, she didn't know which was the right emotion. She crossed her arms over her chest and took Amity's hand in her own; she grabbed Resenta's hand on her other side. They marched down the hall locked together, four women in the same chain formation that made them so formidable during the march. It wouldn't be easy for one man to take them, and besides, they had security.

The security system was developed early in the planning stage, but they made many enhancements in the past few weeks. Some of the male allies were able to help them with suggestions based on their own experiences, and the women were more than happy to implement any suggestions that were feasible.

One man, Stone, worked in security on the outside, and they put him in charge of the security detail. After all, they were new to much of this, and were not above accepting help from men when help was freely offered. The enhanced security made them feel more comfortable, but they still trembled as they prepared to face yet another possible enemy.

"I think…" Linolin started to say something and stopped.

"What?" Lorelei stared at her friend, willing her to finish her thought. "Tell me. I need to know."

"I think…Ogden was too easy. We're destined for something…more challenging." Linolin spoke in a near whisper, but her voice sounded like thunder in the quiet hallway.

Amity nodded. "I was thinking the same thing."

"We won't let anyone take us back." Resenta spoke with conviction, but the quaver in her voice gave her away. She was not as confident as she appeared.

"Look, let's…stop for a minute." Lorelei paused and the other women, still with their arms locked with hers, were forced to stop.

"What?" Linolin nearly crashed into Amity, but prevented collision just in time. She teetered as she spoke, but righted herself and glared at her friend.

"Let's just…breathe." Lorelei paused. It sounded dumb to her now, but it made sense a moment ago. "Let's…breathe. And…I don't know, but…something. We're not ready."

Amity moved around Resenta so she could see her friend, who was blocked from view by the larger woman. "I think we just need to take a minute and…courage. Restore our courage."

"Boy, I could sure use hot beverage right now." Lorelei whispered, and her friends nodded. "Too bad all the hot beverage is with the intruder."

"That's our courage", Resenta said. The others stared at her without comprehending. "Hot beverage. We need hot beverage. The only way to get it is to face down the intruder, because he is keeping us from hot beverage. Focus on hot beverage, not on the man, and we will find our courage."

Lorelei nodded. Resenta had an amazing way of finding just the right thing to say. This woman she avoided for so long had amazing depths and amazing strengths she was only just beginning to appreciate. She grabbed Resenta's hand and held it, allowing the courage of the other woman to flow into her own bruised and battered body.

They stood hand in hand for nearly a minute, gathering their courage and whispering to each other that they could do this. If they could do all the things they'd done, they could do this.

"Hot beverage." Resenta whispered, and the others picked it up.

The words passed through the group and had a strange effect. Just as Resenta predicted, they were able to find their courage. They focused on hot beverage, on their desire for the strength and comfort of the familiar, and they began to move, no longer frozen in fear.

The door to the dining hall creaked as Lorelei pushed it open. Resenta and Linolin entered before her, their bodies blocking her from the sight of the intruder. She wished they would stop treating her like a fragile invalid, but at the same time, she felt like a fragile invalid and was grateful for their protection.

The intruder held out his hand. The two women parted and allowed Lorelei and Amity to move into the room where they could see who penetrated the fortress. Lorelei rushed forward, but was stopped by the cautious hands of her friends holding her arms to keep her from leaping into his embrace.

"Dad!"

Her father watched his daughter with a look on his face that she remembered from when she was five and fell down the stairs. He looked happy to see she was fine, but worried she was hurt. It was an unusual look, one she had not seen often, but the memory of his concern flooded back and she struggled to move toward him. Her friends held her in an iron grip she was not able to break.

"Careful." Linolin hissed.

"We don't know who is friend and who is foe", Resenta added.

Lorelei nodded. Her first instinct was to rush to her father, hold him and be held by him, but that could be dangerous. After all, he was one of them…the men. The archaeologists. One of Ogden's team. He was part of 'the project', and would need to prove himself before she could trust him again.

"I was hoping…to see…your mother", her father stammered. "I'm glad to see you. Is she…all right?"

Lorelei nodded, not trusting herself to speak. She thrust Amity forward, prodding her friend to be the spokesperson for both her and her mother.

"She is fine." Amity crossed her arms across her chest and thrust out her chin. "We are all fine. We do not need our men here. They are in the way."

"I understand. I know you…she…all of you…can survive without us. I've always known that. It's just…I can't survive without you. None of us can."

Amity frowned. "You want us to come home and take care of you again."

"No."

Her father stopped, his single word hanging in the air. He looked at his daughter, still straining against Resenta's grip even as her own best judgment told her not to trust him. Her lifelong attachment to this man was strong, and threatened to overpower her instinct for self preservation.

"What do you want, then?" Amity pressed him, taking her role as Lorelei's spokeswoman seriously.

"I want…to come here. And help you. I want…to join. I heard…there were some men…you allowed inside. You have…male allies. I want to be one." Dad stammered, his usual self confidence hidden behind new emotions, emotions he struggled to express.

"Why?"

Amity wasn't going to be satisfied easily. She put her hand on Lorelei's arm to remind her friend that men were not allowed in just on their word. Lorelei nodded and relaxed. Men must be tested. Even fathers. She stopped straining toward her father and her friends relaxed their grip just enough for her to move two steps towards him.

"Dad? Why?"

Dad paused. He clearly didn't want to mess up his answer and lose his only chance, so he took his time to think through the words he wanted to use. "I've never believed in the inferiority of women. I...your mother...never had anything to fear from me, and she knew it. We had...a good relationship. We loved each other. We weren't always intimate, no, but we were always comfortable. I hoped...I hoped...we would find that sort of relationship for you, but...Ogden...wasn't all we hoped."

"It wasn't your fault." Lorelei put her hand on her father's arm. "It was..." She stopped. She had no idea whose fault it was, and realized it might have been his.

"Your grandfather." Dad paused, then looked away. "I...I allowed my father to make the selection. I had no idea how to begin. I didn't want you to marry."

Lorelei stared. "Not want me to marry? Why not? All women marry." She shot a glance at Linolin, and her friend laughed.

"You were...are...smart. You have spirit. You were not meant to be locked into a kitchen. When it came right down to it, I couldn't do it. I thought my dad...he did such a good job...with your mother and me..."

"He's telling the truth."

Lorelei jumped when she heard her mother's voice. None of them saw her come up the hallway and enter the room until she spoke. Now Lorelei moved to her mother's side and locked arms with her.

"Elyria!" Dad held out his arms to Mom.

"Sandon, why are you here?" Mom stared at her husband, daring him to lie to her.

"I want to join you. I want to be one of you."

"None of the women are with their men right now. It's our agreement."

"That's all right. I'll stay with the other men. I just...want to...be part of something I believe in, something I should have started myself long ago. I didn't have the courage. I needed the comfort of the usual routines."

"So why now?" Lorelei stood firm beside her mother, two women challenging the man who had been so much a part of their life for so long.

"Because…you have shown me what courage looks like. You have shown me what courage can do. I have never seen anyone do what you women did, never seen anyone dare what you women dared…you inspired me. I want to learn how to be like you." Her father stared at his hat as if surprised to see it in his hands. He couldn't look in their eyes.

"No man can join without proving they are trustworthy." Linolin stepped forward and joined the conversation for the first time, sensing the other two women were not able to deal with the decision.

"I am willing. What do I have to do?"

Amity and Linolin presented Lorelei's father with his options. First, he must get the approval of his wife and daughter. If they were willing, he could undergo the tests they had devised. If he passed the tests, he could stay.

"And if I don't?"

"We'll have to kill you." Resenta spoke just behind Lorelei's ear, causing her to jump.

"What?" Her father shrieked.

"You know too much." Resenta winked at Lorelei.

Lorelei nodded, picking up Resenta's cue. "That's right. We can't allow any man to walk out of here alive once he has found our location. It's for our safety, you understand." She stared at her father, a cool detached look in her eyes, and challenged him.

He rose to the occasion. "I understand. I'm prepared."

Linolin looked at Lorelei and her mother, still locked arm in arm as if forming a human chain against the risk presented by the man who cowered in front of them. Lorelei whispered with Mom, but it was mostly for show. They had already made up their mind. They whispered for a few moments, acting like they were arguing, and then agreed to allow him to be tested. If he passed the tests, they were willing to have him enter the fortress.

Lorelei remained behind as Linolin and Amity led her father off to be tested. She and Mom collapsed in each other's arms, exhausted. It drained their energy to remain cool and play the game. Now all they could do was wait.

"And pray", Mom whispered.

Lorelei nodded. "And pray."

Resenta stuck her head between those of the two women, her chin resting on their shoulders. "Don't worry", she whispered. "He'll pass."

56

Dad passed the tests and moved his things into the half-finished men's wing. The working women raced time monster to get a cot built for him before bedtime. Security registered his fingerprints and assigned him a number, something they started doing after the false intruder alert made them aware they needed to check people off more easily during lockdowns. Now he entered the small office shared by Linolin and Lorelei and stood before his daughter, his head bowed in humility and appreciation.

"Dad", Lorelei said. "You don't need to do that. We are all equals here."

Dad nodded and sat in the chair she indicated. It was time to set his assignments in the fortress, and Lorelei paused with pen over paper and wondered. What does one do with an ex-archaeologist? What possible role could he fill here, where tasks were more physical? She wasn't prepared to let any of the management duties go to a man. Those were jobs for the women, and they were all filled with talented, capable women.

"Okay, so, what can you do?"

Lorelei pushed a paper toward him, filled with the lists of jobs that needed doing at the fortress. Her father took the pen and hesitated, reading each job carefully. He placed checkmarks before all the jobs he felt capable of performing, and pushed the list back toward his daughter. She stared with astonishment at the checks he had made. If he was telling the truth, he had a lot more skills and talents than she ever realized.

"You can do construction?"

He nodded, and explained that building things was actually part of the job of an archaeologist. They often needed things at the site that weren't available, and had to build them on the spot. One by one, they moved through the list and verified the skills he claimed. Lorelei looked at him with new admiration. Clearly this man had much more to him than he ever demonstrated to his women. How many other men, she wondered, possessed such a wide variety of skills? Was Ogden able to do all these things?

Lorelei examined the duty rosters and plugged her father into several roles where help was needed. He, like the rest of them, would not serve only one function, but would move through jobs that needed to be done. Plus, she informed him, he would be required to take classes on cooking and cleaning like all the men. The women delighted in facing classes of incompetent men and teaching them basic survival skills.

Once the official duties were over, Lorelei relaxed and settled in for a chat with her father. She wanted to find out what was going on outside, and how the men were faring without the women. This was the most important first role men played when they entered the fortress – a connection with the outside world that helped the women determine what impact the walk out was having, if any.

Dad was eager to talk. He missed his family, and wanted to visit with his daughter. It was the first time he'd seen either of his women since the day of the march. "Ogden came by the night of the march", he began. "He was in a state of chaos. I was sympathetic. I didn't know what to do, either. Then he admitted what he had done to you, and I decided I was going to throw him out."

Lorelei didn't say anything. She wanted to hear about Ogden, but she didn't want to appear like she wanted to hear about him. Showing any interest in individual men could jeopardize the mission at this early stage. She mustn't let any of them know she cared about them, and she had already been too openly eager to see her father. She put on her best detached face and waited.

"He was afraid he'd killed you. We were all afraid he'd killed you. All your brothers wanted to…well, the things they wanted to do to him were not possible, and he had acted legally, so…" Father paused, collecting his thoughts. "No one knew whether you were even alive until Ogden visited that…unmarried woman…you know who I mean?"

"Linolin." Lorelei was terse. She wanted to get information, not give it.

"Linolin. She's here, right?" Lorelei nodded. "Anyway, she told us you were alive, and were going to be okay…she wouldn't tell us anything else, like, where you were or who was with you, or what you were doing."

Father paused. His shoulders heaved a few times as though he was crying, but he didn't emit any sound. Lorelei didn't move to comfort him, though she ached to put her arms around him and tell him it would be all right. She was a warrior now, and she needed to act like a warrior. She waited, watching him until he collected himself and could speak again.

"Ogden came around all the time…he needed…comfort, I guess. I wasn't able to give it, because I blamed him. I thought…if he had been a better husband, if he had given you what you needed, if he hadn't beaten you, none of this would have happened. We would still have our wives and our children. He was devastated when the children disappeared, too."

Lorelei decided it was time for her to speak. She steeled herself to make sure no emotion showed in her voice. "How…did you find us?"

"I followed Ogden. He looked for you every day. I realized yesterday, when he was in here so long…he had found you." Dad looked her in the eyes for the first time, as if daring her to criticize him.

"Good. I was afraid it was getting too easy to figure out where we were." Lorelei was still cold in her manner, but she allowed a trace of warmth to creep into her voice.

"I realized…oh, maybe about a week ago…this wasn't about him and you. This wasn't about whether he was good to you or not. This was about all women, not just whether you were happy with Ogden."

Lorelei hesitated. This was something she'd thought about often. If she had been happy in her marriage, happy in her role as a good wife, would she have been able to summon the empathy and courage needed to lead the other women to freedom? She hoped the answer was yes, but realized it was probably no. So in a way, he was right. It was about Ogden…and her. She thought about how she considered calling it off when she and Ogden started getting along. It was an aspect of the mission that disturbed her, and she didn't like thinking about, and here was her father reminding her again that she wasn't really much better than they were. She decided to change the subject.

"How are the men getting along?"

"Not well. None of us ever learned to cook, you know. It was assumed we would have wives to do that for us, and the men who didn't marry could rely on their mothers and sisters. Now that all the wives…and all the mothers…are missing, we're pretty stumped. We know all these things, but we don't have the skills to take care of ourselves."

"How did you manage when you were away from home on a dig?" Lorelei asked the question that had bothered her for some time, even before she began exploring Ogden's papers.

"We had a woman...sometimes several...to cook." Her father looked sheepish.

"You had women on the digs?" Lorelei couldn't hide her astonishment. "Ogden never told me that."

"Did he ever tell you anything about his work?" Lorelei shook her head. "None of us told. Good wives were not supposed to know there were working women. It was assumed it would disturb you, make you unhappy. And...well, some of the men were...less than...discreet with the women. Not Ogden", he hastened to add. "Ogden never did anything like that. Corydon, of course. Lymon. Even Merris a few times. But never Ogden."

"Merris?" Lorelei felt her voice come out in a squeak, alerting her father to her shock. The one thing Amity had been sure of about her husband was that he was faithful, and never sought marital duties elsewhere. Now it turned out even that was a lie. She stared at her father through new eyes. "Did any of you ever tell the truth about anything?"

Dad nodded. "I never lied to your mother...well, she didn't know about the cooking women, but I didn't do anything with them. I would never treat your mother that way. And I don't think Ogden ever lied."

"He lied about the dig."

"Yes. He had to...it was his job."

Lorelei stood and turned her back. She couldn't continue watching her father, feeling the conflicting emotions that threatened to tear her apart. She remembered the letter in his papers where he outlined the plan to lie, and the project. It didn't come from above, Ogden suggested it himself. Her answer was muffled with anger and tears she couldn't let her father see.

"His job. It was his job to ensure that women never realized their own potential. And you went along with it."

"Yes. I'm not proud of that. I didn't like it, I didn't want to do it, but the instructions came from the top. The Imperial Leader himself gave the order, and I was not in a position to disobey."

236

Lorelei watched her father's face, reflected in the glass window. She saw no sign of duplicity, only pain and shame. She decided to believe him.

"Lorelei, your plan is working. The men are ready to negotiate."

Lorelei turned and leaned over the desk, resting her palms on the solid top. "Are they ready to see us as equals?"

"No. They're ready to negotiate better terms for your marriages, but they aren't ready to give you new roles."

"Then we are not ready to negotiate. We will not take a half loaf like our suffragist sisters before us. That was their mistake, and why they never won complete equality. We will not make the same mistake."

Dad nodded. This was the daughter he believed in, the one he had wanted to protect from the restrictions of marriage. "I thought you'd say that. I think...if you can make this last...you'll get what you want. The men are discovering how much you did for them, and the amount of intelligence it required. Now if they can just translate their knowledge into humility, it could still work."

Lorelei nodded. The conversation was over. She needed to get back to work so the mission had a fighting chance to succeed. She motioned her father toward the door, but he wasn't ready to go. He handed her a slip of paper with numbers on it, written in a careful hand so they could be read without difficulty.

"What is this?"

"The numbers to a bank account I established for the shelter."

"Fortress. We are not helpless women needing shelter, we are warriors."

"Fortress. I like that. Anyway, it contains everything I owned...it is yours to ensure you can keep this going. Here, this number...that's the amount you have to work with."

Lorelei stared at the number her father indicated. She knew he was comfortable and made a good living. She had no idea he was so wealthy. Of course, since men never discussed finances with women, how could she know?

"Just give the bank this number. It's anonymous. It won't give you away to use the money."

Lorelei nodded, her eyes still on the slip of paper. This could keep the mission going long enough to ensure success.

"I also have some suggestions I'd like to run by you at a later date, when you have more time to spare. I think you could make this shelter...fortress...self-sufficient. Grow your own food, sell things for money...making your own money means you wouldn't have to rely on men to help you out."

Dad grabbed his hat off the desk and was out the door before Lorelei could speak, or even thank him. She watched his retreating back, then returned to work. She would definitely have to explore that self-sufficiency thing as soon as she had time. Right now, management duties demanded her immediate attention.

57

Linolin stared at the paper Lorelei thrust into her hands, her face wet with tears. These were tears of joy, not fear. "Do you know what this means? We can keep this place going for years." She let out a whoop that could have alerted the entire city to their presence if the walls weren't so thick. She grabbed Lorelei and spun her in a dance around the room, until Lorelei was ready to collapse from pain. "Oh, I've hurt you! I'm sorry. I forget my own strength when I get so enthusiastic."

Lorelei nodded. She gasped for breath and fanned herself. The dance was energetic, and she sank into the chair to recover. Linolin perched on the edge of the desk, her long legs tucked behind her as she watched women through the mirror carry out the tasks required to maintain a busy community. She tapped her pencil on a paper she brought with her, and turned to business.

"Thirteen." Linolin announced the number as though Lorelei knew what she was talking about. At the puzzled look of her friend and office mate, she realized she needed to explain. "Thirteen women remain trapped in their homes. We've managed to get the rest out, except the two who died..." Linolin paused, remembering the lovely women who were found in such serious shape that they died before they could get them to the fortress. "Thirteen. We need to get them out. I have no idea if they can even walk on their own, but we know they're locked in. We're getting intelligence every day."

"What should we do?" Lorelei had no idea how one went about rescuing women who were locked into their homes by their husbands. Over a hundred women had been rescued from their homes, but the rescue missions took place while she was recovering from her own wounds.

"We need to stage a raid."

"Can we do that?" The idea frightened Lorelei. It sounded like something beyond their capacity.

"I've been talking with Stone. We drew up a plan, and he and I are going in to get them tonight."

Lorelei shook her head. "It's too dangerous."

"We must. These women are in grave danger, and if I'm not willing to face a little danger to get them out, what sort of friend am I?" Linolin stared into Lorelei's face and nodded. "I see you agree.

Good. I have little to lose, and I haven't suffered. I feel sometimes like I don't belong here with all the brave women who risked everything and suffered for your bravery."

Lorelei hugged her friend. "Of course you belong here. How would we have done it without you? And Manx…" Lorelei winced as pain shot from one of her still healing wounds. "I owe him…both of you…my life."

"Then we go tonight."

"Yes. We go tonight."

Linolin stopped, about to exit, and turned back to Lorelei. "No. Not you. Me. And Stone. You will remain here, safe. You've done enough."

"I won't let you go without me. I am well enough."

"The risk…they want you more than any of the rest of us. You are the prize. If they get you, they get the whole group. At least, that's what they believe, and they're prepared to torture you to get that."

"I know. I'm still ready to go. You can't stop me, because I will follow you."

Linolin argued for several more minutes, but Lorelei stood her ground. She was not going to sit in the fortress and worry while her friends were outside facing a danger she understood better than either of them. She understood the homes, the routines, the things that would be done to keep women locked in. They needed her, and Linolin gave in, realizing everything she said was true.

The two women spent the next hour going over the plan. Lorelei was astonished by the audacity of it, just slipping through town under the cover of darkness and grabbing women right out of their homes.

"The women all know we will be coming. We found a way to get a message through, since they are still required to answer voice monster. Thanks for that code you loaned us. You and Amity are quite a pair."

"We never thought we'd use our code for anything like this. We only used it for talking about more interesting things than we were supposed to be talking about. I'm glad it finally is getting some real use."

Lorelei was in her room getting ready for the raid when she felt someone watching her. She whirled, and breathed in relief when she saw it was Grenata. "Don't creep up on me like that! You terrified me."

"I'm sorry. I…wanted to talk to you." Grenata hesitated, but crept over the doorsill when Lorelei invited her to come in. "I'm sorry, I guess you probably think I'm avoiding you."

"It does sort of seem like that. You scurry the other way whenever I'm near. What's wrong?"

"You know. You saw. How can you ever tolerate the sight of me again?" Grenata raised her hand as Lorelei started to speak, and continued. "Yes, I know, I've been the one you had to tolerate, the one who didn't fit, the strange and out of step one. I hoped, when we started this, I might find a place…but…I'm still strange. Still out of place. How could I have expected for people…other women…to like me? I couldn't even manage the basics of being a woman."

Lorelei drew Grenata into her arms and stroked her hair. "We like you…we all like you. Yes, you were different, but that wasn't a bad thing. It made you interesting. It made you alive, in a world where most women were dead. Now all the women are alive, and you are the most alive of all of us. You've never allowed a man to rule you, not completely. I gave in, I took the easy way out, and lived a much easier life than any of my friends. But you never gave in. You never gave up that spark that made you…made you…Grenata."

Grenata pulled out of her friend's embrace. "Yes, but…with what you saw…how can you…how can you…stand to even look at me?"

Lorelei laughed, not a mocking laugh but a friendly laugh. "Dear dear Grenata, I've been working side by side with Linolin ever since that day. Our relationship hasn't changed. Why did you think I would be different with you?"

"You don't understand, do you?"

"No, I don't. I wish I did, but…it seems strange and unnatural. I just…maybe…you could help. Tell me what you feel."

Grenata opened up, and years of pain and suffering flowed out. It wasn't just Lymon and the abuse. It was the marital duties, something she hated even more than the other women. She never developed any interest in being a wife, and she felt strange when other women were around. When she met Lorelei in college…Grenata paused, gulped, and plunged on…she felt…like…she wanted to marry her. She was promised to Lymon, but here was someone she could love and live with. But Lorelei didn't notice her, not in that way. She was just a friend. She thought about running away, finding a way not to marry Lymon, but she realized marrying him would keep her close to the woman she loved...yes, loved, she said defiantly as if Lorelei was about to protest.

When Linolin took her in, the attraction was immediate. She hated to think of living anywhere else, but the men found her and made her go back to that...that...beast. She cried all the time, and he mocked her for her tears. He made her do extra marital duties just because he knew she hated them. He knew...he always knew...and he treated her worse because of her devotion to Lorelei. When he realized she had fallen in love with Linolin, he vowed she would never see that evil woman again. Well, thanks to her friends, she had...and she discovered that Linolin felt the same way about her.

"I know you think it's wrong. I know you don't approve. But...I can't help it. I'm not like you, or Amity, or Corinne. I don't want to give up Linolin, but I will if you will just be my friend again."

Grenata stopped, exhausted from spilling out her heart. Lorelei patted the bed beside her and Grenata sat, staying far away from Lorelei until she knew the other woman's thoughts. Lorelei watched her friend and saw things in her face she'd never noticed before. She had no idea anyone felt that way about her, and in the course of a few months, she found out that two people loved her. It was a lot to assimilate.

"I've never stopped being your friend." Lorelei selected her words carefully. "I wish you'd told me how you felt about me."

"Would you have understood?" Grenata asked her the same question she asked Ogden, and she winced.

"Probably not. It's still new to me, you understand. I've lived my entire life as a good wife, and never knew women could feel that way about women. But you've always been my friend, you will always be my friend, and I would never ask you to give up Linolin. If you're happy...I've always wanted to see you happy."

Grenata smiled with a joy Lorelei had never seen in her before. She grabbed her friend in a giant embrace, releasing her when she winced. "Oh! I hurt you. I'm so sorry!"

"Don't worry about it. I can handle affection. Just...hug me on this side next time, okay?" Lorelei smiled to let her know there were no hard feelings.

"I wish I were going with you tonight."

"I do too, in a way, but the plan would be spoiled with too many people. Don't worry, we'll tell you all about it when we get back. Now hurry to dinner. I have to finish getting ready before I come down. We'll talk later, okay?"

Grenata left, and Lorelei finished her preparations, a new spring in her step. She was doing something that mattered, and she was finally seeing her friends happy. Her father was settling into the men's wing. Her mother was singing as she prepared hot beverage in the kitchen. Today could turn out to be the best day yet.

58

Lorelei and Linolin slipped out just after dinner. The sun was setting; darkness would be their cover. Lorelei pinned and tucked to fit Linolin's pants to her smaller frame, but now she realized why Linolin wore pants. They were comfortable, and they made sense. They wore black, and their faces were painted a shade of black that would keep them from shining in any lights that might pass. There was no moon tonight, so there was little risk of being seen.

Each of them held their hands in their pockets, wrapped around a small bottle of something Stone called 'pepper spray'. He said it wasn't really pepper, it was something else, but that was what the old sources called it. He spent several days in the kitchen alongside the women, using their pots and pans to cook up a concoction that could be used against any man who tried to detain them. He was making larger batches every day, so they would always have some available whenever a woman needed to venture out of the fortress.

They were timing their raid for after dinner because the women would still be in their kitchens. "Probably locked in", Lorelei growled. Her knowledge of the routines served them well, and the women all lived in Lorelei's old neighborhood; all the other neighborhoods had been cleared. Most of the houses in that section of town were built on a similar floor plan, with the kitchen in the back. The women were instructed to be as close to the laundry room window as possible so they could see the commandos – Lorelei liked that word – approach.

They crept around the fortress, staying behind anything that could shield them. They didn't want to risk being seen until they were far enough away from the fortress that they would not reveal its location. Stone joined them on the other side of the building, and the three crept toward the residential zone, dropping and crawling when they had to pass an area where they might be spotted. Few people were out at this hour, and their route and manner of dress would be likely to mark them as suspicious.

The group reached the first house, only a few doors from where Lorelei had lived with Ogden. Linolin felt her friend tense, and gave her hand a squeeze. "I'm right beside you" was all she said, but it was enough.

Stone slipped the lock on the back gate, and the three slipped through. There was a single light in the back of the house, a light in what would be the kitchen. The only other light was upstairs; Lorelei told them that was probably where the husband had his study.

They dropped to their knees and crawled through the backyard. Lorelei shuddered at the memory of her own escape using the same method. She remembered she was a commando and courage surged through her, allowing her to move forward without fear...well, at least without fear of Ogden. She ignored the pain in her back, determined to complete the mission.

Lawanda, one of her mother's Thursday group, was waiting at the laundry room window as instructed. The laundry room was dark; only the small light over the sink provided illumination to see as Lawanda tried to open the window. It was no use. Her husband thought of that possibility and installed a lock on the outside. Stone went to work with a small tool kit and soon had the lock open. Lorelei was astonished that he could do it without a sound, but the lock fell away and Lawanda was free.

As soon as she was out the window, she dropped to her knees. The four crawled to the back gate. When they were free of the yard, Stone re-latched the gate and they were able to stand, except Linolin who had to crouch because she was so tall her head showed over the fence. Lorelei realized she was holding her breath, and released it in an enormous sigh.

Lawanda received instructions from the group and headed off on a pre-planned route toward the fortress. She was now clothed in a black garment that covered her from head to foot so she could be hidden in the night. Linolin closed the pack that held twelve more garments, and the three headed toward the next home where the next woman waited in tense darkness, hoping her salvation would arrive safely and free her from bondage in her own home.

The next several rescues went equally well, though there was a tense moment at the house next door to where Resenta suffered so long. The husband installed some sort of alert system, and showed up just as his wife disappeared out the window. He grabbed out the window and got his hands on Lorelei, who was helping the woman climb out a window too high to safely get out by herself. She froze in panic, then remembered her spray. Using her free arm, she lifted the tiny canister and pushed the button, aiming for his eyes as Stone had taught her. It didn't seem like much protection, but the man holding her yelped and released her arm, screaming in pain.

Linolin frowned. "We're going to have to do something. If that man manages to get to voice monster, he'll alert everyone. We won't be able to release another woman…not tonight, not ever."

Stone nodded and crawled through the window. They heard sounds of scuffling inside, then Stone reappeared, his fist high in the air in the standard group salute. He succeeded, but at what? Lorelei didn't have long to wait for the answer. He was puffed up by success and proud of his accomplishment.

"You won't have to worry about him. He's tied to cold box. He won't be able to move until someone finds him, probably in the morning." Stone grinned.

Linolin gave him a fist bump and Lorelei patted him on the back. Her arm hurt, bruised where the man grabbed it, but that would not prevent her from proceeding. She was part of this team, and she would remain part of this team.

Astra, the woman they rescued, had not said a word. She yelped in terror when her husband's arm came out the window, and she beat at him while he held Lorelei, but she hadn't made a sound since Lorelei sprayed him. Now she burst out sobbing in fear and relief.

"You go back to the fortress", Linolin told her, rocking the sobbing woman in her arms. "Report to Amity; she'll sign you in. Then I want you to have a check up, so go to Dr. Maestro immediately after sign in. Can you do that?"

Astra nodded. She was one of the younger women, and one of the smaller ones, and the entire procedure scared her from the beginning. She overcame her fear and joined the march with the rest, her signs held high, three yellow sashes lined up across her white dress. The bruises on her face and arms suggested she had been beaten, but she had not given her husband any information. None of the women had. Now she dropped to her knees with the others and crawled through the dark to the gate. She donned a black garment and headed toward the fortress, ready to rejoin her fellow warriors.

"Seven down." Linolin looked up from her list. "Only six left. We're more than halfway there, and only one major incident."

"It's too soon to congratulate ourselves", Lorelei said. "There are still six more chances to fail, and we want to guard against too much confidence."

Linolin didn't speak. She hugged Lorelei as if worried she would never see her again. Lorelei understood. None of them knew what would lie in wait for them at the other houses. They knew Astra's husband hadn't been able to get to voice monster because he was still on the floor in pain when Stone got to him, but that didn't mean there wouldn't be leaks or weak spots. Six more chances for the men to win.

The next house was close, and they crept through the backyard as they had done at the other houses. The window was open and Lorelei stepped toward it, waiting for Liata, their current rescue. Her heart nearly stopped when a male head popped out the window. Seeing Lorelei, he nodded and disappeared. Lorelei motioned for Linolin and Stone to stand close. She might need more than her spray this time, because the man seemed to be waiting for them. He was likely prepared.

The face appeared again, a face younger than Lorelei expected. This was another of her mother's group, and none of those women were young enough to have such a young husband. The young man whispered behind him and motioned to Lorelei to move closer. Lorelei inched a single step closer, Stone and Linolin pressed against her on either side. The young man leaned out the window and whispered to the group.

"Dad is gone for a few minutes. I got him out of the house. I'm going to help Mom get out, but I needed to be sure you were legitimate. This could have been a trap."

The face disappeared, and another face, a familiar face, appeared. Liata was framed in the window for a mere second before her son lifted her and handed her out the window, feet first, to the waiting group. Stone grabbed the woman and helped her son ease her to the ground, where she dropped to her knees as instructed by Linolin.

"Take good care of her", the son whispered. "She's a grand woman. She doesn't deserve what Pop did to her. She needs to see a medic."

The young man disappeared and the window closed behind him. Linolin was on her knees beside Liata, who appeared to be in pain. Lorelei dropped beside her on the other side, and the two women helped her crawl across the yard. When they were safely outside the gate, they helped her to her feet. She winced as she stood, and leaned on Stone for support.

"I couldn't have gotten out the window by myself", she whispered. "If it hadn't been for Cameron, I would have died in there."

Linolin hesitated. "Should we send her to the fortress by herself? She might not be able to make it in the shape she's in."

Lorelei agreed. She knew better than Linolin what the woman was suffering, and she didn't know how she would walk back. Stone motioned into the darkness and a young man who was hovering nearby galloped into view. The young man was also dressed in black, and had his face painted like the commandos.

"Marsden, you need to take Liata back to the fortress. She's not going to be able to make it on her own." The young man nodded and lifted the black garbed woman in his arms. At his instruction, Liata wrapped her arms around his neck. He would carry her back to the fortress where Manx would be waiting. He loped off into the darkness, carrying his cargo as if she were a precious treasure.

"And who was that?" Linolin demanded.

"Marsden."

"I know that. I recognized him. Why was he here?"

Stone shrugged. "I thought it wouldn't be a bad idea to have an extra security detail. They've been behind us the whole time, just in case they were needed. I know you women are amazing, but...if the men were armed, or in a group...you might need some help."

Linolin laughed. "You are something, aren't you? I'm so glad you're on our side. But...you should have told us. We almost certainly would not have protested. Right, Lorelei?"

Lorelei nodded. She felt safer now that she knew there was help if they needed it, but she hoped the additional forces didn't alert the men to their presence. Stone assured her his men were trained in stealth, and knew the risks of the mission.

The remainder of the rescues went off without a hitch. Lorelei and Linolin crept through backyards, collected women, and sent them to the fortress. Stone mostly stood back, a security presence should it be needed. Three other women needed to be carried to the fortress, and the women realized the added importance of Stone's extra precautions. Having someone who could carry a grown woman halfway across town was a definite benefit.

Lorelei and Linolin settled in the dining hall with hot beverage. They were exhausted, but it was the kind of exhaustion that exhilarates and energizes. They were still pumped up and knew it would be a long time before they would get a good rest. Linolin was planning to sleep at the fortress so if anything happened she would be present to help. They expected problems in the morning, after the men discovered their wives missing.

"Would you do something for me?" Lorelei didn't look at Linolin as she spoke.

"I will do anything for you…if it's in my power." Linolin put a hand on her friend's arm.

Lorelei went to the kitchen and returned with a pair of scissors. "Cut my hair."

Linolin took the scissors as though they were a serpent. "Are you sure? It's a big step…you've been growing your hair…how long?"

"Since I was…seven." Lorelei gulped. It was a big step. "All the women…none of us were allowed to choose how to wear our hair. I'm going to cut it because I can."

She settled in the chair and closed her eyes, not wanting to see as Linolin removed the curls that cascaded down her back. She heard the click-click of the scissors and felt her head grow lighter as the hair fell away. When Linolin finished, she ran her hands through her hair; it felt different.

"I didn't cut it really short", Linolin said. "I thought…that might be too much. I just cut it to your shoulders."

Lorelei looked at herself in the mirror Linolin handed her. She looked different. She was a new woman. She would need to get used to it, but…well, it looked…good. Maybe.

The brown locks lying on the floor didn't feel like they were hers at all; they belonged to the good wife, and the good wife was dead. Lorelei was free.

59

After the raids, the fortress settled back down to business and things remained quiet for several days. The mood was tense at first, but the women gradually relaxed and celebrated the successful raid once they realized the angry men had not found them. The thirteen rescued women remained in Manx's care until he pronounced them fit, and they received many visitors who were anxious to be reunited with old friends.

Lorelei and Linolin continued to manage the logistics while helping out with the actual labor of the place wherever possible. Grenata spent most of her time painting, but managed to perform her assigned tasks with an enthusiasm she never showed for the work while married to Lymon. Mom and Dad spent evenings sitting quietly in the lounge, not speaking, just holding hands. Amity continued to work and study with Manx, and Corinne bustled around making sure everything was moving smoothly. And it was.

Security relaxed as the days went by without another intruder. It was evident Ogden hadn't told anyone where they were...although the thought did go through Lorelei's mind, and she suspected through Linolin's, that the men could be lying in wait, lulling them into a false sense of security before they struck. She stared at the opal, which rested in a drawer in her room, and wondered what was happening outside. It wasn't safe for any of them to venture out even after dark; the successful raids led to increased vigilance and anger among the men. They made sure all needed supplies were fully stocked before the plan was put into action. Now all that was left was to wait.

Wait for what? Lorelei wasn't sure what to expect next. Something should happen, but who would make the next move? When? Her question was answered about a week after the raids when a loud noise penetrated the thick walls of the fortress. Lorelei and Linolin snuck outside through the hidden door and hid behind the shrubs to listen.

"Women of the town. We know you are somewhere in this town. We are ready to negotiate. Send the two women...the ones who led you...to the downtown archaeology building at noon tomorrow, and we will talk about terms. We repeat, we are ready to negotiate."

The message was repeated over and over on a voice amplifier attached to a mini-transit that appeared to be cruising the entire town, blaring the message into the empty sky hoping some woman would hear and report back. The message ended with the assurance that the women would be safe and treated with respect. The men wanted to talk. They were ready to come to terms. Send out the two women…Lorelei winced as she realized the men either didn't bother to learn the names of the women, or treated them with the disrespect of not saying them, but she understood exactly who they meant. They wanted to talk to her and to Linolin.

The two women huddled in their office discussing the situation and the appropriate response. Resenta burst in, followed by Grenata. They had heard. All the women heard.

"We're not letting you go." Resenta was adamant.

Grenata nodded. "It's too dangerous. They could be lying."

Linolin agreed. "Yes, they could be lying. But what choice do we have? We can't know for sure unless we accept the offer."

"So take Stone along, and his security." Grenata crossed her arms across her chest, firm in her demand that the women she loved not be put at risk.

"We can't. We must go alone. That is what they're demanding." Lorelei spoke for the first time, her voice as firm as Grenata's, her determination as strong.

In the end, it was decided the women would go. The final decision was made by the group as a whole, at Resenta's insistence. The discussion raged throughout the day, culminating just before dinner, and the vote was close. The decision hinged on a single vote and every head turned in Amity's direction, the only woman who had not yet expressed her opinion.

"I think they should go." Amity looked from face to face, acknowledging the fear, but understanding the need for direct action. "If they don't go…we might be here forever. I like it here, don't get me wrong, but I want to be able to walk free. I want to at least be able to go to book room or the park again, to take my children to child mover, or just breathe the air. We all want that. That's why we did this, for freedom, not to spend the rest of our days locked in a fortress. I vote go."

Lorelei and Linolin left the shelter the next morning and weaved through the most circuitous of all their routes, the one most designed to confuse anyone who might follow. They darted behind trees and buildings whenever anyone approached, until they were on a route that would lead anyone watching away from the fortress.

They appeared in full view at the opposite end of town from the fortress and marched with firm steps and heads held high to the large downtown office where Lorelei attended the staff function. They hesitated in front of the big glass door, aware of male eyes staring at them from every window in town, wondering what was going to happen now.

They were greeted by a young man who addressed them with courtesy and led them toward a moving stair. They were swept upstairs and into an office that contained only a desk and three chairs. Clearly this was going to be a small delegation, or else they were not at their final destination. They perched on the edges of the chairs in front of the desk, trying not to look nervous and looking more nervous in the process.

The door in the opposite wall swung wide and a large man moved through and settled across the desk from them. The two women took note of his disheveled state. His suit was unwashed and unpressed, and he had noticeable food spots on his shirt and tie. Linolin winked at Lorelei. This was a good sign.

The man introduced himself as Falwell, Chief Archaeologist, and told them he was going to be in charge of leading the negotiations. He wanted to do some preliminary work before they met the rest of the negotiating team. The women nodded.

"So, I need to have your full names."

The two women provided the information. Falwell noted it on a card, taking pains to check the spelling. He looked at the names for several seconds after he wrote them, as if memorizing every line stroke.

"Your husband's names?"

Linolin smiled. "We have no husbands."

Falwell stared at Lorelei. "No husbands?"

"None." Lorelei held his gaze until he dropped his eyes and wrote 'none' in the space on the form. She noticed his hand faltered as he wrote it beside her name; she was sure he knew who she was, even though she never met him before.

"Now, your address."

Linolin shook her head. "Sorry, we can't reveal that at this time."

"It's an official record. We must have an address."

Lorelei nodded and gave him the address of book room. He wrote it down, then stared at it. He grabbed a large book and cross checked the address. He frowned at the women.

"You do not live at book room."

"You know we can't give you that information at this time." Lorelei stared straight at the man, daring him to…what?

"This is an official government procedure. We must have the proper paperwork on file. You are not negotiating in good faith."

Linolin frowned. "You are the ones who are not negotiating in good faith. You insist on us giving you information that could compromise our position in the negotiation. We cannot give you that unless and until an agreement is reached."

Falwell nodded. Lorelei suspected he hadn't intended to win easily. After all, he had to know that at least one of the women sitting in front of him had been given a severe beating and had not revealed the location of the facility. The women were strong, and he bowed his head in acknowledgement of their strength. He stood and extended his hand toward first Lorelei, then Linolin.

"I like you. You're going to be good negotiators. We'll begin as soon as we assemble the rest of the team in the negotiating room."

Falwell exited as abruptly as he entered. Lorelei and Linolin watched the door where he disappeared. They didn't hear the door behind them open, nor did they hear the soft footfalls across the carpeted floor. They were unaware there was someone else in the room until hands grabbed them out of the chairs and twisted their arms behind their backs.

Lorelei contorted to get a glimpse of the men holding her. There must be at least a dozen men in the room, she thought, right before one of them placed a soft cloth over her nose and mouth. She felt herself getting blurry, and then felt nothing.

60

Lorelei and Linolin woke almost simultaneously. They were in a cold, dark room that smelled musty. Their hands were twisted behind their backs and tied with ropes which were attached to something they could not see in the dark. They were side by side, so close their thighs were touching. There were no other restraints that they could tell, and they were able to adjust position until they were sitting against a wall.

"This…is…a…betrayal." Linolin spoke through clenched teeth.

"This is what Resenta and Grenata expected", Lorelei answered.

"They were right. I knew there was a possibility. But if we just stick to the plan, and stick together, we'll be fine." Linolin grunted and fidgeted, and Lorelei realized she was trying to untie the ropes around her wrists. "No, that's no good."

"Let me try."

Linolin shifted until she had her back to Lorelei. Lorelei fussed with the knots on the rope, her hands hardly able to work the knots because of her own ropes, and also because of her cold fingers. She persisted until she was able to free one of Linolin's hands.

"Let me rest and I can get the other."

Linolin nodded. She pulled her hand out of the loose rope and rested it on Lorelei's shoulder. Lorelei suspected she was smiling, but it was a grim smile that revealed more perhaps than she would want it to. It was a smile familiar to all the women, the smile Linolin always used when something was going badly.

Lorelei went back to work on the other hand after a few minutes. This one was easier to get free, because now Linolin could help. When the other woman was out of her ropes, she untied Lorelei. The two women stood and stretched.

"You don't suppose they'll have been stupid enough to leave the door unlocked, do you?"

Lorelei shook her head. "I think even these men aren't careless enough to leave unlocked doors just because they've tied us up. Those ropes weren't tight. They might have expected us to get loose."

Linolin nodded. "Just what I was thinking. Still, we should check, if we can find the door."

The two women moved around the room in opposite directions, feeling the wall for anything that felt like a door. They met in the middle, unsuccessful, and started around again, each now tracing the path the other had traveled. Lorelei cried with victory when her fingers encountered a switch. She flipped it up and the room flooded with light.

Lorelei and Linolin gasped simultaneously. The room was filled with bones, some nearly complete skeletons, and a lot of skulls. They looked at each other in horror…was this some sort of killing chamber? Were they being left here to die?

Lorelei recovered first. "No, of course not. This is an archaeology center, remember? They dig up bones. These are…specimens. Of course. Why would they have a killing chamber?"

Linolin relaxed. "Of course. I didn't think about it. They dig up old things, and these bones are probably old. Maybe even…you don't suppose some of these bones could be…our women?"

Lorelei shook her head. "I doubt it. Why would they dig up bones of ancient suffragists? They want to ignore the women, not study them."

The two women hugged, relieved. With the light on, they were able to see the door and headed in that direction, bumping into each other in their haste. They laughed and tried again, once again bumping into each other. Linolin bowed and gestured for Lorelei to go first. She did, and when they were both standing in front of the door she turned the knob. Nothing.

"Just like we thought. Locked."

"And possibly blockaded. Hey, don't archaeologists use axes, or something?" Linolin searched the room.

"I'm not sure. I never saw Ogden's tools. What I saw was mostly papers and a few artifacts. Anyway, I'm sure they wouldn't leave something like that lying around when they were planning to incarcerate two troublesome women in this room."

"Do you suppose they plan to kill us?"

Lorelei thought about that. "No, they could have done that already. I think…they want to know where the fortress is. They want the women back. We're no good to them dead."

"If we can retain our strength, we won't be much good to them alive, either." Linolin wore her grim smile.

The women heard footsteps approach. They turned off the light and rushed back to where they were when they woke, wrapping the useless ropes around their wrists. When the men entered and flipped the switch, the women blinked as if the sudden light blinded them.

"So, you're still tied up tight, huh, little honeys? Yeah, I didn't think you were smart enough to get out of your bonds. Ogden, he said you were smart. We laughed at him." The man who spoke stared into Lorelei's face, his face so close to hers she could feel his breath. "You're pretty, though."

The other men were wandering the room, stroking the skulls and skeletons with a sinister motion and a mean look. The women watched but didn't speak. Linolin grabbed Lorelei's hand and gave it a squeeze.

"We're just checking on you. Making sure you aren't getting into mischief." The same man was speaking again. The other men appeared to be just for show. "We'll be back…don't go anywhere."

The men laughed, and the room plunged into darkness. The only light now was from the hallway, but the women could see the cruel men framed in the doorway. The speaker spoke again.

"Your husband will be here soon, pretty lady. We're just waiting for him. He'll settle your hash, he will. He's promised us he won't go so easy on you this time."

The door closed with a click, and Linolin and Lorelei were again alone. Lorelei shrank in despair.

"Do you suppose…Ogden finked?"

Linolin moved across the room in only three steps and restored the light. She knelt beside Lorelei, reading the despair in her face. "I don't think so."

"But…"

"Listen. If Ogden finked, we wouldn't be here."

Lorelei puzzled over that. She shook her head, asking Linolin to explain.

"Ogden knows where the fortress is. They wouldn't need us if he was working with them, because he could lead them right to us. I bet he isn't in on this at all, or at the very least, he hasn't told them he knows where we are."

Lorelei understood. The voice amplifier, the subterfuge in the office, the official government paperwork…all of those things indicated the men did not have the information they wanted. Falwell tried to catch them off guard with the paperwork. Now they were kidnapped, and it was likely they were going to be held until they betrayed their friends.

"Why do you think they wanted us to get out of the ropes?"

Linolin shook her head. "That doesn't make sense."

"Maybe…it's the skulls."

"The skulls?"

Lorelei pulled her closer to one of the tables full of bones. "They think…because we're women…we'll be terrified by the bones. So they wanted us to turn on the lights…see the bones…fall into their arms for protection."

"They think we're weak."

"Do you think…they'll torture us?"

Linolin nodded. "I think they'll try whatever it takes. They want the women back, and they're used to treating women with violence."

"They're also used to it working. Women have been trained to answer commands given by men."

"You've been strong this long. All you have to do is hold out as long as you can. I wasn't trained that way, so I just have to endure whatever pain they give us. I'll be beside you…you'll be beside me. We'll be strong."

Lorelei hoped Linolin was right. She knew from experience the level of cruelty these men could dish out. Even though Ogden had never done more than beat her and lock her in the kitchen, she knew from her friends that many men were much more brutal. Broken bones were common. Concussions were frequent. Some women were cut with knives and burned with matches, or had their hands held on hot box until they were so badly burned they almost lost the hand. Several women had their heads held in the sink or the toilet until they nearly drowned. She whispered these things to Linolin, who nodded. They were no surprise to her, after years of dealing with battered wives.

"We'll manage", was all she said.

"We have to manage."

61

Linolin was the first to be taken. The same men who visited them earlier came in later...Lorelei couldn't be sure how long because her time monster was broken...and dragged Linolin out. Lorelei managed a grim smile when they didn't try to carry the woman who was taller than at least two of them. They weren't going to have it easy with Linolin.

When they brought her back, she was barely conscious. Lorelei knelt beside her friend, stroking her hand, wishing Manx was with them. She had no idea what to do to help, and Linolin had never experienced a beating before. Lorelei turned her over and checked every inch of her body. There were no bleeding wounds, at least. Lorelei wasn't sure what to do with bleeding wounds if there was no bandage box.

Linolin mumbled and groaned for what seemed an eternity. Lorelei continued to stroke her head and murmur soothing words. In here, there was little else she could do. After a long period of quiet, followed by a longer period of moaning, Linolin roused enough to speak.

"Shh. Don't talk. Save your energy."

Linolin shook her head. "No. I have to...prepare you. They'll...come for...you...next." She paused, her effort exhausting her. "They used some sort of...tool...not a belt...some sort of...black ...thing...they called it...rubber...they beat me...all over..."

"Did you...tell them anything?" Lorelei held her breath.

"No."

Linolin stopped speaking and fell into a troubled sleep, her moans piercing the room and causing Lorelei to shudder. She knew all too well the pain her friend was feeling. She wandered around the small room, examining the skulls as if they could tell her something, but their tags contained only numbers. She wondered if it would be possible to use the bones as weapons. She hefted one and realized it was very fragile, but tested others that seemed stronger. She hid one of the larger, stronger bones behind her, and another behind Linolin. Then she tried to sleep herself, which was difficult with the moans Linolin was uttering.

The men came back while they were asleep. She woke when the room flooded with light and saw the same man standing at her feet. She decided it was time to speak.

"Where's Ogden? You said he was going to come get me."

"He'll be here, pretty lady, don't worry. He'll be here in due time. Meanwhile, we thought you might like a preview of what he has planned."

The men grabbed her and untied her hands, apparently not noticing the knots were loose. She thrust her bone behind Linolin just in time, knowing she could not face five of them alone even with the weapon. It felt small and puny in her hands.

They carried her along the hall and down several flights of moving stairs. She struggled against their grip, but they were stronger than her, and there were five of them. She shoved her hands and feet against the wall, trying to prevent them from moving her down the stair, but they merely pried her feet off the wall and moved again.

"One more try on that, little lady, and we will break those bones." Speaking Man had an 'I really mean it' sound in his voice, and Lorelei decided not to try again.

They carried her into a small room with a long table in the center and no other furniture. She could see instruments lying on the table, and contorted to see what they were. She saw a black thing that resembled Linolin's description, but nothing else was familiar. They looked like some of the tools Manx used but she didn't know what they were for.

They dropped her on the table and the wounds on her back protested. She stifled a cry, determined not to let them see her weakness. One of the men picked up the black thing and advanced toward her.

"Tell us where the women are, and we will let you…and your friend…walk out of here." The man was speaking again, but Lorelei turned her head away from him and pretended not to listen.

The man holding the black tool brought it down sharply against her arm. It hurt, but not nearly as much as Ogden's belt hurt. She bit her lip and didn't cry out. He hit her again, this time on her leg. She still didn't cry out.

"Hurts, doesn't it? You can try to hide it all you want, but it's in your face. You're in pain." Speaking Man shoved his face close to hers. "Tell us what we want to know, and you won't have to be in pain any longer."

Lorelei didn't speak. The abuse began in earnest. The man hit her over and over, and after every few hits, Speaking Man would demand to know where the women were. Lorelei steeled herself and didn't answer.

She didn't know how long she had been there when the beating stopped. She felt something warm and wet on her back and worried her stitches broke open. She was sure she couldn't take any more when one of the men lifted her high over his head, carried her up the flights of steps, and dumped her on the floor beside Linolin. She held on to her strength as long as she could and managed to hold the first moan until after the men left. She presented her hands, once again tied, to Linolin, who struggled to a sitting position and untied her.

The two women held each other and rocked. They whispered to each other, phrases meant to strengthen, to uphold, to allow the other to persevere in the face of intense pain. Linolin examined her back and announced she was bleeding, but it wasn't one of the wounds Manx had stitched, it was a new wound and appeared superficial. Linolin tore a strip off her shirt and pressed it against the wound to stop the bleeding.

They were left alone for some time, but with no windows and no time monster it was impossible to know how long. A plate of inedible food was thrust into the door at them and pushed their direction. Lorelei crawled toward it, and the two women divided the food. It was awful, but they were hungry and they knew they needed to keep up their strength.

"Do you suppose this is what the men are eating, with us away?"

Linolin stared at the glop on the plate with distaste. "Serves them right. They should have learned to cook."

Lorelei laughed, and for a moment the pain receded. Linolin joined her, but her usual hearty laugh was impossible around the pain so it sounded false and unusual. Lorelei grimaced.

"We're quite a pair, aren't we?"

They slept. When they woke, there was more food, and a cup of something that sort of resembled hot beverage but was so bitter they could only swallow a couple of mouthfuls. They devised games to play while they waited, guessing games and any other game they could think of to pass the time. One of the greatest dangers was to allow boredom to sap their strength.

Linolin noticed the bone behind her, and Lorelei explained. Linolin nodded and hefted the bone. "We should practice."

The women spent the rest of the day…at least as they could judge by the arrival of food…practicing with their bones and playing guessing games, making up stories about the skeletons and skulls in the room. When they fell asleep, no one had come to fetch them for more torture.

62

The next day they were taken to the small room together. Lorelei was tied to a chair that had joined the table, and forced to watch as the men beat Linolin. They beat her as they did the day before, but they added something new. They beat the soles of her feet with some sort of stick. They called it bamboo.

"Gotta love China", one of the men chuckled as he pulled off Linolin's shoes and socks to expose her feet. "They really knew how to treat women."

Lorelei watched in horror as the stick beat against her friend's feet. She caught Linolin's eyes and could see the pain, but Linolin shook her head and put her finger to her lips. Do not talk. It was what they said to each other over and over yesterday, over and over. Don't make the pain stop by talking. It was easy enough to say when you were alone in a small dark room, but it was harder when you were watching your friend be tortured.

When Linolin didn't break, it was Lorelei's turn. The men stood Linolin on the floor, delight on their faces as she winced when her feet touched the ground. They thrust her into the chair and tied her, then laid Lorelei on the table. Linolin turned her head away; she wouldn't watch. Lorelei had tried the same trick. She knew what would happen. One man stood behind Linolin and held her head so she was forced to watch Lorelei abused. He hissed at her not to close her eyes unless she wanted Lorelei hurt worse.

Linolin held up well as the men beat Lorelei with the black rubber thing. When the man pulled off Lorelei's shoes, Linolin moaned and Lorelei worried they were finished. She cried out "No!" and Linolin nodded. She would not talk, but she knew what her friend was facing. Lorelei clenched her fists and bit her lip to keep from crying out as the stick hit her bare feet over and over.

Speaking Man was absent for most of the torture. He arrived just as the men stood Lorelei on the floor. He noticed her pain and grinned. "This is nothing", he said. "Just wait until Ogden gets here. He has something special planned for you."

"Tell Ogden to come. I can handle him." Lorelei squared her shoulders and threw out her challenge.

"Oh, he will. He's on his way."

"It doesn't take so long to get here from our house."

"He'll be here when we want him here." Speaking Man turned his back and marched out the door. The women were still defiant. They were not prepared to talk.

When the women were dumped back on the floor, their hands retied and the lights off, they were free to express the pain they felt. Linolin managed to untie Lorelei's hands even through her moans, and then Lorelei untied Linolin. The knots were so ridiculously loose it was obvious they were intended to get untied, and she could see the puzzled look on the men's faces every time they opened the door. Surely even women could figure out how to get untied. She knew what was going through their minds.

Linolin examined Lorelei's wounds, and Lorelei returned the favor. Although the men confiscated their little tubes of pepper spray, they had not found the ointment secreted where the men would never look. They anticipated problems, and Manx prepared them. Now they applied ointment to their feet where the wounds were raw and bleeding. The other beatings appeared to have left only bruises, and the ointment would not help with those.

They settled down to try and sleep, but sleep wouldn't come. There was too much pain, and too much fear. They knew the fortress would likely be on lockdown since they had not returned. The women trusted them, but they also knew the level of pain men could inflict, and no one would take any chances. Amity would have had them on lockdown by dinner, and they were no doubt terrified about the future.

"We can't let them down."

"No, we can't. It's all that's holding me together." Linolin grimaced as pain shot through her hip, and she adjusted position. "I can't believe the good wives held out as long as they did."

"Well, to be honest, I don't know of any good wife that was beaten on the soles of her feet before. I have to admit, that was worse than anything I've ever experienced." Lorelei sat up, her back hurting too much to lie down. There was no part of her body that wasn't in pain. "I wonder why they aren't hitting me on the back, trying to open up my stitches?"

Linolin shook her head. "I've wondered the same thing myself. I think…they don't want to do anything we can't recover from, because they want us to talk. Ogden thought he had killed you. Maybe he's instructed them how far they can go."

"So you agree now? Ogden put them up to this?"

"No. I think it's possible. I don't know. And I still think there is no way he told them where we are, or they wouldn't be doing this…at least, they wouldn't be doing it this way. They would have us all on severe punishment once they drug us out of the fortress."

Lorelei fell silent, wrestling with her own demons. She had been nervous ever since Ogden appeared in the fortress, but she wanted to believe he was being straight with her. Why? He hadn't been a good husband most of their time together, and he hadn't given her any reason for thinking he would not betray them. Oh, sure, he promised, but she had learned so much about the lies all the men told that she found it impossible to believe her father when he said Ogden never lied to her. Still, he hadn't showed yet, even though they kept promising…or threatening, really. Where was he? Was he part of this? Why wasn't he showing up?

They finally fell asleep, wrapped together for warmth and comfort, and didn't wake until the door opened to deliver their breakfast. A male face, a young face, peered at them, the same face that delivered their food the day before. He thrust the plate in the door, slid it across the floor, and darted away as though worried he'd catch some dread disease if he stayed too long in the presence of the bad women.

They ate in silence, the grotesque food tasting worse with every bite. It was only the knowledge that they had to keep up their strength allowing them to choke it down. They cleaned the plate and pushed it back toward the door, away from their spot. They spent the day trying to make up stories and games as before, but they were no longer able to do so. They stayed on the floor, unable to walk for any length of time on their tortured feet.

It was obvious the men weren't coming back for them that day. Lorelei wondered if they were amateurs, since they always seemed to stop just at the point where she wasn't sure she could take it anymore, and they gave them long periods of rest between the torture sessions. Linolin insisted it was because they didn't want to kill them, but Lorelei suspected they didn't really know what they were doing. They were used to beating their wives, but those beatings didn't last so long, and maybe they didn't know how much pain women could take.

The men didn't realize they had trained women to take pain with the frequent beatings they administered.

"They assume we're weak", Lorelei whispered to Linolin. "They think we can't take it. They don't know how we're holding out so long."

Linolin agreed. "I don't know how much longer we actually can hold out" was her only addition.

63

Night came, though in the tiny room without windows it was difficult to be sure. They could only measure time by the activities around them. The dinner tray was delivered and picked up by the same young man, but he lingered in the doorway looking at the women, acting as if he wanted to say something. The women looked back, determined not to let themselves be trapped into revealing something just because someone looked young and scared. He started to speak, then caught himself and left. The door closed with a resounding click of the lock.

The two women were stronger now, having been left to rest. Their bruises still hurt but their feet felt better from the regular applications of ointment, though they were still unable to stand. They sat face to face, massaging each others feet, taking care not to touch any open wounds, and talked. They talked about the history of women. They talked about the women in the fortress. They talked about the men who challenged them. They talked about each other…their hopes, their dreams, their fears. The talk helped to strengthen them, draw them closer together, and steel their resolve to not break.

"About Grenata", Linolin began.

"You don't need to explain." Lorelei rubbed a spot on Linolin's foot.

"I want to. It's…well…"

"I know." Lorelei moved positions until she was beside Linolin. She wrapped her arms around the other woman's shoulders. "Grenata and I talked. She's happy. Thank you for making her happy."

The two women nestled close, holding each other to stop their own trembling, partially from cold and partially from fear. Footsteps passed by outside, voices rose and fell, until gradually all noises ceased. The workers had gone home for the evening, and the two women had nothing more to fear until morning. They fell asleep nestled together for warmth and comfort.

Their sleep was interrupted by a loud whisper and a scuffling at the door.

"Shh!" A voice whispered in the darkness.

"I can't see anything…is there a light?" Another voice.

"We can't turn on a light. Someone will see."

Linolin sat up and shook Lorelei. "Someone's here!" she hissed.

The two women grabbed their bones and held them over their head. This didn't appear to be the same men as usual. They never entered in this way, sneaking in the darkness. They entered boldly, with the light at full blast. The women shivered as they listened to a whispered conversation they couldn't understand.

A scrabbling sound at the door, and then the door opened. Footsteps headed toward them. A tiny light picked through the darkness, tracing the path to where the women sat, bones poised over their heads. A light played over the wall as though unable to find the women and rested on Linolin's uplifted bone. A hand grabbed the bone and held on, while the light searched the wall for Lorelei's bone. She swung it in the direction she thought was the head of the person facing her, but she failed to connect. A hand darted out of the darkness and grabbed the bone, wresting it from her grasp.

"Whoa! Not so fast. We're friends." The male voice sounded sinister, in spite of the insistence they were friendly.

The light played over a face leaning over the two women, but Lorelei couldn't tell who it was. The light didn't illuminate any part of the face long enough to recognize it, and it looked eerie in the partial light. She put her fists in front of her, prepared to fight before she would allow anyone to take her or Linolin. A hand reached down and grabbed her hands. The hand felt familiar. Lorelei touched it.

"Amity!" Lorelei started to shout, but Amity shushed her. "What are you doing here?"

"We're here to take you out."

"Turn on the light." Linolin's voice came from the darkness beside her. "There's a switch next to the door."

"We can't. We don't want to alert anyone that we're here."

"There are no windows in this room. No one outside will see."

Light flooded the room and the two women blinked. Hands pulled them up, pulled off the loose ropes, embraced them, hands that belonged to people whose faces they still could not see. As her eyes adjusted to the light, Lorelei recognized not only Amity, but Grenata and Stone. Someone she could not see hovered in the background. He moved into the light and she recognized the familiar figure of her father. He came to take his daughter back from her captors.

Linolin swooned, the pain in her feet prohibiting her from standing. Stone caught her, and Lorelei filled him in on the situation.

Neither of them would be able to walk out. Until their feet healed, they were trapped.

Stone shook his head and lifted Linolin as though she were a much smaller woman. Amity and Grenata each took one of Lorelei's arms and carried her to the door between them. Dad picked her up and slung her over his shoulder, moving with a light step as though he were a much younger man carrying nothing. They stepped into the hallway and were again plunged into darkness.

"Turn the light off." A male voice came out of the darkness, an unfamiliar voice.

Stone switched off the light in the small room and they followed the unknown guide to the moving stairs. He led them through winding hallways until they reached the front door and erupted into the night. In the light from the street lamps, Lorelei cried out as she realized it was the young man who brought them their food.

"Go!" he ordered. "Get them out of here."

"You come, too." Stone grabbed the young man's hand.

"I shouldn't. I should…stay. Mislead them."

"You can't stay." Lorelei heard and felt when Dad spoke, his shoulders heaving with the effort of speaking while carrying her. "They will know who led us in. There is no one else."

The young man swallowed. Clearly he had not thought of such a contingency. "I'll…go. Is there…anyplace I can…go?"

"Follow us." Stone started off at a rapid pace, his long legs tracing the familiar route to the fortress.

Seven men stepped out of the shadows and Lorelei nearly screamed. Dad whispered to her to be quiet, and told her these were friends. Stone had, as usual, brought along an extra security detail. Dad handed his precious cargo to a younger man who stood nearby, and told him to be extra careful. Lorelei twisted her head and was able to see who held her. She was being carried back to the fortress by Raulston. Stone handed Linolin off to Manx, who was helped with his tall sister by two other young men who were recent arrivals in the men's wing.

The odd group headed back to the fortress, taking a circuitous route and watching for a tail. A group of men passed on the other side of the street and the group lunged for the darkness to hide them. The men passed, and the entire group breathed in relief. Stone stepped out of hiding to see if it was clear.

Their relief turned to horror as a policeman stepped in Stone's path. "What are you doing in the streets at this time of night?"

The rest of the group waited in the darkness, holding their breath. Stone dropped his shoulders, put his head down, and looked dejected.

"I'm just…looking for my wife…my baby daughter. I…go out…every evening…hoping. If I could just find her…bring her back home…" He waited. The hiding group waited.

The policeman nodded. "Quite a disaster, right? You need any help?"

Stone shook his head. "I'm…I think I'll head home tonight. I'm going to try again tomorrow, when there's more light."

"When you find her, buddy, beat her a couple extra strokes for me, you hear? And if my wife is with her, you tell her she better get her fat fanny home."

Stone and the policeman shared a laugh and the policeman moved on. Stone watched until he was out of sight, then he raised his fist and motioned to the group that it was safe. The collective sigh could have alerted the policeman to their presence if he had been close enough to hear.

They arrived at the fortress without further incident. Lorelei didn't breathe properly until they were back inside and the obscure door closed behind them.

64

Lorelei woke to a dark room filled with hushed whispers. She heard Amity talking to someone in the doorway before the wedge of light flooding through the door disappeared and the room was empty. She tried to reach the lamp by the bed, but pain in all parts of her body prevented her from reaching the switch. She fell back into the bed, wrapping her arms around the pillow and waiting. She was not sure where she was, though she thought she might be in her room at the fortress. She slept again and dreamt that Molton was sitting beside her, reading her a story.

She opened her eyes again; there was still no light in the room, and her head hurt. The door opened a crack and a face peeked at her. She lay silent, not sure if it was friend or foe, not wanting them to know she was awake if they intended to hurt her. The face withdrew and another face appeared.

"Lorelei?"

Lorelei recognized Amity's voice and motioned for her to enter. The door opened wider and Amity slipped through, followed by Manx and Stone. Stone clicked on the light. Manx held some evil looking instruments on a shiny silver tray, and Lorelei shrank. She'd had enough of instruments to last her a lifetime. Amity settled on the bed beside her and stroked her hand while Manx drew blood and conducted a brief examination.

"Nothing obvious except a lot of bruises, and those lacerations on your feet. Linolin's feet look just like that. How did you get those?"

Lorelei explained how their feet were injured. She was only halfway through her story when Manx leapt up and punched the wall. He drew back his fist and examined his knuckles, now covered with his own blood. Amity handed him his tray of instruments and he went to work bandaging himself while Lorelei finished.

"If I ever believed they could be brought to the negotiating table, I am sure now that I was wrong." Manx stared at Lorelei. "Did you recognize any of the men?"

Lorelei shook her head. "One man introduced himself when we first got there, but we never saw him again. He said he was the Chief Archaeologist."

"Falwell?" Stone leaned forward as he spoke.

"That sounds right."

"If Falwell is involved, this was probably ordered from the top. He doesn't answer to anyone except the Imperial Consul." Stone growled and stomped.

"After they…kidnapped…us, we didn't see him anymore."

"No, he wouldn't do the dirty work. That would be beneath him."

"Most of the men didn't say much. There was one man – Linolin and I named him Speaking Man – that did all the talking."

"You'd never seen him before?"

"I don't know. He might have been one of the men that came to the house when they were looking for Grenata. He looked sort of familiar."

Stone was pacing now, his hands behind his back and his head down. "Did they tell you anything? Ask you anything?"

"They asked where the women were."

Manx nodded. "I imagine that's why they stopped short of fatal wounds. If you died…" Manx gulped, and broke off at the thought of how close the women might have been to death.

"Speaking Man kept saying Ogden was on his way, but Ogden never showed. He said Ogden had really terrible things in store for me. Linolin thought they were just trying to play with my head, but I'm not sure."

"Ogden wasn't to blame." Stone stopped pacing. All heads turned his way.

"How can you be sure?" Amity put the question going through all their minds.

"Because Ogden was responsible for getting me in touch with the kid who helped us get you out. He couldn't go himself because he is being watched, but he knew who he could trust. The kid was terrified. He'd been watching when he brought your food and he couldn't believe anyone could treat someone like they were treating you. He could tell you were in pain. He was ready to help when Ogden approached him."

Lorelei felt a weight lift off her shoulders. It was difficult when she believed Ogden was responsible for the kidnapping, and that he misled her so badly when he came to the fortress. She wanted to believe him, and to believe he hadn't lied to her, but there was no mistaking the fact that they were betrayed in the very place where his work was coordinated.

"Linolin? Is she all right?"

"She isn't awake yet." Amity stroked Lorelei's hair as she spoke.

Manx nodded. "She'll be all right. She's strong. It was difficult for her. She's worked with beaten women for years and thought she knew what to expect. She had no idea. It's different seeing it and having it happen to you."

Lorelei nodded. "She's amazing. I can't believe she held up through that."

"I can't believe either of you held up through that. I don't know many men who can withstand that sort of brutal punishment." Manx paced, still angry and trying to get it under control.

"Most of us have experience. Oh, not that bad for me, no. Ogden was never that brutal, except the once, but he did beat me several times. It's always hard at first, but you learn how to shut out the pain. At least until they start thrashing your bare feet." Lorelei winced at the memory.

"Don't think about it", Amity suggested.

"I need to think about it. It keeps me focused, keeps me angry."

Manx agreed. "You'll need your anger now. This certainly isn't the end."

"Where is...the kid? The one that led us out? Is he...all right?" Lorelei realized the kid was in a lot of trouble. The men who did this to her would not hesitate to do as much...or more...to a boy who betrayed them.

"He's fine. We've given him a cot in the men's wing, and he understands he won't be able to go back. He's joined us for good. I think he'll be a good ally. He doesn't have many skills yet, but he's smart and he'll learn fast. His name is Almuth." Amity stroked Lorelei's head and kissed her brow. "You sleep."

"When can I see Linolin?"

"Soon. I plan to put her in your room as soon as I feel she can move." Manx explained that it would not be possible for Linolin...or him...to return to their home until things quieted down. She was now an official client of the battered women's shelter she helped to build. "You'll heal better together."

Lorelei was falling asleep. She realized the medicine Manx gave her for the pain was making her sleepy, and she welcomed the relief.

Her friends noticed she was dropping off and Manx ushered Stone out the door. Amity remained behind.

"I won't leave your side", Amity promised. "I'll be here as long as you need me. Just let me know if there is anything I can get you."

Lorelei tried to nod, but her head wouldn't move. She was too sleepy to even murmur agreement. Amity pulled the covers up to her shoulders, helped her arrange the pillow under her head, then settled in the chair beside her and held Lorelei's hand as she fell asleep. Lorelei didn't even notice when Molton crept into the room and settled beside her with his book. She began to dream as he started to read to her.

65

Lorelei and Linolin went back to work two days after their return. Manx wouldn't let them get up until they were fully healed, so they persuaded Amity and Corinne to bring their work from the office. Corinne set up a desk in the room so she could work with them and help them when they needed, but Lorelei suspected it was as much to ensure they didn't overwork. The two women were glad to be working again. The day before, when they were no longer sleeping all day, time monster moved so slow they thought the day would never end.

Molton and Micra were sleeping on cots in Manx's office so they could be closer to their mother. Molton bounced in and out, his energy exhausting both women until Manx put him on a strict schedule and told him he had to be less energetic to allow the women time to heal. Lorelei laughed to see him peek in the next day, his hair slicked down, his hands washed, and his best Sunday manner on display. She reached out her arms, and he rushed into them, followed more decorously by Micra, who bounced on Linolin's bed until the other woman moaned and she realized she was hurting her.

"Mama?"

"Yes, Molton?"

"Why do the bad men keep hitting you?"

Lorelei thought. How did you answer a question like that from an eight-year-old? It was something she didn't totally understand herself. She knew the men wanted to keep the women down, but why did they have to be cruel? "I don't know, son. I think...maybe...they're scared of me."

"Gee, Mom, why would any man be scared of a woman?" Molton, sweet Molton, still managed to have the male's view that had been trained into him.

"I'll explain that to you someday, dear. Just...don't say anything like that, again, okay? Because that's the sort of thoughts that make men want to hit women."

Molton nodded, his slicked down hair already escaping and misbehaving. Lorelei tousled his hair, kissed him on the cheek, and told him he needed to let Micra have her turn. The children stayed with their mother and their Aunt Linolin until Manx arrived to shoo them off and rescue the exhausted women.

Grenata popped in at regular intervals to bring them hot beverage, and Mom came by several times a day. Dad visited less often, but his visits were delightful and cheered the women up if they were feeling down. Manx allowed them to work only one hour the first day, but if that went well, he promised, he would add an hour a day as long as they didn't show signs of fatigue. Corinne did most of her work in the little office, but came to the shared bedroom for the hours her recuperating friends decided to work.

Linolin worked out a budget for the money Dad put in trust for them, and Lorelei reviewed the plan for self-sufficiency he worked out while they were in captivity. The plan was detailed and comprehensive, and Lorelei realized they were held captive somewhat longer than she realized.

"A week." Amity frowned as she told them. "We sort of knew where you were, and some of us made nocturnal visits to figure out how to get you out, but we didn't have any luck until Almuth contacted Stone…or I guess, Ogden contacted Stone. I didn't know Ogden had been involved."

Stone hadn't told anyone about Ogden's involvement because he was afraid they would think it was a trap. He knew Ogden before joining the fortress, and was pretty sure Ogden was being straight with him. He insisted on meeting Almuth and seeing the plan before letting the group know anything. He tested Ogden secretly to see if he could catch him in a lie. When Ogden came up clean, and Almuth passed his tests, he went to Amity.

"If Ogden wasn't involved, how did he know where we were?" Lorelei needed to silence the nagging voice of doubt.

"He heard the voice amplifier in the streets. He suspected what they planned to do. He stopped by the fortress to warn you, but you had already left for the meeting. He waited when you arrived at the center, hoping to catch you before you got in the door, but he wasn't able to catch you without anyone seeing. They would have just grabbed all of you then. He knew he needed to stay in good with them if he wanted to get you out. He saw Almuth escort you in and realized who he would need to trust."

Ogden waited to see if they came out. If they did, his suspicions were false. When the men all left for the night, and the women hadn't come out, he knew the worst had happened. He waited in the dark at the fortress, hoping someone would come out that he could approach. He came back every evening, sneaking out the back door of his house to throw off anyone who might be following, and waited until Stone finally appeared on the fifth day.

Almuth came by to visit the women, but didn't have much to say. He stood in the doorway much like he did when they were imprisoned, and mumbled a few words about how sorry he was, then darted away, again as he did when he tried to speak to them that night at the Archaeology Center. Lorelei tried to put him at ease with a smile, but it was no use. He was still too timid to talk to them.

The day after Linolin and Lorelei were first allowed to get up and take a walk, bells rang throughout the building. Women bustled and scurried past their door, which they kept open to avoid being isolated. A handful of men, not security, rushed up and down the hallway but no one stopped in to tell them what was happening. Molton and Micra were their only visitors all morning.

They had no idea what was going on until Manx and Raulston appeared, each offering their arm to one of the women in bed, helping them to their feet and escorting them down the hallway to the dining room. They moved slowly, knowing the women still had difficulty walking. Each woman leaned on the arm that held her, unable to put their full weight on their battered feet.

The dining room was festooned as if for a celebration, but the mood in the room was not festive. A choir of women in the corner was singing a mournful tune, and a group of men accompanied them on various makeshift instruments that Lorelei recognized as kitchen equipment. Children fidgeted in chairs arranged in rows at the front of the room beside the choir; they each held a large pot in their lap. Molton waved at his mother as she entered, but Micra grabbed his hand and told him to focus.

Chairs were lined up in rows as if in church, and a large podium had been erected at the front of the room. Most of the chairs were filled with the women of the fortress. It looked sort of like shelter group, only much larger.

Dad appeared and took Lorelei's arm from Raulston. He escorted his daughter to a special seat at the front that bore a big sign saying

"Reserved for Elizabeth". Manx showed Linolin to the seat next to Lorelei, bearing a sign that announced it was "Reserved for Susan".

The two women settled into the seats, exhausted from the long trek down the hall, and their escorts settled in beside as if to protect the women from anything that might threaten them. A hush fell over the room as soon as the women were seated.

Amity mounted the steps to the podium and raised her fist. The entire group, men, women, and children, raised their fists. Lorelei and Linolin tried to raise their fists but they were still in too much pain for assertive movement. Everyone leapt to their feet when the two women raised their feeble fists and burst into applause. Amity stood silent and waited until the applause thinned down, then raised her fist again for silence.

"We have decided", she began, her voice blooming in the great hall even without the use of a voice amplifier, "that it is time to have a memorial service for our fallen friends. We wanted to wait until the bravest among us were able to be present."

The crowd rose to their feet again, and wild applause, cat calling, and foot stomps grew so loud that Lorelei felt pain starting to rise behind her ears. Her face grew red with embarrassment and she whispered to Linolin that they didn't deserve this applause when their mission failed. Linolin grabbed her hand and squeezed.

Amity raised her fist again and the room grew silent, but the women were clearly restless. She glanced at a paper on the podium in front of her, lifted her head high and proud, and began again to speak.

"We will keep this service short, because we know our brave fallen warriors would not want us to fall behind on the tasks for which they gave their life in hopes of building a better world. We also know Elizabeth and Susan are not going to be able to stay with us for long, as their wounds are more serious than they like to admit."

Amity looked at her friends with a fond smile. "We are proud to announce that, in spite of all the obstacles to our success, pulling off the march and getting the women back to the shelter…." a loud boo from the audience "…excuse me, fortress…in spite of all the beatings and lockings ins and other brutal punishments, we ended up losing only five women. Two were beaten so severely they could not walk, but they managed to crawl out of their houses in their quest for freedom and were on their way back to the fortress when they succumbed. Aliana and Titania, we salute you!"

The children thumped their pots twice in unison. Molton hit his pot again when the other children were finished, and Micra gave him a fierce frown. Two loud salutes rose from the crowd as fists shot skyward. This part had apparently been rehearsed.

"Mala died following an unsuccessful rescue attempt. Her attempt to escape on her own resulted in a fall from a second story window. We were not able to bring her body back to the fortress, as it was claimed by her husband and buried as though she were still a good wife. We will do all we can to erase the shame implied by that inglorious burial."

Another thump from the children, another loud salute, and another group fist raise, and Amity began again.

"The last two, Creana and Saluna, died just two weeks ago when they snuck out of the fortress during lockdown in a failed effort to rescue our friends who were held hostage at the Archaeology Center. With no knowledge of the downtown area, they wandered off in the wrong direction and got lost. During the evening rush to get home, they became disoriented and were hit by a people mover, who didn't bother to stop and see what happened to the women he mowed down. Stone and Marsden found them before they were claimed by their husbands, and we were able to bury them in graves of honor in our own fortunately still small cemetery, as fallen warriors deserve."

More thumps, and more salutes. Lorelei felt her eyes fill with tears. Creana and Saluna were two of Montoya's recruits, and were crucial during the planning process. They were fierce warriors, brave and intelligent. She had become good friends with both women, and it was difficult to hear about their deaths in this manner. She grabbed Linolin's hand and the two women mourned silently over their fallen friends. Dad put his arms around her shoulders and she felt comforted.

Amity said a few more words, but as promised, the ceremony was brief. The choir sang a rousing song, a fitting send-off for warriors, accompanied by enthusiastic loud thumps from the children, while Resenta and Ornata lit five large candles that lined the space behind Amity, their red and purple dresses adding a touch of symbolic color. Then the service was over and Lorelei and Linolin headed back to their room, leaning on the arms of their loved ones. They couldn't manage any more today.

66

A week after the service, Lorelei and Linolin were finally allowed to return to their office. They were settling in to long-neglected duties when Amity appeared to tell them Ogden was asking for Lorelei. She asked Linolin to accompany her, and headed down the hallway to the dining hall where Amity left him.

Ogden was standing by the pot of hot beverage testing it, then drinking something else. Lorelei approached him and held out her hand. He took it, but rather than shaking hands he stroked her palm as he had done when they first met. She gently removed her hand from his and asked what he was doing.

"I'm tasting these drinks and hot beverage to see if I can sort out the tastes."

"And?"

"I like the chocolate. The rest? You can keep them. I'll stick with hot beverage."

Lorelei smiled. She agreed, except she didn't like the chocolate. Most of the women preferred hot beverage, too, but there were a few who liked the other drinks. Grenata was particularly fond of the lemonade, and she actually tried putting it on ice. She said it was much better that way than hot.

"I...wanted to thank you." Lorelei cursed her voice for shaking.

"For what?"

"Your help in...saving me...and Linolin."

Ogden touched her face, gently stroking her bruises. Lorelei remained stiff, not encouraging him but not making him stop. He seemed to be wrestling with demons, and she didn't plan to either help him or impede him. He rested his hand on her cheek for several seconds, then moved away a few steps. He stared down at the table, and poured himself a cup of hot chocolate. He reached for the coffee, but changed his mind. He shuffled his feet. He put his hands in his pockets and rocked back and forth. He seemed embarrassed, and Lorelei left him alone with his emotions. He walked away from her and stared at something on the wall no one else could see. That apparently helped him recover his equilibrium, and he turned back to her and changed the subject.

"I wanted you to know..." He paused, gulped, then started again. "I wanted you to know...I cancelled...Micra's engagement. I think...she should choose her own husband."

"Or...none at all?"

Ogden hesitated before he answered. "If...that's what she wants."

Lorelei almost hugged him. It didn't matter, because she had no intention of letting Ogden...or anyone else...have control of Micra, but it was a gesture that meant a lot to her, especially since it was such a major step for Ogden. "Good. She's finally learning to play and be a little girl. Linolin's teaching her to be rebellious, and Amity's teaching her to be smug."

"And you're teaching her to be strong?"

"I guess so. I hope so. I don't intend for her to ever be a good wife."

An awkward silence was broken when Ogden changed the subject again. "I brought you something."

He reached down to bring up a suitcase by his feet. Lorelei tensed, and Linolin watched him intently from her position near the door where she could summon the waiting guard at a moment's notice.

"I thought you might want some of your things from home."

Lorelei thanked him but didn't take her eyes off him as he walked around the room looking at the things that were laying out, mostly projects the women were working on. She still wasn't sure she could trust him, though no army showed up after his last visit, and Stone was adamant that he was the one who saved her and Linolin. "He really loves you, you know", Stone insisted.

"That wasn't all I brought you." Ogden stopped wandering and stood face to face with her. "I left it in the mini-transit...don't worry. I had him park down the street in front of one of the businesses I frequent. I need help to bring it in. It's heavy."

Lorelei didn't say anything but waved at Marsden, who was standing guard over the dining hall while Ogden was there. She instructed him to help Ogden with his cargo and to check it carefully to make sure it was safe. The young man nodded and loped off to fulfill his instructions.

Ogden returned with an enormous box. Marsden followed with another like it. They placed the boxes on the table, and Lorelei thanked Marsden. He nodded and resumed his guard at the door.

"There are men here." Ogden announced it as fact, but Lorelei realized it was a question.

"Yes. There are men who have come to support the cause. We built them a men's wing. Would you like to see it?"

Ogden nodded, his eyes wide. She took him toward the back of the facility, where the nearly complete men's wing was safely distant from where the women were housed, for safety and propriety. The women built it with an automatic lockdown feature they could activate from Linolin's office if there was ever a need.

Ogden walked around the men's quarters feeling the workmanship on the walls, on the bunks, on the floors. "This is amazing. The women built it?"

"This was designed by the group we call the working women. They worked outside the home. Did you know about that?"

Ogden nodded. Of course he knew. These women waited on him and his friends when they ordered food or needed some service downtown. Some of them accompanied him on digs. He continued to run his hands over the smooth wood of the bunks.

"This is excellent quality work. You should be glad you've got these women on your side." Ogden grinned as though to take any possible sting out of the remark.

"We are. They're amazing." Lorelei crossed her arms and waited.

"Oh, we need to…you need to…open your package."

Lorelei had forgotten the boxes. They headed back to the dining hall, Ogden almost skipping like Molton. The boxes were still where they left them. Lorelei knew most of the women in this facility could be trusted. They might lie and steal and commit petty acts of vandalism at home, where their husbands would be the ones hurt, but they didn't hurt each other. All of them had hurt too much for that.

"I brought you the papers…and the artifacts."

Lorelei stopped opening the box and stared at him. Could it be for real? Were these really her papers? She tore open the box in a hurry, not worrying that Ogden preferred neat unwrapping. He had no rights over her here. She pulled out the first sheaf of papers and ran her hands over them. These were her papers. They were here.

"They don't belong to me...to any of us. They don't belong to the men. They belong to the women. This is your history."

Lorelei nodded. She believed this from the beginning but she'd never dared speak it out loud. "It's your history, too. The men were always a major part of the women's movement. After all, if men didn't keep women down, women wouldn't have needed to rise up."

Ogden threw back his head and laughed. Clearly he never thought of it that way, and hearing his wife so neatly summarize the battle of the sexes amused him. "You're right, you know. The only reason I ever needed to beat you was because...I beat you. If I had just...loved you...you would have stayed with me because you wanted to, not because you had to."

Lorelei nodded. "I thought, the night before the march, that...well, that you were finally learning how to be a good husband just when I was on the verge of transgressing my role as a good wife."

Ogden put his arms around her. She didn't make any attempt to move away, but she didn't return the embrace.

"I know this is too much to ask", he whispered in her ear. "But do you think you will ever...I know, probably too soon...but maybe in the future...I could...you know, court you?"

Lorelei slipped out of his embrace. "I think...before that comes, you need to figure out where you're going to live."

"What?"

She pointed to the papers. "You can't go back home."

Ogden understood. He looked worried. Plainly he hadn't thought about the consequences. Lorelei slipped her arm in his.

"You like the men's quarters?"

He nodded. "It's very nice. Looks very comfortable."

"Go home and pack before anyone finds out what you did. Then...you can come stay here." She paused at the look on his face. "No. I'm not saying we're back together. But...you can stay in the men's quarters for as long as you need...and as long as you follow our rules."

Ogden looked worried again. "What rules?"

"No regimentation. No force. No beatings."

"I can follow those...well, you might have to remind me about the regimentation."

"And…women run things here. Men operate in roles determined by need and skill, and no men are in management."

He nodded. "It seems perfectly fair. I agree."

"If things work out…maybe you'll become one of us. Maybe you'll understand why we need to be free. And maybe…someday…if things go well…I might let you court me."

Ogden smiled. She allowed him a quick hug, then sent him home to gather his things before she changed her mind. "Molton and Micra will be glad to see you. Just don't…let Molton find out you were the one who…beat me up. He wants to kill that person."

Ogden took her hand. "He's a good son. He's right. I think I want to kill that person, too."

He left, promising to return with his overnight bag and a few things he couldn't live without. Linolin entered the dining hall as he left, determined to watch over Lorelei. She exclaimed over the papers, which meant as much to their movement as her ancestor's books. Lorelei told her she invited Ogden to stay in the men's quarters. Linolin approved. She understood he would never be able to return after he delivered those papers to Lorelei. Lorelei found a letter on top of the second box, the carbon copy of a letter Ogden mailed to his boss, and to the newspapers. He was announcing the find, without permission, without authorization, and as honestly and openly as if Lorelei herself had written the letter.

Corinne rushed in from the loading dock. "There's a truck here!"

Lorelei and Linolin raced to the dock. They were not expecting any deliveries today, but a large truck was backing up to the door, marked with the logo of the supply company that brought the fortress their food and building products. No orders had been made, and no supply truck was expected.

Stone and Marsden joined them, and the women noticed they were armed. Stone nodded behind him, and the women realized he had brought a security detail in case the truck was delivering an army.

The truck reached the dock and stopped. A young man jumped out of the front seat and headed toward the back of the truck. He came up short when he realized he was facing an armed security detail.

"Hey, I just got some packages I was told to deliver."

Stone moved the young man aside and eased open the back door of the truck. The only obvious load was cardboard boxes, more than a hundred. The men advanced with care on the boxes, ready to act if a man should leap out. Stone reached down and opened the closest box. It was full of papers. The second box held more papers. Stone motioned to the young man that he could begin unloading his cargo.

The dining room overflowed with boxes, all of them filled with papers, books, and artifacts from Ogden's study, from his office, and from a downtown warehouse where overflow was stored. Clearly the find at the dig had been larger than any of the women realized. Ogden had it all delivered to the women, hundreds of artifacts and thousands of papers and books. It was going to take Lorelei a lifetime to read all of this.

Linolin took Lorelei's hand and they danced around the hall. It wasn't over, they hadn't won, and probably wouldn't win for a very long time. But this was a major breakthrough, and they were on their way to at least making the men sweat. And men who were trying to take care of themselves for as long as the women had been gone were talking about negotiating – seriously, not the type of negotiations they were offered by the Archaeology Center. So far the men offered too little, but in time…with no hot beverage, inedible meals, and no clean clothes, they would eventually have to offer more.

"You know what?" Lorelei looked at her friend, and Linolin looked back.

"What?"

"It's time to build a new wing."

"Another one?"

"Yes. We need to build a women's history and library wing. These papers…these artifacts…and our own stories, the ones Resenta is collecting…need a home."

Lorelei and Linolin locked hands and stared at the pictures on the wall. Grenata continued to add new pictures to the collection, some of them more cheerful visions of the future than her previous paintings. But no matter how many pictures she added, the centerpiece of the collection would always be the same – the Declaration of Rights made at Seneca Falls in 1848. Resolved: that woman is man's equal.